PEASANTS AND KINGS

EMMA SLATE

Tabula Rasa Publishing

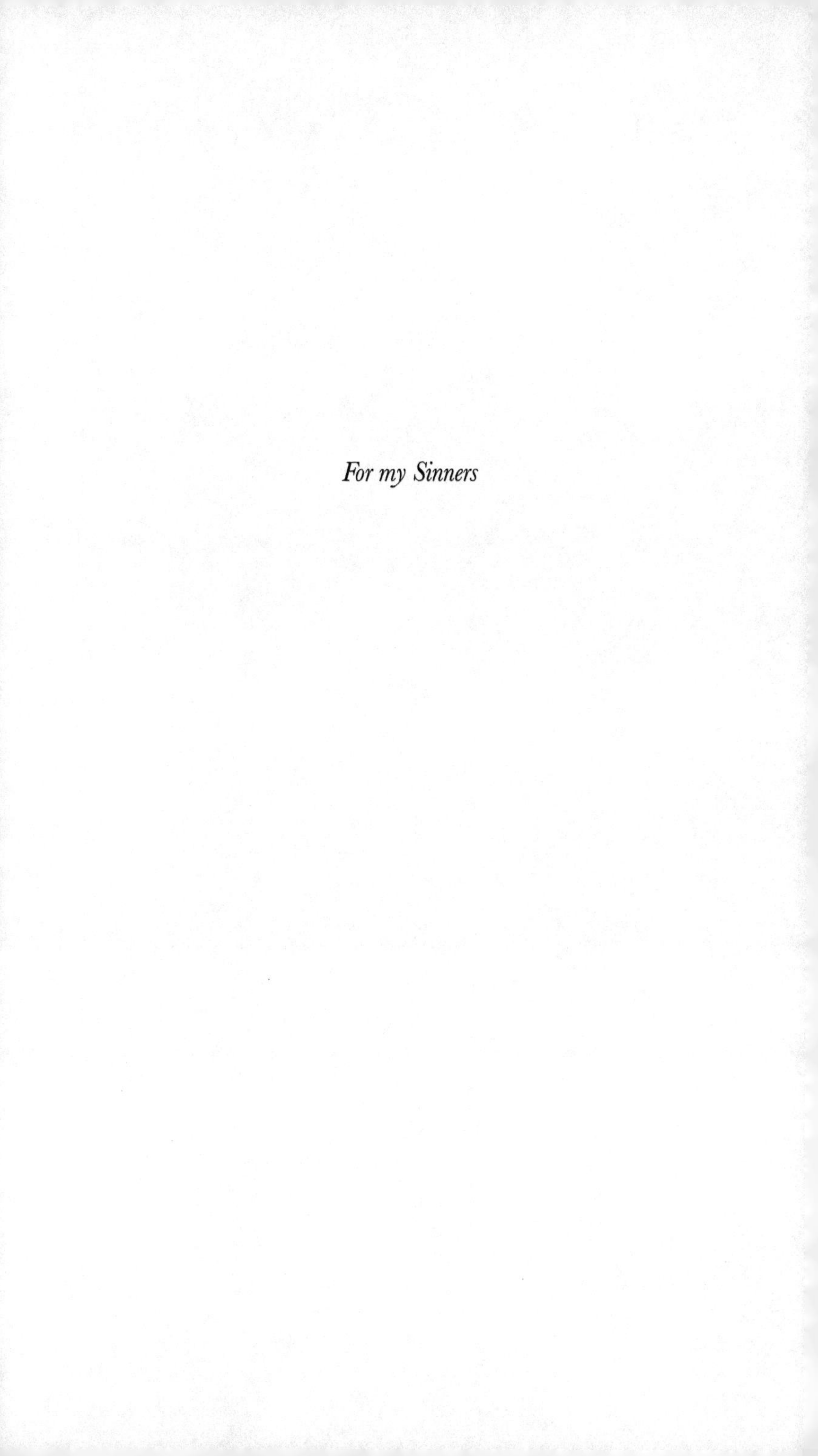

For my Sinners

Prologue

My heart thumped in my chest like the beat of a solemn war drum as I stared at the newly churned earth over my mother's grave.

The pulse of my blood reminded me that I was alive, and she was not.

Ominous clouds dotted the sky. Thunder boomed in the distance, announcing impending weather. A warm, gentle breeze tugged at my hair.

I clasped my hands together, my jaw clenched as I tried to keep my emotions locked inside me. If they were allowed to escape, allowed to run free, I might never be able to wrangle them back under control.

My mother had been a devout Catholic, but she was now buried in a nondenominational cemetery in a town I'd never heard of. When the minister had called to inform me of her death and that her funeral had already been scheduled and paid for, my mind jumped into overdrive.

Had she been sick? No. If she'd been sick, she would've tried to get into contact sooner than a week ago. I'd silenced her call and hadn't even bothered listening to her voicemail. She called again and again. I'd deleted every message.

My chest was tight with guilt, each breath like jagged glass puncturing my lungs and shredding my heart.

I hadn't cried. Not even when I'd gotten the phone call from the minister.

What the hell was wrong with me? Was I in shock? Or was it something more?

A lifetime of resentment had stood between us, and what began as months of not speaking so long ago had melded into years.

Grief, shame, and confusion…it was an ongoing battle of emotions, the victor still unclear. Feelings consumed me like a tidal wave, and just when I was able to break the surface and breathe, another emotion would crash down on me.

The soft tread of footsteps on damp grass momentarily diverted my attention. An older woman in a thick black sweater dress, black hose, and rounded-toe heels came toward me. Her chestnut hair was heavily laced with gray and her brown eyes were warm with compassion as they met my gaze. Her face was lined with age, smile parentheses bracketing her mouth and wrinkles at the corners of her eyes.

She held a manila envelope. Her nails were perfectly manicured, and she wore a dainty diamond tennis bracelet.

Who was this woman? She clearly had money, but it was more than that. She had class.

This town didn't showcase either of those things. When I'd driven down Main Street, I noticed the decayed state of the buildings. Those that weren't boarded up were dilapidated and required renovation. Most needed new roofs and some were too rundown to inhabit, even for a business. No one had paved over the crumbling brick streets, not bothering to conceal the fact that the town had once been a bustling hub of economic activity at the height of an era when small-town America reigned. It was a time I'd only seen in vintage movies that my mother had loved to watch when I was a child. All that remained now were memories of what once was, a nostalgia that was nearly tangible.

"Ms. Miller," the woman greeted, hand outstretched with the envelope. "I'm very sorry for your loss. Your mother…was a good person."

She released the envelope as I grasped it and then turned to leave.

"Wait!" I called to her.

She looked over her shoulder.

"Who are you?" I asked.

"It doesn't matter. You'll never see me again. Good luck, Sterling."

I swallowed as I watched her vacate the immaculate grounds of the cemetery. The lawns had been mown; the flower beds along the sidewalks were all pruned to perfection. It was as though the town cared more for the dead than the living.

I looked down at the thick envelope. My finger toyed with the edge of it, wanting desperately to rip into it so I could devour my mother's final words to me.

I headed to my old blue Toyota Camry that was parked along the curb. It wasn't going to turn heads, but it was reliable enough to have made the drive all the way from Dallas without a worry.

As I drove back toward the cheap, outdated motel I was staying at near the edge of town, I kept glancing at the envelope that rested on the faded and cracked leather passenger seat. It taunted me, intrigued me. I didn't know what I'd find when I opened it, and I wasn't sure I was ready.

I pulled into the parking lot of the motel. It looked like a crime scene waiting to happen. I'd only booked it for one night, but I wasn't sure I even wanted to stay. I contemplated buying an energy drink and hitting the road—after I read my mother's letter.

I unlocked the door to the motel room and went inside. The old air conditioner kicked on as I entered, groaning and whirling, clearly struggling despite the fact that it wasn't sweltering outside. The back of summer had broken, and it was nearly autumn, but still, the unit could barely keep up.

The room smelled of must and decay, of a place long forgotten and hardly used. Everything was tan and brown, and the faded taupe carpet bubbled at the corners of the floor.

I kicked off my heels and sat down on the edge of the bed, and finally, with a deep breath, ripped open the envelope.

There was a folded letter inside with my name scrolled in her elegant handwriting.

But that wasn't all. I grabbed the thick envelope and turned it upside down so its contents spilled out. Bundles of bright green bills tumbled onto the questionable paisley bedspread.

I reached for the letter and unfolded it. It was written in Italian, my mother's native language.

Dear Sterling,

I've started this letter so many times, never feeling like I said everything I needed to say or that I was able to say it coherently.

So, I guess I'll start writing and pray this is a decent goodbye.

God, I wish there had been more time.

There are so many things I want to tell you. So many moments I wish I could do over. Our estrangement hurts me more than you know. And you may not understand this because you're not a mother, but everything I did, every choice I made, and every town I moved us to was to protect you.

It's always been about you, Sterling.

There is nothing—NOTHING—a mother wouldn't do to protect her child, as I've tried to protect you. Even by committing this cardinal sin, I have to believe that God will forgive me because in taking my own life, I have given you a chance to live yours.

It was the only way.

All these years, I've let you think the worst of me. That I was unreliable, that I couldn't ever hold down a job long enough to give you roots or provide a good life for you. The lie was easier to believe than the truth, a truth I never wanted to share with you, but now I must because your survival is at stake.

What I'm about to tell you means life or death for you, Sterling.

Do you remember the stories I told you when you were a child? About a beautiful princess who rode bareback on a great black stallion through the luscious green forest and rolling hills of her family's estate? An estate so grand and opulent that it rivaled the great palaces of Europe? Those stories weren't fiction. They weren't made up to lull you to sleep with your head full of dreams and whimsy. Those were stories from my own childhood.

I come from a family called Moretti, and we can trace our lineage back to The Crusades. Within our veins runs the blood of the Compagnia Bianca del Falco, known as The White Company. We are fantastically wealthy Italian mercenaries that yield great power and influence amongst Western Europe, and our family name is known within elite circles.

We are one of the five powerful families who control Italy. The other families are Lanza, Borgia, Sforza, and the Foscari.

Power, bloodlines, archaic alliances…that is all my family—and the other four families—care about. A feud had erupted between our family and the Foscari, but in our world, grievances can be mended if bloodlines are united…

For that reason, before I was even born, I was promised to a Foscari for a grand marriage that would unite two great Italian families, putting an end to past injustices. But when I was seventeen, I fell in love with a boy who was not my intended. Foolish, young, and drunk on first love, we married in secret beneath the stars. We plotted and planned how to flee, wishing to escape the bonds of our social classes. We chose love over family and obligation.

When the Foscari learned of my betrayal, they found and murdered my husband—your father—in cold blood. After the punishment was complete, the families still wished to join our bloodlines and even though I was no longer a virgin, the Foscari were willing to forge ahead with the marriage. Secrets can be kept within families, but a public failure to unite the bloodlines was impermissible.

Grieving the loss of my love, I was numb to everything around me. I had plans to go through with the marriage. After all, I saw the power of the Foscari firsthand, the brutality of them. What choice did I have?

But then I realized I was pregnant with you.

For myself, I was willing to be a sacrificial lamb. But God knows what they would've done if they'd realized I was pregnant with a peasant's child. The child of a man they had no qualms about murdering. What would they do to you to protect their own family name, their own legacy?

I went to the Catholic Church to seek guidance, and there I crossed paths with a nun, Sister Agatha, who was sympathetic to my situation. She saw my marriage to your father as valid in the eyes of God and believed her duty was to protect you and me from such horrible people at all costs. You were not even born yet, but she knew what would happen when you were. Risking her own life, she helped me escape to the United States and stayed with me here until you were more than a year old. I changed my last name to Miller, wanting *nothing more than to disappear and to blend in, leaving the Moretti name behind forever. I wanted to shield you from what I feared most in this world…*

I know it sounds like I've lost my mind, but you need to trust me, Sterling. It's all so very real.

I know how hard it's been all these years, never settling down long enough for you to form lasting friendships, never letting you get too close to anyone except for Tiffany. Against my better judgement, I let you have one summer. A golden summer of fun and laughter. It was dangerous, but necessary. I've never seen your smile so carefree as I did that summer. Tiffany saved you in a way that I couldn't.

I'm sorry I had to rip you away from that small glimmer of normal life. I'm sorry for the years of animosity between us, but I hope you can understand why it had to be this way.

You are in great danger, Sterling.

The Foscari have never stopped hunting me, and even though I've managed to evade them, they finally found Sister Agatha. Something went wrong. A slip of the tongue, a comment in passing, someone she knew who had connections back home. She died a horrible death to try to protect us, but no one can withstand torture. She knew you were alive, knew your given name, and she had already seen you begin to grow as a child. There was no hiding your eyes from her…

You have a genetic trait called heterochromia. That in and of itself is not unheard of, but once or twice every generation, a Moretti woman is born with one turquoise colored eye and the other a vibrant green. It wasn't random like I told you when you were a child.

Though Sister Agatha knew about your Moretti trait, that was all she knew. She couldn't lead them directly to you, only tell them that twenty-four years ago, I had borne a healthy baby girl.

But I know everything. What you look like as an adult, where you've lived in the past, people you've known, everything. If they find me, they'll torture me until I tell them where you are.

And Tiffany? I can't let your best friend get hurt too. If the Foscari find me, you'll both be in danger.

You must disappear. You have to acquire a new identity. Leave everything and everyone you know behind. Sever all ties. Say nothing of your life, me, or anything you know to be true about who you are. Conceal your eyes from the world. Don't speak Italian and try to blend in. If you must, use the information I've given you to avoid anyone connected with the Foscari and never look back.

The Foscari have been wronged and I don't want to imagine your future if they find you.

There are some things worse than death.

This next part is the most important of all—you cannot go to my family. The Moretti will not protect you. They would rather turn you over to the Foscari to honor their debt than they would defend you. Even though you're only half Moretti, they still value your bloodline. I have dishonored the family in an irrevocable way, and I have no doubt they'll make you pay for my sins.

I left Italy to give you a chance to live. I left Italy because I didn't want anyone to use you as a pawn to further their agenda of seeking wealth and power.

I'm so sorry, la mia bellissima figlia. I'm so sorry to leave you with such a bitter truth. I chose love when I married your father, and now I'm afraid that following my heart has changed the course of your life.

I love you more than you can possibly know. I wish I could've given you more. A father. A family. A home.

I never told you his name, but that never stopped you from wanting to know about him. Your father's name was Gianni Russo, and he would've loved you more than anything in this world. He was a good man, Sterling. The blood of him is within you, but so is that of a Moretti.

I have left you all that I have—twenty thousand dollars in cash to help you disappear. I'm sorry it couldn't be more.

Be safe, be smart, and above all, survive.

All my love,
Your mother

. . .

I crumbled the note in my hand so I wouldn't see the streaky ink of her words, smeared from the tears she'd shed while writing the letter, and smeared once again from my own.

When I was done crying, I flattened the paper and read it over and over. Names from the letter stared angrily back at me. Moretti. Foscari. Russo. *Compagnia Bianca del Falco.*

Guilt and shame over ignoring her phone calls and attempted overtures over the years clawed at me. I finally understood why she'd been relentless in trying to get my attention, but anger from my childhood had clouded everything that had to do with her.

My mind whirled in an attempt to process the truth. How was I supposed to reconcile her sacrifices? Everything she'd done had been to make sure I lived. She'd protected me at every turn. But because of her secrets, our relationship had been tainted. At eighteen, I'd left the house and never looked back, tired of the excuses and nonsensical nature of our lives. Nothing had made sense.

It made sense now.

I cried for the loss of her, not just for her death, but for the years of misunderstandings. Why hadn't she told me earlier? Why hadn't she told me the truth? Why had she waited until there was six years of silence between us before coming clean? Would I have been brave enough at eighteen to even hear the truth?

I'd never know.

All I knew was that she'd taken her own life to protect me.

Flopping back onto the bed, emotions washed over me. I stared at the nicotine stained white popcorn ceiling of the motel room, hating that I couldn't stop the tears from leaking down my cheeks.

My heart lurched in my chest. She'd loved me. More than she should have. I was undeserving of it.

Be safe, be smart, and above all, survive.

Terror bloomed in the midst of grief.

The fear of the Foscari finding me had motivated her to take her own life. I would not let my mother's death be in vain.

But how the hell was I supposed to get a new identity? She'd said it in the letter like it was easy enough to go to the store and grab a new one off the shelf.

A thread of resolution curled through me and I reminded myself that I still breathed air into my lungs, that it wasn't too late for me yet. The Foscari might've been looking for her all these years, but they'd never found her. If she could run for so long, I could too. They knew less about me than they knew of her. She'd found a way to disappear, to create a new life. And I had to do the same. I wouldn't risk staying out in the open. Not after reading the letter and understanding the direness of the situation.

I had twenty thousand dollars to start a new life. Twenty thousand dollars and my mother's blood in my veins.

Something in my brain snapped into place, and as fast as emotions had come pouring out of me, it was like the faucet had suddenly been shut off. My tears dried on my cheeks as I moved around the motel room, throwing my toiletries into my suitcase and zipping it closed.

I put the letter and the money back into the manila envelope and then rolled it shut and secured it with a hair tie.

Looking around the room, I made sure I had all my belongings and then left. I hoisted my suitcase into the trunk of my car and didn't bother checking out of the motel. I'd prepaid, planning on leaving early the next morning.

But my mother's final words had lit a fire of urgency, and I refused to sit still, to give in to the paralyzing emotions that threatened to pull me into their undertow.

I had a full tank of gas and no idea where to go. So I just drove.

I thought about my father. Gianni Russo. How had he met my mother? How had a sheltered young Moretti woman come across an unsuitable boy not of her echelon?

Their love had been so powerful that they'd been willing to risk everything to be together.

I never truly believed that kind of love existed, but clearly it did. My parents were lucky enough to have found it, but not lucky enough to be able to grow old together.

They were tragic, star-crossed lovers.

Grieving and with only the help of Sister Agatha, my mother had somehow found the courage to escape Italy and come to the States. How had she done it? Sheer force of will? She came from the bloodline of Italian mercenaries. No doubt, the strength of her resolve was buried deep in her DNA, perhaps the reason for her tenacity.

I'd never heard of a family of Italian mercenaries in existence since The Crusades. It sounded ridiculous. And yet, my mother's words rang true. I knew it in my bones.

Afternoon turned to evening as I drove farther and farther from the plot of land that was my mother's final resting place.

I replayed pieces of my childhood in my mind, pouring over every memory, every conversation I could muster. I tried to see those recollections through the lens of an adult, knowing what I knew now. But it would take longer than a car ride to nowhere to unravel the myopic emotions that steadfastly clung to my memories.

Just because she'd told me the truth didn't mean I was suddenly full of forgiveness. Compassion, maybe, in the distant corners of my angry heart.

Guilt, definitely.

Her letter was only a window into her psyche. Now she was gone and had left me with half-truths. The window was shut. And just like that, the numbness of the adrenaline faded away, leaving a tempest of wrath.

Hours later, my skin still tight with anger, knuckles white from gripping the wheel, I knew I had to think about stopping for the night. I'd been heading east for hours and exhaustion was setting in.

I drove through yet another city that looked like all the rest, every stop at a red light an excuse for my rage to flicker again.

Estrangement from my mother wasn't anything out of the ordinary. I'd been safe and loved, but it didn't make up for the lack of friends, the lack of attachments I longed for, or my inability to connect with others because I'd always been terrified that as soon as I made a friend, Mama would rip me away and drag me to a new place.

It wasn't a true sob story, but it was *my* story.

"Mama, why?" I asked, hitting the steering wheel.

My mother's letter had told me just enough to crack the lid on a Pandora's box of my background. I wanted to know it all, but I hadn't been given the chance.

And then I had the worst thought of my entire life: My mother might've died to protect me, but what if it had also been a way out of her own personal pain? What if she no longer had the strength to continue living? She'd never dated. She'd never made connections, either. What if she'd been too tired, weighed down by her past, knowing her future would be just more of the same?

She'd been completely alone.

Now *I* was completely alone, destined to feel what she felt.

Tears I thought were long gone suddenly welled at the corners of my eyes and blurred my vision. There was a faceless enemy tracking me, bludgeoning me with anxiety and fear.

I pulled off the highway, not bothering to look at the signs. I drove through the small town, passing quiet streets.

When I found an empty parking lot, I turned into it, put the car in park, and then let loose the sobs I'd been attempting to hold back.

They came from deep inside, from the depths of my soul and marrow. I purged it all. I flogged my heart with thousands of lashes in the form of detrimental, guilt-stricken thoughts.

And when there were no more tears, I finally leaned my throbbing head against the cool window and took a deep breath.

I fell into a light sleep and woke when the new day appeared on the horizon. I stretched my sore body and rubbed my tender eyes.

A choked, maniacal laugh escaped my lips when I realized where I'd spent the night.

In the parking lot of St. Mary's Church.

Here. Here, I'll be safe.

Chapter One

One year later

I rode the elevator to the top floor. When the steel doors opened, I rushed down the long white hallway with slate gray carpet and came to the last condo. I pounded on the light wood door for what seemed like forever.

The door to the apartment opened and Tiffany stood in front of me, all long-legged, blonde, and staring at me with glittering aquamarine eyes.

"Sterling?" she asked in shock. "Where have—I haven't seen you—where the *hell* have you been?"

Without waiting for a reply, Tiffany grasped me gently around my wrist and all but hauled me into her luxury condo. She released me and then shut the door.

I clenched my cold hands into fists and looked around the room. It was an open floor plan with a modern kitchen and stainless-steel appliances, yet the living room was inviting and airy. Light gray walls matched the accent pillows on the white couch and high-end white trim carpentry highlighted the room. The last time I'd been over had been two years ago when she'd just moved in and she'd had no artwork to display. Now, expensively framed and expertly hung black and white photos brought the entire ambiance together.

I glanced at the clock on the microwave, noting the time. "Crap. I didn't even think—I just came over. Were you asleep?"

She snorted in wry humor. "I'm a night owl."

I nodded. "Right."

"Sterling? What's going on? Where have you been this past year? I've called and called—"

"I got a new phone number." I pinched the bridge of my nose. "Can we sit? There's a lot we have to—can we please sit?"

"Yeah, absolutely. Should I get a bottle of wine?"

"How about something stronger?"

"Glasses?"

"Don't bother."

She let out a long exhale and then went to the kitchen. Tiffany came back with a bottle of rye whiskey. Unscrewing it, she took a swig and then handed it to me.

"You look like hell," she said, studying me carefully.

When I'd had my fill, I handed the bottle back to her.

"I haven't had my hair cut in over a year."

"That's the least of it. You've got shadows under your eyes. Are you sleeping?"

"A few hours a night."

She paused, holding the bottle of rye between her legs. Staring down at it, she said, "I thought you ghosted me."

"Shit," I muttered. "I didn't want you to think that, but

there was no way for me to explain it all to you. Now I'm here and I don't know what to do and you're my best friend—my *only* friend—and, oh fuck, I probably put you in danger just for being associated with me and…"

I grabbed the bottle from between her legs and took another fortifying sip.

"Danger? What are you talking about?" Tiffany asked.

"My mother died last year," I said quietly.

"Violetta died? Did she have a funeral?" When I nodded, she frowned. "Why didn't you call me? I would've gone with you."

"I know." I shot her a tiny smile. "But I—I didn't think about it, honestly. I just kind of…went into a daze. I packed a small suitcase and drove to Kansas for the funeral."

Her eyes were somber. "She was so young. What happened?"

I stared at my hands. The home manicure I'd given myself a few days ago was already chipped and my nails needed attention.

I lurched off the couch and began to pace across her wooden living room floor. My cheap shoulder bag rested on the end table and I reached for it and unzipped it. I felt around at the bottom of the ripped lining and dug out the letter. I hadn't had the heart to burn it. The money had all but run out and the letter was the only thing I had left of my mother.

I showed the letter to Tiffany.

She frowned. "It's in Italian."

I nodded. "It explains everything, Tiff. My childhood, why we moved all the time, why she wouldn't ever let me stay in one place too long. This explains it all."

Her eyes were bright like glowing gemstones.

I enlightened her about the contents of the letter, including what my mother had said about our lineage.

Tiffany's gaze widened. "You can't be serious. You honestly don't believe—"

"Yes, I believe her," I said. "The letter alone might've given me pause, but the twenty grand that went with it made it real."

"Twenty grand? Where did she get that kind of money?"

"I don't know. The letter didn't say. It was all she had left."

I told her of the extreme measure Mama had taken to protect me.

Tiffany's hand went to her mouth, almost as if to stop the sounds of horror from escaping her lips.

I fell silent, giving Tiffany a chance to process everything I'd said. I'd had a year to replay everything again and again, on repeat.

"Jesus, Sterling, I'm so sorry. I can't even imagine. Can you tell me the rest? I want to hear it all."

Nodding resolutely, I continued. "After her funeral, I drove southeast. I wound up in a little town in Arkansas, and by some miracle, I was able to get a job under the table and rent a small apartment. But nothing happened. No scary men came looking for me, it was just *boring*. I started to think I was nuts for doing this, for living a life under the radar. I started to doubt everything. I didn't want a life like my mother's, always running. I knew why she did it, but I…anyway, I spent a lot of nights awake, wondering how it all could've turned out this way."

I bowed my head, needing a moment to compose myself. It had been so long since I'd been able to confide in someone. I'd kept to myself this past year, not wanting to make connections, not wanting to get involved, knowing I'd inevitably have to leave at some point.

"There was a car accident a few days ago just outside the town I was living in. I wasn't involved, but I saw it happen. One of the cars rolled into a ditch. The other smashed into a guardrail and caught fire. I didn't think, Tiff. I just pulled over and before I knew what I was doing, I was running to the car on fire. It was a mother and her young boy who'd been hit. I couldn't get the driver's door open; it was smashed shut, but it didn't matter. She was gone. The boy was screaming in the back seat and the fire..."

I shuddered at the memory.

"Oh my God, is the boy okay?" Her voice sounded very far away and pulled me from the memory of my recent past.

I nodded my head. "He's fine. He has a few scratches from glass, but nothing major. The fire...I got smoke in my eyes and couldn't see. The paramedics were washing my eyes out for me, and my contacts had to come out. But someone caught the whole thing on video and it's gone viral. Our local news station picked the footage up, and I freaked out. My face is all over TV. All the footage is high definition, it's everywhere. Local TV, online, all over."

"Shit." She shook her head. "You've worn contacts for as long as I've known you. I've never even seen you without them. But that's not enough, is it? How could they possibly know you're a Moretti? Your mother said in the letter that heterochromia isn't that uncommon."

"They published my legal name, Sterling Miller," I said with a grimace. "I've been giving people fake names for a year, and I lied to the paramedics, but then the police showed up and started to document witness accounts and asked for my

ID. I thought about getting a fake ID when I went on the run, but I didn't know the right people to ask, and I didn't want to draw any attention to myself by getting involved with criminals, you know? And fake IDs are not foolproof. You can tell a fake a mile away." I let out an exhale and shook my head. "I might've been able to stay on the run, but Sister Agatha knew my legal name *and* my trait, both of which are now public. And now my face is all over the media. The Foscari have every piece of the puzzle they need to identify me."

"Here, take another drink."

I threaded my hands through my hair. "I'm sorry that I brought this to your door. But I—I had nowhere else to go."

"No. You were right to come to me. I'm glad you did," she said. "You should've come to me a year ago. You shouldn't have had to do this alone. You're stronger than anyone I've ever met."

The adrenaline had worked its way out of my bloodstream, and I leaned back against the couch cushions in exhaustion. "Strong. Yeah."

"I'm serious. You did what your mother said to do. You disappeared. You tried to start a new life. And then you screwed it all up by rescuing some kid." She smiled. "You're not just strong, you're a good person. So good, Sterling."

Emotion fizzed in my throat. I couldn't speak through the tightness, so I reached out and squeezed her fingers.

Tiffany raised the bottle of rye. "To Violetta."

"To Mama."

We passed the bottle back and forth until I was too tired to keep my eyes open. When I finally lay my head on the couch's accent pillow, my legs strewn across Tiffany, I could almost pretend we were teenagers again, gossiping about the boys in our class and rating them on a sliding scale of hotness. I could almost pretend we had our entire lives ahead of us.

My eyes drifted shut, and I let myself believe I was still that girl who didn't know what the future held.

"Sterling?" Tiffany whispered.

"Hmmm?"

"Do you trust me?"

Chapter Two

"Psst. Hey. Hey, Sterling. You're drooling."

I opened my eyes and caught Tiffany's grin as dreamy morning light filtered through the large glass living room window. She held out a cup of coffee to me and I reluctantly sat up, realizing I'd fallen asleep on the couch.

"What time is it?" I asked, taking the coffee from her.

"Nine."

"I don't even remember falling asleep," I murmured, stifling a yawn.

"I tried to get you to move to the guest room, but you flung me off. So I covered you with a blanket and left you to it."

I looked into the coffee mug, steam rising toward my face. "Thanks."

"How are you feeling?"

"I don't know. Exhausted. Numb. Confused."

Her aquamarine eyes were clear, and her skin was flushed with health. She didn't look like she'd been up late pounding rye whiskey and talking to me about my past and my very screwed up present.

"There's a clean towel in the guest bathroom. Did you bring a suitcase with you?"

"I left it in my car in the parking garage. I should grab it real fast."

"I'll have Jerry get it." She called down to the security desk and a few minutes later Jerry stood at Tiffany's threshold and she was giving him my car keys.

Jerry came back within ten minutes, handing off my suitcase. I thanked him as Tiffany closed the door.

"You passed out last night before I could offer you leftovers. You must be starving." She smiled.

"I haven't eaten anything since yesterday morning," I admitted.

"Take a shower. I'll have eggs ready by the time you get out."

"Eggs would be good. Tiff? What am I going to do about this mess?"

"Shower first, food second, discussion third," she said, her tone not allowing for argument. "There's a fresh bottle of my favorite lavender body scrub. I swear it's transformative." She pointed in the direction of the guest room. "Go."

I saluted her and grabbed my suitcase to wheel it into the bedroom. Once I closed the door, I settled the suitcase in the corner and unzipped it. I pulled out an old pair of faded jeans, clean undergarments, and a gray threadbare T-shirt. With my toiletry bag in hand, I headed into Tiffany's guest bathroom.

The water was hot, and the pressure was perfect; the lavender body scrub soothed my senses. I hid for as long as I could, blocking out my hopeless reality.

But I knew I couldn't hide in Tiffany's shower, no matter how nice it was, and so I finally climbed out and towel dried my hair.

I got dressed and then went to the kitchen, lured by the aroma of eggs. My hunger kicked into high gear.

"You made this?" I asked in surprise when Tiffany slid a plate across the counter. I hopped up on a bar stool and reached for my fork.

"You think I made eggs Benedict?" She laughed. "You're cute. I called out for it. There's a café around the corner, and I tip well so they're fast."

"Well, thanks," I said in amusement. "It smells great."

"Eat."

"You didn't get anything for yourself?"

"I'll have a smoothie in a bit."

While I devoured the eggs, Tiffany stared at me pensively over her cup of coffee. "I've been thinking about your situation, and I think I have a solution."

"I'm all ears," I said.

"I know someone who can get you a new identity…a real one." Tiffany paused for a moment and then said softly, "You need to talk to Genevieve."

"Who's Genevieve?"

"My boss. She can get you a job at The Rex and a new identity."

"You work the Concierge desk, Tiff. How in the world can your boss get me a new identity?"

"I need you to trust me, Sterling." Her eyes glowed like flames.

"Of course, I trust you," I said automatically. "I came here, didn't I? I told you everything."

She smiled slightly. "You wouldn't have told me anything if you didn't need my help."

"Probably not," I admitted. "I wish I didn't have to come to you. I wish I could have left you out of it and protected you. I don't want you to run into any trouble because of my—"

"Hey, take a breath," she said softly. "You shouldn't have had to deal with this alone, Sterling. I'm happy you came to me."

"I couldn't live with myself if anything happened to you."

"Nothing is going to happen to me."

She came around the corner of the counter to embrace me, and for a moment, I let her. It had been so long since I'd felt the comfort of another person's touch.

"Thank you," I said again.

She pulled back and rested her hands on my shoulders. "I'm sorry for your loss, Sterling. But I want you to know that I admire you."

"Admire *me*? Why?"

"Because I don't know anyone who would've been able to do what you've done. You've got a lot of courage and determination."

I stared into her eyes.

"I'm tired, Tiff."

"I know."

She took my empty plate and brought it to the sink to rinse it off. "When you talk to Genevieve, don't lie to her. She's going to push and prod for information. She's going to want to know why you need a new identity and why you want a job at The Rex. You can't hide it from her."

"That goes against everything my mother's letter said —and against all my natural instincts."

"I told you, you're going to have to trust me. You can trust Gen, too. You *have* to trust Gen."

I paused for a moment. "I don't really have a choice, do I?"

"Not really. Not unless you want to take your chances and run again. I'll give you cash if that's what you need, but I don't have the connections to get you a new identity unless you speak with Gen."

"I can't take your money," I said. "As generous as the offer is, I'd never be able to pay it back and I couldn't live with that."

"Then we're back to you trusting Gen."

"Do I have to tell her everything? Can I leave out The White Company? Can I just tell her about the Foscari?"

"I think that might be okay." She stared at me as she bit her lip. "I'm worried about you."

"Don't be," I hastened to assure her. "We have a plan of attack now, right? I'll talk to Gen and state my case. I'll do whatever job I have to do to get a new identity and disappear."

"I didn't mean about your meeting with Gen. I meant I'm worried about *you*. Emotionally."

"Ah."

"You should fall apart. Cry, scream, throw shit. You've been holding it together since you got here."

"I have to hold it together because I'm afraid that if I fall apart, I'll never be able to piece myself back together."

"Have you really grieved for your mom?"

"Yes," I said, ducking my head so she wouldn't see my eyes.

"I know you. You haven't really grieved. You haven't had the time this last year. Not if you've been worried about the Foscari coming for you. You've been in survival mode. You've mashed it all down."

"I've grieved," I insisted. "Alone and in private."

She peered at me. "Alone to process everything you've learned about who you are and your mother's history?" She shook her head. "I'm afraid that if you don't deal with this, deal with your past, your mother's death, the truth of it all, you'll think you've got it handled and it will all come at you when you least expect it."

"There's nothing more to deal with," I insisted. "I haven't cried for her in over a year. It's done. I don't want to look back. I want to look forward."

"Don't take this the wrong way, but you're kind of like…"

"Like what?"

"A feral pet."

"*What?*"

"You've always been prickly and hard to comfort. You don't let anyone into your world. I get it. I understand why, but it seems even more so now than ever before." She paused. "I talk about things. I let it all hang out there. I don't care. But you guard your feelings like you're afraid someone is going to use them against you. You've been that way since the day we met."

"And you wanted to be my friend, why?"

"Because you didn't judge me for the cheap gold studs in my ears, and your offer of friendship was unreserved."

"Are you saying I have some winning qualities despite my rough edges?"

"Something like that." She grinned. "I called Gen while you were in the shower."

"Yeah?"

She nodded. "She'll see you on Monday, which means I have a day to get you ready."

I looked at her warily. "Get me ready?"

"Yeah. You didn't think I would send you into the lion's den without any weapons, did you?"

"Lion's den?"

"You're beautiful, Sterling. You're smart, you speak two languages fluently—"

"Three," I corrected.

She frowned. "Italian, English, and what else?"

"French."

"Okay, that's new."

"There wasn't a lot to do this past year while I was trying to remain under the radar."

"So, you used your time to learn another language. Sure, yeah. Because everyone does that."

"I'm not like everyone else. I wish I was," I said, staring over her shoulder to the window. Bright sunshine poured through the glass. "I just wanted normal. That's all I ever wanted to be. Instead, I have this—*legacy*—I have to contend with."

"Normal is overrated."

"It would've been nice to have had a choice, you know? Instead, my mother's history is dictating my present and my future." I shook my head. "Okay, enough with the feeling sorry for myself. That won't help. Can we go back to what you said about having to get me ready?"

"You've got the goods, but the packaging doesn't do anything for you."

"I don't know what any of that means."

"No offense, but your wardrobe leaves a lot to be desired. And your nails…" She shook her head. "Your hair is pure luxury, but you've neglected the hell out of it. You've got to *wow* her."

"Wow her," I repeated dumbly.

"The Rex is a glamorous hotel. You can't walk in there looking anything less than your best. Doesn't matter if you're a server in the Bar and Restaurant, a concierge, or a maid. You have to look your best because The Rex expects the best."

I sighed. "I know beggars can't be choosers, but I'd love nothing more than a job that lets me blend in, sit behind a desk, and stare at a computer all day long."

She looked at her watch, a dainty little piece. "Can you be ready to go in an hour?"

"Go? Go where?"

"I have a dress fitting at Folson's."

"Folson's?" I asked in surprise. "A dress fitting?"

"There's a corporate event I have to go to," she said breezily.

"I don't have nice enough clothes to get me through the front door of Folson's," I said to her, looking down at my worn-in-the-seat jeans and threadbare shirt.

She waved away my objections. "I've got a dress that will fit you."

"I'm three inches shorter than you, Tiff," I said dryly.

"It hits me mid-thigh. The length on you won't be an issue."

"But my shoes—"

"Will you stop?" she asked in exasperation. "I've got it covered, all right?"

"Why do I feel like you're not telling me everything?"

"Because I'm not."

Chapter Three

An hour later, I was wearing a black floral print dress with a belt that cinched my waist and a pair of black ballet flats that Tiffany had sent out for. I knew she was doing well at The Rex—a downtown luxury condo was nothing to sneeze at—but the fact that she could send out for breakfast and shoes gave me pause.

"You look great," Tiffany said, as she looked in the hallway mirror and tied a pink headscarf into a makeshift headband.

"Me? You're the one that looks amazing." She was dressed in an A-line blush dress with a sweetheart neckline and three-inch matching high heels. She looked completely out of time and place in the 1950s getup, and she rocked it easily.

"Let's go," she said, grabbing her matching clutch and opening it to ensure she had her favorite lip gloss.

We rode the elevator down to the underground parking garage, and I followed Tiffany to a corner space with a shiny, candy-apple red Audi TT RS backed into its spot.

"No way," I said softly. "You bought it?"

She grinned. "Yep. Signed the papers last week."

Tiffany hit the clicker and the doors unlocked. I climbed into the passenger side, my body melting into the black leather. I had to stifle a moan of pleasure.

Tiffany turned the key and the car's unique five-cylinder engine came to life. She grabbed a pair of black cat-eye sunglasses resting on the console, made sure they were clean, and placed them on her head.

She put the car into drive and wove her way through the parking garage at far too high a speed. Bright sunshine caressed my face when we got out onto the street, and I squinted at the change in light.

"There's a pair of spare sunglasses in the glove box," she said.

"Thanks," I said gratefully.

They were a little big for my face, but I didn't care. She pressed a button and a radio station playing jazz filtered through the speakers. I reached over and lowered the volume so we could talk.

"You're doing really well, Tiff. Aren't you?"

"I do okay," she averred.

"I've been hiding away, and you've been buying cars and sending out for breakfasts…"

"I got a promotion. I want to enjoy it." She turned up the music so we couldn't talk anymore.

What the hell wasn't she telling me?

I'd bared my soul to her and come to her for help, but clearly, it wasn't a two-way street. It made me embarrassed that I'd been honest with her and she wouldn't do the same.

The rest of the drive was silent and charged with tension. Finally, she turned into the department store parking lot. Tiffany cut the wheel and revved the engine loudly before parking the car directly in front of the

Folson's store entrance in the closest spot she could find, surrounded by other cars.

"Why didn't you park farther away? Aren't you afraid the car is going to get dinged?" I asked, as I grabbed my purse and opened my door to get out.

There was a whistle from a group of guys, followed by, "Sweet ride!"

Tiffany tilted her sunglasses down on her nose and then looked at me and said, "*That* is why I parked near the front."

When we arrived at the entrance to Folson's, a young man darted in front of her and held the door open, gazing at her with open worship. His Adam's apple bobbed as he gave her a long, lingering look.

Tiffany smiled and blew him a kiss, and despite my uneasiness, I grinned in amusement.

We passed both the men's and women's sections and kept going until we found the back of the store, a secluded area with a small, clean desk. A female attendant with her hair pulled into a top bun watched as we approached. Her lips formed into a polite smile.

"Hello, how may I help you?" she asked.

"My name is Tiffany Bristol and I have a dress fitting at 11:45."

The woman typed a few keys and then nodded. "Excellent. Would you follow me to the dressing room? I'll have the gown brought to you."

"Thank you," Tiffany said.

I marveled at the expensive designer gowns on display and had to stop from running my hands over the gorgeous fabrics. The attendant showed us into a room with three mirrors in a semicircle around a small, elegant platform.

"May I get you something to drink?" the attendant asked.

"Two glasses of champagne, please," Tiffany answered, as she began removing her heels.

The attendant nodded. "Deidre will be fitting your dress. Please don't hesitate to push the buzzer if you need anything."

The woman inclined her head and then shut the door. I looked back to Tiffany, who was watching me with an amused expression.

"Champagne?"

"You need it. You're wound tighter than a spring."

"No disagreement there." I looked at the dressing room door. "I've never seen that kind of service before."

"I *love* being waited on. I love people knowing I have money when I walk into places." She paused. "I've gained so much from my time at The Rex. Confidence. Financial freedom…purpose. They've been good to me."

"How did you get your job at The Rex?"

"You mean, what made a luxurious hotel take a chance on a high school graduate from a poor background?"

"I wouldn't have phrased it that way."

"Why not? It's the truth." She shrugged. "I'm not embarrassed about how I grew up. The Rex…they see potential. They're willing to take chances. Even though they want the best, and demand the best, if they see someone they can mold into an ideal Rex employee, they'll do it. That's why they're different than any of their competitors. They appreciate people who are willing to work hard."

I took a seat in the chair that rested in the corner of the private dressing room. "It sounds like you found your dream job, Tiff. I'm happy for you."

Smiling, Tiffany slithered out of her dress and hung it up on a hanger. She stood confidently in a strapless bra and white thong. A delicate golden key pendant on a fine gold chain rested against her smooth skin. She had no reason for modesty: she was tan, slender, and in-your-face beautiful. Stunning, really.

Tiffany had started her life out with distinct disadvantages, but she had managed to pull herself up from the bootstraps and make something of herself instead of falling into a life like her mother. Tiffany hadn't settled, and for her it would've been so easy to settle.

There was a knock on the door and two people entered after Tiffany told them to come in. One woman held a tray with two champagne flutes, the other—Deidre—held Tiffany's dress. It was an off the shoulder floor length, bright pink gown.

"That dress is Academy Awards worthy," I remarked.

Tiffany laughed. "If only the kids from Holy Trinity could see me now." She grinned. "Think they'd still call me names?"

"Kids are assholes," I said.

"And yet they can do so much damage to your long-term self-esteem, you know?" She shook her head.

I held the two champagne flutes as Tiffany slid into the gown. It fit her perfectly, from what I could tell, but she immediately started directing Deidre to make alterations. She was polite, assertive. There was no small talk; it was all business.

"I'll be in four-inch heels, so we should take that into account as well," Tiffany said.

Deidre nodded and began alternating between pinning the dress in places and scribbling down measurements on a notepad. I got up and handed Tiffany her drink. She gently tapped her flute to mine and we both took a sip.

It was not cheap, hangover-in-your-teeth champagne. It was complex and crisp.

I wasn't immune to the polish and luxury. It was seductive, to say the least. Especially after years of living modestly and memories of a childhood spent in rented apartments and bungalows with lawns that were more dirt than grass.

But I didn't need a job that paid what Tiffany's job paid. I just needed enough to live, enough to be comfortable, enough to be secure. I would take whatever job Genevieve offered me because it would give me a new identity, and that was my primary concern.

The fitting didn't take long and we left the dressing room. I was feeling buzzy and bold from the glass of champagne as Tiffany linked her arm through mine. She all but dragged me through the women's department.

"You need something bold but classy," she said. "Something that compliments your naturally golden complexion. How do you feel about wearing white?"

"White? Seriously? No one can get away with white unless you're a bride."

"It's hard to pull off," Tiffany agreed. "But I think you're cut out for it."

"If you say so," I muttered. "Tiff, hold on a second. I can't afford Folson's. I can't even afford Target. How am I going to—"

"I've got an account with Folson's. Don't worry about it, okay?"

"Stop telling me not to worry about it," I hissed. "This feels very…I don't know. What's the word I'm looking for?"

"Like charity?" she supplied.

I glared at her. "I was going to say sketchy. There's something sketchy going on here."

"What do you mean?" Her eyes were open wide with sham innocence.

"I mean, what aren't you telling me?"

"A lot. I'm not telling you a lot," she admitted. "But it has to be this way. You have to be a blank slate; you can't know anything when you first talk to Gen."

"Why all the mystery when it comes to The Rex?"

"You'll understand after your interview. We can talk about it all then."

Without another word about it, Tiffany changed focus and waved down a department store retail attendant and told the woman what she wanted, gesturing to me.

Before I knew it, Tiffany was ushering me back to the private dressing room and the attendant was carrying a few dresses by their hangers.

She hung them up and told me if I needed anything in a different size to let her know.

I quickly closed the door to the dressing room and looked at the options hanging in front of me. They were beautiful gowns and demurer than I expected.

"Have you got a dress on yet? I want to see."

"Hold on," I said, quickly grabbing a garment on a hanger.

"Too many ruffles," Tiffany said, when I opened the door.

The next dress was a fail, too. The asymmetrical hemline cut me off mid leg, and she immediately rejected it.

By the time the attendant returned with a pair of three-inch white patent leather pumps, Tiffany had given me the stamp of approval on the last dress. It was a form-fitting contraption that made me look more hour-glass than I was, with a modest neckline. It hit just at the knee, so it wasn't scandalously short, but timeless and sexy.

Even the retail attendant—Rachel—agreed it was perfect.

"She has to wear her hair down with that dress," Rachel said, giving her opinion.

"Yes," Tiffany agreed. "I think…long waves. Old Hollywood come back to life. It needs a good trim and a salon shampooing. I want her hair to gleam."

Rachel nodded. "I've called down to Macy in the makeup department. She's expecting you now, and I've made an appointment in the Salon for Ms. Miller."

"Thank you so much," Tiffany said, as Rachel handed her an appointment slip for the salon. "Sterling, let's get you out of that dress. We'll have it—and the shoes—sent to my place. Jerry will sign for it."

After I got dressed, we headed to the makeup department. The price tag on some of the products made my head spin, but after the dress and pumps, I realized it was useless to protest. We spent some time finding the perfect colors for my complexion and after a short while, we said goodbye to Macy and then headed to the elevators.

Tiffany pressed the "up" button.

"We're not going to the salon?" I asked.

"Not yet. The appointment isn't for another hour." She shook her head. "I'm hungry. Aren't you?"

The buzz of champagne had worn off and I'd burned through the eggs. "Yeah. I could eat, actually."

We rode the glass elevator to the fifth floor and walked to the patisserie café. The tables were covered in lace tablecloths and white china. Each of them had a tea service set and a three-tier cake stand. Tiffany sashayed up to the hostess, who looked us over.

"We don't have a reservation. I'm Tiffany Bristol." Tiffany absently touched the key pendant around her neck.

The hostess's eyes settled on Tiffany's neckline and her flat lips curved into a smile. "We have just the table for you, Ms. Bristol. Right this way, please."

We followed the young woman through the room to the back corner and arrived at a table tucked near a large window. It was private and intimate.

"Your server will be right with you. Please let me know if there's anything I can do for you."

She inclined her head and then stalked away, the sound of her heels fading as she retreated back to her hostess stand.

Two servers arrived. One carried a tea tray complete with a teapot, two cups on saucers, sugar cubes, and milk. The other brought an elegant three-tiered cake tray.

Tiffany thanked them and then they left. She took her napkin and rested it in her lap. "Have you been to high tea before?"

"No."

"Start with the tea." She held up her strainer and set it on her teacup. "We're drinking loose leaf." She lifted the teapot and poured it over the strainer and then set the pot down and gestured for me to do the same. "I like milk and sugar in my tea, so I'll add both." She grasped the tongs and picked up a sugar lump and gently eased it into the tea, avoiding any plop or splattering. She then took the creamer and added a splash of milk, as elegantly as if she had been born and raised by a prestigious family from Chelsea in west London.

"When you stir," she explained. "You don't do it in a circular motion, but in a six-twelve motion. This prevents the clinking sound and it also dissolves the sugar quickly."

She demonstrated and I nodded.

"We'll eat the finger sandwiches on the bottom tier first —with our actual fingers." Tiffany grinned. "And then we move onto the scones. And I'll show you how we do it when we get to it. Sound good?"

"Yeah," I said. "But why are you showing me all this?"

"It'll come in handy when Gen appraises you."

"Appraises me? I'm not a piece of jewelry. This is making me uncomfortable."

She peered at me over the delicate china and tea. "I've never wanted to tell you the truth more than I do right now, but I can't…"

"Do you really work for The Rex, Tiff? Or have you gotten yourself into a situation—"

"I work for The Rex, and there is no situation. Now drink the tea before it gets cold."

Chapter Four

Tiffany reached out to smooth an errant curl over my ear. "There. Now you look perfect."

I grinned. "Are you sure the red lipstick isn't too bold?"

"Oh, it's super bold, but it makes you look fearless. Besides, it's the only color you're wearing. The white dress makes it pop."

Tiffany had given me a mild sleeping pill the previous evening to ensure that I'd rest the night before the interview instead of tossing and turning, wondering about what I was walking into. I'd had a solid eight hours of sleep, and combined with the magic of high-end concealer, I looked my best.

"How are you feeling?" Tiffany asked.

"About how I look? Fine." The white dress and pumps that Tiffany had picked out for me made me feel strong, powerful. Like I was wearing armor. "I think I get why you like going out with a full face of makeup, your hair done, and wearing designer clothes. I feel like a warrior. I mean —a very pretty warrior—but a warrior nonetheless."

"Let me hear your battle cry," she said with a grin.

"I'm yelling on the inside," I replied. "You sure you can't give me one tiny inkling about what I'm walking into?"

"Nope. Now get going. There's a car waiting downstairs for you."

I frowned. "What? I was going to drive myself."

"No offense, but you can't show up to The Rex in your car."

"What's wrong with my car?"

"If you have to ask…" She grinned impishly. "It doesn't make the right impression. Take the car downstairs. Dan will drive you to The Rex, and he'll bring you back here when you're finished." She took my rudimentary flip phone and programmed Dan's number into it. "There. Now, don't worry about a thing. Remember to smile."

I saw my reflection in the mirror by the door. I looked like myself, but felt more settled into my own body, somehow. Same dark brown hair the color of maple syrup, only now it gleamed from the treatment and trim at the salon. Same golden-brown eyes thanks to the contact lenses I'd worn since I was seven. Same lush mouth that was quick to snap a snide retort.

But I felt more like me than I had in a long time. Maybe because I was in the presence of my oldest friend, someone I trusted implicitly.

I squeezed her hand and then walked to the door.

"Sterling…"

"Yeah?"

"I never realized it before, but you walk just like your mother. I can see her in you. Be strong."

"Thanks Tiff." I flashed a smile and then went downstairs to the black town car waiting for me. I kept my manicured nails clasped in my lap on the drive to The Rex as I stared out the window from the back seat of the car. My mind began to wander, but I forced myself to think of the looming interview. Nothing else mattered at that moment except my meeting with Genevieve. If I had any hope of disappearing and staying safe, then I needed to convince this woman that I would be an asset to The Rex.

I arrived at The Rex fifteen minutes before my scheduled meeting at eleven. I tried to project confidence as I strode across the marble floor of the hotel. I turned a few heads in the process and that did a lot for my ego. For a year, I'd tried to be invisible, but now raw, feminine satisfaction at being noticed curled through me.

I sat down on a white couch in the lobby and watched the patrons of the hotel. Men in well-tailored suits walked through the room heading to the Bar and Restaurant, the front desk, or to the elevators. People shook hands as they met to dine, and some laughed and spoke as though they had known each other for years.

There was a palpable energy in the hotel. I couldn't put my finger on it, but it felt like I was witnessing the elite in their natural habitat. Hotel rooms went for no less than six hundred a night. You had to have some serious cash to stay at The Rex, but judging by the amount of people in the lobby, the price tag didn't seem to be a deterrent. If anything, The Rex was selecting its own customer base, weeding out those that couldn't afford to stay there. The hotel projected pure opulence and luxury, and it catered to those who wanted nothing less than the best.

A young woman with dark blonde hair in a low bun at the nape of her neck strode across the floor wearing a black pencil skirt and a white, pressed button-down. Her steps were long and confident as she approached me, surveying me up and down with intelligent eyes behind a pair of black frames.

I stood and smiled.

She reached out a hand before she'd even come to a stop. "Ms. Miller?"

"Yes." I took her hand and gave it a shake.

"Welcome to The Rex. My name is Annika. If you'll come with me, I'll show you to Genevieve's office."

"Thank you." I dropped her hand and walked beside her as we went toward the elevators.

There was no idle chitchat as we waited for the doors to open. A soft bell chimed, signaling the arrival of a car. The doors pinged open and Annika gestured for me to proceed first.

She pushed the button for the fifteenth floor and the light turned a golden orange and the doors closed in front of us, but the elevator didn't move. She then reached into her blouse to pull out a golden skeleton key on a chain, similar to the one Tiffany wore. Annika took off the necklace and placed the one-inch long key into a single, tiny unmarked keyhole next to the button for the fifteenth floor. With a gentle turn, the elevator came to life and we started our ascent. She removed the key from the keyhole and placed the necklace back around her neck and tucked it into her blouse, hiding it from sight.

We were silent, which I was grateful for. The steady beating of my heart was enough to occupy me. I held my clutch, determined to appear poised instead of nervous.

The elevator came to a halt and the doors slid open to reveal a room with cream brocade patterned wallpaper and an antique oak desk with detailed scrollwork on the legs. The air smelled of lemongrass and instantly made me feel welcome.

Annika stepped out of the elevator and I followed her, my gaze roving across the walls and artwork. She walked to a closed door that hadn't been visible from the elevator and rapped on it before pushing it open. "I have Ms. Miller for you."

"Thank you," came a distinctive feminine voice. "Please show her in."

Annika turned around as she pushed the door farther open. "Genevieve will see you now."

"Thanks," I said as I strode past her into the room.

The door closed behind me and I took a moment to marvel at the space. It wasn't at all like the front room I'd just walked through. It looked like an English library, complete with leather couches, a gas fireplace, and shelves lined with leather bound books.

A woman with a brown chin-length bob wearing a short-sleeved black silk dress sat on one of the small couches that faced the fireplace, papers spread out on the dark wood table in front of her.

She looked up and gave me a cursory glance. "Have a seat," she commanded. "I'll be with you in just a moment."

I did as she said and sat down in one of the leather chairs—the one facing away from the window so I wouldn't be distracted by the view of the outside world.

While the woman ignored me and focused on the papers in front of her, I let my gaze wander around the room again. It didn't look at all like the sort of place one would conduct an interview. It wasn't a sterile environment meant to keep someone on edge, but rather warm and hospitable.

"What do you think?" Genevieve asked.

I jumped and then let out a small laugh. I'd been so engaged with the thoughts in my own head that I'd forgotten she was there.

"It's stunning," I admitted. "Completely at odds with the front room." My gaze met hers.

Genevieve set down a black fountain pen and then casually leaned against the couch. She lifted her arm so her elbow rested on the back of the leather sofa as she peered at me.

"I spend a lot of time in here. I wanted it to be comfortable."

I nodded, setting my clutch aside, wishing I had something to do with my hands.

There was another knock on the door and Annika came in with a tea tray. She set it down and then discreetly left again.

I looked at the tea tray and held in a snort of laughter.

Tiffany, you wily bitch.

We spent the next few minutes fixing our tea. I held my teacup like a shield, waiting for Genevieve to direct the interview. So far, all she'd managed to do was peruse me from head to toe. Her eyes gleamed with shrewd intelligence and I wondered what thoughts were circulating through her mind.

"Tiffany told me you need a new identity. Why?"

I sucked in a breath, unprepared for such directness, but then I told her. It was an abbreviated version, and I essentially explained that the Foscari were after me without telling her about my family, The White Company. When I divulged the Foscari name, I watched to see if there was a flash of recognition in Genevieve's eyes. There wasn't.

She took a sip of tea, acting like I hadn't just revealed an outlandish story.

Hating her lack of reply, I continued to speak. "I didn't bring a resume, but I'm not picky. I'll take whatever job is available, as long as I can get a new identity."

"Whatever job is available," Gen repeated. She set her

teacup down in its saucer, which rested on the coffee table. "Do you know why you're interviewing with me on The Fifteenth Floor and not downstairs with the rest of the staff?"

I shook my head.

"What is it you think Tiffany does for a living, Sterling? You've seen her condo and her clothes, her car, the way they waited on her at Folson's. There's no way you actually believe she works the concierge desk, do you?"

She didn't give me a chance to reply.

"The Fifteenth Floor is a brothel, Sterling," Genevieve said plainly.

I blinked. "*Excuse me?*"

"A brothel."

My head spun.

Gen went on, "Tiffany is a Rex girl, a courtesan."

"She never told me," I murmured in a daze. "Even when I asked her—I knew she wasn't telling me the full truth but—"

"Of course she didn't tell you the truth. She's not allowed to. None of the girls are."

Tiffany had sex for money.

My best friend, the only person in the entire world I fully trusted, had lied to me about what she did for a living and sent me into an ambush.

It all made sense; why she'd insisted on dressing me, doing my hair and makeup. She had groomed me so that when I met with Genevieve, I looked the part.

Looked the part of a high-end call girl.

The cage door of my emotions flung open and boiling hot rage poured through my blood. I stood slowly.

"You both must think I'm a world-class idiot," I said, seething. "She let me come in here and all but beg for a job

—any job—but apparently the only job I'm suited for is spreading my—"

"Sit down," Genevieve commanded firmly, not bothering to rise from her seat.

I held her stare. The woman was cool and composed.

"Sit down," she said again, this time more softly. "Or, walk out of here and take your chances trying to find someone who can do for you what *I* can do for you."

Desperation bloomed in place of my animosity and I collected my emotions and bottled them. With a deep breath, I sat.

"Don't blame Tiffany. She wasn't allowed to prepare you. When I interview new girls, I need to see their true emotions when I explain what it is we do here. It tells me a lot about who they are, yourself included. If you'll allow me, I'll give you some more information, and then you can take your time and make a decision. You can leave anytime you want, Sterling. I won't stop you or beg you to stay. I haven't even technically offered you anything. But bear this in mind, if you do walk out of here, that's it. You won't be given another chance. Ever."

"So, I have to decide if I want to do this before I leave your office?"

"You don't even know what *this* is or what it entails." She peered at me. "Besides, if anyone has the right to be upset right now it's me."

"You?"

"You can't be that naive, can you? That story you told me, about your mother and the Foscari." She shook her head. "I'm crazy to even entertain this meeting."

I frowned. "Why are you, then?"

"Tiffany has never vouched for another girl. She's never even asked me to *meet* with someone new."

"That can't be enough of a reason, can it? I mean, no matter how amazing of an…employee she is."

She paused, her expression pensive. "I owe Tiffany a great debt. And in our world, you pay your debts. And that's all I'll say about it. But frankly, I'm not sure you're cut out for this line of work. It takes a certain type of person to do this job—and I'm not just talking about the business transaction of sex. To be a Rex girl…it's not just about being beautiful. Which you know you are. But so are many other girls. No, it's about something more. That *je ne sais quoi.*"

She lifted the teacup and took a sip. "Our clients aren't looking for normal women. Boring women. Stupid women. These are wealthy men, powerful and decisive. They're the movers and shakers of the world. They thrive on success and challenges. They buy eight hundred-dollar bottles of Barolo they don't even finish. They have private art collections that rival the world's best museums and yet have never been seen by the public, and on and on. Why? Because they *can.*"

Genevieve's gaze scanned me from head to toe, cataloguing me again. "You're hot headed and repulsed by what we do. It's written all over your face. Girls like you normally don't even make it through my front door." She leaned toward me as if to ensure I didn't miss what she said next. "But as I mentioned before, I owe Tiffany. You have bravado, I'll give you that, but I can see the fear in your eyes. I'll give you a new identity, but nothing in life is free. To earn it, you must become a Rex girl and have skin in the game."

"I speak three languages fluently and—"

"Even better. Our clients are from all over the world."

"No, I meant—"

"I know what you meant, but I don't care," she said, her tone hard as she interrupted me for a second time. "You want a regular job in an office cubicle. I'm not offering you that. You'd be wasted in an office. If you become a Rex girl, you'll be given every luxury you can imagine by the men you spend time with. Gifts, jewelry, clothes. You'll be able to travel and spend time on private estates. You'll experience places that most of the population doesn't even know exist as you see the world in first-class style. Are your morals so unwavering that you can't be tempted by those things?"

"It's not about morals."

"It's not? Then what's the problem?"

My heart pounded so loudly in my ears that it drowned out everything else. I wasn't sure why I was so shocked. My best friend had been doing this for years and seemed no worse for wear. Not only did she have every luxury she wanted, but she didn't seem jaded. She didn't seem... *broken.*

Genevieve's gaze was unwavering. "You have a choice, Sterling. We all have a choice. But you have to ask yourself if your pronouncement still stands. What are you willing to do to be safe?"

Genevieve paused, waiting for my answer.

An answer I didn't know if I was ready to give.

There was a knock on the door. Annika popped her head in, her hand still on the knob. "Sorry to disturb you," she said. "Ramsey is on the phone for you."

"Tell him I'll be right with him."

Annika nodded and then closed the door. I turned my attention back to Genevieve.

"I have to take this call, but we're not finished with this discussion," Genevieve said finally. "I'm willing to give you some time to think over what I've just told you. Please wait in the restaurant in the lobby. Have lunch and I'll be in touch with you shortly."

I tamped down an audible sigh of relief as I went to the door, ready to escape the room.

"And Sterling…" Gen called from behind me.

I looked over my shoulder.

"Give it some serious thought," she said. "There are far worse things in life than becoming a Rex girl."

Chapter Five

The lobby wasn't as busy as it had been when I'd arrived for my interview, yet the few people present still moved about with purpose. The Rex suddenly reminded me of a hive of insects all united toward a common goal.

I headed to the restaurant. A young man dressed in a white button-down shirt, a charcoal gray vest, and a skinny red tie stood at the host stand. His brown hair was parted and styled like a 1950s businessman and he welcomed me with an authentic smile.

"Hello," he said. "Do you have a reservation?"

I shook my head. "I just had an interview with Genevieve and—"

"Enough said. Right this way, please."

He picked up a menu and led me to a two-top in the corner of the room and then went to one of the chairs to pull it out for me.

"Do you mind if I sit at the bar?" I asked.

"Not at all." He pushed the chair back in and gestured toward the bar.

When I was settled on a stool with a menu in front of me, I was able to turn and survey the restaurant.

The decor was old-world yet inviting. Gaslight sconces graced the walls, casting the restaurant in dim but romantic lighting. It was classic in a way that was not only for those on dates, and I had the sense that a lot of business deals were made over perfectly seasoned steaks and handshakes.

A cute, blond bartender approached and set down a Rex Hotel coaster in front of me. "May I get you something to drink?"

"Just sparkling water, please."

I glanced at the menu again but didn't register any of the dishes. I wasn't really hungry. Not after *that* meeting.

My thoughts swirled in my head like smoke. The truth about The Fifteenth Floor hadn't fully sunk in yet, but for some reason I was strangely intrigued by Gen's offer, by the picture she had presented. I wasn't immune to opulence and wealth. I couldn't ignore the fact that The Rex world was seductive. They sold sex, clearly. But was there more to it than that?

"May I get you something to eat?" the blond bartender asked, jarring me out of my thoughts.

"No thanks," I said. "I'm not really hungry."

He inclined his head and then moved away, leaving me alone with my questions.

Two older men walked into the Bar and Restaurant, dressed in tailored suits. The host sat them at a table in the center of the room. They commanded the space around them and when the server came to take their order, neither of them looked at their menus before speaking.

They knew what they wanted and how they wanted it, and there was no hesitation in their choices.

Would these be the type of men I spent time with if I became a Rex girl?

The man who faced me moved his head and met my gaze. He arched an eyebrow and a slow smile spread across his face.

I hastily turned around, wanting to hide, wondering if I would learn to flirt and be comfortable being valued for my physical being.

I wasn't a prude or a virgin. I'd had relationships. They'd been underwhelming and unsatisfying, fizzling out as quickly as they'd started. I'd often wondered if there was something inherently wrong with me, since I could never find a man that held my interest.

Swallowing, I thrust that idea away. If I thought about all the reasons I couldn't or shouldn't be a Rex girl, I'd chicken out. I'd walk out of the lobby and never look back, and then I'd have to take my chances on the run again from the Foscari.

But if I said yes? If I said yes, a whole new avenue would open up before me. I didn't know nearly enough about The Rex world or what it meant to work on The Fifteenth Floor, but I knew that my back was to a wall. I'd lived on borrowed time the past year, and I was exposed and out of money. I wouldn't survive, not on my own. If I walked away from the offer in front of me, I might never have another chance at starting a new life.

Genevieve wasn't convinced I was cut out to be a Rex girl, and I agreed with her. I didn't *want* to become a Rex girl. But if I wanted to survive, as my mother had told me to do, I didn't see any other choice.

I was staring into my glass of sparkling water, watching the bubbles fizz and pop when I noticed a man approach the bar.

Even though I was distracted, I couldn't help but spare

a glance in his direction. He unbuttoned his black suit jacket before sliding his large body onto the stool right next to mine. There were a few other seats available at the bar, and I wished he'd used one of them.

His hair was blond with subtle hints of red.

A male strawberry blond. In the wild.

The thought made me smile.

My grin somehow pulled his attention because he looked at me head on. His stormy blue-gray eyes were mesmerizing, and when I was able to pull my gaze away from them, I was finally able to see the entire picture of his face. He had a bold, unapologetic nose which was the slightest bit crooked, no doubt from a fight. His jaw line was chiseled and cut.

He sat close enough that I could detect the faintest trace of expensive aftershave, and it made me wonder at the color of his beard. Would it be blond? Red? Darker auburn? I suddenly had to know.

I'd never seen a man like him in my entire life. Brawny and impressive—and though he filled out the expensive, tailored suit perfectly, it looked like a shield from a world he didn't belong in. He appeared to be fighting his natural instinct, hiding something in the darkness to seem civilized in public.

"Like what you see?" His voice was a sensual Scottish burr, and it had me shooting my gaze to his face.

He didn't look at all like he was joking, and there was no hint of a smile on his cruel mouth.

Cruel because his lips were temptation. Full and rich. Designed perfectly to drive hopeless women to the brink of stupidity.

He was too angular, too sure of his countenance to be anything but assertive, and it was clear he wore his natural confidence better than he wore a suit.

Desire pulsed low in my body.

"Cat got your tongue?" he pressed.

His tone did not come out teasing, as if he couldn't be bothered with banter.

It made my spine snap straight. I would not give him the satisfaction of retreating, of trying to lie and pretend I hadn't been physically assessing him. If I was interviewing to be a high-class call girl, then why not practice the art of flirtation on a complete stranger I'd never see again?

I took a sip of my water and dropped my chin so that I could look up at him through the sweep of my lashes. "Yes. I think I do like what I see."

He clenched his carved jaw and refused to turn his eyes away from mine. If anything, his gaze darkened. The mood transformed from stormy to tempest.

What would he be like unleashed?

The fear of the Foscari and the complete lack of control over my own life, the crossroads I was at, all melded together in a stew of lust which I hadn't felt in far too long. I was ready to do something dangerous.

I wanted to lean toward this stranger, place my lips against his, and get lost in the feel of him for a few hours. It was out of character, it was destructive, it was playing with gasoline and a lighter.

The bartender returned with a platter of bone marrow and set it in front of the man next to me. "Compliments of the house," he said. "Would you like something to drink?"

"SINNERS neat. Thank you."

After the bartender set the glass of amber liquid on a coaster, he said, "Enjoy." He moved away to the other end of the bar to talk to another patron.

The stranger scooped up a dollop of marrow and placed it on a slice of grilled Tuscan bread.

"Do you eat?" he asked.

My mouth flickered up in amusement. "On occasion. Why? Are you asking me to dinner?"

He looked at me. "Why go to dinner when there's food in front of us right now?" The man took his bread plate and set down the grilled Tuscan bread slathered with bone marrow and placed it in front of me.

"Are you adventurous?" he asked.

I boldly met his gaze. "Are we still talking about food?"

His jaw clenched again and the muscles near his neck pulsed lightly, and without bothering with a piece of bread, he spooned out the bone marrow and slid it between his lips.

I picked up what he'd set in front of me and took a bite. The bone marrow tasted like rich, decadent sin sliding down my throat. With my eyes focused on him, I couldn't help but wonder how *he* tasted.

I devoured the bone marrow in a few bites, not caring how it came across. As I ate, he watched me with resolve.

"If I didn't have a very important business meeting soon, I'd ask if you wanted to get a hotel suite for the afternoon."

"Just the afternoon?" I breathed.

He nodded slowly.

My nipples tightened as a shot of desire zinged through my veins, and a gentle throbbing pulsed between my legs.

He leaned forward ever so slightly toward me. "What are you doing later tonight?"

The reality of my circumstances, and the fact that I was waiting to finish an interview to become a high-class escort came crashing back, effectively obliterating the bubble of desire I would've gladly remained in.

"I'm busy."

"Too bad." His cell phone rang and he reached into his

breast pocket to pull it out. He looked at me, his blue-gray eyes hard when moments ago they'd been openly lustful. "When you change your mind, leave your name and number with the front desk of the hotel."

He got up from his stool, and without a backward glance, put the phone to his ear and strode out of the Bar and Restaurant.

When I change my mind?

Arrogant ass.

My nipples didn't seem to care that he was an arrogant ass.

He didn't ask for my name; he hadn't cared to. I didn't even know his, since he'd never offered it.

I looked at my phone, and saw it was already two o'clock. There had been no word from Genevieve.

Was this a test? Was she waiting for me to decide one way or another, refusing to coerce, instead leaving the choice to me?

It would make her life easier if I walked out of The Rex and never returned.

I opened my clutch and pulled out a few bills and left them next to my water glass and then I hopped off the stool.

The blonde reservationist at the front counter was in the middle of a phone call, and I impatiently waited for her to give me her attention. She smiled at me as she hung up.

"Hello, ma'am. Checking in?"

"Actually, I'm trying to get ahold of Genevieve."

I watched the desk agent's blue eyes widen in understanding. "Absolutely. Who shall I say is calling?"

"She knows."

The woman lifted the receiver and pressed a button. A moment later she said, "Hello? Yes. I have someone for

Genevieve." Her eyes rolled over my appearance as she waited for the person on the other end to finish talking.

"Yes, that's correct. Great. I'll send her up." She placed the phone down and looked at me. "Take the farthest elevator and press the button that says WR."

I frowned. "WR?"

"It's the Whisky Room."

"Thank you," I said, wasting no time in trekking across the lobby to the elevators.

As I ascended the floors, my pulse drummed in my ears. I had to expect the unexpected with Gen. I was prepared for that now.

The elevator doors opened to a view of the Dallas skyline. It felt like I was floating among the clouds and the world was at my feet. It stole my breath.

I stepped out onto the dark stained wood floors into a room that was filled with leather chairs, couches, and coffee tables. An unlit gas fireplace graced the center of the room. The Whisky Room was deeply masculine and smelled of pipe and cigar tobacco, sandalwood, and leather.

Genevieve sat alone at the bar off to the right, a tumbler in her hand, and a slight smile on her face. She took a sip of her drink as I approached.

"Why is it called the Whisky Room?" I asked as I strode to her. I placed my clutch on the wooden bar, perched on the stool next to her, and crossed my legs.

"It's what we serve the most of. Scotch whisky, Irish whiskey, American whiskey. There are actual casks of it through that door." She pointed to a discreet wooden door that nearly blended into the wall. "Including Flynn Campbell's own signature scotch, SINNERS."

That's what he'd been drinking.

"Flynn Campbell," I murmured. "The owner of The Rex Hotel empire."

She inclined her elegantly styled head. "What's your poison?"

"What are you drinking?"

"A glass of SINNERS, of course," she said with a wry smile.

"Then I'll have that, please. The same way you're drinking it."

She set her glass down and hopped up. Genevieve went behind the bar and grabbed a clean rocks glass, and then swiped a bottle of SINNERS, popped the cork, and poured me a stout, three-finger glass.

Shit's about to get real.

Genevieve set the bottle down, slid the glass across the bar to me, and then came back around to sit on her stool.

I frowned as I grasped the tumbler and looked into the glass of amber beauty.

"Something wrong?" Genevieve asked.

"No. It's just—well—you're treating me differently than you did in your office."

She reached for her glass again but didn't move to take a sip. "I'm not often wrong about first impressions. I'm still not sure I'm wrong about you, Sterling. I have my doubts that you're cut out for this, but you didn't leave the hotel, which means you've thought this over somewhat, and you took it upon yourself to ask to speak to me again. I'm still willing to give you a chance. If you want it."

My hand grew slick around the glass, but I refused to fall at her feet to thank her.

"Want has nothing to do with it. I need this."

"Fair enough."

I finally lifted the glass of scotch to my nose and

inhaled. Peat and citrus teased my senses. I took a sip and held it on my tongue a moment before swallowing.

Genevieve's eyes studied me, but she didn't ask what I thought. "I'm about to tell you things that can never be discussed with anyone, ever. Before we proceed, you need to understand that what you're about to get involved in won't be supported by attorneys or NDAs. We have…*other means* of dealing with people who violate our trust. Are you with me?"

I nodded.

"Good. The one rule we have is utter secrecy. You'll learn the ropes as time goes on, but secrecy begins immediately. You can discuss any and all things pertaining to The Fifteenth Floor with me and anyone I approve of, and no one else. Do you understand?"

"Yes."

"Excellent, Sterling," she said. "Now we can finally get down to business. There are three types of keys. Rose gold, yellow gold, and platinum. Rose gold is the lowest tier. The platinum key is the highest tier. Each key represents something different. Rose gold means a man will have the pleasure of your body, but anal is off limits and you don't swallow. Yellow gold: He gets your body as he wants… nothing is off limits. Platinum: You behave like the yellow gold level, but you're also available for threesomes or multiples." Her grin was wry. "Have I shocked you?"

"A little," I admitted with a nervous laugh. "I suppose I'll have to get over it though, right?"

"When we speak, I'll be forthright and honest. When you're with a man, it's all about seduction, but right now you have to know the rules. If we can't get past discussing sexual acts, then you won't be able to go through with this."

I all but gulped the scotch in front of me, waiting for Gen to continue.

"All girls start at the rose gold level. You will too. Some girls wish to remain at the rose gold level for their entire career. That is entirely up to them. They don't earn nearly as much, but the choice is always theirs. So is the choice to leave, at any time after their first year is complete. Let's be clear, if you accept the terms of working here, you must work The Fifteenth Floor for one year *minimum*."

"And if I decide I'm not cut out for this? And want to leave before the year mark?"

"What The Rex giveth, The Rex can taketh away. You don't want to find out what happens when you cross us."

It wasn't a full-on threat, but it was enough.

"I won't screw over your hotel. I'm one person against an empire. I know you could bury me."

"Let's operate on good will then, okay?" she said with a small smile of understanding.

"Okay."

She took a sip of her own scotch before setting it down. "Do you want to know about the earning tiers? I figure it's not overly crass discussing money, considering we're talking about men buying certain holes of yours for the night."

I choked on the last of my drink and coughed. Tears leaked out of the corners of my eyes and I gasped air.

Genevieve let out a chuckle. "You're going to have to get over that prudish instinct."

"What exactly says prude about me? Because I literally choked on the word 'holes'?"

Genevieve's humor could no longer be contained, and her chuckle gave way to a full-on belly laugh. "Fair enough. Rose gold earns two thousand a night. Yellow gold is five thousand. Platinum, seventy-five hundred. Of course, we take our cut, and you get what's left over. It's plenty. Just ask Tiffany."

My head spun at the numbers she'd thrown out.

"Rex girls aren't just grouped by keys. They're also divided by tiers. There are two of them," she said, speeding right along. "Tiffany is in the regular tier. She keeps her birth name, her normal life, and when people she knows in the outside world ask where she works, she tells them she works at The Rex, just like she told you. Everyone knows The Rex is high-end. When she's with clients, Tiffany has a persona and they don't know who she really is. They don't get personal. They may be powerful, but they also know our ground rules and no one, at any level, gets to violate them. The regular tier girls' persona is just a reference for the next time a client of theirs calls. Regular girls have clients that are wealthy, but that's about it. The men have enough money to play the game, but they aren't the movers and the shakers."

She paused and looked at me. "Still with me? Do you need more scotch?"

"I'm good."

Nodding, she continued. "Then there's the Elite tier. The girls that go that route give up their real name, their identity, everything, because they're with men who can't be seen doing what they're doing or ever be connected with that part of society under any circumstance. We protect all of our clients, but for these men we also take care of travel and security. They don't just walk into The Rex. They show up in private cars to events and use service entrances in the night. These are politicians, judges, powerful men who shape the world. Those are the men the Elite girls entertain. You will become an Elite girl." Gen touched the corner of her coaster. "Do you have questions?"

"Yes."

"Ask them."

"All right." I took a deep breath. "How does this work, exactly? How do I meet clients?"

"We don't have a dedicated room where men come to meet our Elite girls. We hold events. Some of the events will take place at The Rex, where we are the hosts. Some will be at other locations. Mansions, private estates, nightclubs, even ski resorts. Those sorts of places. We are their guests at such events. Sometimes we fly girls out to private locations, with security of course. Dubai, Paris, London."

"Okay," I said, gripping my thigh to keep myself steady and alert.

"But you will choose the men you sleep with. Every girl does. No man can claim a woman; he can only make her an offer. The choice is always yours. Security does not tolerate any sort of force whatsoever when it comes to our girls. You will be protected by men who are absolute professionals.

"The keys I discussed earlier, the pendants; they are more than symbols. The keys signal to our clients what you're available for, but they can't take them from you or claim you. They will have to"—she paused and smiled—"*woo* you into choosing them for the evening. Once you choose a client, you give him your key. No money exchanges hands from them to you, and you *never* ask for, or talk to them about money. All of that is already taken care of, and security knows every client by face and name. They are all vetted and have accounts with us. You and our clients are watched like a hawk from the moment you begin speaking to them to the moment you begin to entertain them."

I blinked in confusion. "Hold on. I really get to choose?"

"You get to choose," she repeated.

"But isn't that—well, doesn't that seem counterintuitive? If a man wants to pay for sex, why are we giving them hoops to jump through?"

"These men are alpha males. They enjoy the chase; no, they *thrive* on it. The Rex is not an average hotel and The Fifteenth Floor is not your average brothel. Just like our clients, The Rex is elite. Everyone who works here is elite in some fashion. The bartenders, security, everyone. The Rex stands for the best, and in our world of decadence and sin, our girls are desired worldwide.

"The way we operate means that our clients never grow bored. It's not just about sex, Sterling. It's about the art of seduction, and the keys given by our women are like trophies to them. You're not regular prostitutes," she emphasized. "You're courtesans. We use our femininity, our sensuality, and our minds to charm them into wooing us. It's reverse psychology at its finest, a clever game of cat and mouse where they see a woman they want, and even if they've already been chosen by her in return, they have to earn their time with her. After a night with you, they will feel like they have really won something of value that can't be bought with any amount of money, and they'll have a key to prove it."

She cocked her head to the side and studied me. "If it was just about sex, we'd do things like every other high-class escort business. They'd come in, pick a girl on looks alone, have sex with her, and then leave. But that market is saturated, and believe it or not, men grow bored of that. Particularly these men."

She'd thrown a lot of information at me, but the only thing I focused on was the fact that Rex girls got to choose who they slept with.

"I need to use the restroom," I murmured, slipping off the stool.

"Other side of the room." Genevieve pointed.

I grabbed my clutch and almost jogged to the bathroom, but I forced myself to keep my steps steady. I was retreating—and I was sure Genevieve knew it. It was one thing to discuss the idea in the abstract. It was quite another to venture forward with the details.

I quickly found the empty restroom. I took a moment to grip the marble counter. Forcing my gaze into the glass, I studied my reflection.

"You can do this," I whispered to myself. "You *have* to do this. Stop looking scared. Stop looking like a wounded bird. She sees it all."

I opened my clutch and found the mint tin and popped a tiny breath freshener. After the quick reprieve, I headed back to the bar.

Gen impassively watched me stride across the empty room toward her. She was a keen observer and even though I didn't know her, I found that I admired her shrewd acumen, her discerning eye, her ability to cut through the bullshit and tell me what I needed to know.

I settled on the stool and set my clutch aside.

"Better?" she asked with wry amusement.

I arched a brow. "Better than what?"

She chuckled knowingly and then picked up where we'd left off. "All of The Rex girls go through a six-week training period—"

"I don't have six weeks. The car accident…I'm on camera…I need a new identity now."

Genevieve paused for a moment and then said, "Okay. There's an event three days from now. You will be there." Her eyes bored into mine. "Due to your circumstances, I'll skip the formalities and you can train later. If you give your key away to a client at the event, the job is yours and you will become an Elite tier Rex girl. We'll get you set up with a new identity, a new social, a new name. Your old life will be dead to you. As far as the world will know, you'll have suffered a terrible car accident and been buried hastily, without family. We'll publish an obituary in the local paper to confirm your death. The old you simply won't exist. That's what we do. You'll be completely anonymous in your new life, and more importantly, you'll be safe. Now, pour yourself a second drink and finish it quickly so we can move on to phase two."

I blinked. "Phase two?"

"Phase two is the physical exam."

Chapter Six

Hours later I was back in Tiffany's plush apartment, curled up on the couch with a red and black wool blanket around my shoulders. My mind glided over the events of the afternoon—and I realized I was processing everything with a clear sort of detachment.

I'd seen a doctor who had drawn my blood to test for any abnormalities or blood-borne diseases and to confirm I was actively taking birth control, and then she'd given me a gynecological exam. She'd been gentle and efficient, but I felt violated, nonetheless.

I'd also had to stand naked in front of Genevieve, who'd studied my body like I was a piece of livestock. It was beyond intimate, and there was no part of my being that hadn't been examined.

Somehow, I'd managed to remain aloof and disconnected, realizing that at some point I'd have to bare all to a man I'd give my key to.

"We're not looking for perfection," Genevieve stated after I'd slid back into my dress. "We're not looking for a perfect stomach or a size four woman with a specific hair color. Women come in all shapes and sizes. This is about making sure you aren't trying to hide track marks or scars from self-harm."

Genevieve had told me to come back to The Rex the next morning at nine for my spa and salon appointment. After, she'd get me sorted with an outfit for the event.

I was beginning to feel like a doll being dressed up. None of it felt real and I was having trouble wrapping my mind around what I had agreed to do.

Tiffany blew through the door and then locked it before striding across the floor, her heels clacking against wood.

"Hey gal," she said, eyeing me warily. She set her clutch down on the coffee table and took a seat next to me, crossing her legs. She was wearing dark skinny jeans and a rhinestone bustier. She looked oddly ready for a night out. I glanced at the clock. It was only seven p.m. Fatigue made it feel like two in the morning.

"How was the interview?" she asked.

"Long," I said.

She plucked the mug of tea from my hand and sniffed it. "There's no bourbon in this."

I smirked. "No. Just good old-fashioned chamomile."

She fell silent and then said, "Okay, let's hear it."

"Hear what?"

She groaned. "I'm sorry, Sterling. I wanted to tell you about my job so many times, you have to believe me."

I nodded slowly. "I've been sitting here for hours, going over and over everything." I frowned. "I felt betrayed, at first. That you sent me to Gen without telling me a damn thing."

"I couldn't."

"I know."

"And I—"

"Hold on, let me get this out." I paused and then looked at her. Her gemstone-colored eyes gleamed in the light, but they were steady and piercing. "I came to you, without a doubt in my mind that I could trust you. I told you the truth about my mother, about her past, the letter—all of it. You not telling me about The Rex and what you really do for a living? Yeah, it hurt. It made me feel like you didn't trust me, but once I got past all my anger, I realized you kept your word. You didn't betray The Rex and tell me the truth, which is how I know I was right in coming to you." I grabbed her hand. "You're trustworthy and I'm—I'm honored that you went to bat for me."

She swallowed and tears welled in her eyes. "Damn you. All this time, I thought you were going to tear me a new one…"

I shook my head. "Gen said you've never asked her to meet with a girl on your recommendation."

"I haven't."

"She also said she owes you one. What's that about?"

She smiled slightly. "Iron vault, remember? She offered you a job, didn't she?"

"Yeah. I'll work the event in three days and go through the training period after."

"That's not normally how it's done. The training period is to get you ready for—"

"I don't have time. I need the new identity now."

She paused. "It's a serious commitment. It will make you question everything you've been taught about morality. You'll have really intense moments where you think you're doing something wrong, but then you'll make your peace with it."

"I can't stop thinking about right or wrong."

Tiffany cocked her head to the side. "Do you think it's wrong?"

"Well, it's illegal."

"So, laws are always right?"

"No. Definitely not. Damn, this is all sorts of weird. I'm talking about making my living by selling my body. How did you reconcile it when you first began?" I asked.

"You've been on dates, right?"

"Of course."

"Have any of the men you were with paid for dinner?"

"Yeah. Most of them, but that's not the—"

"Did you sleep with any of them? I mean, after they paid for dinner and held doors open for you and treated you like a queen?"

"A few."

"So technically, in a roundabout way, you've slept with men for money. I mean, it was food, and society doesn't like to call a spade a spade, but basically you got something and were treated a certain way, and it made you feel good and then they got something in return."

"I disagree. I slept with them because I *wanted* to. There was no coercion or demands. I could've gone home alone. A lot of the time, I did go home alone."

"So, we're talking choice, right?"

"I guess so, yeah."

"I have a choice," she said. "I don't *have* to do this job. I choose to do this job. I choose who I want to spend my nights with, and you will have that choice too. I don't feel used or dirty or ashamed. I get paid for something that most people give away for free. It's like going on a date where at the end of the night you get to keep a shitload of money. None of it is forced. Sex is the oldest profession in the world. Why aren't we allowed to use what we have to our advantage?"

"It's an odd sort of rationalization, but I see what you mean. Your life seems pretty charmed." I flashed a smile that wasn't genuine. "How do you feel? I mean, from when you started until now?"

"I'd be lying if I said I didn't have an adjustment period. The act itself wasn't the problem," she admitted. "It was all mindset. I had to forget everything I'd been taught about sex, you know? The Rex taught me to value myself—to have pride in my body and to own my sexuality. I earned my condo and my car. I earned the three hundred-dollar highlights in my hair. I earned the salt scrubs, the trips to Monaco, the designer clothes, the jewelry given to me as thank you gifts."

It was all about the presentation, I realized. How she rationalized using her body for her financial security and outright luxury.

"The first time is the weirdest because you're deconstructing your programming. You're unraveling everything you've been taught to think about sex. Rex girls aren't normal prostitutes."

I flinched at the word.

"It's not ugly, Sterling. I go to Rex events or fly to private estates for parties. And even though everyone knows why I'm there, I still get to choose who I want to spend my night with. Do you know where I was last month?" she asked suddenly.

"No. Where?"

"Monte Carlo. Me. In Monte Carlo. Do you know how much money I lost at the casino? Ten thousand Euros. Do you know what the duke I was with did? He laughed and gave me a diamond necklace just because." She leaned back against the plush cushions of her custom designed couch. "People can judge me all they want. But I don't have to answer to any of them." She shrugged. "I make more than plastic surgeons in LA. What does that tell you?"

"How can The Rex get away with running a brothel?" I asked quietly. "It's illegal."

"Not if you grease the palms of the right people. The world is a different place if you have money, Sterling. Remember that."

Tiffany gently took the teacup from my hands and set it down on the coaster. "You need a real drink. And a place too loud to think. Come on, get dressed. I'm taking you out."

"Too loud to think about the fact that I'm about to become a high-class hooker?"

She waved her finger at me in admonishment. "I have one rule. And one rule only."

"What's that?"

"You're not allowed to call yourself a hooker or an escort. You're a courtesan. Got it?"

"Got it." I paused. "Can I ask you something?"

"Sure."

"Have you ever had a client not treat you well?"

"Yes. But that was agreed on before he ever laid a hand on me."

I frowned. "I don't understand."

"He was into darker stuff. But he didn't surprise me with his wants. We talked about it, and I let him school me on a lifestyle I never thought I'd be into."

Her hand absently went to fiddle with the key pendant around her neck. I finally was able to get a good look at it, and my eyes widened in surprise and I let out a gasp.

"You have a yellow gold key," I murmured and leaned forward to examine it more closely. "It's gorgeous."

"You know what's strange?" she asked.

I shook my head.

"This apartment could burn to the ground. My clothes with it. All the furniture and artwork. But this necklace? I value it above all things. It represents my power and my freedom."

"Thank you, Tiff."

She lightly smacked my thigh in a signal to end the deep and dark discussion. "Let's get a move on."

"I'm not in the mood to go out."

"Sterling, we should at least go out and say goodbye to your old life. You know?"

"What, get drunk and talk about my mother and the past I wish I didn't know about?"

"We don't have to talk about that. In a few days, you're going to have a different name, a different persona. It will be like you never existed."

I paused and then said, "I have nothing to wear except for my interview dress."

"I have a whole closet. What's mine is yours. We'll find something that fits you."

My interview makeup was still on, aside from the lipstick that had faded. I touched up my lashes with more mascara and swiped my lips again. I brushed out my sprayed waves and pulled my dark hair into a high pony-tail. I made sure all the flyways at my temples laid flat.

"You cannot wear those jeans. I won't allow it," Tiffany said. "They're one good wash away from falling apart."

"Yeah, and they're just now perfect." I pointed to a black skirt on the bed. "What is that?"

"A leather miniskirt."

"No. Absolutely not. I adamantly refuse."

She grinned. "I thought you might say that. I might've bought you a pair of black skinny jeans when we were at Folson's the other day." She skipped out of the guest bedroom and returned a moment later with a shopping bag.

"How did you do this? I never saw you—"

"Oh, it was easy. I did it while you were in the dressing room. Now say, 'thanks, Tiff'. And don't look at the price tag."

"Thanks, Tiff," I said with a winsome smile.

I slid into the designer jeans and had to admit that I felt like a million bucks. I donned the emerald satin tank she'd laid out on the bed and wore the black flats I'd worn to Folson's. I borrowed a pair of small silver disk earrings from Tiffany.

"You look great."

"Thanks," I said.

"How's the mood?"

"On the upswing," I admitted.

"Told you. You can't sit around and stew."

"Yeah. You're probably right."

"The event you mentioned, the one that happens in a few days...I'm going, too," she said.

I let out a breath. "Good. That'll be good."

"Yeah, a familiar face." She squeezed my hand.

My gaze dropped to the key she wore around her neck, and I wanted to ask her all sorts of questions about it.

"I wore a rose gold key for two years, Sterling."

"I didn't ask you anything, did I?" I looked her in the eyes.

"You were clearly mulling it over." She grinned. "Yes. Two years before I went to yellow gold."

"What made you decide to—ah—advance?"

She laughed. "I was just ready. I felt comfortable enough with my status, but I wanted more. So, I offered more."

"Any plans to move to platinum?" I asked, super curious at the path Tiffany had taken.

"Eventually," she said. She paused before she went on. "Do you know how Gen got her position as a Madame?"

I shook my head.

"You have to hold a platinum key for at least three years to even be considered for a Madame position. Ultimately, I'd like to retire the key and run an entire floor of my own."

"Really? You're not going to take the cash and run when you've done it long enough? Maybe buy yourself a home on a beach somewhere?"

"Nah, I'd grow bored in retirement." Her eyes twinkled. "I know this sounds odd, but I'm really good at this business. Not just the sex—which I'm sure you've learned by now it's not even about that. Not really. But the idea of running my own floor at another Rex location…well, I feel like it would be a really good fit. An amazing challenge. And then, one day, I won't just be a courtesan. I'll be something more."

"I thought being a courtesan doesn't bother you."

"It doesn't. The Rex…it's safe, it's familiar. It's addictive."

"What's addictive? The power of sex?"

She smiled, looking amused and secretive. "You don't know what The Rex can do for you, Sterling. It can open doors you didn't even know existed. You will meet men who have the power to change the face of the world. You know what this job has given me?"

I shook my head.

"Lessons in how to own myself. How to own my body and sensuality. And how to use that knowledge to my advantage. It's powerful, what I do. I have *real* power." She squeezed my hand again. "We can talk more about it at the bar. You ready?"

"Yeah. Are you calling a car?"

"The place I want to take you to…you don't really arrive in a chauffeured town car."

"What kind of place is it?"

She held out her hand. "The kind of place where we should take your beater."

"You drove us to Waco," I accused.

Tiffany swerved my dated Toyota into a parking spot and cut the engine. "Yes. This is my favorite spot."

I looked out the window and saw a bright sign blinking the name *Shelly's* across the roof. Motorcycles were parked out front and a few grubby overweight men wearing leather vests were smoking cigarettes, looking like their broad shoulders could prop up the walls of the establishment.

"Your favorite bar is a biker bar?" I asked in amusement.

She shrugged. "Sometimes I want swarthy instead of suits. What can I say? Let me buy you a shot of tequila."

Tiffany locked my car and shoved the keys into her clutch. With brazen bravado, she stalked toward the entrance. The men who were smoking quickly jumped to like they were eighteenth century, leather-clad tattooed dandies and opened the door for us.

"Thank you, boys," Tiffany flirted, shooting them a winning smile.

The bar wasn't seedy or even a dive. It was a lot of dark wood and dim lighting, but it felt welcoming, despite the rough customers who sat at the tables.

We bellied up to the bar. I watched a petite brunette pick up a bottle of bourbon and pour it quickly into three shot glasses before sliding them to a scruffy blond biker who was waiting at the end of the bar.

"That'll be fifteen dollars," she said to the attractive biker.

"I thought family drank for free," he stated with a flirtatious grin.

"What, you don't get enough free stuff while you're here?" she demanded.

"Awww, Mia, come on," he whined. His eyes slid to Tiffany who was looking on in amusement. "Can you talk some sense into her?"

Tiffany shook her head. "Solidarity for sisterhood. Pay up."

The biker sighed and then looked at me. His flirtatious expression morphed into something else when his eyes met mine.

"Oh, Lord," the bartender—Mia—muttered. "Boxer, grab your shots and get out of here."

"But I want to stay and chat with," he paused, obviously waiting for me to introduce myself, which I had absolutely no intention of doing.

I wasn't looking for trouble. And Boxer looked like pure trouble.

"She's not going to tell you her name," Mia said. "Now get. Colt's waiting on you."

"You're more of a hard ass now that you got married." He shook his head and grasped the three shot glasses. "Ladies. It's been a pleasure."

The biker took his drinks and sauntered away from the bar, disappearing into the back, down a long hallway.

"Sorry about that," Mia said with a sassy grin. "Boxer is like the older brother I never wanted. Sometimes I have to school him. What are you drinking?"

"Two shots of tequila," Tiffany stated.

"Better make it four," I interrupted. "I'll nurse the second one."

Mia stared at me for a long moment and then nodded. "Tequila. Got it." She quickly poured the shots. "They're on me tonight."

"Oh, you don't have to do that," I protested, reaching for my clutch.

She waved away my protest. "My bar, my rules. And any gals that come in and ask for multiple shots of tequila —well, I know what that means. So, enjoy your drinks."

"Well, will you do a shot with us?" I asked.

Mia grinned. "Thanks for the offer, but I'm pregnant."

"Congratulations," Tiffany said with a wide grin. "Damn girl, where are you hiding that baby belly?"

Mia tugged on her flowing black tank and dragged it close to her body. Sure enough, she had a baby bump. She glanced at me.

"Drink one for me, yeah?"

An hour later, Tiffany and I were sitting in a corner booth when the blond flirt plopped down next to me and curled his arm around my shoulder.

"Excuse me?" I squawked.

Tiffany laughed when she saw my indignant face. She'd only had two shots of tequila, and then had switched to club soda.

"You know what I was doing while I was sitting with my boys talking about club business?" the blond asked.

"Can't even imagine," I said, brushing his arm off my shoulder.

"I was thinking about you."

"Seriously, dude," I said to him with a laugh. "You're ballsy."

He flashed a grin. "Have I got your attention?"

I gently pushed against his chest, noting the solid muscles beneath his white cotton T-shirt. "I'm flattered. Seriously. But I'm not interested. I'm just here to have a good time with my friend."

He sighed but inclined his head. "Alright. But if you change your mind, my name is Boxer. I'm a Tarnished Angel, and me and my boys run Waco. If you need anything, you come to me."

I raised my eyebrows but nodded. Boxer held my gaze and then reluctantly slid out of the booth and sauntered his cute butt up to the bar where he no doubt was attempting to coerce Mia into giving him another free drink.

"Nicely handled, doll," Tiffany said, slinging back the rest of her club soda.

"The last thing I need is a complication right before I…"

"You're also not allowed to get involved with anyone outside The Rex."

I leaned back against the booth, my gaze flitting to the bar where Boxer stood. He caught me watching him and gave me a mocking bow.

"Would you have gone for it? If you weren't in the situation you're in?" Tiffany asked.

A vision of the hot Scot I'd met that afternoon flashed in my brain. If there had been anyone to make a mistake with, it would've been him.

"Sterling?" Tiffany prodded.

I shook my head and came back to the moment. "The biker is hot. Clearly. But no."

"Because he's not white picket fence material?"

"Pretty much, yeah." I frowned. "Though I guess that dream is null now. I mean, what man wants to marry a… well, what we are." I shrugged. I shot back the rest of the tequila, embracing the burn. "What do you plan to do, Tiff? I mean, when you run your own floor. Can you date then?"

"Yes. I could date then. But I don't want to get married and have babies. I never have. I want what I've always wanted. Wealth, the ability to travel, nice things. I plan on choosing lovers who don't care what I've done for a career. It's different for me than it is for you."

I wondered what I'd become in a few years. Would I still recognize myself? Would I resent the woman who'd been the catalyst for all of this?

No, it wasn't fair to blame Mama for how I chose to disappear, how I chose to hide and find a way to live with the repercussions of her actions.

But I could blame her for leaving me this mess.

I knew she'd loved me. She'd said it in her letter which I'd read often enough. The lengths she'd gone to protect me from her family as well as the Foscari couldn't be denied.

And yet, I condemned her. For leaving me alone. For not telling me the truth. For taking the coward's way out. For ruining my only chance at having a normal life, when that's all I'd ever wanted. For putting me in a position where I had to go on the run. For making me live this strange half-existence where I could never be *me* ever again.

"I need to get out of here," I said, feeling the tequila infusing my blood with rage and destruction. "I need to get out of here before I do something catastrophically stupid with a really hot guy. Rex or no Rex."

"Say no more. Let's go."

I slid out of the booth and looked around the room. Boxer was sitting at the bar, talking to another man in a leather vest. A big, brawny man who leaned over the plank of wood and kissed Mia on the lips.

My eyes slid to Boxer who was watching me with a glittering gaze.

He'd offer me solace. He'd offer me a night of forgetting. And then I'd wake up with a whole host of other problems because from the moment I'd let The Rex doctor examine me, my body was no longer mine.

It belonged to The Rex.

With a sigh, I turned my back on him and stalked toward the exit. A black town car was waiting for us at the curb, and a bunch of bikers were looking at us with interest.

"Why did you call a car?" I asked. "You didn't drink that much. You could've driven us back in my car."

"Your car is gone, Sterling," she said softly.

"What did you do, Tiff?"

"*I* didn't do anything. Someone from The Rex came and got it so they can use it to fake your death."

"How did you—"

"Okay, truthfully, Gen asked me to bring you here. I mean think about it, the last place anyone sees you and your car is a biker bar where you're doing shots of tequila. They're going to hang onto your car for a couple of days until after the event. If you commit, then they'll burn your car and some friends on the police force will retroactively date a few reports, a coroner will get a fat envelope to write some things out, and it's done."

Tears threatened my eyes. The car was a piece of shit, used, and the paint was chipped and faded. But it had been mine. It was all I had of my old life.

A life that no longer existed.

A life that hadn't been much of a life anyway.

Chapter Seven

I entered The Rex two days later at nine a.m. on the dot. My hair was pulled back into a sleek ponytail and I was wearing skinny jeans and a white blouse. Annika met me in the lobby and took me to The Fifteenth Floor and showed me into Gen's office.

Gen handed me a black jewelry box. Inside, was a rose gold key on a delicate chain. "This will allow you access to the elevator. You don't need anyone to accompany you. We also need to discuss the fact that you can't use your real name anymore. Even though you don't have a new identity yet, I still don't want you going by your given name."

And so it begins.

"Have you thought of a name you like? You'll use it as your persona and it will be the name on your new ID."

"No. I thought you were going to assign me a name."

"The choice is yours. A lot of girls choose gemstones," Gen supplied, trying to guide me. "And I suggest something common for a last name."

After a moment I said, "Eden. Eden Smith."

She smiled slowly. "Head on down to the salon. They will be expecting you, Eden."

I nodded, and in a daze, I took the elevator and used my key for the first time. It was surreal. I could only imagine how I'd feel when I attended my first event.

I walked across the lobby, glancing around, wondering if I'd run into the Scottish mystery man I'd met only a few days ago. I couldn't seem to get him out of my mind. His arrogance, his assurance, his audacious virility all called to me.

When I arrived at the salon and spa entrance, I was greeted by the desk agent. After giving her my name—my new name—she handed me a salon gown and told me to follow her.

The salon was as glamorous as The Rex's lobby but more soothing, with cream-colored walls, potted plants, and rows of chairs that were lined in a communal setting so friends could gab while getting their hair styled. It was as thoughtful a room as anything else I'd seen concerning The Rex. They had done nothing half-measured, which I appreciated.

I could see why Tiffany was loath to ever walk away from a career at The Rex.

When I was seated in a salon chair, the check-in girl asked me if I wanted anything to drink.

"Hot tea would be great," I said with a smile. "Thank you."

"Black? Green? Herbal?"

"Black, please. Earl Grey if you have it."

"Excellent. I'll have that for you soon. Jase will be along shortly. She's still talking to Genevieve about what to do with your hair."

I swallowed nervously and hoped they left my hair intact. I loved the length and style, but I was a canvas for them to paint, a lump of clay to mold. They would make sure I was attractive enough to draw the attention of men who I'd be spending time with, and they knew what those men wanted.

My hands were clasped in my lap as I waited for the desk attendant to come back with my tea. She returned with an elegant silver tray and a delicate white cup with a silver rim and a steaming pot of water with loose-leaf tea steeping. Milk, sugar, and honey adorned the tray in small containers with spoons. I strained my tea into the cup, added some honey, and stirred it. I lifted it to my nose, inhaling the soothing aroma. It was still too hot to drink, but it was enjoyable to have something to hold.

After a few minutes of sitting in a chair in the empty salon, a woman finally strolled toward me. Her brown hair was cut into a severe bob that highlighted her cheekbones and warm brown eyes.

"Hi. Eden? I'm Jase."

"Nice to meet you," I murmured, taking a sip of my tea, trying to remember to answer to my new name.

"Sorry for the wait. Gen was talking to me about your hair."

"You're not going to do something really dramatic, are you?" I blurted out. "I'm sort of fond of my hair."

She removed my ponytail holder so that my dark locks spilled down my back. Jase ran her fingers through my mane in an almost seductive manner as she examined me, but otherwise didn't answer.

I looked at my reflection in the mirror and waited.

Finally, Jase nodded. "I'm going to give you a gloss to bring out the richness of your hair. I'll take it up about four inches from your last cut—right now you're overwhelmed with length and it's too much for the shape of your face. I'll add in some light layers and give you some frames."

I let out a breath and nodded. "Okay. Yes. That sounds —well, I was worried you were going to chop it all off and I was scared."

She let out a laugh. "Very few of the girls get their hair chopped. Need to have something to grab onto." She winked and I felt my face flame.

I really needed to get over blushing every time someone at The Rex alluded to anything to do with The Fifteenth Floor.

⁓

"Holy crap," I murmured after Jase turned the salon chair around to show me the final result.

She laughed. "Well? Didn't I tell you to trust me?"

"You did," I said, swiveling my newly styled head from side to side. My maple syrup colored hair now fell a few inches past my shoulder blades; the face frames highlighted the wings of my eyebrows and somehow drew everything all together.

I ran my fingers through the rich glossy locks and marveled at the change. It wasn't super dramatic, and yet, the effect was stunning. I wondered how I'd look with a full face of evening makeup and a dress for the occasion. If anything, I could believe I'd look like a woman headed to a night at a gala and not really what I was about to become.

"Thank you." I looked up at her and smiled. "I'm overwhelmed."

She bowed mockingly. "It's not *exactly* what Gen had in mind, but I know she'll be happy with the results."

"You went against Genevieve? Are you even allowed to do that?"

Jase chuckled. "This is one arena where Gen yields to me. She trusts me. After all, I'm the best in the business."

My stomach rumbled, reminding me that it was lunchtime. I'd been in the salon chair all morning and I wasn't even close to finished. The afternoon would be spent getting waxed, a manicure, pedicure, facial and skin treatments, a massage to relax my posture and then for the final addition, I'd see Gen to be dressed.

"Are you hungry?"

"Starving," I admitted.

"I'll have the restaurant deliver food here." She opened a drawer at her station and pulled out a menu. "Choose what you want."

We chatted over our salads. I liked Jase. She was friendly and confident, and I hadn't detected an ounce of judgement about The Fifteenth Floor.

"I've been working here for five years," she stated. "I've styled a bunch of girls."

I itched to ask questions, but something told me my curiosity wouldn't be welcomed. There was an air of mystery at The Rex.

I wasn't naive enough to think that Jase was my friend. If anything, she was another test I had to pass. Any questions I posed to the stylist were bound to get me into trouble with Genevieve.

If I wanted answers, I'd talk to Tiffany, and even she had to talk around some issues.

After I ate my salad, Jase led me to the spa area. She put me in a room with a table covered in a sheet.

"Thanks again for the amazing haircut," I said when her hand was on the doorknob.

"You're welcome." She smiled and closed the door.

An hour later, freshly waxed and groomed, the esthetician showed me to the nail station for a pedicure.

Tiffany and another woman were sitting next to each

other, talking in hushed tones. When Tiffany saw me, she gasped. "Oh my God!"

"What?" I asked in trepidation.

"Your hair! It looks amazing!"

I relaxed and smiled. "Thank you. Jase did a good job, didn't she?"

"Such a good job!" Tiffany's companion said. "I'm Julia."

"Hi, I'm…Eden," I said, going toward her with my hand out.

Julia shook my hand and then pointed to the chair next to her. "Sit here."

"Okay, thanks." I climbed into the chair and rolled up my jeans. Tiffany and Julia were both dressed casually in floral print dresses, their toes soaking in tubs of water and essential oils.

I glanced at Julia's yellow gold key and smiled awkwardly before shooting Tiffany a pleading look for help.

"So, Eden is working her first event ever at The Mansion tomorrow night," Tiffany said, effortlessly turning attention away from my gawkiness.

"Ah," Julia said with a secretive grin. "Parties at The Mansion are always a good time."

Tiffany laughed like they shared a secret I wasn't privy to.

"What can I expect?" I asked. "I'm nervous."

"Don't be," Julia said. "But remember, what happens at The Mansion stays at The Mansion."

"That's reassuring," Tiffany muttered, looking around. Satisfied that we were still alone for the time being, Tiffany continued, "You should just wait and see what goes on. It's really hard to explain. But don't be afraid. You have to remember you're a Rex girl now. You're safe, always."

"We've all walked into it completely blind." Julia winked and then leaned her head back against the massage chair.

Three technicians appeared, and we all fell into silence. Tiffany and Julia were finished before I was, and they left, leaving me to sit and wonder about what I could expect.

The wardrobe room on The Fifteenth Floor rivaled a magazine stylist's closet. There were rows and rows of high-end designer clothing on racks and heels to match every outfit imaginable. It was like the hotel's own personal department store.

"I think silver," Petra said, holding a clipboard in her hand.

"Silver is perfect for her coloring. Plus, it's her first appearance and it will help her make a splash," Genevieve said.

"What do you think? Audrey or Liz?"

Genevieve looked me up and down. "Definitely Liz."

"Liz?" I piped up, feeling like a mannequin in a store window.

"Elizabeth Taylor," Genevieve explained. "All of our gowns are designed after the Golden Age of Hollywood stars, but with our own Rex flare."

"Oh. I see," I said with a nod.

"Definitely Liz. With vixen curves," Petra said to me, but then she directed her next statement to Genevieve. "Sultry eyes and pout. A modern Liz Taylor."

I blinked. I'd never heard of myself talked about in such a way.

"Too bad she doesn't have violet eyes. It would've been

perfect." Gen shrugged. "Oh well. What do we think then? The Maggie Pollitt?"

"Absolutely," Petra agreed. "She'll make an entrance."

I thought about what Julia and Tiffany had been talking about and the air of mystery surrounding The Mansion party.

Genevieve gave me a lingering look and then turned to Petra. "Why don't you get the dress?"

Petra nodded and left the room.

Genevieve faced me once she was sure we were alone. "You're nervous."

"Uh. Little bit," I said.

"Why?" Her gaze shrewdly narrowed. "What did Tiffany say?"

"Nothing."

"I don't believe you."

"No, really." I bit my lip, not wanting to throw Julia and Tiffany under the bus, but damn it all, I was still curious. "She was vague and cryptic, and said nothing specific, only that the party is always a good time."

"You want to know what you're walking into," she stated. "I was going to tell you tomorrow right before the event. I didn't want you to have too much time to over-think things. But I guess you'll overthink this no matter what."

She gestured to the white L-shaped couch. I took a seat.

"Just like there are different keys for the girls, there are different rooms in The Mansion. Each of them caters to different tastes. Some are tamer than the others."

"Tamer," I repeated. "Like one room is a sex dungeon or something?"

She inclined her head in affirmation.

I swallowed. What level of debauchery was I walking into?

"Like I said, you have no reason to be nervous. You will be wearing a rose gold key. Our clients know what that means. Should you wish to explore and…observe…you're welcome to, but it's not mandatory. I need to reiterate here that you will not be forced to do anything you don't want to do."

Petra chose that moment to return with the most gorgeous dress I'd ever seen. It looked exactly like the dress Elizabeth Taylor had worn in the movie *Cat on a Hot Tin Roof*, except it was silver instead of white. It was a chiffon, knee-length cocktail dress with a low neckline, cinched at the waist.

I reached my hand out to touch the fabric. "It's incredible. Are you sure—I'm afraid I won't do it justice?"

"Try it on," Petra said.

I needed both their help to slip the dress over my head. I stood in front of the mirror, and even without my hair styled to match the dress and still barefoot, I couldn't help but love what I saw.

I felt like I'd been transported to a different era. Back to a time when women were encouraged to be beautiful and feminine; where dressing well wasn't seen as anything except a way to compliment the wearer and fit in with societal expectations. A time when women wanted to be wanted.

I clasped the rose gold key pendant around my neck, and it rested against my skin. It felt like it belonged there.

"Oh," I said, coming to understand why The Fifteenth Floor was different.

"I never get tired of seeing a girl try on one of our dresses for the first time," Petra said with a knowing chuckle. "It's always incredible watching their trans-formation."

Genevieve pushed against my hip with her hand to get me to turn. "I don't even think we need to take it in."

"No, it's perfect," Petra said. "I brought the crystal slippers." She picked up a shoebox, pushed back the tissue paper, and pulled out a ballet slipper garnished with tiny crystals.

"I guess they'll work," Genevieve said, a frown marring her face. "I would've liked for her to wear a heel of some sort."

"I think these work better."

"You're the stylist," Gen said.

Petra knelt in front of me and helped me step into the ballet flats. They were comfortable, yet oddly heavy due to the crystal beadwork.

"I think the shoes look fantastic," Petra stated, rising. "Besides, I think they offset the vixen quality of her persona with an air of innocence."

"No, you're absolutely right," Genevieve said.

I turned back to look at myself, marveling at the changes in such a short amount of time.

Vixen? No one had ever used that word to describe me.

My mother had been the one to turn heads wherever we went. I swallowed, thinking of her. She'd left Italy, pregnant, and on the run to protect me. She'd been seventeen and she'd done what she had to do. I was twenty-five. I could do this.

I could be Eden.

Chapter Eight

After I changed into my street clothes, Genevieve told me to follow her. We left the wardrobe room and headed through the hallway back into the reception area. Annika wasn't at her desk and Genevieve pushed open the door to her office.

I followed her inside. "Should I sit?"

Genevieve shook her head in negation as she went to her massive ornate desk and picked up a brown leather binder that resembled a photo album.

"These are the photos and personas of the girls who work The Fifteenth Floor. You'll need to memorize their names."

I took the binder. "You want me to learn all these names and faces by tomorrow's event?"

She smiled. "There are only thirty women in the binder."

"So few?"

"Exclusive and elite."

"Ah, right."

"All the ladies working tomorrow night's event are sleeping here tonight."

I frowned. "Why?"

"Call time is seven a.m. for the stylist chairs. We fly down to Austin mid-day. It's going to be a long day tomorrow." She paused. "And a longer night. Take the binder, memorize the faces and names. Annika will show you to your suite."

"But I don't have a change of clothes—or pajamas."

Genevieve grinned. "We're a luxury hotel. We sized you during the dress fitting. You have clothes waiting for you, and every comfort item from a toothbrush to room service is now at your disposal. You're completely provided for."

The idea of ordering every dessert on the room service menu made me giddy.

"Sleep well," she said.

I inclined my head, wondering how I was possibly going to sleep with the adrenaline coursing through me.

I left Genevieve's office. Annika was back at her desk, her bun compact and devoid of flyaways. I wondered about her. She had a key to The Fifteenth Floor. Was she just Genevieve's assistant, or would I find her face in the binder?

"I like your hair," Annika said, rising from her desk. "I don't remember if I told you that."

I blinked. "Thank you. Jase did a great job, didn't she?"

Annika nodded. "She's a master." She waved me down the hallway. We passed the wardrobe room and then turned the corner. There was a door at the end of a short corridor and as we entered, the decor changed immediately. It finally looked like a hotel floor complete with numbered wooden doors.

"This floor is reserved for our girls. No clients are

allowed in these rooms, even if you want them to come, so don't bring them."

"What happens when there's an event at The Rex and someone wants to be with a girl for the night?" I asked. There was no end to my questions. As soon as I had one answered, a few more popped up to take its place.

"Girls only go into our clients' hotel suites."

"And there's no worry about mistreatment?"

"No. Our clients are vetted. They're screened thoroughly as a prerequisite to entering our world. These are not random men from the streets. Besides, security screens every room for cameras or anything suspicious or out of place. So you don't have to worry about a video of your night with a client hitting the internet, and neither do they. *Everything* we do is controlled."

We arrived at suite number twenty. She inserted a universal key into the lock and pushed the door open but made no move to step inside.

I went in and looked around, listening with one ear as Annika continued to speak.

"Key to the suite is on the coffee table next to your new cell phone. It's been pre-programmed with all the numbers you'll need. Genevieve is speed dial one. I'm speed dial two. You contact Gen for high-level inquiries or major problems only, and me for everything else. I'll answer any questions you have about scheduling and the like. New clothes are in the dresser. Dinner will be brought up for you at seven. Anything you need that is standard hotel fair, dial the front desk and The Rex will see to it. Food, towels, clean sheets, etc. Got it?"

"Gen for the important stuff, you for admin, The Rex for comfort. Got it. Thank you," I said, marveling at the decor. Cream and gray lush carpet and furniture adorned the room. I wondered what the bedroom looked like but would wait to explore until Annika was gone.

"I know this is daunting and overwhelming," she said. "If you need to talk to someone about all of this, please know that you can talk to me."

I said slowly, "No offense, but I hardly know you."

She smiled.

"Sorry, I know that was rude, but I—"

"Genevieve is the Madame. She's our boss. She's not a Girl Scout leader. She won't offer you platitudes or sit with you while you process this *very* out-of-the-box situation." Her face hardened. "She won't be there for you the morning after your first time with a client."

"But you will be?" I pressed.

"Yes. I have a master's in psychology with an emphasis on post-traumatic stress counseling. That's my real job here; the rest of what I do just fills the gaps between the time I spend with the girls."

A laugh escaped my lips. "You're a counselor to courtesans?"

Annika's stare was penetrating and finally she said, "Speed dial two, Sterling."

"My name is Eden," I corrected.

Her stare was intractable. "Speed dial two," she repeated softly. "I'm here for you when you need me. I hope you remember that."

With that final pronouncement, Annika closed the door, leaving me alone in a very beautiful suite with nothing but my riotous thoughts.

I set the binder down on the coffee table and reached for my new cell phone. I unlocked it and scrolled through the numbers. Genevieve, Annika, Security, and the front desk were on speed dial. I added Tiffany to the speed dial list.

I set the phone aside and then went into the bedroom. A heavy wooden bed rested in the center of the room. A matching dresser sat across from it. I opened the top drawer and the scent of lavender wafted to my nose, tickling my senses.

Lingerie and undergarments in my size were neatly folded. I pulled out a bra and panties set.

Lace. Delicate. White.

I put the garments back in the drawer and shoved it closed.

The middle drawer had pajamas. A pink satin set with a button down top and bottoms. They were classy and stylish, and not at all what I expected.

I took out the pajamas and set them on the bed. A knock on the door startled me and I went to answer it.

"Hey girl," Tiffany said from the doorway of my suite. "Just wanted to check in on you."

I waved her inside. "That was thoughtful. Come on in."

She wore a pair of black yoga pants and a faded T-shirt that hung off her shoulder and revealed a red bra strap. Her blonde hair was piled on top of her head in a messy bun and her face was free of heavy makeup.

She crossed the threshold and took a seat on the couch. Tiffany ran a finger across the leather binder.

"It's not completely altruistic of me to visit," she said. "Genevieve told me to give you a run down. Basic rules, that sort of thing. She also asked me to help you learn the names and faces of the girls."

I let out an exhale. "I thought I wanted to be alone. You know, to process everything in silence, but I think it's better that you're here."

"Have you eaten?"

"Annika said dinner will be sent up at seven," I said,

moving toward the bedroom. "I'm not that hungry right now, but I could use a drink."

"Ah, one of the rules I have to tell you about. We're not allowed to drink the night before an event. We need to get a good night's rest, and alcohol…well, we all know what that can do."

"I don't even know how I'm supposed to sleep tonight." I left the door of the bedroom cracked so I could hear Tiffany speak while I changed.

"There's a light sedative in a medicine bottle by the sink. The same one I gave you the night before your interview. You should take it in a few hours. It'll conk you out, let you rest, but you won't feel hungover in the morning."

I quickly kicked off my shoes and then slid out of my jeans. The satin pajamas were cool against my skin, and I breathed in the soothing scent of lavender as I adjusted the shirt collar.

When I came back into the living room, I saw that Tiffany had flipped open the binder and she was looking at the first page. She glanced up when I joined her.

"What do you want to do first? Memorize? Or get the run down?"

"Let me look at the photos first. Let them sink in. Then we can talk. I'll review the photos later again tonight before bed."

"It won't be difficult to learn them all."

"Will they all be there at the party tomorrow night?"

"Yes."

"Is that standard? Every girl works every event?"

Tiffany shook her head indicating it wasn't. She picked up the binder and handed it to me. I took it and sat down in the chair, tucking my feet underneath me.

"There are some events—events of the season, if you will—where every girl works. It's non-negotiable. Elite or not. The Mansion party is one of them. Other events are more intimate. Depending on what the client is looking for, The Rex might only send gold and platinum girls. Or even just platinum. Very special requests, they send only Elites, or just a select few girls of the client's choosing."

"What about emotional attachments?"

"Emotions are messy, and in this business we can't afford messy. The Rex won't let you be with a client more than twice in a year. That way no one gets attached. It's important that we keep the clients happy so they keep returning."

I thought about her words and tried to shut out the knowledge that I would be entertaining many different men.

I'd be *sleeping* with many different men.

Gen and The Rex could call us whatever they wanted. They could dress it—and us—however they wanted.

But I knew what I really was.

Tiffany gently squeezed my hand. "Look through the binder. We'll talk more later."

Chapter Nine

I was a stranger to luxury.

I'd never been to Europe, but as a kid, I'd decorated my school lockers with photos of castles on rolling hills I found in old travel magazines. I'd had dreams of walking the halls of Versailles and roaming the gardens, visualizing the flamboyance of the French court in its heyday.

And even though I saw the wealth that Tiffany had been accumulating, it didn't at all prepare me for flying on a private jet from Dallas to Austin.

I'd never been on a plane in my entire life, and my first experience definitely set the bar high.

As if being chauffeured in a Mercedes directly to a private jet with fine leather seats and elegant woodwork hadn't been enough of a shock, The Mansion itself rendered me speechless. It was forty-five minutes from the airport in Austin. It was a tan, Spanish-style home nestled on private acreage. The structure was complete with window arches, columns, and a balcony that overlooked the front entrance, so the owner of the home could stand out and look down, like a king reigning over his subjects.

It was old-world, titanic wealth.

Hours had passed and now I was standing in the wings on the second floor of The Mansion with the other Rex girls, waiting to be announced like a nineteenth century debutant.

"You didn't tell me we were going to have to walk down a two-tiered staircase," I hissed at Tiffany.

Tiffany reached out and adjusted the rose gold key necklace that rested against my warm skin. "You'll be fine. Trust me, there is no better way to make an entrance."

"Yeah, God forbid we just walk among them like the mere mortals we are…"

"We're not mere mortals and neither are they. You have to get used to being on display, Eden," she said.

The previous night, after I'd memorized the faces of the women in the binder, Tiffany had given me a rundown of the explicit rules followed by a few pointers.

No drinking the night before an event.

No drinking at the event.

If a man gives you a cocktail, find a way to dump it into a plant, excuse yourself to the restroom and "conveniently" forget your drink or find some other way of disposing of it.

Your key is not to be given to anyone who places you under duress or coercion.

No boyfriends.

No discussion of past clients in any form to anyone except Genevieve, ever.

No discussion about anything you see or hear while with a client ever, to anyone, under any circumstances. These men do not exist outside the events.

No sexual relationships with anyone who is not a client.

Any event garments aside from undergarments will be returned to The Fifteenth Floor.

"You look amazing," Tiffany said. "You should know that."

"Thank you," I murmured. "You look incredible too."

She inclined her blonde head, the waves of her hair falling over her face in pure Veronica Lake fashion. Tiffany's persona, Hazel, was announced. She threw a smile over her shoulder and said, "You can do this."

As she walked away from our spot toward the top of the stairs, I watched her shoulders rise and her chin lift. She embodied sensuality. I was fairly certain I embodied terror.

Life or death, I reminded myself.

I took a deep, calming breath. When the butler called out the name Eden, I started forward, my ballet slippers sinking lightly into the plush red brocade carpet. As I'd been directed by Tiffany, I paused at the top of the stairs, staring out into a sea of guests.

My gaze locked on a man with stormy, blue-gray eyes. I held my breath and didn't look away. I could easily pick him out in a room full of strangers. He wasn't just tall—he loomed, making the others appear small. Though he was in an immaculate tuxedo that spread the breadth of his shoulders, he didn't look like he belonged in it and I recognized who it was.

My hand reached out to rest on the ornate wood banister as I began my descent, our eyes remaining fixed on one another. The crystal chandelier in the center of the ceiling made everything twinkle in golden light. The party, the guests, the decor—it was all so civilized, so grand. Not at all the sort of place one would expect debauchery to exist.

When I stepped foot onto the marble dance floor at the bottom of the staircase, I was immediately surrounded by men in tuxedos all vying for my attention. I was too short to see over the men standing in front of me, and the stranger I'd met in The Rex Bar and Restaurant disappeared from my sight.

I looked around in a moment of panic, only to find Tiffany plagued with just as many admirers. She caught my gaze and winked, and then mouthed *Eden*.

Eden wouldn't be concerned with the amount of attention she was getting. Eden would be confident. Eden would thrive in this environment.

I am Eden Smith.

The men were effusive in their compliments, and I found myself smiling in genuine amusement at the measures they took to woo me. The art of flirtation began to blossom as I wore my new persona.

Out of the corner of my eye, I saw Julia—who went by the name Pearl—being whisked off the dance floor by two men, her head thrown back in humor as she laughed.

Suddenly, the men surrounding me parted like waves of the ocean to make way for the Scottish stranger who was clearly out of place and time. He strode toward me with command and purpose.

When he stood no more than three feet away from me, he stopped. We stared at one another, the people around us fading into nothing. I couldn't read the expression on his face.

Finally, he held out his large hand to me. Without pause, I took it.

There was a collective murmur from the other men as they realized they'd lost the chance to seduce me.

"Shall we?" he asked, his voice a deep, sensual purr. His brogue was thick and seductive and brushed tingles of awareness down my spine.

"Bold move," I murmured when we were off the dance

floor standing near a marble column at the edge of the room.

"You seemed to enjoy it," he said. His eyes dipped to my throat and his expression tightened.

I touched the key around my neck and met his gaze. Our eyes clashed and tension mounted, turning tacitly sexual.

"I don't want to have this conversation out in the open," he said, pitching his voice low. His hand settled at the small of my back as he gently escorted me off the main floor to a library. It was a private place, a place of civility and gentlemanly pursuits.

He led me inside and I heard the door to the library click shut behind me, but the man made no move to come deeper into the room. Instead, he stood by the door, his eyes appearing flinty in the dim, romantic light.

"What's your name?" he asked, his voice like a crack of thunder in the silence.

"Eden."

"Not your persona, I mean your real name."

"You didn't care enough to ask me my real name the other day at The Rex. Why do you want to know now?"

His gaze narrowed. "You're trying my patience."

"Excellent," I said as I tossed my hair. "But you know I'm not allowed to give out my real name."

He took a deep breath. "Let's start over."

"Great, I'm going to go back out onto the floor and—"

"Eden," he warned.

"Excuse me, but you're acting very possessive of me right now. You don't have that right. I don't even know your name."

"Hadrian Rhys."

My mouth flickered in amusement. "You're named after a Roman emperor?"

"Aye."

"Your mother certainly had a high opinion of you."

His gaze went glacial.

I was at a loss for what to do, what to say. The man in front of me—Hadrian Rhys—was still a stranger, despite the fact that I'd met him a few days earlier by sheer coincidence, and despite the fact that it had been one of the most sexually charged encounters of my life—and he hadn't even touched me.

"You never changed your mind," he said.

"Hmm?"

"You never left your name with the front desk."

I smiled slightly. "No, I didn't."

"Aye, but now I know *why* you didn't. You're a Rex girl."

I arched a brow. "You never even considered the fact that perhaps I didn't *want* to meet you later that evening?"

It was his turn to look amused. "Of course, you did. You just weren't allowed to act on it."

"Ah, your arrogance. Back in full force. How could I have forgotten?"

"There's nothing wrong with admitting you want me, Eden."

"Are you kidding me right now?" I asked in exasperation.

He took a step toward me. "I'm not a man easily surprised, but when I saw you walking down the stairs, I was. Were you surprised to see me, too?"

I inclined my head but gave no vocal affirmation to his words.

"You wanted me that day in the bar—your eyes held nothing back." He took another small step toward me, like a lion that didn't want to spook its prey. "When you came down the stairs tonight you looked regal and composed.

Until I got close enough to see your eyes. You didn't do a good enough job, Eden."

"Good enough job of what?" I demanded, trying to stem the breath from leaving my lungs.

He reached up slowly and his large hand gently cupped the back of my head. "A good enough job of hiding the fact that you don't belong here. Hiding the fact that behind your beautiful face there is fear and anger. You're so very angry."

I was disturbed, and it had nothing to do with the drum of desire beating in my chest. No, it was something else. This man, this stranger, could see through my veneer.

And it was terrifying.

"Why are you here, Eden?" he asked again.

"Why are any of us here?" I countered.

"Don't."

"Don't what?"

"Don't deflect. I want you to be the woman I met in the bar."

"I am. My name is Eden——"

His hand moved and his thumb stroked my jawline, freezing my speech. I couldn't stop the shiver of pleasure.

"Your reaction to my touch is enough truth for me." His finger glided lower to rest at the rapid pulse of my throat. "Eden. That's so tongue in cheek."

My fake name spilled from his lips like a taunting mockery.

I smiled. "I'm glad someone noticed."

"I'm not just *someone*."

He was so much larger up close and my neck was getting a crick while I stared at him. He was dynamic and I felt his pull. Pride demanded I do something, anything, to get away from him.

But my body had other ideas.

I hadn't expected to feel arousal for a man in this setting. But maybe it would be easier this way. My first time…with a man I already wanted. A man who already knew I wanted him.

A Rex girl could choose who she gave her key to, and at that moment it was all I could control.

"How old are you, Eden?"

"Twenty-five."

"Christ," he muttered, shaking his head. "I knew you were young, but I didn't realize how young."

"You're awfully condescending, Hadrian." I rolled my eyes. "Are you afraid this crowd will corrupt me?"

"Say it again." His voice was low, demanding, and his brogue slid over me like mink on naked skin.

"Say what again?"

"My name."

I licked my suddenly dry lips. "Hadrian."

His gaze darkened with heat and promise.

"Spend your night with me."

My breath hitched.

"You're safe with me, Eden. Pretend it's the night we first met and that we aren't here in this place. I won't demand anything of you that you don't want to give."

He waited, not making a play to coerce or convince me further. His body was taut with alertness and his gaze was unwavering as he waited for my answer.

I'd already committed to becoming a Rex girl. Wouldn't my first time be better if it was with a man I would've gladly slept with for nothing in any other time and place?

He was more arrogant than anyone I'd ever met, yet he wasn't wrong about his pronouncements.

This man standing in front of me was not like any of the other men in the ballroom. He elicited something inside of me that I'd never felt before. An emotion I couldn't name. Some strange combination of desire, fear, and safety that I couldn't rationalize.

I wanted to feel the weight of him against me, I wanted to know how his lips tasted.

There was no point in weighing my decision any longer. Sometimes, you just had to go with your instinct.

I reached up behind my neck and unclasped my key necklace. I took his hand and turned it over. His skin was warm, rough. I gently placed my key into his palm, and when I did, his fingers curled around it.

With his other hand, he grasped my hip and tugged me flush against his body.

My fingers splayed across his chest, feeling the muscles beneath his tailored, crisp shirt.

"Let's find Genevieve, aye?" he asked, his voice raspy with desire.

I nodded, unable to speak. He released me and then laced his fingers through mine. He stalked out of the library, his strides long and confident. I stumbled in an attempt to keep up with him. Hadrian had a purpose and he clearly wanted the business side of this arrangement dealt with.

Genevieve was standing in the corner of the ballroom, conversing with Annika. We approached them immediately.

Without a word, he showed my necklace to Genevieve.

"Eden?" she asked me, but without removing her eyes from Hadrian.

"I'd like to give my key to Hadrian," I said.

"All right." Genevieve's gaze slid to mine. She waited for a moment to see if I was sure, and then nodded. "Enjoy the rest of your evening."

Hadrian's hand tightened ever so slightly on mine and

he turned, all but dragging me away. I looked over my shoulder at Genevieve and Annika. Their eyes were trained on me.

I wasn't able to hold their gazes long since the man who'd claimed me marched us from the room.

Nothing had been decided between us. What he liked. What he expected. I wore a rose gold key. I was a novice. He knew what the key's patina meant…right?

"Where are we going?" I asked, breathless.

Hadrian looked at me and instantly slowed his trek. "Sorry. I forget that I'm a beast compared to you."

I blinked. "A beast?"

He flashed an arrogant grin. "My size."

"I—oh, you mean your stride."

We walked through a long hallway until we came to a door. He turned the knob and suddenly we were outside underneath the stars. I gulped a breath, feeling my lungs expand.

Lit torches had been staked throughout the grounds to illuminate the garden pathway. Groomed and manicured bushes added to the pristine luxury of the estate.

"Why are we out here?" I asked. "Why aren't we inside? There are plenty of rooms…"

He looked out over the gardens as he replied, "I wanted to take you someplace intimate."

Hadrian's head turned and the intensity of his eyes had me sucking in a breath.

I was lost in his gaze. My skin felt stretched too tight. I wanted to throw myself against him, beg him to make me forget why I was really here with him.

"Hadrian," I whispered, an aching plea of acceptance.

His mouth sealed over mine as he dropped his hand to wrap it around my waist. He assaulted my senses. He pillaged my mouth like a conquering warrior sacking a city.

My heart leapt into my throat and my breathing turned shallow. I needed more of him.

I reached up to grasp the lapels of his jacket and dragged myself closer.

"Eden," he murmured against my mouth.

The name of my persona on his lips reminded me that this wasn't real. But I wanted him anyway.

I wanted to spend the night with Hadrian, circumstances be damned.

"Take me to bed, Hadrian," I whispered back.

"Are you sure?"

I nodded.

"No. Say the words."

"I'm sure."

He slowly let me go and then took my hand again, leading me into a garden maze. We wandered through it in silence, his hand solid against mine adding to the charged air between us. He seemed to know where he was going but didn't clue me in.

The maze opened into a large flat area to reveal a glass gazebo. Hadrian came to a halt and I sidled up next to him, looking at him with silent longing.

Though it was dark, the torches around the maze cast dim light into the gazebo.

I saw three shadowy figures moving on the other side of the glass, like dancers on a stage. They glided together. Arms twining around necks, fingers plowing into hair, heads thrown back in pleasure.

A sound escaped my throat, dragging Hadrian's attention to me. His eyes glimmered with desire as he gently pulled me to stand in front of him. The heat of him was at my back and more warmth traveled through my body when Hadrian's fingers splayed across my shoulder, rooting me in place.

My eyes had adjusted to the flickering light of the torches that illuminated the gazebo, and I watched the scene unfold.

Two men. One woman. They circled her like they were wolves and she a sheep. They were tall, well built. Attractive. One had dark hair, the other light. Two devils, intent on debauchery and seduction. Their gazes were riveted on the woman, who turned her face toward the glass, and when she did, I knew instantly who it was.

The girl called Raven.

Her face was a picture of languid sensuality. As if she had all the time in the world, as if she wanted nothing more than to be their conquest.

Raven held out both arms and the men came to her. The dark-haired one stood in front of her and brushed the hair away from her neck to kiss the curve of her shoulder.

The blond cared nothing for kissing and moved behind her. He hiked her dress up and questing fingers sought the place between her legs.

I swallowed, shrinking back against the wall of Hadrian's chest, wondering why my gaze was riveted to the erotic scene. I felt like I shouldn't be watching such a display of abandon. In the real world, what they shared would have been private, but here…I couldn't look away.

A dull pulse took up residence between my thighs and my nipples hardened.

Hadrian's hand gently slid from my shoulder to the top of my chest and into my cocktail dress. He held my heavy breast in his palm and his thumb skated across my nipple.

Raven placed her hand on the dark-haired man's shoulder and gently pushed him down. He dropped to his knees and soon his face was between her legs and he guided her underwear to the side and began to taste her.

The blond, not to be outdone, ran his fingers down the front of her dress, slipping beneath the fabric to caress her breasts, tweaking the tips of her nipples.

Like Hadrian was doing to me now.

Raven's face was a mask of pleasure, intimate, on the verge of coming.

Hadrian pinched my nipple, causing me to inhale and a sharp needle of desire pierced me between my legs.

The blond man turned Raven's chin and sealed his lips over hers, driving his tongue into her mouth. She reached around his neck to pull him closer.

I watched the three of them slowly sink to the floor like they were one entity. They all grasped for each other's clothing; buttons popped on white starched shirts, zippers were lowered, but Raven was the only one who found herself almost entirely naked. Only her lace white thong and heels remained.

The blond lay on his back, pumping his massive erection. Raven eagerly crawled toward him and took him into her waiting, wet mouth. His face screwed up into a picture of desire as his fingers plowed through her already tangled locks.

The dark-haired man watched his acquaintance being pleasured and reached into his pocket for a condom. He tore the wrapper off and then sheathed his impressive length. He positioned himself behind Raven, spreading her legs wider as he nudged aside her scrap of underwear. Soon, he was guiding himself inside of her.

Raven lost her rhythm as she was being filled by the dark-haired man and the erection in her mouth sprang free.

The blond coerced her to him and reached out to play

with her nipples. She went back to devouring him, her body shaking and shuddering.

Hadrian's other hand slid down my waist to pull up the fabric of my dress. His fingers slipped across the lace garter I wore and danced across my skin to the apex of my thighs.

I instinctively widened my stance.

His fingers dipped inside my French lace panties and gently began to stroke me.

My gaze was still riveted on the erogenous picture. My breathing was heavy as I watched the blond empty himself into Raven's eager mouth.

The dark-haired man continued to thrust into Raven from behind and eventually, his face grew taut as he came.

Hadrian continued to tease me between my legs as his fingers played with my nipple. I pressed back against him, unable to ask for what I wanted, but unable to stop the call of desire that crowed through my blood.

The three players in the gazebo collapsed to the ground. Raven reached for both of them, her arm sliding around the blond's neck.

After a few moments, they collected their clothing, but didn't bother to dress. They plodded from the gazebo, no doubt to find a bed so they could pleasure each other until dawn.

It wasn't until they'd gone and we were alone that Hadrian murmured against my ear, "You liked watching them. I know you did."

I didn't reply. Instead I closed my eyes and focused on his hands and the desire they were eliciting.

"Want me to stop? I'll stop."

"No," I whispered. "Don't stop."

"Then tell me you liked watching them."

I'd never wanted to come more in my life. Every stroke

from him caused a new tremor to race between the juncture of my thighs.

"I liked watching them."

No sooner had the words spilled from my lips than Hadrian slid a large finger into my waiting, welcoming body.

He said something in a foreign language.

I focused on the feeling of him inside me. It wasn't enough. I wanted more.

His finger was ruthless as he thrust it in and out of me. And when he added another finger, my violent orgasm made me clamp around him as all the stress of the evening and my primal instincts came together in a fantastic release. My legs turned to jelly, and I would've sunk to the ground, but Hadrian braced me against the wall of his chest.

He left his fingers inside of me until I stopped quivering, and only then did he leave my body. Before I could say a word, he scooped me up into his arms and carried me off into the night.

Chapter Ten

My cheek rubbed against Hadrian's lapel as I breathed in the spicy, aromatic scent that clung to his skin. I wondered what he smelled like beneath the cologne.

I was in a post orgasmic, catatonic state. It was the only logical explanation for why I was doing what I was doing.

He hadn't said anything after he'd lifted me into his arms. Instead, he'd carted me like I weighed nothing as he walked around the glass gazebo and eventually entered the other side of the garden maze.

"Where are you taking me?" I finally asked, my voice coming out low and strained. Like I'd spent hours screaming my pleasure.

"To the carriage house," he said.

His brogue was sinful, a potent caress.

We finally came to the end of the maze and I saw a structure—far larger than the gazebo—made of wood and brick.

Hadrian managed to open the door with me still in his arms and then gently set me down onto the floor. He closed the door, standing in front of it for a moment, staring at me.

I looked everywhere but at him, taking in the gas fireplace and the expensive leather furniture in the overtly masculine living room.

"It's nice, but what is this place?" I asked.

"It used to be a carriage house, but it's been converted to a small guest house."

"Are we allowed to be in here?"

"I'm…an associate of the man who owns The Mansion. He won't mind."

Though the carriage house appeared small by The Mansion's standards, it was just as grand. An expensive rug covered the floor of the front room. Artwork hung on the walls and ornate trinkets adorned the mantle of an elegant fireplace.

Without a word, Hadrian brushed past me into the living room and went to a silver and glass bar cart.

"Drink?" he asked.

"Ah, I'm not supposed to drink on nights that I work."

"I won't tell." He picked up a crystal decanter and poured two glasses of amber liquid.

He stalked toward me, glasses in hand, and gave me one and then clinked his glass against mine.

"Saluti," I murmured before taking a small sip. It burned and made my eyes water.

I quickly set the drink aside, resolving not to touch it again.

Hadrian saw my reaction and grinned before taking a hearty sip of his drink.

"What the hell was that?" I demanded, pressing my hand to my chest. "I think it singed my throat."

"Brandy."

"Yuck. Maybe it's an acquired taste."

He chuckled at my reaction. "Do you speak Italian?" he queried, peering at me with interest.

I'd let my guard down for a mere moment, and part of my past had barreled its way into my present.

I might've been going by the name Eden, but I still was very much Sterling. Sterling who spoke fluent Italian.

"Eden?" he prompted. "When I ask you a question, I expect an answer."

I did not like his tone or his high-handedness. And I did not like the fact that he'd had his fingers inside of me not ten minutes ago and now he treated me like he owned me.

But for the night, he did.

"Yes. I speak Italian," I gritted out.

I tore my gaze from his and stepped away, moving further into the living room and pretending to understand the artwork I was seeing.

Now that we were inside the carriage house, in privacy, I expected Hadrian to rip my clothes off me and drive his body into mine. But he hadn't made a move to touch me.

I was primed for him, and our conversation felt forced and awkward since I knew what was coming.

"You look exhausted," he said finally.

I startled. "I'm not."

"Eden," he began. "You don't need to lie to me. If you're tired, you're tired."

"Okay, I'm tired."

"Then let me show you upstairs."

I frowned but nodded. He was a strange man, Hadrian. Alpha. Mysterious. Demanding. He had played my body like an expert and then seemed done with it, all at once.

"You look confused," he said, setting his glass down on a dark wood end table and stalking toward me.

"Don't you want more?" I blurted out.

He arched a brow but said nothing as he clasped my hand and led me up the wooden staircase. We walked down the hallway, past two bedrooms and a bathroom, to the last door.

"Master bedroom." He waved me inside. I stepped in and looked around, my gaze landing on the large ornate sleigh bed.

What sorts of things will he do to me?

A shiver of want raced down my spine in anticipation. I turned in time to see him fling his bowtie onto the chair in the corner and then he went for the cufflinks at his wrists. He set them on the bedside table.

My gaze was riveted on the column of his strong throat that was now revealed. He shrugged out of the crisp linen he wore, tossing his shirt on the chair.

"Do I want more?" he asked, picking up the thread of my question. "Aye, Eden. I want more. I want more than you're willing to give—but I said I wouldn't press you to do anything you didn't want to do."

"I don't understand."

"I know you don't. Christ, you're only twenty-five years old."

"What does age have to do with anything?" I demanded.

"A lot. I'm twelve years older than you are. Your life is just getting started and you don't even realize it yet."

"And you've got one foot in the grave?" I frowned. "I still don't get what you're saying to me, Hadrian."

He shifted so that he was standing right in front of me. He took my hand and placed it on his fly. "This is what you do to me when you say my name and look at me with those wide, innocent eyes."

"I'm not innocent," I protested. "And frankly, I'm offended that you think I am."

He let out a rumbly laugh. "So you're pissed that I'm calling you innocent? Would you rather I call you something else?"

I yanked my hand away from him, anger in my cheeks. "What is all this? Are you feeling a stab of guilt because you bought a woman for the night?"

"I have no guilt over that, believe me. And for the sake of honesty, you should know I didn't have plans to procure a Rex girl this evening."

"Procure?" I shook my head. "So I was an impulse purchase?"

"Is that how you view yourself? As something to buy?"

"It doesn't matter how I view myself. It only matters that you want me."

"I disagree. It matters very much how you view yourself. Because if you were honest about it, then maybe you'd be honest about how you feel about what's happening between us tonight."

Oh, I wanted Hadrian Rhys. And I wanted him in a way that I'd never wanted anything in my life. I wanted to feel his raw, unrestrained power as he thrust inside me. I wanted him so deep that I'd be sore in the morning.

But I also wanted to remain aloof, detached—and Hadrian was doing everything in his power to make this something it wasn't. He wanted us connected in a way that wasn't allowed, and I remembered what Gen had told me; these men were alpha males who thrived on the chase.

Hadrian was pushing for more than I wanted to give, and it was hard to resist.

Entangled. That's what we were becoming.

If I'd chosen another man tonight, he would have been different. He would've wanted the fantasy and sexual satisfaction. I doubted he would've cared to spend any time discussing anything else.

Maybe that was my mistake, choosing a man I already desired. I thought it would've been safer, but there was no going back, and I refused to be a coward.

I reached up to the pins in my hair and I tugged them free so that my dark locks fell in large waves across my shoulders. And with my gaze trained on his, I removed my dress, letting it drop to the floor. I stood in front of him in nothing more than crystal beaded ballet slippers and French lace undergarments with garters.

He took a long time staring at me, his gaze slowly traveling from the top of my head down to my feet.

Hadrian was bare-chested, muscled arms by his sides with his fists clenched.

I approached him slowly and when I was standing in front of him, I grazed my fingers across the fair skin of his chest.

"Do you ever see the sun?" I asked, my breath teasing his flesh.

His muscles bunched beneath my fingers and I flattened my palm, wondering if I could absorb his power by mere touch.

"I'm from Shetland."

"I don't know what that means."

"It means I'm descended from Vikings and Celts," he explained. "I'm fair skinned by nature."

"I should've known you were a modern-day Viking," I murmured.

My fingers danced across his body to skim over a thick, angry red scar that cut along the right side of his ribcage. It was clearly an old wound and was now healed, but even I could tell it had been deep.

What happened to him?

I wanted to ask, but that would send us deeper into the realm of personal, so I decided to ignore it. I slid around to his back and was unable to stop my feminine sigh of appreciation when I saw the naked breadth of his shoulders.

He turned suddenly, making my hand drop from his body. Hadrian cupped my butt and hauled me toward him, his mouth finally descending toward mine.

His kiss wasn't gentle, but forceful.

Viking, indeed.

Ruthless and savage, I'd known from the moment I saw him that Hadrian in a suit had been nothing but a facade.

His hands traveled down to the back of my thighs, spreading them, urging my legs to wrap around his middle.

I jumped into his arms, the heat of me pressing against the straining erection behind his fly.

He carted me to the bed, and without letting go, laid me down. His body covered mine.

My hands and lips wanted to be everywhere, but Hadrian was a conqueror and I was at his mercy.

So I accepted his seductive assault and drowned in the feeling of him.

He lifted his lips from mine and raised his head. His blue-gray eyes raged with lust and the corded muscles of his neck were tight with restraint.

Hadrian scrutinized my body as his hands cradled my breasts. He pressed a kiss to the column of my throat and then inched lower to take a nipple into his mouth through the fabric of my lace, teasing and taunting.

"It's beautiful," he commented.

And then he ripped the delicate garment in half, leaving me almost naked.

Hadrian sieged my skin with his hot mouth, kissing and licking, devouring and removing lace as he went.

When I was completely disheveled and bare, he finally lifted himself off me, but only to remove his tuxedo trousers and black silk boxer briefs.

Hadrian, in all his nude glory, made my insides quiver with desire and fear.

He took himself in hand, caressing his member, all the while keeping his eyes on mine.

I swallowed, but couldn't look away, and even went as far as bending my leg to reveal the wet sliver between my legs.

Hadrian made a noise of appreciation.

I was witnessing a man in his most basic element, and he was ready to take me like a mindless animal that cared about nothing except mating.

My hand slipped down between my legs.

"Don't touch yourself," he commanded harshly. "Let me."

I arched a brow and continued to stroke myself. "I was never very good at taking commands."

"You'll learn."

He released his member and kneeled down between my legs, inhaling slowly, as if absorbing my scent, my arousal having already perfumed the air.

His tongue lashed my skin, which caused me to buckle and cry out.

"Your punishment," he reminded me. "Because you didn't listen."

He devoured the flesh between my legs. Hadrian knew the perfect masterful pressure to exert to bring me to the edge, only to pull back before my climax. And then he'd start all over again, tirelessly, for what seemed like eternity.

"Hadrian," I moaned, mindless with my need to come.

"Tell me what you want, Eden," he commanded. "Maybe I'll give it to you."

"Fuck me," I whispered, the fever of desire making me mindless.

"I don't have a condom. I told you, I didn't plan on being with a Rex girl tonight."

"I'm on birth control and I just had a physical. I'm clean."

"So am I." Hadrian grinned, revealing his feral intensity. He slid up my body and positioned himself at my entrance. He thrust inside of me in one expert movement, causing my breath to hitch at the sudden invasion of him.

I felt him everywhere, deeply.

Hadrian didn't take his eyes off me as he started to move, slowly at first and then when my body began to give into him, make room for him, he picked up speed. His thrusts became ruthless and dominating, his hand clasped the back of my neck as he brought my lips to meet his.

His tongue plunged with the rhythm of his body. Desire had me digging my nails into his back.

"You like that?" he whispered harshly, his mouth against mine. "What about this?"

He rammed into me and angled his pelvis so that I had no choice but to come.

Waves of pleasure consumed me. I arched my back, wanting to drag it out for as long as possible.

With a curse in a language I didn't understand, Hadrian clasped my hips in a bruising grip and emptied himself.

We stilled and Hadrian propped up on his elbows to stare into my eyes.

He smiled slightly and pressed a quick kiss to my lips before sliding out of me. I watched him heave his mighty body off the bed and pad naked to the bathroom.

I wasn't usually a fan of brawny men that looked like they could crack skulls for a living, but something about the way Hadrian strutted made me appreciate his sensual grace despite his size.

I didn't know what to do now. Was I supposed to get up and sleep in one of the guest rooms? Give him his space?

He came back from the bathroom and climbed into bed. I got out of the other side and went to the bathroom to clean up. After I did my business, I looked at myself in the mirror. Tousled waves, bright eyes, flushed cheeks.

I headed back to the bedroom. Hadrian was in bed, the covers pulled up to his waist. He had one arm tucked beneath his head and his seductive gaze tracked my every movement.

"So, I guess I'll sleep in the guest room," I said awkwardly.

"Why would you do that?" he asked.

"Because—well, sleeping together isn't *sleeping* together."

"Eden," he began. "How am I going to take you in the middle of the night if I roll over and find you aren't there?"

Heat crept up my cheeks at the mention of his desire. I was already tender between my legs, but I knew I'd want him again too.

He flipped the covers back in a silent command for me to climb into bed, and then he turned the bedside lamp on.

I flipped off the main light and then went to my side of the bed, sliding between the sheets, naked.

I mirrored his pose, lying on my back, arm tucked underneath my head to stare at the ceiling.

He flicked the lamp off and we were blanketed in darkness.

I let out a slow exhale.

The scent of Hadrian after sex drifted toward me, a scent I couldn't describe. Sated male, warm skin, and the aroma of an expensive shave cream and masterfully chosen cologne.

"Is your shave cream Italian?" I blurted out.

After a moment of silence, he said, "Aye. How did you know it was Italian?"

"My mother," I said softly, smiling in remembrance. "She used men's Italian shaving cream for her legs. She refused to use anything else."

"Are you close to your mother?"

I swallowed in an attempt to tamp down the sudden lump in my throat and realized it was best if I didn't say more. "No."

He paused for a long moment and then his hand reached out to pull me into his side. It was intimate, and blurred the line of what we'd just done, and for what reason.

But I couldn't stop from placing my hand on his chest, feeling the strength beneath my fingertips.

"Good night, Hadrian."

His arm tightened around me. "Good night, Eden."

I awoke to early morning sunrays streaming through the expensive blinds. I winced, feeling like I was hungover, even though I'd gone to bed completely sober.

True to his word, Hadrian had turned to me in the middle of the night, rousing me from sleep with his wandering hands and tongue. He'd kept me on edge for hours before finally letting me come. I felt like a wrung-out dishrag, and no doubt, if I looked in the mirror, I'd see bags under my eyes.

I rolled over, expecting to find Hadrian in bed next to me, but he wasn't there. Neither were his clothes.

Frowning, I slowly sat up and ran a hand through my tangled hair.

I heard the faintest sounds coming from the kitchen and deduced Hadrian's location. I looked at the clock on the bedside table. It was a little past seven. I still had some time before I had to get back to The Mansion.

I went into the bathroom and grimaced when I saw my reflection in the mirror. Last night's makeup was ringed around my eyes. I turned on the faucet, let it warm, and then I scrubbed away the residue with the luxury soap on the counter.

There was something oddly sobering about washing off face paint in the early morning light.

Though I'd found pleasure in Hadrian's arms, I definitely couldn't dismiss the truth. In the dark, in the shadows, pleasure reigned. I had enjoyed what I'd done.

But in daylight, the cold transaction of business was first and foremost.

Hadrian was an amazing lover. And for my first Rex experience, I couldn't have hoped for better. But that's exactly what it was—my first experience. The first of many.

There would be other men who would be amazing in bed, but would any of them wrench desire from my body? Would any of them look at me the way Hadrian did? Like he could see past the name I called myself and the smile I plastered across my lips?

Would any of them slide between my legs and fill me so completely that I'd forget why I'd taken this job in the first place? Would any of them make me feel like a sensual, powerful woman? Or would I wake after mornings with them and have regrets about the life I had chosen?

I had no regrets now.

But I also knew I was feeling emotions that I shouldn't be feeling. Not for a client.

I wanted more of him. I wanted another night where I was the one who climbed on top of him and made *him* beg.

I grabbed the hand towel and gently dabbed my face dry. I twirled my hair into a loose side ponytail, securing it with a strand of hair and pins.

Hadrian had ripped the lace undergarments from my body, so I slid into my dress, wearing nothing underneath. It felt mischievous and secretive.

I left my ruined undergarments and slipped into my crystal slippers before padding out of the bedroom and down the hallway.

My steps were quiet as I made my way down the stairs and headed toward the kitchen. Hadrian's back was to me and he was standing at the counter. I was just about to announce my presence when his phone trilled. He reached into his black tuxedo pants pocket and pulled out his cell.

"This is Rhys." He paused a few moments. "I didn't agree to that. No. The price is the price. It's non-negotiable."

I hesitated, not wanting to alert him that I was eavesdropping on a business conversation. A few more moments of silence passed.

"Have you forgotten who the fuck you're talking to?" he demanded. "I'll give you a few days to reconsider your position, but only a few. After that, I'll be happy to remind you exactly who you're dealing with."

Ice flew through my veins, freezing my blood.

I didn't like his tone or the fear that rippled down my spine. It was a conversation I never should've heard.

He hung up and set his phone aside.

His business was his business.

I finally mustered the courage to face him. Slapping a

smile on my face, I entered the kitchen. "Good morning," I greeted.

He looked at me over his shoulder. His eyes crinkled at the corners, and his grin made my heart soar in my chest.

"Good morning," he murmured huskily.

I swallowed my desire. He'd been inside of me most of last night, but I wanted him again.

Desperately.

"I'm going to go," I blurted out.

"Coffee first." He went to a cupboard, pulled out a mug and filled it. "How do you take it?"

"Black, if it's drip," I replied. "I prefer espresso."

He arched an eyebrow but came toward me and held out the cup.

"Thanks." I took it from him, trying not to be too overt as I studied him. His blond hair and natural strawberry highlights would've looked downright feminine on a lesser man. But Hadrian wasn't lesser. He was huge and looked out of place in a modern kitchen. He wore his white formal shirt from the night before, but it was open at the neck and rolled up to the elbows. He was wearing his tuxedo trousers, but his feet were bare.

He looked casual and relaxed. Sexy as hell.

He looked even better naked.

"You're up early," I said, striving to break the awkwardness that had sprung up between us.

"I'm an early riser. Plus, I'm dealing with jet lag."

I nodded and tried to take a sip of coffee, but it was still too hot to drink so I set it aside. "I really do have to get going."

A grin appeared on his lips. "Do you?"

"Yes, I do." I cleared my throat. "Thank you."

"For what?"

"Last night. It was…well it was…"

"Go on."

"I'm glad it was you. For my first Rex experience."

His gaze darkened. Hadrian took a step toward me, crowding my space, breathing my air. He wrapped his arms around my waist and hauled me against him and I felt his erection.

A pulse of desire drummed between my thighs.

As much as I wanted Hadrian one last time, I knew it would be a mistake.

"I didn't know it was your first event. What's your real name?"

"I'm still not going to tell you that," I said, pushing against his chest, trying to get free.

"I noticed you wear colored contacts. Why?"

"It's part of my persona," I lied. "It fits the look of a Rex girl."

"Show me your real eyes."

"No."

He released me, his gaze intense. "I'll walk you back to The Mansion."

"Thanks, but I don't need—"

"Eden," he growled.

"Fine," I muttered. "Can we go now, please?" Without waiting for him to reply, I turned and marched out of the kitchen and waited by the front door.

Hadrian was slower, as if he didn't have a care in the world. He sat on the couch to put on his socks and formal shoes.

The silence between us was making me antsy, but I had nothing to say to him. I'd fucked him for money and the next morning he'd just poured me coffee and acted like we were some domestic picture of normalcy.

We weren't.

I was glad I wasn't allowed to tell Hadrian my name.

Then I'd become real and this would no longer be a fantasy.

We had to remain a fantasy. That's what The Rex sold: the perfect evening, with the perfect girl and no strings attached—unattainable to all but the most wealthy and coercive of men.

Hadrian got up from the couch and walked to me. Grasping my hand in his, he reached for the doorknob.

The morning was quiet, and the air was fragrant with the perfume of the manicured gardens.

I attempted to tug my hand free of Hadrian's grasp, but he was having none of it.

"Stop fighting me," he commanded, tightening his fingers around mine. His grip wasn't painful, but strong. There was no getting away from him.

We wandered leisurely through the maze, past the glass gazebo that had been the stage of the most erotic performance I'd ever witnessed. I was immediately transported to the previous night, watching writhing bodies find their pleasures. And then I'd found my own pleasure, many times, under Hadrian's relentless, unyielding demands.

I shook off the sensual trance. The closer The Mansion loomed, the more despondent I grew. I couldn't understand my own reaction. It wasn't shame or even regret that fluttered in my chest. No. It was something else.

Something I didn't dare give a name.

He opened the back door of The Mansion and allowed me to step inside first. It was dark and quiet. Either the house was so large that sound didn't travel from one room to the next, or everyone was still asleep.

"You can leave me here," I said. "I know the way to the kitchen."

Hadrian paused a moment and then slowly released my hand.

I thought if he was no longer touching me, the intense physical chemistry between us would disappear, but it went nowhere.

Before I could think anything of it, I stood up on my tiptoes and brushed a kiss to the corner of his mouth and whispered, "Thank you for last night."

I didn't wait to see his reaction. I turned and bolted down the hallway, refusing to look behind me.

When I got to the swinging door of the kitchen, I pushed against it and went in. There was a buffet of hot dishes lined up on the long granite counter tops. Girls in different states of dress sat in groups of twos and threes, chatting and drinking their coffees.

Genevieve was nowhere to be found and I breathed a sigh of relief, not yet ready to face the Madame to give her my report on the evening.

I went through the kitchen, dodging girls with plates and mugs, and made my way into the dining room.

Tiffany and Julia sat at the corner of a long table that looked like it had once belonged in a medieval castle. They quickly waved me over, and I walked toward them across the wooden floor.

Julia's gaze ran up and down my body. "Good morning."

"Morning," I replied.

"How was your night?" Tiffany asked. Her face was clear of makeup and she was wearing a white satin robe secured at the waist. Julia was wearing the same garment in a shade of rose.

"My night was good," I said.

Julia frowned. "Good? Your first night with someone and all you have to say is good? I didn't see who you left with. So, who was it?"

"Fish for information all you want. My lips are sealed." I smiled to take the sting out of my reprimand.

We weren't at liberty to discuss who we'd spent the night with—it was inevitable that we'd see each other leaving with men, and sometimes women, so it wasn't like it was ever a complete secret. But discussion about our sexual proclivities went against Rex policy. We had to protect our clients or at least give the illusion of discretion.

We'd all meet individually with Genevieve and tell her about the night and make a note of whether or not we wished to see that client again. It was a way for The Rex to keep tabs on clients without them realizing they were being intently monitored.

For any psychological upheaval, we would speak to Annika.

But Gen and Annika were the only two people we were allowed to discuss details with. Everyone else was off limits. Even the girls.

"Did you guys have a good night?"

They both nodded. Tiffany appeared like she wanted to say more, but she held her tongue and went back to eating a strawberry on her plate.

"I need coffee and food." I stood, and as I approached the buffet area and grabbed a chocolate croissant and some fruit, my mind wandered back to Hadrian.

It had felt like regret when I walked away from him.

Chapter Eleven

The flight back to Dallas was quick and quiet. Most of the girls dozed, including Tiffany, who slept with a pink sleep mask over her eyes and a pair of noise canceling headphones.

When the private jet rolled to a stop on the tarmac, Genevieve stood up and said, "Well done, ladies. The event was a success, and we've been invited back for Elijah Padgett's spring party. Before you leave for the day, please check in with Annika. She will hand out your necklace replacements." Her eyes locked on mine. "Eden, I'd like to see you in my office when you get back to The Rex."

I nodded, feeling my heart kick up in trepidation.

We got off the plane and slid into waiting town cars that drove us to The Rex. Because many of the girls were in some version of lingerie, we used the service entrance and took a private elevator to The Fifteenth Floor.

Annika was standing at her desk with black jewelry boxes labeled with Post-it notes.

One by one, the girls grabbed their boxes and then went to their rooms on the floor, no doubt to shower and clean up before leaving to enjoy their free day. Some looked like all they wanted was an empty bed to crash in for a few hours.

I hung back and waited until I was the only girl left. Annika handed me my jewelry box and said, "I'm here if you want to talk after you chat with Gen."

I nodded and then went to Genevieve's office door. When I knocked, I was told to enter.

Genevieve looked surprisingly well rested despite the fact that she'd been awake all night, overseeing the girls and making sure to be available if there had been any problems.

Then again, she hadn't spent any time in a client's bed, so she was one step ahead.

"Something to drink?" she asked, not rising from her leather couch.

"No thanks," I said, sinking into the comfortable leather chair.

Genevieve kicked off her heels and tucked her legs underneath her, all of a sudden looking much younger than she appeared.

"So," she began, her gaze direct. "How was your night with Hadrian?"

"Fine."

She peered at me. "You're allowed to be more forthcoming than that with me, you know."

"I know." I smiled slightly. "I just don't want to be."

She paused for a moment and then said, "I had my doubts about you, but I'm glad to see that you've proven me wrong. I think you'll do very well as a Rex girl."

"Thanks," I murmured.

"The training program will begin in a few days. As it stands, you now live at The Rex. When you complete the training period, you will be able to live off premises if you decide you want to, but many of our Elite girls choose to live here. They travel a lot and don't want to rent an apartment or buy a condo. Besides, if you live at The Rex, room and maid service are complimentary. As promised, a new identity will be created for you. Your current residence—do you have roommates? Or do you live alone?"

"I've been staying with Tiffany. Everything I own is at her place."

"Fine. We'll get you a completely new wardrobe, but more importantly is there anything you want to keep from your old life? Photo albums? Yearbooks? Anything?"

The only thing of value I had was the letter from my mother, which was at Tiffany's condo.

"No. I don't have anything I want to keep."

She stared at me for a long moment. I wondered if she'd ask me why I wasn't sentimental, or worse, why there was nothing to be sentimental about.

"Good, that will make it easier to kill the old you. We have your car, and we'll take care of it from here. You'll be guided through the process of adopting your new identity during the training period."

"Thanks." I headed for the door.

"Oh, Eden? Welcome to The Fifteenth Floor."

I went to my room and slid out of my crystal slippers. I took off the dress and put on a bathrobe. After examining the garment, I placed it on a hanger and hung it on the hook outside my hotel door, along with the shoes.

Then I showered off the remains of the previous night, trying to wash away Hadrian. But he refused to be banished from my mind. When I closed my eyes and let the water spray me, I pictured his body moving over mine.

A quiver of desire shot between my thighs.

But then I remembered the phone call I'd overheard.

He was dangerous. Involved in something dark. But with me, he hadn't shown any of that. Yes, he'd been demanding and rough, but he hadn't hurt me.

I got out of the shower and grabbed a fluffy white towel to dry off and then quickly dried my hair before heading to the bedroom.

The black jewelry box was propped open, resting on the nightstand. The key within appeared different in the light of day. It looked like any other piece of expensive jewelry, yet it was a symbol of my newfound power over the direction of my life.

I needed to talk to someone about my night. About Hadrian. About how I was feeling—and that shame and guilt weren't part of it. I briefly wondered if there was something inherently wrong with me.

Why wasn't I ashamed? Shouldn't I have been ashamed? This was what Tiffany had been trying to tell me. There was no reason for shame.

I didn't want to confide in Annika. She didn't know me, and even though she was a trained psychologist, I didn't want to be another case she studied.

My new cell phone was still on the coffee table in the living room. I called Tiffany.

"Hello?" she asked groggily.

"Sorry, were you asleep?"

"Almost. What's up?"

"Can we talk? I need someone to—"

"Give me five minutes, I'll come to your suite. Order coffee, I'm dying."

I let out a laugh. "Rough night, Tiff?"

"Rougher than yours, no doubt," she quipped.

Tiffany knocked a few minutes after I hung up with room service. I hadn't bothered to change out of my robe.

Even though Tiffany was gorgeous, she wasn't spared from looking like she'd been up all night after being with a client.

She was dressed in a pair of sweats and a T-shirt, her damp blonde hair braided down her back. "Is it okay if I lay on your couch until the coffee arrives? I'm barely able to stand upright."

"Have at it," I said. "Is that why you didn't bother heading back to your condo?"

"Yup. Besides, I don't know what the hotel mattresses are made of, but there's something magical about them." She dropped onto the couch and spread out like she owned it.

"How was it?" she asked softly. "Really?"

"I thought we weren't allowed to talk about it," I evaded, despite wanting to tell her everything.

"You're allowed to talk about your feelings. No one has to know any details. Whatever you say stays between us."

"I know." I smiled. "That's why I called you."

"Talk fast," she commanded. "I'm exhausted. I doubt I'll even make it until they bring coffee. After I nap, I plan on taking a steam and getting a massage."

"That sounds like heaven," I admitted. I paused and then confessed, "I enjoyed myself."

Her aquamarine eyes turned bright with interest. "That's great. Really."

I nodded. "Yeah. It wasn't—he wasn't—what I was expecting. In a good way."

"Clearly. Don't take this the wrong way, but you look like you got good and fucked."

"*Tiffany*." I laughed.

She giggled. "Well, it's true. You look relaxed."

"Is it weird that I don't feel ashamed?" I asked her. "I mean, aren't I supposed to feel that way?"

"Says who? Society? Prudes?"

"Yeah." I frowned. "I guess I'm just trying to rationalize not feeling how I thought I was going to feel."

"Odd, isn't it?"

"Very," I agreed.

We fell into silence for a moment and then she asked, "Anything else you're trying to wrap your mind around?"

"I liked him."

"And you wouldn't mind seeing him again?" she guessed.

I nodded eagerly.

"Let me give you a piece of advice. *Don't* see him again. Even if he asks for you, say no. He was your first client. And I'm guessing he was good in bed based on how slow you're walking. You like him. You enjoyed him. Let it be that and nothing more. If you see him again, it will get complicated. Trust me."

"Did this happen to you?" I asked.

"It happens to most girls early on," she said slowly. "If you want to do this job long enough to make it through your first year and keep your new identity, don't see him again. Don't even put yourself in a position to get attached."

I nodded. "Yes. You're right. Absolutely, one hundred percent."

"Say it again."

"What?"

"That I'm right."

I rolled my eyes. There was a knock on the door, and I went to answer it. It was room service with our coffee and a light snack. I'd only picked at the food I'd eaten during my morning at The Mansion with the girls, and my stomach rumbled with hunger.

I tried to take the tray from the room service waiter, but he insisted on bringing it into the room as a matter of professionalism. He turned and then closed the door on his way out. I spun back to Tiffany; her eyes were shut, and she looked dead to the world.

With a sigh, I took the room service tray to the bedroom. I slid into a pair of comfortable pajamas and then ate the fruit on the tray.

After I finished, I climbed into bed and pulled up the covers to my chin. Before I knew it, I drifted off to sleep.

Chapter Twelve

After we'd woken from our naps, Tiffany bailed on her massage and steam idea and we headed back to her condo. I needed to grab my suitcase and the few meager belongings I had left at her place.

"You sure you don't want to go out with me and some of the other girls tonight?" Tiffany asked.

I shook my head and set my new cell on the kitchen counter. "I'm not a night person. Besides, I'm still kind of groggy even though I slept most of the day."

"You know," Tiffany began. "When you're done with the training period, you should just move in here."

"And be your roommate?" I asked with a smile. "That's really sweet of you. You sure you want a roommate?" When Tiffany didn't reply, I lost my smile. "What?"

"I'm flying to London this week."

"Okay," I said with a frown. "Client?"

Tiffany paused. "I have a job interview. At The Rex in London."

"An interview in London? That means you're—you're leaving Dallas?"

"Maybe. Probably." She shrugged. "There's an opening to work on The Fifteenth Floor at The London Rex. I've always wanted to see London."

"I—God, I don't know what to say."

"These opportunities don't come along often, and I have to—"

I shook my head. "No. Of course, you have to go. Were you waiting to tell me?"

She shrugged. "It's been in the works for a while. I told Gen I'd love to move there if there was ever an opening."

"Well, yeah. You have to make headway while you can. I get that. I do." I looked around her gorgeous condo. "You'd let me live here, in the home you worked your ass off for? Why are you so good to me?"

She arched an eyebrow. "Good to you? I just need someone to make sure my plants don't die."

I let out a strangled laugh. "You don't have any plants."

"See? You could get some. Make this place homier." She bit her lip in concern. "You're not mad? I mean, with everything you're dealing with, I could stay. I *should* stay."

I shook my head adamantly. "No. You need to live your life, Tiff. You've already done so much for me."

She paused, looking at me thoughtfully. "Did you ever think—well, this is where life would take us?"

"Not in a million years."

"Promise me we'll always be friends. Promise me that we'll always remind each other of where we started and what we've overcome."

"Why do you want to remember all of that?" I asked quietly. "I'm trying to forget it."

There wasn't anything more to say after that—what could she say? She was aware of my situation. She knew what had brought me to her doorstep and into the world of The Rex.

I brushed past her and headed to the guest room to gather my belongings.

"Sterling," she said.

"Eden," I corrected, looking at her over my shoulder. "My name is Eden."

She stared at me for a long moment and then nodded.

I went into the guest room and began to pack up the few clothes I'd brought with me to get them out of Tiffany's apartment.

There was a knock on the bedroom door and a moment later Tiffany came in, dressed and ready for a night out.

"You look great," I said. Her hair was in a loose side braid and her black satin tank emphasized her toned arms.

"Thanks. Are you really sure I can't convince you to come out? I'm worried you'll sit here and stew all night."

"I won't stew. I'll ponder—and besides, I want to get back to The Rex. Gotta rest up for that training program."

"Has she told you what the training even entails?"

"Not yet."

"They get you on an exercise regimen and a meal plan. They outfit you for your wardrobe. They teach you tea service and how to navigate events."

"So, like charm and beauty school for courtesans?" I asked with an impish smile.

"Something like that. It's not hard. You won't work again until you finish the training program. They want to get you into a routine and check in on your well-being. Which is partly why they want you at The Rex in a suite."

"That makes a lot of sense."

"During training, you also talk to Annika three times a week."

"Are you kidding me? I have to bare my soul to a shrink?"

She cocked her head to the side. "I imagine you could sit in silence three times a week, but they want to make sure your body and your mind are equipped to handle this very unusual lifestyle. They don't need girls going off the rails or developing addictions."

"When I met Annika, she made it seem like I had a choice in whether or not I spoke to her."

"She was planting the idea in your head early so you felt comfortable, but no, you don't have a choice."

"I feel like I've been expertly outmaneuvered," I muttered. "I hate the idea of mandatory check-ins with her."

"Don't worry about it. I still check in with her once a week," Tiffany said.

Her phone buzzed in the back pocket of her jeans. She pulled it out and looked at the screen. "Julia is here with her driver. I'll see you later. Dinner, before I fly to London?"

"Absolutely."

In an uncommon show of physical affection, I hugged her. "Thanks. For…well, being you."

She squeezed me back and then quickly left the apartment. When I heard the front door shut, I looked back at my suitcase, which was now zipped closed. I had no reason to linger.

I went to the bedside table and opened the drawer. The letter from my mother was folded, but I didn't need to read the delicate scroll of her handwriting to know its contents. I had it perfectly memorized after reading it for a year straight.

The letter was dangerous. Not only did it give away every piece of truth about my parentage and ancestry, but it was a physical link to my mother.

From the moment I got the phone call that she'd

passed and the date and time of the funeral, I felt like I was living someone else's life. It was like I was watching myself from above with a weird sort of detachment.

I'd been running from a faceless enemy for a year. The Foscari, though a very real threat, hadn't presented them-selves to me. They hadn't showed up on my doorstep. I hadn't come face to face with the horrors of them.

I took the letter and went into the kitchen. I turned on a stove burner and set the paper on fire. As it burned, I dropped it into the sink. Only when it was a pile of ashes did I run water over it, letting it wash down the drain.

I'd never forget her words. I'd never forget the smudged ink from the tears my mother had shed while writing the letter. I didn't need a physical reminder of my past life because somewhere, in the back of my mind I was already worried that my past wasn't going to remain in the past, no matter how much I tried to keep it there.

The next morning, I woke up in my hotel suite at The Rex. It took me a moment to process where I was—I'd been bouncing around so much it was hard to feel settled.

Autumn sunlight streamed through the curtains I hadn't bothered closing the night before. I'd wanted to wake up with the sun. I looked at the alarm clock. It was just past seven. I got up and showered and was just about to call room service for breakfast when my work cell phone buzzed with an incoming text.

Genevieve: Meet me in my office in an hour.

I sent back a confirmation text and then ordered breakfast. There were a few items of clothing in my closet, and I was able to piece together a decent outfit. I wore the black ballet flats Tiffany had called out for.

Five minutes prior to my meeting with Gen, I grabbed my cell and suite key and left the room and headed for her office.

Annika smiled at me as I arrived. "You look like you slept well."

I paused and then nodded. "I did."

"You can go on in. She's ready for you."

"Thanks."

I knocked on the door of Gen's office and then entered. The woman didn't know the meaning of dressing down. She was in what I was learning was her signature look. Another black, form-fitting dress, sheer black hose and three-inch stilettos.

She was perched on the arm of the leather couch and in the matching chair was a man with dark curls. His green eyes peered at me with interest as I came into the room and shut the door.

He rose slowly and I noted the breadth of his shoulders and the three-piece suit he wore.

I frowned in confusion.

"Eden," Gen greeted. "Thank you for coming."

It was a formality, of course, since I worked at The Rex and Gen was my boss.

"Ramsey Buchanan," the man said in a Scottish brogue, stepping forward and holding his hand out to me.

I took it as I studied him.

He reminded me of Hadrian. Not physically, the two men were not built similarly. And I could tell Ramsey wore his suit and polish comfortably, unlike Hadrian—who seemed like he would've been content wearing animal pelts and carrying an axe covered in the blood of his enemies.

"Nice to meet you," I murmured.

He gestured to the empty chair across the coffee table and I sat.

"You don't know who I am," he said.

I shook my head.

"I run The Dallas Rex." He studied me. "I watched your interview with Genevieve."

"Watched? You mean I was being filmed?" I asked, feeling my cheeks heat with embarrassment.

"Honey, you've been filmed from the moment you stepped out of the town car outside The Rex," Genevieve said dryly.

Ramsey knew, then. About my past and why I'd come to The Rex for help.

"The reason I'm here," he continued, "is because something unusual has happened. You've been offered an exclusive contract with a client."

"I don't understand…"

"The client you were with at The Mansion," Ramsey added.

"Hadrian?"

"Yes," Genevieve said.

A thrill of excitement shot through my belly, but I forced myself to remain visibly unmoved. Cold. Detached.

I wasn't sure continuing any sort of relationship with Hadrian was a good idea. In fact, I knew it wasn't.

"We're not at liberty to divulge specifics. He wants to be the one to discuss the contract with you directly, and of course your compensation," Genevieve continued.

"What about my training period?" I asked.

"If you agree to his terms, then you'll forgo the training period until you come back to The Rex," Gen said.

I blinked.

"You can get on a plane this afternoon and be in New York to have dinner with him this evening if you agree to meet with him."

"He's in New York?"

"He had some business to deal with," Ramsey said. "But he wants to meet with you immediately."

I wondered if his business had to do with the phone conversation I'd overheard.

"If you're concerned about your safety—" Gen began, as though I had failed to hide my emotions.

"I'm not," I interrupted. "He wasn't forceful. He treated me…it was fine."

"Fine?" Gen repeated with a look at Ramsey.

"Am I allowed to refuse his contract?" I asked.

"Of course," Gen said. "If you refuse his contract, you will come back here and continue with the training program like we had originally planned. Nothing changes."

"No, I mean, am I allowed to refuse right now? And not even fly to New York to meet with him?"

Ramsey glanced at Gen and then back to me and said, "I don't normally discuss our clients, but I know Hadrian personally. He's a man of his word—in all regards. You *want* to meet with him. Trust me on that."

"I don't trust anybody," I said before I could hold it back. "You're vouching for Hadrian, but you said you know him personally. Does that mean you're going to tell him who I am…tell him about my past?"

"No. You're a Rex girl, and the rules don't get bent for anyone, not even Hadrian. Meet with him and then decide. What do you have to lose?"

Chapter Thirteen

"Would you like another glass of champagne, ma'am?" the flight attendant asked with a pleasant smile.

"No, thank you, I'm fine. Just a glass of water, please."

She nodded and scooped up the empty champagne flute and moved through the rest of the empty cabin of the private aircraft.

It was only my second time on an airplane, and I was being flown on a private jet to New York City to meet with a man I couldn't stop thinking about.

I could grow used to this.

Two hours after my meeting with Ramsey and Gen, I was on my way to the airport in the back seat of a jet-black Mercedes Maybach with a driver dressed in a bespoke suit, and a new ID and social security card in my purse.

I had become Eden Smith. They'd come through for me.

The Great and Powerful Rex.

I didn't take any luggage—not that I had any appropriate clothes to pack anyway, and Gen had assured me my wardrobe would be taken care of when I got to New York.

A woman named Elodie would greet me at The Manhattan Rex.

"She's the New York version of me," Gen had explained. "You can take her into your confidence, and you can discuss with her anything you would discuss with me."

Before takeoff, I remembered to text Tiffany and quickly filled her in on the fact that I was leaving for New York. I hated that we wouldn't have a goodbye dinner before she flew to London, but she understood.

The champagne fizzed in my blood. Or maybe it was excitement. I couldn't tell which.

I'd tried to play it cool in front of Gen and Ramsey, but inwardly, I was warring with myself. Yes, I wanted to see Hadrian again. Of course I did. Our night together had been spectacular. But the other part of me didn't think it was a good idea. I could already feel my clear-headed judgement clouding.

Curiosity had gotten the better of me. After I heard his demands in New York, I could still walk away and return to The Rex.

"We'll be landing soon," the flight attendant said, startling me out of my thoughts.

I lifted the slat on the window and peered through the white clouds. Before I knew it, we were descending. I stepped down the ladder of the aircraft directly onto the tarmac and saw another Maybach waiting for me. The driver stood by the open rear passenger door.

"Ms. Smith," he greeted.

"Hello."

"I'm Kent. I'll be driving you to The Rex. Get comfortable, and please, let me know if there is anything you need. There are drinks and snacks in the back for you."

After I scooted in, he closed the door. I looked around at the luxurious interior as the driver climbed into his seat up front.

As we sped away, my eyes were glued to the stretches of dirty highway, busy billboards, and the New York City skyline. Traffic flowed despite the numerous cars on the road. Kent didn't attempt to talk to me, which I appreciated. The silence was welcome, and I was able to think in relative solitude.

When we pulled up to the curb of The Manhattan Rex almost an hour later, a hotel doorman opened the car door.

The Dallas Rex Hotel had nothing on its Manhattan sister. Though they were similar in decor, there was something unique about the New York location.

Maybe it was the city. Maybe it was the overall energy, the frenetic pace of life here. I couldn't put my finger on it. Though it was familiar to me because I'd spent the last week at The Dallas Rex, The Manhattan Rex felt like its own entity, the queen bee of the hive.

"The original," a woman said, approaching me. "There's nothing like the original. Even if we copied the exact floor plan and decor and put it in another city, The Manhattan Rex is one of a kind. Iconic."

I looked at her. She'd apparently been watching me take it all in, noting my expression.

"Elodie?" I asked.

She smiled. "Yes." She held out her hand to shake mine. "Don't lose that," she warned.

"Lose what?"

"Your ability to get lost in a time and place. It's good to have that in your arsenal."

"What does that even mean?"

"It means that there's still an innocence about you. A

naive wonderment. Hold onto it as long as you can. In our industry, it's easy to become jaded."

I didn't know what to say in response, so I said nothing.

"Come on, I'll show you to your suite." We strode across the immaculate lobby toward the elevators. She was a stunning woman, with elegant caramel highlights in her perfectly styled light brown hair. Only average in height—a little shorter than me—there was something about her that drew the eye. Confidence, no doubt. She walked with regal grace and I wondered if it was her natural gait or if it had been taught.

Elodie pressed the "up" button on the elevator.

"Can I ask you something?" I said.

She glanced at me. "Sure."

"Is this usual? Contracts, I mean. Does this happen at The Rex often?"

She paused and then said, "No. It's not the norm. It happens from time to time. But usually our girls stay with The Rex."

I pondered why Hadrian would want me for an exclusive contract. Sure, we'd spent the night together. An *incredible* night. But was that enough to make him want me again? And if so, why not come to another event and ask me for my key? Or did he think that was too much trouble?

As my thoughts swirled, the elevator arrived, and we stepped in. The carriage was empty save for an operator. When we reached the twelfth floor, we got out and Elodie started talking again. "There will be a car waiting for you at eight to take you to the restaurant where you will meet Mr. Rhys." She headed to the door of my suite and opened it for me, and I went inside. "If you need anything, call the front desk. Otherwise, I'll see you at six to bring you your clothes for the night."

She turned to leave. The door clicked shut and I was alone.

I lay down with the intention of taking a quick catnap. It seemed like I was only asleep for a few minutes when my phone jarred me awake with a buzz. I cracked an eye open and reached for it on the bedside table. It was a text from Tiffany telling me to enjoy my night.

I'd been asleep a lot longer than I thought. Early evening sunlight streamed through the gauze curtains. It was just past five, and I still had more than enough time to get ready, but I needed to get moving. I took a shower and blew my hair dry. The suite had been supplied with makeup, hair products, and other styling tools. While the heating wand was warming up, there was a knock on my suite door.

I went to the front room and looked through the peephole. Opening the door, my eyes immediately went to the garment bag slung over Elodie's arm. In her other hand, she carried a brown shopping bag.

"Your dress," she said, brushing past me and entering the suite.

I closed the door and then turned around. She placed the garment bag on the couch and unzipped it. Elodie pulled out a black beaded dress and held it up for my inspection.

"Elodie, if you're the New York version of Gen, why are you bringing me my dress in person?"

"You have no idea who Hadrian Rhys is, do you?"

"Should I?"

"It's short," she explained as she ignored me, twirling the hanger to show me the gown. "But it has a high neckline with long sleeves and also conceals your back."

I took a step closer so I could reach out and touch the exquisite dress. "Are those pearls?"

She nodded. "Black seed pearls."

"It's stunning."

Elodie's gaze bored into me. "It doesn't take long."

"What doesn't?"

"Getting used to this lifestyle." She shrugged and then let out a laugh. "You'll come to expect it eventually. And you won't ever want to go back."

I swallowed, not liking the finality of her statement, but Tiffany had said the same thing.

"In the brown bag are a pair of black stilettos and the appropriate jewelry for your evening. What were you going to do with your hair and makeup?"

"Big curls but leave it down."

Elodie nodded.

"Subtle eyes and a bright red mouth," I went on.

She grinned. "He won't know what hit him."

Chapter Fourteen

I climbed out of the car with the aid of the driver. With my black beaded clutch in one hand, I strode toward the heavy oak doors of the restaurant. I approached the hostess and smiled.

"Good evening," she greeted, setting a cordless phone down in its cradle. "Do you have a reservation?"

"My name is Eden Smith and I—"

"Welcome, Ms. Smith," she said. "We've been expecting you. If you'll follow me."

She led me through the subdued, romantic restaurant, past people enjoying their bowls of spaghetti and meatballs and veal scaloppini.

We headed through the kitchen where there were two tables set so VIP customers could dine while their food was being prepared, and then continued on to another room at the back of the restaurant.

The walls were dark wood, and the light fixtures emitted a soft glow. It was dreamy and quixotic, with black and white sketches of vineyards and tables laden with food.

The atmosphere was a blend of extravagance and earthy Italian home.

There was only one table and it was set with a white tablecloth, a breathing bottle of red wine, and a bread basket.

"Mr. Rhys will be joining you shortly," the hostess said. "May I get you anything while you wait?"

I shook my head and set my beaded clutch down on the table. "I'm fine. Thank you."

She cocked her head. "Enjoy your dinner."

The hostess left me alone. There was no menu on the table, so I assumed that meant the order had already been taken care of.

I hadn't eaten anything since that morning, so I took the olive oil shaker and dribbled it onto a bread plate. I added pepper and salt and then dunked a piece of bread into it before setting it in my mouth. I inhaled deeply as the aroma of freshly baked bread reached my nose, and then I exhaled in enjoyment.

"Eden," a low, masculine voice greeted.

My spine snapped straight in surprise. I hadn't heard anyone enter the room.

But that wasn't what startled me.

It was the pleasure in hearing his voice.

Deep.

Brogue.

Familiar.

I turned slowly, needing time to prepare and steady my nerves.

Hadrian Rhys stood arm's length from me, dressed in an immaculate three-piece gray suit. His blue-gray eyes surveyed me from the top of my head to the tips of my toes.

He sauntered toward me and I had the insane urge to

take a step back, to flee. It was a mistake agreeing to meet with him alone. When all I wanted to do was—

Despite my mind trying to talk me out of this meeting, my body remembered him longingly. It wanted him; it yearned for his touch. And my body was telling my brain to shut up.

"Thank you for coming," he said.

I hadn't been prepared for his polite countenance. If anything, I expected to meet Hadrian again and immediately do battle with his arrogant side.

"Shall we sit?" he asked pleasantly.

"In a moment," I said, finally shaking off the spell of desire that came with Hadrian's presence. "Why wasn't I allowed to know the stipulations of the contract you're proposing before coming to meet you?"

"I wanted to be the one to make you the official offer. And I had a feeling that if Ramsey and Genevieve had relayed information to you on my behalf, you'd have found a way to say no."

"I could say no right now."

He smiled in genuine amusement and it softened the harsh planes of his face. And it had me catching my breath.

"You *could* say no right now," he agreed. "But I haven't fed you yet. Maybe you should wait until after dinner. The pasta here is the best in the city."

"I won't be able to enjoy my dinner unless we discuss why I'm here."

Hadrian picked up the wine bottle that rested on the table. He poured two glasses and handed me one. He grasped the other, holding it in his large hand—a hand that had brought me to the heights of pleasure.

I was suddenly transported to that evening, when I'd felt his fingers slide into me.

"You're flushed," he noted. He cocked his head to the side. "Thinking about our last time together?"

"No."

His gaze was intense. "I haven't been able to stop thinking about you."

I sighed. "Damn it, Hadrian."

"What?"

"You make it impossible to play coy."

"Playing coy is beneath you. I like you for your honest reactions."

Hadrian set his glass down and then gestured to my chair before coming to pull it out for me.

I slowly moved to sit down and when Hadrian leaned over to help me scoot closer to the table, he said softly, "You look beautiful."

"Thank you," I said, hating that it came out breathy.

Hadrian took his seat.

We stared at each other over the glasses of wine and bread basket. The air was pumped full of tension.

"I want you to spend the next six months with me in Shetland."

My fingers played with the stem of my glass. "You don't mince words, do you?"

"Waste of time. I know what I want."

"Six months is a long time," I said.

"I'll make it worth your while financially."

All the tender feelings I had begun to feel instantly vanished. How could I have forgotten why I was truly here?

"I wasn't referring to the financial aspect of it," I announced coldly. "I meant in relation to time. Six months is a long *time*."

"Do you think I'll get bored with you?"

"No. I think *I'll* get bored with *you*."

He took a sip of his wine. "You won't. You're intrigued by me. And besides, I'm unlike any man you've ever met."

"Ah, I finally recognize this version of you."

"I don't want to do battle with you, Eden. It's very simple. I want to spend six months with you. I'm offering you a million dollars for that time."

"A million?" I asked with a gasp.

I hated myself in that moment. I hated him too. For reminding me of what I had become.

"There will be clothes and jewelry. Anything I give you as a gift, you can take with you when the contract ends."

"Stop," I said. "Please stop."

He frowned. "What did I say wrong?"

"I just need a second to process—"

"No, you don't. It's simple."

I glared at him. "It's simple for *you*, maybe. You're not the courtesan." As soon as I said the words, I immediately wanted to take them back. Admitting to Hadrian that I had trouble reconciling why I was meeting with him, why I'd spent the night with him in the first place, showed weakness.

"During your time in Shetland with me," he said, his brogue thick, "you won't be a Rex girl."

"What will I be?"

"Mine."

I shoved back from the table. "I need some air."

He rose when I did, but he made no pursuit to follow me.

I rushed through the restaurant with my head bowed so I didn't have to see anyone. I was sure people knew. Could they read it in the way I held myself? Did they know I was questioning my own worth?

Any other girl in my situation would've jumped at the

money Hadrian offered, so how was it that a million-dollar exclusive contract made me feel cheap?

Once I was on the sidewalk outside the restaurant, I gulped in a breath of air and willed my heartbeat to slow down.

The sun had set, and I was shrouded in shadows except for the city lights. Here, away from Hadrian, I could admit it.

It wasn't about the money.

He could've asked me to go for nothing and I would've jumped at the chance. He made me feel alive and bold, made me feel like I wasn't a desperate orphan in need of a new identity to escape a dangerous family.

He made me feel like I wasn't alone.

His presence—his body—commanded my attention and refused to let it go.

The door to the restaurant opened and then Hadrian was standing next to me.

"You didn't leave," he said.

"I told you I needed air." I looked at him as we stood next to each other on the street, taxis whipping by us in the night. "You expected me to run."

"Aye."

In a daring gesture, he turned toward me and his hand reached out to caress my face, his thumb stroking the apple of my cheek.

"What is it you're afraid of?" he asked.

I stood in silence.

"Come on, what is it?"

"What if," I began, "after a few weeks, you want me gone, or I want to leave. What happens then?"

"I won't keep you prisoner, if that's your concern. If it's a monetary issue, you don't need to worry about that either. You'll get one hundred thousand dollars up front just for accepting."

My brow furrowed.

"Take the contract, Eden."

"Don't rush me," I snapped.

"I want this finalized. One million dollars. Six months. Exclusive. In Shetland with me. I will not be with another. And I will *not* share you."

The contract was too good to be true.

There was a catch.

There had to be.

But I was too inexperienced to look for hidden meanings or play the game Hadrian was a master at.

It didn't matter. I knew what my answer was going to be the moment I realized it was Hadrian who'd offered the contract.

"Yes," I whispered.

"Are you sure?" he asked. "Because once you say yes, you're mine. The contract begins immediately."

I nodded because I was unable to speak. His intense gaze captured mine, clipping my wings.

He gently grasped my elbow and escorted me inside the restaurant. When we were in the private back room, Hadrian released me. He looked at me for a long moment and then with one confident move of his massive arm, he swept the dishes, the glasses of wine, the bottle itself to the floor. Glass shattered, wine spilled, bread and olive oil went everywhere, and I didn't care.

"Lay on the table," he demanded. "Spread your legs."

His blue-gray eyes were trained on me as he waited for me to do his bidding.

Like a puppet, my limbs moved. I crawled onto the table and flipped over, flat on my back, and opened my legs.

Hadrian walked toward me but didn't touch me. Instead, he stared down at me, an inscrutable expression on his angular face.

My heart began to drum with excitement and nerves. I had no idea what to expect, and the anticipation made me wet between my thighs.

He reached out to caress one of my ankles. His touch was tender, light, and then his fingers were gliding up the inside of my legs, dipping into the hollow behind my knees.

It tickled, and I let out a laugh.

His hands didn't stop, but continued higher, pushing up my dress so that it gathered around my waist.

I was wearing a scrap of lace that barely passed as underwear. He touched a finger to it and made a noise of approval. And then he was on his knees, pushing aside the lace, his tongue at the heat of me.

I couldn't stop the scream that erupted from my lips, not caring that the kitchen staff was only a few feet away.

Hadrian gripped my hips to keep me pinned to the table as he continued to devour me. Voracious, he feasted like a warrior at a banquet.

He pleasured fast and ruthless, leaving me no choice but to come against his mouth.

And when he lifted his head, he swiped his tongue across his lips.

"I will ruin you, Eden," he murmured.

I was sure it was already too late for that.

Chapter Fifteen

Hadrian helped me off the table and aided in straightening my dress. My cheeks were on fire and I looked everywhere but at him. The room was littered with the remains of our wine glasses and china, scattered across the floor.

Without a word, Hadrian clutched my hand and led me to the restaurant's bar. While I settled onto a stool, Hadrian spoke to the bartender and asked for a bottle of wine.

"Please tell the kitchen we've moved and would like our salads," he said.

The bartender nodded, poured our wine, and then left the bar to speak to the kitchen staff.

I wasn't sure what to say to Hadrian—the formalities of the contract had been addressed, but I was tongue tied. All I could do was stare at his large hand as he grasped the delicate wine glass. His scarred knuckles stood out and it reminded me of the scar on his body.

The bartender returned, carrying our salads. He set them down in front of us, asked if we wanted fresh cracked black pepper, and then went to help another customer.

"How is this going to work?" I inquired.

"You pick up your fork and—"

"Not that. I mean, *this*." I gestured between the two of us.

"I don't understand. I thought things worked quite nicely in the back room." He arched his brows as if daring me to vocalize what had occurred.

"Yes, I know how that went. I meant…after. Do you want me to talk? Do *you* want to do the talking? Or do you want six months of silence between us?"

He peered at me. "You're nervous."

"I'm not nervous."

"Liar."

I scoffed. "Fine. I'm nervous. I don't know how any of this is supposed to work. I don't know if you even want to talk to me, or if you'd prefer it if I was a nice quiet trophy—"

"What's your real name?" he interrupted.

His question made me pause and then I said, "I'm still not telling you that."

"Where did you grow up?"

"Here and there."

"Do you have any siblings?" he asked.

"What is this, an inquisition?"

"I'm trying to learn about you."

"By firing questions at me? Haven't you talked to another human being before?" I asked in exasperation. "It's called a normal conversation, Hadrian."

"I don't have time for normalcy."

I reached for my wine glass. "Why not? That makes me curious about you…"

"It does?"

I nodded.

"Okay, what do you want to know?"

Everything.

In a gesture that surprised both of us, I stroked my finger along his jawline. It was stubbly, the beginning of his beard growing in.

He turned his head ever so slightly so that his lips grazed my fingers.

"I'm going to learn everything there is to know about you."

"That sounds like a challenge," I said lightly, dropping my hand and lifting my glass of wine.

"Not a challenge. A promise," he vowed.

I had to stop the arrow of nerves that shot through my belly. The danger wasn't that Hadrian was determined to learn everything about me, it was that I wanted to confide in him all that there was. But I could never entrust anyone with the knowledge I possessed—the knowledge I'd burned to ashes and washed away.

Our dinner was leisurely and as the wine flowed, I felt myself relaxing in his presence. In spite of the alcohol, I managed to keep my wits about me, knowing that Hadrian had the force and drive of a battering ram, and that he would stop at nothing to get something genuine out of me.

He cut off a sliver of his steak and set it on my plate. "Try it."

The meat was tender and rich, and I had to stop a moan of delight. I took my time savoring it and was just about to ask if I could have another piece when Hadrian obliged without me having to say a word. He grinned, obviously pleased that I was enjoying myself.

"What will I do?" I asked him in between bites.

"Do?"

"I assume you'll be occupied during the days, doing whatever it is you do that allows you to offer me such a generous sum for my time…" It was as close to an outright question about how he made his money as I would dare to ask.

"Aye."

Disgruntled that he hadn't taken the bait about his work, I repeated my question. "So, what will I do?"

"You mean how will you occupy yourself while you're waiting for me?"

I scrunched my nose at him.

He chuckled. "I have horses. You can ride."

"I've never ridden a horse."

"Then I'll teach you," he said. "I'm sure I can drag myself away from work long enough to show you how to ride properly."

I stemmed the flow of excitement for the possibility of getting to experience something that I had never had enough money to pursue. "Okay, what else is there to do in Shetland?"

"I have a pool. You can swim. I have a library. You can read. You can walk on my beach—"

"*Your* beach?"

He paused, as if weighing what he was about to say. "Aye. My beach."

"Like, your own beach?" I asked, seeking clarification.

Hadrian nodded once, a quick slash of his head.

How much money did he have that he could afford to own a private beach? I dismissed the thought, realizing he had enough money that he wouldn't miss a million dollars.

"Do you get to enjoy your own beach?" I asked. "Or do you constantly travel for work?"

"Actually, I don't travel for work often. I prefer the seclusion of Shetland and work from home most of the time."

We continued to devour our entrees—and much to my

surprise, Hadrian let me have his entire steak when he saw how much I relished it.

He was strange, this man. Commanding, intense, mysterious, and yet his focus was on me and my pleasure. Even when it came to food.

"Are we going to have dessert?" I asked when the dinner plates had been cleared.

Hadrian's mouth curled upward. "You have a sweet tooth."

"You don't?"

His gaze dipped down my body making me feel warm and flushed.

"Panna cotta," I stated. "If they don't have panna cotta, I'm going to doubt the integrity of this Italian restaurant."

Hadrian laughed and called to the bartender, "One panna cotta. Two spoons."

When the dessert arrived, covered in fresh berries, I let Hadrian have the first bite. I wanted to watch him. His face lit up, and for a moment he looked incredibly boyish.

In fact, he enjoyed the dessert so much I was only able to get two spoonfuls before the entire thing disappeared.

"Oh, I see how it is. You'll share your steak without a thought, but when it comes to dessert, I'm on my own," I said with a laugh.

He didn't even look chagrinned when he replied, "I'll get you another."

"No, it's okay," I said. "I've had enough actually."

We lingered over the last few sips of wine, but inevitably our dinner came to an end. A spark of excitement lit in my belly when Hadrian stood up from the bar and helped me from my seat. His hand rode the small of my back as he guided me to the exit. The pressure of his palm against my dress sent a gentle pulse of pleasure between my legs.

A black Rolls-Royce waited for us at the curb with a driver standing at the door ready to open it for us. I'd been impressed by the car that had driven me to dinner, but the Rolls took it to a whole new level.

Hadrian's hand rested on my thigh, lazily stroking circles across my skin, but he remained silent as we drove. When we arrived back to The Rex, Hadrian helped me out of the car.

Much to my confusion and surprise, he didn't take me to his hotel room. He escorted me to my suite, pressed my body to the door, and then kissed me so deeply that my thoughts scrambled, and my brain short-circuited.

Just as I grabbed the lapels of his suit jacket, he pulled away. He gazed down at me and smiled thoughtfully. "I have a business meeting before we fly out tomorrow. Meet me in the lobby at eight a.m. Good night, Eden."

Chapter Sixteen

Second thoughts clawed at the back of my head. It was easy to silence them when I was in Hadrian's orbit, but he'd left me alone in a plush hotel bed. Instead of sleeping, I thought about how he'd touched me and my response to him.

I couldn't believe I'd met the man only a few days ago, and now I was about to fly to Shetland to spend six months with him.

Eventually I fell into a fitful sleep and woke up sometime around dawn. I dragged myself into the shower. Hot water sprayed me, but it wasn't at all restorative.

I dried off quickly and went to the suitcase Elodie had packed and left for me while I was out to dinner with Hadrian. I dressed in a pair of pre-chosen dark jeans, a cozy gray turtleneck sweater, and black ankle boots. I blew out my hair so it fell in loose waves around my face, applied the barest of makeup, and then gathered my belongings.

I put my work cell phone into a brand-new black leather shoulder bag and wheeled my suitcase to the door. I took one last look around, not for anything I might've left —I didn't own anything—but because it felt like I was finally closing the door on my past.

Strange, nonsensical thoughts continued to plague me as I stepped into the elevator. When the doors opened into the lobby after a short ride down, I forced a serene expression, hoping it would aid in calming the rapid beat of my heart.

Hadrian stood at a cream-colored couch with his phone to his ear as he stared at the exit. He wore a charcoal gray suit and his strawberry blond hair was styled off his forehead. A beam of sunlight streamed through the lobby windows, highlighting his strong, angular jaw.

A delicious shiver worked its way down my spine. A bead of warmth curled through my stomach.

His expression was stoic and gave me no insight into his thoughts. As I approached, I was able to hear the tail end of his conversation.

"Good, I knew you'd come to your senses," he said. He hung up and then his head swiveled, his gaze meeting mine.

I nearly faltered, but I forced my pace to remain steady as I stalked toward him. When I was a few inches away from him, I stopped. My chest rose and fell quickly, and his eyes drank me in.

Did he know I was trying to breathe him in? I wanted to memorize his scent forever.

He removed his hands from his pockets so he could take my chin between his thumb and forefinger and study me.

"You didn't sleep," he stated.

I wasn't sure if he expected a reply, but when he gently pinched my chin, I opened my mouth and said, "No, I didn't sleep much."

"What kept you up last night?"

I swallowed. "Thoughts of you."

"Honest response. What kind of thoughts about me?" His gaze seemed to darken.

I blushed and looked away from him.

Thankfully, he didn't continue the line of questioning. He took my hand, linking his fingers through mine. I looked down at our clasped palms.

Hadrian did not strike me as one who enjoyed public displays of affection, but maybe this wasn't that at all. Maybe this was nothing more than a show of possession, of command.

He stalked toward the exit of The Rex Hotel with me in tow. A doorman opened the door and we stepped out into the cool Manhattan air.

A driver in a chauffeur uniform waited by an idling Rolls. With a nod from Hadrian, the driver opened the back door and then took my suitcase to store it. Hadrian gestured for me to get in first.

The reality of the situation dawned on me and panic hit me hard and fast in the chest. My instincts screamed to escape.

It was as if Hadrian knew how I was feeling because when he climbed in next to me, he placed his hand on my thigh. I could feel his touch through the designer jeans I was wearing, his body warm and solid next to me.

The door closed and then Hadrian whispered, "Easy."

I felt like a spooked horse, but when Hadrian wrapped his arm around my shoulder and pulled me toward him, I gave up the fight of appearing sure of myself and my convictions. I leaned against him, pressed my nose to the collar of his shirt, and closed my eyes, attempting to battle back the feelings of what-the-fuckery.

"Are you having second thoughts?" His voice was sinful velvet, a caress in the dark.

I kept my cheek to his chest but managed to look out the window. I thought of how to answer him. I wasn't having second thoughts. Not at all. I was afraid of what he made me feel. I settled for giving him something truthful. Something that wouldn't cost me a lot.

"I've never been out of the country."

"Never?"

I shook my head.

"Ah, now I understand. That was the real reason you said yes to me. You want to be an international woman of mystery."

A companionable silence fell between us as we drove out of the city. He didn't seem inclined to want me to move, and at the moment I was comforted by his strength.

We arrived directly on the airport tarmac and my breath caught in my throat when I saw a private jet that was sleek, powerful, and the epitome of wealth.

"Okay, that's twice the size of the one I flew on to get to the city." I gaped.

"It's even more impressive on the inside," he assured me. "It took two years to build, but it was worth the wait."

I gawked at him. "This is *your* jet? Yours. This one isn't from a charter service?"

"I only charter jets for people when I'm not flying with them. Otherwise we take mine."

I swallowed. "A million dollars really isn't anything to you, is it?"

"Does that mean you're impressed?"

"Impressed? No. Overwhelmed, yes."

We got out of the car and he escorted me toward the jet's stairs, his hand riding my hip. I gripped the railing and boarded the plane. When I got inside, I held my breath. It was light wood and white leather, very much the opposite of old-world luxury. It was modern and utilitarian. I suddenly understood something about Hadrian. Though he was wealthy and money was no object, his taste wasn't flashy or gaudy.

Immediately up the stairs was a station for the flight crew. Past that was a small dining area with a sophisticated table on each side of the aisle and chairs across from one another, one facing forward, and one facing rearward so that people were seated as though they were having dinner at a fine dining restaurant.

I stepped toward the first section of the plane.

"Take this one," he said softly, gesturing to an elegant white leather seat near one of the windows. "You can look out as we fly."

I glanced at him and smiled. "Thank you."

He took the seat across from me on the other side of the table and pressed a button to raise the sun slats over our windows.

While we were getting situated, a flight attendant approached from the front of the aircraft.

"Good morning, Mr. Rhys," she greeted. Her gaze slid to mine and she smiled. "Good morning, Ms. Smith."

"Good morning," I murmured.

She was beautiful. A glossy haired brunette with an hourglass figure wearing a vintage blue dress with white piping and pumps. It added to her femininity. Her smile was kind and genuine when she asked, "What can I get you to drink, ma'am?"

"Sparkling water, please."

"And for you, sir?"

"I'll have the same. Thank you."

She nodded and went to fix our drinks, and then returned a few minutes later to set our glasses and two cloth napkins embroidered with 'H.R.' on the table between us. Hadrian and I sat in silence as we sipped our sparkling waters. I stared out the window and watched airport crew moving next to the plane, inspecting everything to ensure we were ready for departure.

The pilot came to personally speak to Hadrian. "Sir, we're on schedule and are clear for takeoff. Would you like to depart?"

Hadrian reached over and made sure my seatbelt was buckled tight, letting his hands linger for a moment. He smiled slightly and then settled back into his luxurious leather seat before looking at the pilot and saying, "Aye."

I glanced out the window as the engines whined and we taxied away from the gate, excitement bubbling in my stomach. A few minutes after takeoff, the pilot announced that we'd hit altitude and could travel around the cabin.

Hadrian unbuckled his seat belt and stood. "Come on, I want to show you the jet."

We left the dining area and I followed Hadrian down the aisle to the rear of the plane. We passed two additional sections. One area sat four people close together and the other was a work and entertainment area with a large television and a small, stylish desk. When we got to the end of the aisle there was a wall with a small door between it and the rear of the plane marked 'Private'. Hadrian pushed open the door to reveal a tasteful bedroom, and an aircraft-sized, well-designed bathroom.

"It's not as big as some," he said with a wry grin. "But I use the plane mostly for business. And a little bit of pleasure."

I looked at him and raised my eyebrows. "Pleasure?"

Hadrian gently urged me into the bedroom and quickly followed. He shut the door behind him.

"Get on the bed," he ordered, his voice steel.

I looked away from the king-sized bed with beautiful slate gray satin sheets and light wood accents to stare at him. "You want me on the bed?"

"The bed," he commanded again.

"You don't really want me to…with a flight attendant up front?"

"Eden," he said, voice low. "Get on the bed."

It was clear Hadrian did not like my hesitation. He waited, silently commanding me. I settled myself in the middle of it, on my back, and peered at him.

He remained by the door, his body taut. "Unbutton your jeans."

My fingers fumbled with the button of my pants.

"Unzip them."

I unzipped.

"Touch yourself."

My eyes widened. "While you watch?"

"You did it the night we spent at The Mansion," he reminded me. "Why are you shy now?"

"That was different," I protested.

"Why?"

"I didn't think I'd ever see you again," I admitted. "And that was only for a few seconds before you—"

"What about when you're alone? Don't you touch yourself when you're alone?" he asked, his mouth turning up at the corners.

"Of course I touch myself," I exclaimed. "But I've never done it in front of someone…"

"It's the first of many new things we'll do together, Eden. Now touch yourself. And make yourself come. I want to see you."

"I don't know if I can."

"Close your eyes," he said. "Pretend I'm not watching you. Make me the center of your fantasy."

His eyes were stormy with want.

I kicked off my boots and shimmied my jeans down my legs, tossing them aside. Hadrian's eyes roved hungrily over my bare legs and lace.

Black. French. Taunting.

"Close your eyes," he said again.

I shut my eyes and skimmed my fingers up and down my upper thighs before resting my hand on the seam of my body. I slowly began to play with myself over my underwear, enjoying the tease of my fingers through the lace.

I pretended my fingers were Hadrian's, rougher, blunter, more commanding than I could ever be. I finally slipped inside my underwear and touched myself.

Skin to skin.

I ached with the desire to be filled. I spread my legs wider and heard his breath catch. Could he see that I was wet through the fabric? Wet for him? Could he see what this was doing to me? Could he see how much I desired him even though he wasn't even touching me?

I slid my fingers into my body, my thumb stroking the bundle of nerves between my legs.

"Hadrian," I whispered, my eyes opening.

Our gazes locked; his cheeks were heightened with color and I could see the rise and fall of his chest.

"Keep going," he orchestrated.

My free hand ventured underneath my sweater to pluck my hardened nipple.

"I want you to touch me," I gasped.

"Not yet," he said ruthlessly, his jaw clenched.

I closed my eyes and pleasured myself, knowing he watched, knowing he enjoyed the scene of me writhing on his bed.

I thought about how much better it would be if he was the one inside me, his fingers taking away the empty feeling. Pleasure bloomed between my legs and I shamelessly rode out my orgasm, my eyes shooting open to stare at him.

I'd barely made a sound when I came, my mouth open in a silent scream. No sooner had I removed my fingers than Hadrian unbuckled his belt and shoved his pants down including his boxers. He sprang free, large, ready— so damn appetizing, I wanted my mouth all over him.

But he didn't give me time to ask for what I wanted. Before I knew it, he was on me, spreading me wider and impaling me to the hilt.

I was primed and ready and another orgasm quaked. His lips took mine in a savage kiss, his hands gripping my hair as he pounded into me. Fervent, intense, it was like he was trying to purge everything that he was.

We were two animals in a mindless frenzy, and I realized there was never going to be a moment of embarrassment with this man. He would fulfill all my deepest, darkest fantasies, and be the cause of new ones.

Our bodies were battlefields of desire. To be taken and pleasured, dominated and touched, and suddenly the contract no longer mattered, because I knew what was really between us.

Hadrian gripped the back of my neck and pulled me close, angling his pelvis against me at that primal spot that only he seemed to be able to find.

I came hard and furious, clamping around him. He muttered something against my lips, something I couldn't understand, and then he came.

Hadrian stilled over me, not moving his heavy body from mine, but he lifted himself up to stare into my eyes, his hands cradling my face. He swept his thumbs against the apples of my cheeks and kissed me so deep I felt him all the way down to my marrow.

"You should get some sleep," he said. "I have some work to do. I'll wake you in a bit." He gently eased out of me and went into the bathroom to clean up.

I thought about asking him to stay with me, but I didn't want to come across as needy or insecure, especially after everything we'd just shared.

He kept his eyes on me as he tucked his shirt back into his trousers. Hadrian leaned over and kissed me quickly before leaving me alone in the bedroom.

I waited until the bedroom door closed before getting up and tending to myself. We hadn't used protection—there had been no need for it. I was on birth control and for the next six months we were exclusive.

Dreamily floating back to bed, I thought about what our next time together would be like. I pulled back the covers and climbed into bed. Snuggling into the pillow, my mind was blissfully clear. I conked out.

Chapter Seventeen

"Eden. Eden, wake up."

I rolled over feeling groggy and exhausted, my body languid from the attention Hadrian had paid it earlier.

I stretched and yawned. "How long have I been asleep?"

"About three hours."

"Three hours!" My eyes shot open. "How am I supposed to adjust to the time change if you let me sleep three hours?"

His eyes gleamed. "I have a few ideas about how to exhaust you later."

My body perked up at the thought.

"Splash some cold water on your face," he suggested. "I'll see you out there."

The door shut and I flung off the covers. I slowly got dressed and then went into the bathroom and washed off my makeup. After patting my face dry, I looked in the mirror. The nap had given me some natural color in my cheeks.

My stomach growled. I quickly slipped on my boots and then left the safety of the bedroom.

Hadrian looked up when I approached, setting aside his phone and closing his laptop. He smiled.

"What?" I asked, unable to stop the grin from stretching across my face.

"I like you with no makeup. You look…vulnerable."

My smile slipped. I didn't like the idea of being vulnerable around Hadrian. My body wanted him; I could accept that, but vulnerability led to other things—like intimacy.

I took the empty seat next to him, not knowing how to reply. When I tightened the seatbelt, my stomach rumbled again.

"Hungry?" he asked with a wry grin.

My gaze dropped to his lips. "Yes."

He laughed and pressed the button over his head. A moment later, the flight attendant in her smart, navy-blue uniform appeared.

"Sir?" she asked.

"We're ready for lunch," he said. "Thank you."

She nodded and then disappeared up front to her private domain.

"How long is the flight?" I asked.

"About twelve and a half hours. Shetland is farther north than the mainland of Scotland." He picked up his phone, tapped a few buttons, and then showed me a map across the screen.

"Lerwick is here," he pointed to the town along the eastern coast.

"You live in Lerwick?" I asked. He paused and I looked away from the screen to his face. "Hadrian?"

Hadrian cleared his throat. "No. I don't live in

Lerwick. I live on an island which is a few hours away by yacht. About ten minutes by helicopter."

"Are we taking a boat or a helicopter?"

"Depends," he said with a wry smile. "Have you ever been on a *yacht*?"

I shook my head. "I haven't been on a helicopter, either."

"We'll take my yacht. The view from deck when we come into the harbor is…well, you'll see."

"What's it like?" I asked. "Your home."

"It overlooks the ocean. It's built partly into the side of a mountain."

"Sounds like a fortress," I said lightly.

He peered at me and then nodded. "That's exactly what it is."

I swallowed a bout of nerves that fluttered in my belly. I looked out the window so I could stare into the clouds, so Hadrian couldn't see the confusion I was feeling.

Who was Hadrian Rhys…and why did he need a fortress?

The hours of travel bled together. I dozed a few more times, only to wake up and find Hadrian studying me. When he wasn't engaging me in conversation, he was on his phone.

The man never seemed to tire. He got up long enough to stretch his legs and make a private phone call before returning to his seat.

"Can I ask you a question?" I queried.

"Sure."

"The first night we were together…"

"Aye?"

"You spoke in a foreign language when you were…"

He smiled softly. "When I was what?"

"Coming," I finished, wondering at my bout of sudden shyness.

Shyness should have no place between a courtesan and her lover.

"It was Norwegian," he answered.

"You speak Norwegian?"

"Fluently. Along with French, Italian, and Shetlandic. Do you speak any languages?

"French and Italian," I admitted. "Shetlandic? I've never even heard of that."

"Shetland has both Scottish and Norse influence. So, the language is made up of Scot dialect and the Norn language—which is now extinct." He shrugged.

Shrugged. Like it was nothing.

I looked at him in awe. "You're not just a pretty face, are you Hadrian Rhys?"

"No more than you are, Eden Smith."

I saw Lerwick from the back of a Mercedes that drove us to the marina where Hadrian's yacht waited for us. It was past dinner time and my stomach growled in protest.

"I haven't forgotten to feed you," he assured me with a grin. "I just wanted to wait until we were on my yacht. Can you wait a few more minutes?"

I nodded.

"Do you like lobster?" he asked.

"I think so," I said.

"You think so? Have you never had lobster?"

I shrugged and looked out the window again into the

night sky. "There wasn't a lot of money growing up to have lobster."

The admittance tumbled out of my mouth and my heart pounded with sudden nerves. I hoped Hadrian didn't drag me down a lane of my past, asking questions about me.

He took my hand and gave it a squeeze. "You'll try the lobster—and if you love it, I'll make sure you have it whenever you want."

"You really won't spare any expense, will you?"

"If something makes you happy and I can provide it, then I will."

The car stopped in front of the marina and a man in a stretch golf cart greeted us.

"Mr. Rhys. Right this way."

The car driver placed our luggage on the back of the cart and then we were off, headed through a small gate down to the illuminated docks. We drove for a minute or two and then the golf cart came to a stop in front of a massive yacht. It was lit from above and below with well-placed nautical lighting. I could see the hulls through the water at the rear of the yacht.

My mouth gaped. "This is yours?"

"It's a power catamaran, and yes, it's mine."

Hadrian took my hand and guided me onto the steps at the stern of his yacht on the right-hand side. As we stepped up onto the vessel, my chest tightened when I was confronted with the magnitude of opulence. Even though I'd just been on his private jet, this…this was something else. I could rationalize a private jet. It was for travel, for business.

But a yacht?

A yacht was supreme luxury, a toy for the elite.

There was seating for eight people and a table for

dining outside, all lit up perfectly to showcase expert crafts-manship and a real teak deck. A man appeared from a staircase just to the right of a set of sliding glass doors and he began to speak to Hadrian in low tones before disap-pearing again.

"I know just as much about yachts as I do jets," I said to him, gliding my hand across the sleek stainless-steel handrail I'd been gripping.

Hadrian smiled. "Then I won't bore you with too many specifics. This is Aegir. She's an 80 Sunreef power catamaran, one of only seven like her in the world, and fully customized for me. But I promised you dinner. Take off your boots. I have deck shoes for you, or you can go barefoot."

"Yes. Food and then bed, I think," I said, my body tired from travel. I quickly pulled off my boots and followed Hadrian's massive form across the deck.

Hadrian opened the sliding glass doors and we walked into a magnificent salon and dining room area with its own helm in the corner of the room, complete with a captain's chair and all sorts of gadgets for navigation. He guided me toward a seat at a dining table and I slid into it, completely overwhelmed.

"You don't even look tired. How is that possible?" I asked.

"I don't sleep much to begin with," he said with a rueful smile. "Maybe four hours a night."

"Four hours?" I marveled. "How do you even function?"

"I'm a machine."

One of the yacht crew came from below deck up a flight of stairs into the salon. He placed two steaming, unshelled lobsters in front of us along with a container of freshly melted butter. He then poured us two glasses of white wine from a bottle that had been chilling in an ice bucket on the table.

"I figured, why bother with salads?" Hadrian said.

I nodded. "Good, vegetables are gross anyway."

Hadrian started to laugh, a booming sound that echoed off the walls of the dining area.

I derived a strange sort of pleasure from making him laugh. He didn't strike me as the kind of man who laughed a lot and the thought made my heart lurch in sadness.

"Do you have friends, Hadrian?" I asked suddenly.

"Do you?" he countered.

I smiled.

He glowered. "What's that smile for?"

"It's not fun being on the receiving end of personal questions, is it?"

Hadrian leaned back in his chair and played with the stem of his wine glass while he surveyed me. "I think I may have underestimated you."

"What do you mean?"

"I think you're as tenacious as I am. So, you're a talented linguist. How did you learn to speak three languages?"

"How did you learn to speak five?" I countered.

He sighed. "And here I'd hoped that after a long day of travel you'd be a little more..."

"Malleable?"

"Forthcoming," he corrected. "You're a conundrum. The day we met at the Bar and Restaurant, you were flirtatious and confident. The night at The Mansion you were terrified—which I now know was because it was your first event. You said there wasn't money growing up for you to enjoy the finer things in life, and yet your table manners are perfect, like you come from a wealthy family."

He leaned forward. "You're evasive in conversation,

and the only time I feel like I truly have a grasp on who you are is when you're in my bed. And for a man who reads people, for a man who knows when people are lying, I know there's something you're not saying. Something big."

His words terrified me. No matter how much I thought I could bury my past and have it stay there, I seemed to wear it like a badge for Hadrian to see. And even though he didn't know exactly what I was hiding from him—from the world—Hadrian wasn't a man who would let it go.

He was relentless, and he wouldn't be happy with anything less than my complete and utter surrender. Not just in his bed, but in life, too. He'd never stop asking questions, he'd never stop digging. I was a puzzle he had to piece together.

"Can't it be enough?" I asked, meeting his eyes. "Just being together physically."

"You tell me." His eyes blazed with heat. "I'm not the only one who wants questions answered."

I nodded slowly. "You're right. I am curious about you, Hadrian. Why were you at The Mansion if you weren't there to spend your night with a woman? Why do you live on an island off the coast of Shetland when Lerwick looked absolutely adorable and is clearly remote already? Why is your home built into the side of a mountain? And how do you have so much money that you can throw it away on a girl you don't even know?"

Silence reigned between us and then he suddenly smiled.

I did not like that smile. It was a smile of victory.

Hadrian arched a brow. "You are no better at the art of subtle conversation than I am. How the hell were you ever planning on being a Rex girl?"

I glared. "I have no problem conversing with other people. My problem is *you.*"

He said nothing and then he began to eat, but his gaze remained on me. A shield had been erected and his expression was unusually stoic.

"Why do you bring out the worst in me?" I asked quietly.

"I don't bring out the worst in you. I bring out the honesty in you. And I think you haven't been honest with yourself in a very long time. If ever."

"You are exceedingly arrogant. Not to mention presumptuous. Don't think I don't know what you're doing."

"What am I doing?"

"Trying to fluster me enough into telling you all my deep and dark secrets."

"You have deep and dark secrets?" He raised his eyebrows.

"Eat your lobster, Hadrian," I groused.

We devoured our food as the boat rocked gently from side to side and the waves lapped at the hulls. It was as much about eating as it was about having something to do. I didn't like the uneasiness that had sprung up between us. It felt like we were on uneven ground, but I wouldn't be intimidated into answering questions about myself.

"The nuns taught me," he said, crushing the silence.

My eyes flew to his. His face was stoic, unyielding.

"You were taught by nuns?" I asked. "So was I."

He shook his head. "I was raised by them."

I frowned in clear lack of understanding.

"I'm an orphan, Eden."

My eyes widened in surprise. He'd opened himself up, just a bit, giving me a tiny glimmer into his past.

It felt uncharitable not to give him something in return.

"I'm an orphan too." I took a sip of my wine. "My mother's first language was Italian. It was all we spoke in the house when I was growing up. She was an immigrant and didn't speak English well for some time."

"And French?"

"I taught myself French last year," I evaded. I suddenly felt my stomach lurch and hastily set my fork down.

His eyebrows snapped together. "Eden? What's wrong?"

"I don't know," I said slowly. "I feel funny."

"Funny like you're having an allergic reaction, or funny like—"

"Seasick!" I quickly pushed back from the table, my hand going to my mouth, and then I ran from the salon. I sprinted downstairs, having no idea where I was going, and no sooner had I found a bathroom than I upchucked the rich lobster.

Nausea swam in my belly and I felt clammy and sweaty. I managed to slide across the floor to close the bathroom door and lock it.

I threw up again and groaned.

"Eden," Hadrian commanded a few moments later through the door, trying to turn the doorknob to enter. "Let me in."

"No," I moaned. "I don't want you to see me like this."

"I have something that will settle your stomach. I've got some sparkling water and an anti-nausea pill which works almost instantly."

"But how am I supposed to keep them down if I'm vomiting every—" My head went back over the toilet, effectively proving my point.

"Eden," he barked. "Open the damn door."

I reluctantly dragged myself across the floor and unlocked the door. I didn't bother getting up, but I did move out of the way so it wouldn't hit me when he opened it.

Hadrian loomed. His crisp white shirt was open at the collar, his sleeves rolled up.

I stared at his boat shoes while trying not to embarrass myself by throwing up in his presence.

"You look like hell," he said lightly.

"Screw you." I immediately covered my mouth—not to stop the spewing of my curses, but the spewing of the contents of my stomach.

He crouched down next to me and held out the glass of sparkling water. "Drink this. And take this." He plopped a tiny pill into my hand. "It works well, but it will make you drowsy."

I did as he said and downed it with some water, wanting anything to stop the rolling of my stomach.

My belly reeled, but I closed my eyes and willed it to settle.

"This isn't even choppy water, and we're on an eighty-foot catamaran," he said in wry amusement. "How in the world are you seasick?"

"Not all of us are modern day Vikings born to sail the open sea."

Hadrian chuckled. He leaned past me and turned on the shower. I managed to get some more water down—and it stayed down.

"So. A Viking?" Hadrian teased.

I glared at him, which only made him grin.

"Do you have fantasies of me wearing animal pelts?" he tormented.

"Oh God. Stop," I muttered, closing my eyes. "I knew you'd give me hell as soon as I said it."

He outright laughed. "The shower is ready," he said, taking the glass away from me and setting it on the counter next to the sink. He then helped me stand, and before I could tell him not to, he began stripping me out of my clothes.

"What are you doing? I'm not an invalid."

"Humor me," he demanded.

"Fine, but you have to leave me to bathe in private."

"Why?"

"Pride."

He didn't bother replying and continued to undress me. He took my jeans off, but he left my lace thong alone. He urged the sweater over my head and then removed my camisole.

There was no reason to blush over my nudity, but I did blush when I managed to look in the mirror and see my reflection. Ashen complexion, limp hair damp at the temples.

I slithered out of my thong and tossed it aside before taking his hand and letting him help me into the shower. I breathed a sigh of relief when I leaned against the wall, the water coming down hot and steamy over my body.

Hadrian started removing his clothes.

"What are you doing?" I asked, my gaze riveted on the skin he was baring.

He cocked his head to the side. "Getting naked. Obviously."

"Stop right there," I commanded him, holding up my hand when he stood before me completely and gloriously nude.

He was a sight to behold. Long angular lines, muscles, scar.

"Stop? Why?" Hadrian asked.

"You are not climbing in this shower with me."

"Why not? Do you still feel sick? The medication should've started working by now."

"The pill worked." I nibbled my lip. "You have to promise not to kiss me."

"Excuse me?"

"I haven't brushed my teeth," I blurted out. "And I just"—I waved my hand in the direction of the toilet—"many times."

Without a comment, he marched to the sink, pulled open a drawer and took out a brand-new toothbrush. He tore off the wrapper and then doused it with toothpaste, ran it under the sink, and then brought it to me.

"Brush your teeth, Eden. And I promise not to kiss you. That's not what this is about."

I took the toothbrush and scrubbed my teeth and tongue, turning around so he could only see my backside, somehow embarrassed that a man who had fucked me would watch me brush my teeth.

Hadrian took the toothbrush from me when I was done and then got into the shower, settling himself behind me.

I turned to face him. My finger traced the scar along his abdomen. His skin danced under my touch.

"Knife," he said gruffly.

"I didn't ask," I whispered.

"You didn't have to."

I looked up to stare at him, like I was truly seeing him for the first time.

"Who are you, Hadrian?"

His eyes were intense as they bored into mine. His hand reached out to touch my jaw. "A man with his own past."

Hadrian's thumb grazed my bottom lip and a pang of lust slid down my belly to settle between my legs.

"Lean back against me," he said gruffly.

I reluctantly turned around and settled against him, resting my head on his chest as we stood with the hot water running over us. He made no move to do anything other than cradle me from behind.

He gently nudged me forward and then squirted shampoo from a pump attached to the wall into his hands. "Let me wash your hair."

He was taking care of me in his commanding fashion, but I couldn't say I didn't enjoy it.

"Will you tell me more? About your childhood?" I asked as his hands began to massage my head and suds foamed in my hair.

He brushed his lips along the curve of my shoulder. "No. Not right now."

"Why not?"

"Because you haven't earned it."

"Earned it?" I whipped my head around, staring at him as shampoo bubbles dribbled down my temples and neck. "You don't mean I have to—"

"For God's sake, woman," he muttered. "I just meant I'm not going to tell you everything there is to know about me when you refuse to do the same."

"That's emotional blackmail!"

"Aye," he said, completely unperturbed by my accusation.

His blunt fingers massaged my scalp and I couldn't help the slight moan of pleasure from escaping my lips.

After a stretch of silence, he said, "You weren't interested in my cufflinks or my watch."

I frowned. "What? Were you expecting me to rob you after you'd fallen asleep or something?"

He laughed. "No. I just mean—I'm wealthy, aye. And it didn't matter to you. My wealth, my diamond cufflinks, my two-hundred-thousand-dollar watch, you didn't even notice. You didn't notice when we met in the Bar and

Restaurant and you didn't notice the night we spent together."

I blinked. "You spent two hundred thousand dollars on a *watch*?"

"It's a Roger Smith," he answered gruffly. "I offered you a million dollars and you acted like—I don't even know. There was no calculating gleam in your eye. You weren't going to ask for more. You acted like…well, you weren't worth a million dollars. The Rex world is glamourous and elite, and it didn't turn your head. The only time you were really impressed was when you stepped foot on my yacht."

"A yacht is in-your-face wealth, Hadrian."

"So is a private jet."

"I expected the jet. Businessmen have jets. I didn't expect the yacht. Not on this grand scale. I'm starting to think you have more money than sense."

"You know why I offered you a six-month contract?"

"Because you can't be bothered to date?" I quipped.

"Because your reaction to me wasn't staged or faked." He paused for a moment and then went on, "You weren't born to be a Rex girl, Eden. You won't be able to seduce and flirt and pretend that you feel nothing. You feel far too much, so you try feeling nothing at all, and you don't seek out emotional contact."

I moved away from him so I could rinse the shampoo out of my hair, but also to compose myself.

Hadrian might've asked questions, but he didn't need to; not when he clearly saw who I was.

It didn't matter that I called myself Eden. Eden was a sham, a shell.

"Am I that easy to read?" I asked, finally opening my eyes and meeting his gaze.

"To those who care enough to pay attention, aye."

"And you paid attention."

His hands moved to my tense shoulders.

I pushed away from him so I could leave the shower. A towel hung on the rack and I quickly grabbed it and wrapped it around myself, not even bothering to dry off. I just wanted to get away from Hadrian.

"Are you feeling better?" Hadrian asked as he climbed out of the shower, tacitly agreeing to change the subject. Water sluiced down his muscular body, making me want to drag him to bed.

I thought about his question. My skin was flushed and warm from the shower, and dried sweat no longer clung to my body. "Yeah. I feel better."

"Are you drowsy yet?"

"Not yet."

He wrapped a towel around his waist. His damp skin glistened, and in spite of pushing him away moments ago, I couldn't stop myself from reaching out to caress him.

"I love it when you touch me," he said, his brogue enveloping me in a sensual haze.

"I can't seem to stop," I admitted. I slid my hands up and down his chest. My arm suddenly felt heavy.

Hadrian stepped toward me and scooped me up into his arms.

I nuzzled my cheek against his warm skin. "I think picking me up is your signature move."

He chuckled. "I like carrying you."

"I like being carried," I admitted.

"I love when you fight, Eden. But damn if I don't love your surrender."

"I'm not surrendering," I protested lamely. "I'm just— using you for your brute strength."

He laughed and then stepped out of the bathroom with me and set me down on the bed. Hadrian managed to get the towel off me and then slid the covers up around my shoulders.

"I'm sorry," he said, brushing a tender kiss to my shoulder.

"Why are you sorry?" I asked. My eyes were closing, and I was helpless to keep them open.

"If I thought you'd get seasick, we would've taken the helicopter."

"More money than sense," I murmured into the pillow before drifting off to sleep.

Chapter Eighteen

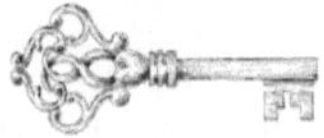

I woke up to sunlight and the scent of ocean mist from an open window in the cabin. My head was foggy from the medicine I'd taken the night before as well as the time change, but I didn't detect any sea sickness.

Sitting up, I nestled myself against the pillows at my back and dragged the covers up to my chest. Hadrian had put me to bed naked, and I'd woken up that way. His side of the bed was empty, and I wondered how long he'd been awake.

Embarrassment washed through my cheeks when I remembered the previous evening. Our dinner had been a series of questions that was clearly the beginning of something intimate. Hadrian's assessment of me, and the fact that he was so in tune with me, made me wary. He'd used our time in the shower to remain close while he continued his attempts to battle through my armor.

The more I endeavored to dance out of his verbal embrace, the more he was determined to twirl me back into his arms.

Was I just a challenge to him? Though I'd admitted

easily our physical attraction and he appreciated that level of honesty, he still demanded more.

How was I supposed to keep my wits about me when the man had taken care of me after I'd gotten seasick?

I brought a pillow to my face and moaned into it, thinking about Hadrian seeing me when I hadn't been at my best.

Some courtesan I turned out to be.

His words came back to plague me; he'd said numerous times that I didn't have what it took to be a Rex girl.

I wasn't sure he was wrong.

What would my life look like in six months when my contract with Hadrian was over? I would be a million dollars richer, but I'd have to go back to work at The Rex for at least a year to fulfill my end of the bargain for a new identity. Would Gen count my time with Hadrian? Or was this all off the books and something entirely different?

Not wanting to drown in thoughts of the future, I turned my attention to the present.

There wasn't a clock in the bedroom, and I wondered about the time. Though the sun was aloft, I had no idea the true hour. All I knew was that I hadn't gotten to fully enjoy my lobster from the previous evening, and I was hungry.

I flung off the covers and climbed out of bed, shivering in the cool air. A pair of blue silk pajamas had been left on the chair by the bed and I grabbed them and threw them on. Slippers lined with soft fleecy wool were at the foot of the bed.

I'd gone to sleep with a wet head and when I looked in the bathroom mirror, I nearly gasped. I was a hot mess. I brushed my teeth and tried to get my appearance under control and then went in search of food and Hadrian.

I went back upstairs to the salon and found the table

laden with fresh fruit, chocolate croissants, and yogurt. Three glass canisters full of different fruit juices rested on a bar at the center of the room toward the bow.

I grabbed a chocolate croissant and wondered about coffee when one of the crew members, dressed in khaki trousers and a white button down, entered the dining room from below. His face was angular; he was young and muscular, and his dark hair was combed off his forehead.

"Good morning, Ms. Smith," he greeted, his Scottish accent thick. He set a tray of lox down on the table.

"Er, good morning," I greeted, feeling awkward that I was still in my pajamas.

"Can I get you something to drink?" he asked. "American coffee? Espresso? Something else you may enjoy?"

"I'd love a cappuccino," I said. "Please."

He bowed slightly which had me frowning in confusion.

"Mr. Rhys is on deck. You're welcome to join him if you like. I'll bring you your cappuccino."

"Thank you, ah…"

"Angus, ma'am," he supplied.

"Thank you, Angus."

I saw Hadrian through the large sliding glass door, sitting at a table on deck, his head bent over his plate as he took a bite. He was dressed in a thick wool charcoal gray sweater and a pair of dark trousers.

Before venturing out to meet him, I took a moment to study the view of the ocean. Waves crashed against the beach with craggy mountains in the distance.

When I opened the door to the deck, Hadrian turned his head and smiled. "How are you feeling? Any trace of seasickness?"

"None," I said with a shy smile and a shiver, feeling my nipples pebble.

I really should've taken the time to find undergarments before coming on deck, I realized.

"Come here." He gestured to the other chair next to him. "There's a heating lamp to keep you warm."

"Maybe I should change," I said.

"Don't bother. You won't even notice the bite to the air. I promise."

Nibbling my lip, I padded over to the seat next to Hadrian and sat down. Apparently, I wasn't close enough because he grabbed the arm of the chair and pulled me toward him.

"Good morning," he said, brushing his lips against mine in a quick greeting before sitting back. He'd barely touched me, and I was already breathless.

"Is it? Morning?" I asked. "Not afternoon? There wasn't a clock in the bedroom."

The doors to the deck slid open and Angus appeared with my cappuccino in hand.

"Thank you, Angus," I said with a genuine smile.

"Can I get you anything else, Ms. Smith?"

"No. I'm okay, thank you." I took a bite of the chocolate croissant.

"Bring her a crab omelet and a side of fruit," Hadrian commanded.

"Yes, sir." Angus retreated before I could tell him not to bother.

I raised an eyebrow at Hadrian instead. "I don't usually eat a heavy breakfast."

"Humor me."

"You're in a really good mood."

"I slept for six hours last night," he said. "That never happens."

I took a moment to study him. The shadows under his eyes did look less pronounced and my heart kicked up with emotion when I thought that maybe, he'd slept well because I'd been in bed next to him.

"You sleep like a corpse," he said. "Did you know that?"

I chuckled. "I did know that."

"Because a boyfriend told you?"

"Boyfriend?" I looked at him in confusion. "No. I've been that way since I was a kid."

"How many men have you been with, Eden?"

"Jesus, Hadrian. Can't I have at least a cup of coffee first?" I sighed. "Just when I thought we could get through a meal without an interrogation."

"It was a simple question."

"One that has no bearing on us," I pointed out. "I have a sexual past. You have a sexual past. Let's leave it there. In the past."

"You're not curious about the women I've been with?"

"Not really, no."

"Why not?" he demanded.

"Because it doesn't matter."

"I'm insanely jealous," he clipped.

I looked at him while I took a tentative sip of my cappuccino. "Why?"

"I hate the idea of any man before me bringing you pleasure."

Angus took that moment to return with my plate of food. "May I bring you anything else, Ms. Smith?"

"No, this looks great. Thanks, Angus." I shot him a smile of gratitude and he beamed before leaving.

"Stop smiling at my staff," Hadrian groused.

"I was being polite."

He shook his head and glared at the sea.

"You're a mysterious billionaire who can have any woman he wants. Why do you care so much about my past? You're so Victorian, Hadrian," I baited, picking up my fork.

"How am I Victorian?" Hadrian demanded, a bite in his tone.

"You expect me not to have had lovers, yet you were completely willing to be a one-night stand."

"I'm possessive."

"So I've noticed," I said dryly.

He examined me. "You're different this morning."

"How so?"

"Last night you ran when you didn't like the direction our conversation was going. Now you're facing me head on. Why?"

"I have my own pride, Hadrian," I said softly. "Everyone wants to be wanted. I knew you were possessive when I said yes to your contract." I shrugged. "And I can't change my past. I can't rewrite it to make you feel better."

"Just tell me how many men you've been with."

"Why, so you can torture yourself with the knowledge? One or one hundred, it doesn't matter. I wasn't a virgin when we slept together."

"I wish you had been," he said, brogue thick and sensual. "I wish there had been no one before me so that you knew nothing except me. I wish I could've been the one to worship you first."

My hand reached out to gently clasp the back of Hadrian's neck, my thumb stroking his jaw, forcing his gaze to mine. I leaned toward him and settled my lips on his.

I was unable to stop my body's reaction to him.

Hadrian's hands reached out and grasped my hips, all but hauling me onto his lap. He became the aggressor.

I knew what it was like to want to change the past, but the past was already written. It could not be stricken from the book of who we were any more than a thread could be pulled on an old sweater without destroying what it was.

We could only look to the present.

"Hadrian," I whispered against his mouth.

"I told you I wanted every part of you," he growled against my lips.

"You can't have something that never belonged to you," I said, pulling away, just enough so that I could rest my head on his shoulder, in the crook of his neck.

Lust coiled inside of me and raged in my blood, and I chose to believe that was the reason I wanted to offer him something truthful, a small measure of comfort.

"It doesn't matter who's been before you. None of them compare to you. Okay?" I lifted my head to look into his turbulent eyes.

"Okay," he said, his voice whisper-soft.

Shivering, I tried to climb off his lap, but he wouldn't let me. So I ate my breakfast from the confines of his embrace, wondering what the hell I'd gotten myself into.

Hadrian was silent, content to hold me and every now and again brush the hair off my shoulder or steal a hand across my back.

When I was finished, I said, "I'm just now realizing we're not moving."

"I had them drop anchor in the middle of the night."

"Why? I thought you wanted to get home."

"I do, but I also wanted you to have a view of the island during breakfast," he said. "The truth is, we could have been home in a couple of hours at top speed, but I had the captain take his time overnight so we'd be here this morning."

I couldn't stop the smile from blooming across my face. "Are you trying to seduce me?"

"No trying about it," he said, humor tingeing his own lips. "I *am* actively seducing you. I'm Hadrian Rhys."

After another cappuccino, Hadrian and I returned to the master cabin and the yacht began to move again. I got dressed for the day and put on some makeup, despite the occasional interference of Hadrian's wandering hands. While I was pulling on a pair of dark jeans and a blue sweater, I heard a bell sound over an intercom system.

I looked at Hadrian.

He grinned back at me. "We're home."

I slid back into my boots since we were about to leave the yacht and let Hadrian escort me to the deck. The yacht was docked at a private pier and I had an expansive view of the island. Sunlight highlighted the gray, craggy mountains that seemed to loom over the entire beach.

On the paved road a few feet from the pier was the hottest car I'd ever seen.

"*Oh my God,*" I breathed.

"The view?" he asked in amusement.

"No." I dropped his hand and ran toward the vintage muscle car. "You own a mint condition '67 Shelby Cobra convertible with a blue and white racing stripe paint job?"

"This? This is what turns your head?" Hadrian asked with a laugh, following me at a leisurely pace. "Not the jet, not the yacht? This car?"

"I know you're rich, Hadrian," I said with a look at him, "but now I know you also have style." My hand glided up the hood of the convertible. "What do I have to do to get you to let me drive it?"

"I have a few ideas," he quipped. "I'll drive us to my home so you can enjoy the view."

"But you will let me drive this car, right?"

"I'll let you drive it, yes," he promised.

I squealed in excitement, which made Hadrian raise

his brows. He walked around to the passenger side of the car and opened the door for me.

Hadrian then went to his side and tucked his large body into the muscle car.

"The car was just sitting, waiting for you," I said. "Isn't that a bit…"

"Bit what?"

"You left it out for anyone to steal."

"No one would've stolen it," he assured me.

"How do you know?" I pressed.

He turned the key, and as the engine roared to life he said, "Because I own the island, Eden. Now buckle up."

I did as he said, clipping into a four-point harness in the racing seat. As soon as he saw that I was buckled in, he depressed the clutch, put the car into first gear, and then stepped on the gas.

"You own the whole island?" I yelled over the thunder of the straight pipes as the wind began to pick up and kick my hair around.

"Actually, I own this island, and the four neighboring ones."

I started to laugh uncontrollably.

He glanced at me in confusion and then focused back on the road. "What's so funny?"

Shaking my head, I tried to get my hilarity under control. "You've done it, Hadrian. You've actually impressed me."

He let out his own booming laugh as we ripped around a curve. "Finally."

Chapter Nineteen

We drove in companionable silence, the humor lingering between us as the sounds of the car's engine filled our ears.

Hadrian was so fantastically wealthy. His money transformed desires into existence. Desires most people would never experience, and because of chance and sheer circumstance, I was with a man who tied me into knots of lust, a man who was possessive and caring, a man who had swept me away from my former life.

But I couldn't forget what I was—a Rex girl.

His wealth reminded me that there was a clear divide between us. No matter how much I enjoyed his company and banter, no matter how much I longed to stay in bed with him and watch the sun set from the embrace of his arms, I knew the truth.

Every time I forgot that I was a courtesan, something happened to remind me that I was.

Cool raindrops began to fall around me. Hadrian stopped the car quickly and raised the top of the convertible and locked it into place. We rolled up our windows and then continued on through the light rain. After a few minutes of driving, the wall of mountains broke away to reveal the other side of the island. I pressed my nose to the glass when I finally saw Hadrian's home on the top of a craggy cliff with waves crashing against the rocks below.

A memory from my childhood pierced my heart so quickly I was helpless to stop it. I hastily wiped my cheeks. The tears had come unbidden.

"Eden?" he asked as he eased off the throttle.

"I'm fine," I muttered.

The car came to a stop, and he stuck the gear shift in neutral and put on the parking brake. Hadrian reached over and brushed away the tears coating my cheeks.

I was suddenly embarrassed at the show of emotion. But knowing Hadrian, he wouldn't continue driving until I told him what I was feeling. Yet he wasn't pushing me to talk.

The rain began to pour, beating against the glass. The sound of it resonated in my chest.

I wanted to tell him. To share it with him.

"It was the waves," I said softly. "Below your home." I peeked a glance at him.

His expression didn't change as he let me go on.

"When I was a kid, my mother used to read me a story about the last unicorn in the world. The unicorn didn't know where all the other unicorns had gone, so she went on a journey to find them. They'd been pushed into the sea. Captured by one lonely, unhappy king who thought if he owned all the unicorns in the world, his heart would be happy." I shook my head wishing I hadn't said anything at all.

I hoped he would put the car into gear so we could continue on our way. I hoped he'd forget that the tears spilling down my cheeks were temporary, and that we could return to normal if we just ignored the moment.

But Hadrian was no ordinary man.

"King Haggard," he said finally.

My gaze flew to his.

He nodded. "I know the story."

"Did someone read it to you, too?" I asked.

Hadrian paused and then said, "A girl I used to know."

His expression was shuttered, like he wanted to lock down every feeling that threatened to bubble to the surface.

We stared at each other and something like understanding, mingled with compassion, bloomed between us. Neither of us pressed the other to say more, and I was glad for it.

He finally put the car into gear again, and we headed straight toward the mountain. There was no road in front of us and it looked like we were about to crash. I was about to scream when a door slid up, Bat Cave style. Suddenly we were in a tunnel that opened into a well-lit garage with stark white walls. Six other luxury cars were parked next to each other, all spotless and ready to roll at a moment's notice.

I glanced at him and he shrugged like it was nothing.

He cut the engine but left the key in the ignition. Hadrian unlatched his racing harness and got out of the car. I was slower to move, and Hadrian came around to help me. Once I was standing outside the vehicle, he closed the door. He lifted me up and set me down on the rear quarter panel of the wet muscle car and then pressed up against me.

"I need to touch you," he said, voice low.

I nodded in agreement. Whatever passed between us in the car during the rainstorm, whatever unspoken burdens we'd shared, neither one of us wanted them to linger.

Touching each other was the easiest way to put us back on ground we understood.

His hands were everywhere, tugging at zippers, diving into my panties. I somehow managed to get his pants undone and then my hands were on him, too. I clasped him in my grip, making him groan.

Hadrian felt like steel and silk.

"I hate you in pants," he growled against my mouth. "They're too hard to get into."

I chuckled against his lips but wanted him naked, too. And suddenly, I felt like I'd die without being able to touch the skin of his chest and feel him moving inside me.

Somehow, I managed to push him away. He looked annoyed and thwarted, but when he saw me quickly trying to undress, his grin returned and then he did the same.

When we were naked, he raised my legs to hook them around his waist, and then he thrust inside me while my back was down against the rain-splattered car.

Our eyes met and I breathed him in as he leaned over me, wanting him deeper, needing him there.

He moved slowly, like he had all the time in the world to make it last. And he did. We did. Because there was nothing but that moment.

But when I clawed his back, he quickened his thrusts, using his brute strength to overwhelm me.

His hand slid down between our bodies and teased me until I came. I shuddered around him, clenching hard. My nails dug into his skin as I rode out my pleasure.

Hadrian gripped the back of my neck and pressed his forehead to mine as he came. His jaw was clenched in strife and I found him beautiful.

When our thundering hearts returned to their normal cadence, he gently eased out of me. His stare was unapologetically hungry.

I sat up and began to gather my damp clothes.

"It was a mistake to bring you here," he said, his voice gruff.

It was like he'd thrown a bucket of ice over my head, and I couldn't stop the expression of hurt that crossed my face.

"It was a mistake to bring you here," he repeated, "because there's no way in hell I'm going to be able to get any work done. Not when I've got a woman willing to let me fuck her against a vintage muscle car."

My smile was brilliant.

Hadrian chuckled as he reached for his pants. When we were fully dressed, he took my hand and led me through the garage, past all the sleek and shiny cars.

"Do you drive them all?" I asked.

"Aye. Not often though. When I'm here, I usually take the golf cart unless I'm driving down to the pier to take the yacht somewhere."

He stopped in front of two chrome doors and pushed a button on the wall. The doors opened, and we stepped into a clear glass elevator and began our ascent. I could see the stone of the mountain through the glass and the steel that had been put in place for the elevator shaft, and as we rose, the stone passed faster and faster. My free hand —the one not held by Hadrian—touched the glass, as if I could reach through it and caress the walls of the mountain.

The elevator came to a halt and the doors opened directly into a mudroom. Black rain slickers were hung up on hooks and matching rubber boots lined the wall.

An umbrella bucket rested in the corner and there was a sink. He didn't slow down long enough for me to be able to remove my shoes. Hadrian went to the door opposite the elevator and pressed his palm against the flat glass plate and it chimed. The door opened and Hadrian entered first, guiding me inside.

I looked around at the modern, open decor. His home was spacious, just from the front room alone. "Huh," I said softly.

"What?" he asked, watching me look around.

"I wasn't expecting something so…contemporary. I expected…something else."

He raised an eyebrow. "Something else? Like dogs asleep on fur rugs by a stone fireplace? Or how about massive wooden tables set with rudimentary chalices? Battle axes in the corners?"

I blinked at his teasing tone. "Kinda, yeah."

He laughed. "Sorry to disappoint."

We moved through his home. As much as I appreciated the open, airy concept that let in a lot of sunlight, I found that I didn't care for the hard lines and sterile feeling. But it wasn't my home and so I made polite noises of interest when Hadrian explained how the home had been built into the mountain.

He led me up a staircase to the second floor. We went down a long hall and on the landing were three doors.

"Home gym," he stated as he opened the first door. There were a bunch of machines that I wasn't sure of their purpose, but I recognized the exercise bike and treadmill. "You're welcome to use anything in here."

He closed the door and we moved to the next room that was a home theater. An L-shaped leather sectional faced a blank wall that had been painted for a projector.

"Oh, wow," I murmured.

He closed the door and then brought me to the last room. It was three times the size of the others, with a masculine, heavy wooden bed on a platform. The bedroom had a gas fireplace, with a leather loveseat in front of it and a coffee table. I placed my hand onto the rich, supple leather.

"Sometimes I sit and read or work at the table," he explained.

There was a liquor cart with a few crystal decanters.

"Scotch?" I asked.

"And brandy."

I nodded. "So, I noticed…well, you don't have any guest rooms."

"No. I didn't build the house with any intention of ever having people stay here. Besides, I have guest cottages on the other islands."

"Where am I going to sleep?" I asked with a raised brow.

"In my bed."

I swallowed. "And clothes? My clothes I mean?"

Without a word, he strode to a door and opened it to reveal a walk-in closet. He gestured to the racks of women's clothes, along with dressers pushed up against the side walls. He opened a drawer and showed me a plethora of lace undergarments.

"Anything you need is here. If you want something, just say the word."

There were more clothes than I could ever wear in six months together. I blinked. "How did you make this happen so fast?"

"The Rex sized you during your dress fitting, and I had them send everything over after the night we spent together at The Mansion. My staff took care of the rest."

"That was presumptuous."

"I always get what I want, Eden." He frowned. "You look upset."

"Not upset. Surprised—and a little taken aback. It's very generous, Hadrian. But I—we—we're sharing space."

"Aye."

"Like we're living together."

"We *are* living together." He arched a brow. "I'm not following your line of thought."

"You don't want your own space?" I asked. "I mean, you seem like the kind of man who wants—"

"This isn't about me and space. This is about *you* and space. You want space? Great. You have an entire island to wander to get space, but you sleep in my bed next to me and you don't worry about it."

My mouth dropped open in surprise. "I just would've thought that as an eccentric, mysterious multi-millionaire, you'd want more privacy."

"Billionaire."

"Excuse me?"

"You said eccentric, mysterious multi-millionaire. I'm actually a billionaire."

"Of course you are. I don't know what I was thinking," I muttered. "A mere millionaire wouldn't have his own chain of islands, would he?"

"Definitely not," he agreed with a roguish grin and then he let out a laugh.

"What's so funny?"

"You. You're funny."

Hysteria was bubbling up inside of me, and I was afraid I was about to do something stupid. It was as if Hadrian knew, because he directed my thoughts away from the current matter by saying, "Let me show you the best part of the room."

He went to the dark, heavy curtains along the far wall and drew them back to reveal a set of French doors. He pulled them open and I was immediately hit with the sounds and smells of the ocean and a view as far as the eye could see of glistening water.

"No way," I whispered, rushing toward him. I stepped out onto the balcony and breathed it all in. A moment later, I felt Hadrian at my back.

We stood in silence while I marveled at the crashing waves hitting the craggy boulders along the shore below us. Ominous storm clouds that had doused us when we'd been driving had abated now and lingered off the coast. The wind had blown them out to sea.

"What do you think?" Hadrian asked, his mouth close to my ear.

His warm breath, his husky voice caused a shiver to run down my spine.

"I think I understand why you chose this place as your haven," I murmured. "With a view like this, how do you ever leave?"

Hadrian's arms tightened around me, but he didn't reply.

I wondered if the real reason he'd asked me to come was due to extreme loneliness. There was plenty of beauty in the world, but if you had no one to share it with, what was the point?

Turning in his arms, I pressed my cheek to his chest, willing the dangerous thoughts to drift away like morning mist on a beach.

I shivered, attempting to burrow deeper under the covers. The French doors were still open, letting in the cool ocean air along with sunlight.

"You're awake," Hadrian said, coming to stand by the bed. His hair was damp and his chest was bare, and he stood in a pair of dark corduroy pants.

"How long have I been asleep?" I asked.

"Not long. An hour maybe."

After we'd lingered on the balcony, I'd stripped off my clothes and gotten into bed. Between my raging emotions, jet lag, and the intense coupling against the Shelby Cobra, I'd been worn out. No sooner had I pressed my head to a pillow than I'd fallen asleep.

Now I felt refreshed. I rolled onto my back and tucked my arm behind my head and watched Hadrian close the French doors.

"Take your time getting up," he said, walking over to the bed. "But I'll be in the kitchen when you come down."

I nodded and he leaned over and kissed me briefly before stalking out of the bedroom.

I took a few minutes to myself, enjoying the feel of the pillows at my back and the sheet tucked around me. Finally, I pulled myself out of bed. I found the clothes I'd shed before sliding beneath the covers and hastily put them on.

I went into the bathroom and splashed some cold water on my face and ran a brush through my hair. Hadrian's master bathroom was a work of art in and of itself, which included a massive porcelain tub big enough for three people and a glass shower with one showerhead. Everything in the bathroom was expertly crafted, but simple, and clearly designed for one person.

He was such a dichotomy. It was clear by the structure of his home that he hadn't factored in a potential live-in girlfriend. There was one sink in his master bathroom, not two. And yet, Hadrian didn't seem at all concerned about having me in his personal space. Shouldn't he have been afraid of the intimacy? Instead, he seemed to be leaning into it. Our clothes shared closet space. That was about as intimate as it got as far as I was concerned.

I knew our time together was finite, but Hadrian wasn't

a normal man. Maybe sharing space was nothing to him. Maybe he didn't have any stronger feelings for me than wanting pleasure and companionship and six months together wasn't going to change that for him.

His head was stuck inside the refrigerator when I entered the kitchen.

"What are you in the mood for?" he asked, not removing his head to look at me. "Mutton stew? Left over mutton chops? Mutton and potatoes?"

"I'm sensing a theme," I said with a grin as I leaned against the island. "Mutton? That seems a bit outdated."

"Mutton that came from my sheep."

"Excuse me?"

He looked at me over his shoulder. "I am a self-sustaining entity. I have four islands to produce my own food and food for the livestock. I have farmers who tend to the livestock—sheep, cows, pigs, chickens. I have others who work in the greenhouse growing food. Elgin—who's married to my housekeeper—is a fisherman, along with his son. Whatever you eat here, I've had it produced on the islands. The families that live on the islands have helped create this sanctuary."

"You mean there are actually other people here? I didn't see any of them."

"My housekeeper and her husband, my helicopter pilot, the stable master, and Patrick, my head of security, all live on this island. Everyone else who works for me lives on the other islands."

"But-but why go through the trouble? You're a billion-aire. You have the money to fly in anything you could possibly want."

"I hate relying on others for anything. So I vowed that when I was able, when I had enough wealth, I'd hire people to produce my own food. No matter what happens in the world or with my business, I'll never be without."

My curiosity went haywire. I wanted to ask him more questions about his wealth and how he'd come to acquire it, but it wasn't warranted nor was it any of my concern. "What about liquor? Wine? Do you have a vineyard too?"

He smiled in gentle amusement. "I get my scotch from Flynn Campbell. He owns his own distillery."

"He owns hotels *and* a distillery? Is the man ever idle?"

"He doesn't make the scotch himself. It's just his operation," Hadrian stated. "The only wine I drink when I'm on my island comes from a specific vineyard in Italy. Brandy, port, and anything else, I have chartered in. There are some things that would be too much trouble to produce. Even for me."

I mulled over his explanations, finding myself even more in awe of him. Why he wanted to know anything about me was bizarre—he was the interesting one. And I was fascinated.

I paused in reflection a moment before saying, "Mutton stew, please."

While the stew was heating on the stove, he cut up a loaf of thick, brown bread.

"I'm guessing you didn't make that," I said.

"My housekeeper, Ingrid, baked it. She's the only reason there's cooked food in my refrigerator."

I grinned.

"What?"

"I'm just glad to know you're not good at everything."

He frowned. "What do you mean?"

"I mean, you don't cook."

"Who said I don't cook?"

"You."

"I *can* cook. I just choose not to," he explained.

I wrinkled my nose at him. "That's annoying."

"What is?"

"Being around someone who's good at everything."

He smiled but didn't rise to the bait.

"Where is she? Ingrid, I mean."

"I wanted you all to myself today, so I gave her the day off. You'll meet her tomorrow."

"What does she do for you?" I asked, pleasure at his words warming me.

"She oversees my household. She cooks my meals and handles my laundry and other services. Her two daughters come and clean a few times a week, and if I need anything at all outside of the ordinary, Ingrid will get things sorted."

I nodded. What must it be like to be so wealthy that you had people to cook and clean for you? Well, for the next six months, I'd find out.

"Wine?" he asked.

"Sure."

There was a nondescript bottle resting on the kitchen island. Hadrian opened a drawer and pulled out a corkscrew.

When the food was ready, Hadrian plated it on a tray. I grabbed the wine glasses and the bottle of wine and followed him into the dining room, which felt just as modern and stiff as the rest of the house. It wasn't warm or inviting.

I reached for the pepper grinder in the middle of the table, but Hadrian's hand stopped me.

"Taste it first."

"It needs pepper. Everything always needs pepper."

"Eden."

"Hadrian."

"Trust me."

I sighed but put down the grinder and picked up a

spoon. I waited for the spoonful to cool and then took a dainty sip of broth.

"Go ahead," Hadrian said with a wry grin. "I'll wait."

"For what?"

"For you to tell me I was right."

"Just for that, I should season it."

"And ruin a perfectly good mutton stew? No. I don't think so." He began to eat. After a moment, he said, "What do you think?"

"It's delicious."

He shook his head. "I know. I meant, what do you think of my home?"

"It's impressive," I said, ladling another spoonful into my mouth and not meeting his gaze.

"That's a diplomatic answer if I've ever heard one," he said in amusement. "Tell me the truth. What do you really think of it?"

"It's cold and," I paused, searching for the right word, "sterile."

"Sterile," he repeated.

"It's not inviting. At all."

"Good," he said.

We fell into a charged silence. I kept my eyes on my bowl, consuming every bite and relishing the rich, hearty flavors on my tongue. I would've gladly kept eating just to have something to do, just so I didn't have to talk to Hadrian.

He'd asked my opinion and I'd told him the truth, and he hadn't liked what I'd had to say.

"Are you ready to see the rest of my sterile house?" he asked, his tone dry.

"There's more?" I asked in surprise.

"Aye," he said quietly.

I had no inkling what he was thinking and instead of trying to apologize for being honest, I merely nodded.

We stood from the table and gathered our empty dishes. After we went into the kitchen and placed them in the sink, Hadrian took my hand and led me to a nondescript door that looked like a broom closet—only it wasn't a closet—but a passage to a fully enclosed glass walkway. We were fifteen feet in the air and if I looked down, I could see the sandy beach below. The glass walls were thick, and I could stare out at the ocean. Birds flew across the beach and then rested in nests nestled within the rocks.

"I designed this home so that I'd never feel trapped. The open, airy concept has a Scandinavian influence."

I nodded at his explanation. "It makes sense, it's just—well, there's nothing personal here, nothing to make it seem like you."

"Seem like me," he repeated. "And who do you think I am?"

"I don't know." I frowned. "I know you like functionality over flash. That makes sense. But I guess—where are all your personal touches?"

"Such as?"

"Pictures? Artwork…anything…"

"Pictures. Do you mean photographs of me through the years?"

"Something like that, yeah."

It took me a moment to realize I'd made an insensitive mistake. He didn't *have* photos that marked the passage of time.

"You don't have any of those, do you?" I asked quietly.

"No, I don't."

I nodded, my heart fracturing just a tiny bit. I wanted to offer him some measure of understanding, and before I could think about why I wanted to share another insight from my past, I dove in. "We moved around a lot when I was a kid. There was never any point in putting up photos. We'd just have to take them down again."

"They were more trouble than they were worth?"

"Yes." I didn't tell him that there hadn't been any photo albums either. No moments captured on film of my first few years of life, and even less later on as I developed into what I would look like as an adult.

There hadn't been anything personal in my childhood because my mother had felt the need to shield me from people who would do terrible things if they found me. People my mother had fled for good reason.

"Don't pity me," he snapped.

I looked at him in confusion. "I wasn't pitying you. I was pitying myself."

The words were out of my mouth before I could stop them. I clamped my jaw shut, wishing I hadn't let emotions get the better of me.

I thought for sure he'd pounce on my vulnerability. Instead, he gently touched my hand and said, "I love standing in the middle of this walkway when there's an ocean storm."

I let out a breath of relief. "Where does it lead?"

"You'll see."

The enclosed glass bridge connected Hadrian's main house to an Olympic-sized pool. The walls looked like chiseled stone, and I knew we were inside another mountain. Dim lighting fixtures cast shadows on the gray stone walls.

"I feel like Gollum," I said with a laugh. "Traveling deep within a mountain full of tunnels."

"Fancy a swim?" he asked, letting go of my hand and going for the buttons on his shirt.

"What about showing me the rest of the house?" I asked.

"I'll show you later. Right now, I want you naked again." He bared his skin and then reached out to tug the collar of the sweater I wore.

"Aren't you tired?" I asked in enjoyment.

"No. Now, stop stalling and get naked."

While I was still removing my clothes, Hadrian took the pool stairs until he was standing waist deep.

I stuck a toe in and shivered from the warmth. "It's heated," I said with a smile.

"It's also saltwater."

I waded into the water, and Hadrian immediately placed his hands on my hips to drag me closer. I wrapped my legs around his body, his hands moving underneath my bum to hold me up.

My fingers dragged up and down his pectorals and then his abs, lingering on the scar on his body. He was such an enigma.

"Do you really pity yourself?" he queried quietly, pressing his lips against the apple of my cheek.

I sucked in a breath, wishing I'd never let my weakness show. "I don't know if pity is the right word," I said slowly. "It's just, well, it would've been nice to live in the same place long enough to have photos on the walls."

His fingers drew up and down my arms. "Why did you go to work at The Rex? It can't just be because you were poor."

"That was blunt," I said dryly.

"Was it?"

"There are less complicated ways to earn a living, Hadrian."

"So I'm right. It wasn't about the money then," he stated.

"It wasn't about the money," I agreed.

"You needed a new identity, didn't you?"

I froze. "No. I wanted something new. Something different."

We stared into each other's eyes, and I knew he could see right through me.

"Money doesn't motivate you," he said. "Aye. I knew that already. I knew it the night I met you."

I hesitated. "It motivates you though, doesn't it?"

"I grew up with nothing," he said, his tone hard. "I knew that money would make everything easier. But this isn't about me. It's about you."

"Has it filled the void?" I deflected.

"Void?"

I inhaled a shaky breath. "The void that comes with being an orphan…"

Hadrian released me and I almost went under, splashing in an attempt to catch my balance. While I got my bearings, Hadrian was wading toward the pool steps to leave.

"I have some work I have to do," he stated as he climbed out of the pool and walked to a shelf with folded white towels. He wrapped one around his waist, hiding his stunning body from me. "Feel free to use the home gym or the theater room. If you get hungry, make yourself something to eat."

I stood in the water a moment contemplating what to say, but he left before I could ask him when I'd see him again. I blinked in confusion and spread out onto my back to float while thoughts swirled in my head.

When he'd gone, he'd taken his dynamic, robust energy with him. His mercurial mood left me bereft. I swam to the edge of the pool and hoisted myself up over the ledge and trod naked to the shelf. I grabbed a towel and quickly covered myself.

Hadrian hadn't bothered taking his clothes, instead

leaving them in a makeshift pile. I scooped them up, along with mine, and carted them out of the pool area. I walked through the covered glass walkway, shocked to find that the sky had darkened and droplets of water were already beating against the glass.

A flash of lightning in the distance over the ocean made me stop and stare for a moment. I'd never seen an ocean storm because I had never been to the ocean. Mama had moved us through small towns in the middle of the country. I'd been to lakes and rivers but never the ocean.

What other firsts would I experience with Hadrian?

I made my way through the quiet house. I had no idea where Hadrian had gone and peeked into his bedroom, but he wasn't there. I threw our clothes into a hamper in the closet and then went to shower. I didn't take long and when I got out, part of me hoped he would be sitting on the bed and we could make amends.

I'd asked him a pointed question, sure, but it wasn't fair for him to leave me. Whenever he wanted to know about me, he would battle his way into my brain with relentless queries. Why couldn't I do that to him?

Hypocrite.

Righteous anger coursed through my veins. It was a good thing that Hadrian had disappeared. He wasn't going to like what I had to say when he saw me again.

Chapter Twenty

I woke up alone. My hand went to Hadrian's side of the bed, but the covers were undisturbed, and it didn't look like he'd slept next to me.

For a moment, I stared at the ceiling, letting the fog in my brain clear. Weak morning light peered through the half-drawn curtains of the balcony doors.

Stifling a yawn, I sat up, perching on the side of the bed for a moment.

I needed caffeine. And then I'd find Hadrian and have it out with him. I felt like I was being punished and we needed to clear the air.

After using the bathroom and quickly brushing my teeth, I went to the walk-in closet. I opened the drawer on one of the dressers that had been relegated for my use. I pulled out a pair of gray cashmere leggings and a black wool sweater that fell to the middle of my thighs.

I padded my way to the kitchen, peeking my head into the rooms as I passed. No sign of Hadrian.

A woman with graying blonde hair pulled back into a

ponytail and dimpled cheeks smiled at me when I walked in.

"Good morning," she said in Norwegian-accented English.

"Hi," I said. "You must be Ingrid."

Ingrid continued rolling the dough in front of her with a rolling pin as she nodded. "Yes."

"I'm Eden," I introduced.

"I know." She winked and then brushed a stray lock of blonde hair that had fallen across her forehead with the back of her hand. "Coffee is on, and the biscuits are going into the oven in a few minutes."

"Biscuits?" My mouth watered at the thought of buttery, flaky biscuits. Perfect to eat on a cool morning.

"Biscuits and gravy. They're worth the wait, I promise."

"They sound delicious. I'll definitely wait." I moved around the kitchen to grab a mug and filled it with coffee. I drank it black, so I had to wait for it to cool.

"Do you know where Hadrian is?"

Ingrid didn't reply right away as she used a glass to make perfect circles in the dough. "He's gone."

"Gone?" I repeated. "Gone where?"

"Left this morning on business." Ingrid didn't meet my eyes.

Gone the morning after he brought me here? After he'd just admitted that he didn't travel often for work?

"You know something," I accused.

She shook her head. "I know nothing."

"You're his housekeeper."

"Hadrian doesn't confide everything in me."

I continued to stare at her. "You *do* know something. Otherwise you'd be able to look me in the eye."

She set the raw biscuits on a cookie sheet and then placed the entire thing into the oven. Ingrid pressed a few buttons, including the timer, and then faced me directly.

"I've known Hadrian for a decade," she said. "He's my employer, but I also take care of him the way I take care of my own children."

"Your loyalty is to him, then," I said with a nod. "I get it. But did he really have business? Or was that the excuse he gave you when he left?"

She shrugged.

"I guess it doesn't matter. He left without saying goodbye though."

"He'll call."

I wasn't sure that he would.

"I'm not hungry anymore," I murmured. "It was nice meeting you, Ingrid."

Not wanting to see her look of pity, I turned and left the kitchen, coffee mug in hand. I took it back to Hadrian's bedroom. I plucked my cell phone from the nightstand and went out onto the balcony.

There were no texts or calls from Hadrian. Disappointment washed over me.

I set my coffee on the balcony table and took a seat in a comfortable chair. I found Tiffany's number in my favorites list and called her.

"I was *just* about to text you," she greeted.

"Really?"

"Yup. You're a wench. Did you know that?"

Despite my low mood, I laughed. "Why am I a wench?"

"Because you didn't call and tell me everything that happened the night you had dinner with your mysterious benefactor. All I got was a lousy text message saying that you were getting on a plane to Shetland."

"It wasn't just a plane. It was his private jet," I said drolly. "And mysterious benefactor? Can you not call him that? It makes *me* feel like a—"

"Kept woman? Mistress? Courtesan? You *are* those things. You know that, right?"

"Yeah, I guess I am." I sighed.

"What's wrong?"

"Nothing."

"Not nothing. You should be squealing like a girl who won the lottery, because you kind of did. So come on, tell me every detail."

"I can't tell you every detail," I reminded her.

"No, I guess you can't. But you can tell me some things. I'm going mad here. I'm dying to know who this guy is and how this even happened. You were only at *one* event and you gave away your key to—oh. Is it him? The guy from that night?"

"Yeah," I said slowly. "It's him."

"Wow. You must've rocked his world."

"Oh my God, will you stop?" I laughed.

"How was the flight over?"

"The flight was amazing. First, we flew on his private jet to Lerwick, and then we took a yacht to his island."

She whistled. "That sounds kind of awesome…so, why do you sound so despondent?"

I fell silent while I pondered what I wanted to say next. "He makes me forget," I said finally.

"Forget what?"

I let out a slow exhale. "Forget why I'm really here."

Tiffany paused for a moment and then asked, "How much did he offer you?"

"It doesn't matter."

"Bullshit. I think it matters very much. Your time is *literally* money."

It was cold and callous and…true.

"A million for a six-month exclusive contract."

"You're shitting me."

"I'm not," I said. "I don't even care about the money. I would've taken the contract for half that. A quarter that."

"You would've taken the contract for free, wouldn't you?"

I closed my eyes. "Yes."

"Oh, Sterling, no."

"No? No, what?"

"You have feelings for this guy."

"Damn right I have feelings for this guy. Annoyance, frustration… We've only just gotten here and he's already left. His housekeeper said he went away on business, but he hasn't called or texted or—"

"You're *not* his girlfriend," she said gently.

It was like a slap to my cheek. "I know."

"If you know, then why are you expecting him to behave like a boyfriend?"

"I haven't told you the reason he left. I—I dug into his past and he didn't like what I asked him about. So, he ran."

"He's still not your boyfriend," she said. "It doesn't matter what you say or don't say. All that matters is that you're paid to entertain him. God, Sterling, this is what the training is for, to teach you how *not* to get involved in shit like this."

"So, it's okay for him to ask questions about my past and demand answers, but I can't do the same?"

"He's asking questions about your past?" she queried.

"Yes, and no matter what I say, he won't stop."

"Okay, every time he asks you a personal question, just find a way to occupy his brain in a different way."

I let out a laugh. "If only that would work. He's relentless."

"You *so* like him."

"I do like him." I sighed.

"As long as liking him doesn't turn into something more. He's a client. It's about the money. You have to remember that."

"I don't know if I can be that heartless."

"You're not being heartless. It's business."

"It doesn't feel right."

"That's your programming talking. Take the money. You can afford to have principles later."

"He wasn't supposed to do this," I murmured. "It was supposed to be six months of pampering and sex and laughing. Nothing like this. Nothing heavy. He went and changed the rules on me."

"Babe, hate to break it to you, but you don't even know what game you're playing."

There was a muffled sound on the other end of the line and Tiffany said, "Sterling? I gotta go."

"But you haven't told me about London yet," I protested.

"Magical, beautiful, everything I could've hoped for." She paused. "Listen, every time you forget why you're there, or you find yourself thinking that you want to know more about him, remember the money. Remember the freedom it will buy you. Okay, that's the last of my lecture. Cheerio, poppet."

We hung up and I set my phone on the balcony table.

Lifting the coffee cup to my lips, I stared out across the endless horizon. It was tranquil here, a true haven. But this wasn't my haven and deluding myself into thinking I was anything but a Rex girl was detrimental. Tiffany was right.

Hadrian was a client—a client I liked and enjoyed, in and out of bed. But I refused to let it become more. We could be friendly, we could laugh and talk, exchange stories of our pasts, but I wouldn't let it develop further.

"I wanted to tell you breakfast is ready," Ingrid said, startling me into splashing lukewarm coffee all over the front of my sweater.

She came to my side and had the grace to look sheepish. "I'm sorry, I didn't mean to—"

"It's okay," I said, throwing her a genuine smile. "I didn't hear you and the coffee wasn't hot. Thank you for the food. That's very thoughtful."

"Change your sweater and then come to the kitchen to eat your breakfast. I don't want it to get cold."

Ingrid left the balcony before I could reply. It seemed she and Hadrian were cut from the same cloth. Both of them commanded and expected their orders to be obeyed.

I didn't have the energy to protest. I changed my sweater and then headed to the kitchen. Ingrid was pouring a glass of orange juice when I entered.

"Sit." She waved to a kitchen stool at the island and pushed the plate in front of me.

"This looks delicious." I picked up my napkin and set it in my lap and then I reached for the fork and knife. I cut into the flaky biscuit doused in brown gravy and stuck a bite into my mouth.

I moaned in delight. "How is Hadrian not five hundred pounds? Your food is unbelievable!"

She smiled and preened at my compliment. "I'm glad you're enjoying it."

Ingrid cleaned up the kitchen as I continued to demolish my food. I was quickly becoming a convert of hearty breakfasts.

"Hadrian has never brought a woman here, ever," she said as she poured herself a cup of coffee.

I swallowed the last bite of biscuit and patted my mouth. "Never?"

"Never. The fact that he brought you here speaks volumes," she said.

I clamped my mouth shut. I wasn't going to ask her if she knew the circumstances of how I'd met Hadrian. He was a private person, and she had already told me he didn't confide everything in her.

"He has his life and everything money could buy. I'm just…a diversion," I said.

She shook her head. "He has people here. He takes care of them. That's what Hadrian does. He takes care of people, but he refuses to let anyone take care of *him*. He's never let anyone in. Until you. He *needs* you."

"He doesn't," I insisted.

"Hadrian brought you here. *You*, not someone else. That was a big step for him. Don't let him push you away."

"So, I should give him a medal?" I asked dryly. "I should give a rich, mysterious billionaire the benefit of the doubt all because he brought me to his island home?"

Ingrid's smile was slow—and not at all expected. She looked out the window. "It promises to be a clear day. You should go out and enjoy it."

"Are you sure you don't want me to stay the night?" Ingrid asked. "It's no trouble. I can drive the golf cart to the other side of the island, get some clothes, and then come back. Hadrian won't mind."

I shook my head. "The good weather has kept as long as it's going to. It will storm. Stay inside, stay warm."

She frowned. "I don't want you to be alone. Hadrian told me—"

"It doesn't matter what he told you," I said. "I don't mind being here by myself. I actually prefer it."

"Let me give you my number. Just in case."

I handed her my cell. Ingrid plugged in her number and then gave it back to me.

After my walk on the beach, I'd gone for a swim. My phone had rested on a chair next to the pool, but it had remained steadfastly silent.

During the afternoon, Ingrid plied me with food and conversation, keeping it light and bubbly and Hadrian-free.

"I'll be here at eight tomorrow morning," she said.

I bit my lip. "Is there enough food to last a few days?"

She frowned. "Yes. It's been stocked with fresh eggs, cheese, frozen meat pies I made just last week in the freezer. Why?"

"Take the next few days off," I told her. "You don't have to come here and entertain me."

"But I took yesterday off," she said, her tone perplexed. "And I'm not supposed to leave you alone. Hadrian's orders."

I smiled slightly. "Hadrian's not here, is he?"

"Well, no."

"Will he fire you? If you don't comply?"

"No. He won't fire me."

"Then please, Ingrid. Let me have some space?" I stared at her and widened my eyes, beseeching her to give me what I wanted.

She studied me for a long moment and then she nodded. "All right. I'm calling him to let him know, though. About what you've asked. Okay?"

"Okay."

Ingrid nibbled her lip. "Have you talked to him today?"

"No. Have you?"

"He called once to let me know he got to Edinburgh safely."

Hadrian cared enough to let Ingrid know where he was, but he couldn't—wouldn't—offer me the same courtesy. Not even a text.

It was another reminder of the truth of our relationship.

Tiffany was right. I couldn't think of myself as Hadrian's girlfriend.

Thunder rumbled ominously in the distance.

"You better get home before it starts coming down," I told her.

She headed for the mudroom to catch the elevator that would take her to the garage. "I like you, Eden," she said with the same forthright honesty she'd used with me from the moment I met her.

"I like you, too," I said.

She looked like she wanted to say more but decided against it when she closed her mouth and nodded her head. When she got to the door of the mudroom, she said, "If you change your mind, please call. Even if it's the middle of the night."

"Thank you." I wouldn't take her up on the offer. I wanted to be alone. I wanted to sit in the dark with a glass of something strong and stare into the flames of the gas fireplace.

When Ingrid left, I did exactly that. I poured myself a glass of brandy from one of the crystal decanters, sipped on the amber liquid, and turned on the fireplace in the den. The sky darkened outside the massive living room window and the threat of rain drew closer. I watched from the couch as the storm finally arrived.

My conversation with Tiffany filtered through my mind. Hadrian was not my boyfriend and I was not his girlfriend.

This was a business arrangement.

A billionaire's private island was my playground.

It was time to have some fun.

Chapter Twenty-One

Three days later, I blew into the house windswept and disheveled. I dropped my pair of sunglasses on the front table and sashayed into the living room and came to a stop.

Hadrian's stoic face greeted me as he slowly rose from the couch. "Where have you been?"

I raised my brows. "Me? Where have *you* been?"

His jaw clenched. "I don't owe you an explanation."

I shrugged. "You're right. You don't."

Hadrian's brow furrowed. "What are you playing at?"

"I'm not playing at anything," I assured him. "If you'll excuse me, I need to fix my hair. I really should've worn a head scarf while driving with the top down." I hastily tried to gather my tangled locks into a makeshift ponytail.

"Driving with the top down?" he inquired.

I grinned cheekily at him. "I took your Shelby Cobra for a spin. That car is sexy, Hadrian. You really should drive it more."

His eyes glittered with an unfathomable emotion, and I wondered if he would lay into me for driving one of his cars without him present.

"Dinner tonight on the rooftop terrace at seven," he said sternly.

I saluted him and then attempted to move past him to the staircase, but his hand on my arm stopped me.

"You haven't greeted me properly," he admonished.

"I haven't, have I?" I murmured, looking up at him through the sweep of my lashes. I gripped his lapels and raised myself up on my tiptoes.

I was still too short to reach his mouth, so his head dipped and took my lips with his.

His tongue thrust into my mouth, boldly claiming me.

Four days without Hadrian's dynamic presence and all it took was one kiss for my body to flare to life. I leaned into him, my breath hitching when his arms swept around me. He hauled me closer and continued to ravage my mouth.

I was about to suggest moving things to the bedroom and giving him a pleasurable afternoon when he pulled away.

His thumb swept across my lips, now swollen from his attention. "Dinner," he reminded me. "Don't be late."

Without a farewell, he stalked from the living room toward the elevator and then he was gone again.

I frowned in confusion. I could tell Hadrian had wanted me.

What game was *he* playing?

I didn't see him all afternoon or into the evening. Two hours before dinner, I started my transformation. I showered and scrubbed my body with luxurious citrus body wash. After I dried my hair, I curled it and let it fall across my shoulders. My makeup was soft and demure except for my dramatic red lips. Then I went into the closet to pick out a dress.

I chose a sleeveless black gown that clung to my curves

and paired it with spiky black heels. I had only the jewelry I'd worn when traveling from New York, but it didn't match my outfit, so I left myself unadorned. We were dining on the rooftop terrace and I knew it had heat lamps, so I didn't bother bringing a wrap.

I left the bedroom and still didn't see a sign of Hadrian. It was nearly seven o'clock when I took the stairs to the rooftop terrace. I opened the door to the roof and strode to a table that had been covered with a cream table-cloth and two place settings. In the center was a gourmet charcuterie board, olives, and other antipasti, and an unopened bottle of red wine.

The sun was still aloft but the air was cool and teased the hair at my nape. Heating lamps dispersed around the terrace roof were on full blast, and I didn't even shiver. I walked to the terrace wall, which was four feet in width and breastbone high, designed as a stronghold against the powerful Shetland wind. I rested my hands flat against the gray surface and stared at the vast ocean below me. There wasn't a cloud for miles, and I hoped the weather held.

The door to the terrace opened and the sound of Hadrian's steps approached. He came to stand next to me, mimicking my pose by placing his hands on the wall. Hadrian was still in his suit from earlier and he reached into his inner breast pocket and pulled out a black velvet jewelry box, setting it down in front of me.

"A gift from Edinburgh," he said.

"Thank you." I ignored the box and kept my gaze on the horizon.

"Most women would be more effusive in their grati-tude." His brogue was thick and heavy, and it settled over me like a warm blanket.

I looked at him and grinned. "I'm not most women."

He surveyed me slowly, taking his time, his eyes

lingering on my lips. "No truer statement has ever been uttered." Hadrian opened the jewelry box and presented me with a set of pearl earrings. "It's why I bought you black pearls instead of white."

"They're beautiful," I said. "Thank you." I swept my hair away from my ears and put them on. I then angled my neck so he could see the pearls against my skin. "Well?"

His thumb swept my lobe and then danced across my jawline. "Perfect."

He then took my hand and led me to the table. Hadrian held out my seat for me, reminding me of the night we'd discussed the contract. It already seemed so long ago, like another chapter in the book of my life.

I placed my napkin in my lap and watched Hadrian open and pour the wine into our glasses before taking his seat.

He lifted his glass toward me, and I did the same. We clinked and then drank. The bold red wine was heady and smoky, and it lingered on my tongue. When I was done savoring the taste of it, I set my glass down and looked at Hadrian.

There was an unresolved tension between us, like we were both dancing around each other.

"What have you been doing the last few days? Aside from driving my favorite car?" he asked, eyes glittering with amusement.

"I've been walking the beach and swimming in the pool. When the weather is clear and there's sun, I've been coming up here to sunbathe topless."

His eyes darkened with desire.

"I've had to turn the lamps on to stay warm, but it's been worth it not to have the tan lines. Evenings are spent making a simple meal for one—I don't know if Ingrid mentioned it to you, but I told her not to bother coming over to clean up after me since I'm perfectly capable of doing it myself. All in all, it's been a pretty relaxing few days."

"How did you spend your nights while I was away?"

"I watched a movie in the theater room while drinking your high-end scotch. And then I went to bed and made sure to sleep diagonally and really stretch out."

"Is that all you did?" he asked, his voice low and sensual.

"No." I pinned his stare with mine. "Every night before I fell asleep, I touched myself and pretended it was you."

He paused for a moment and then he rose from his seat. "Stand up," he ordered.

I pushed away from the table and rose.

"Go to the terrace wall and place your hands on it."

I shivered from the intractable command and walked slowly to the terrace wall and did as he bid. Excitement bloomed in my blood, heating me from the inside out.

A few moments later, I felt Hadrian at my back. His hands gripped my hips and hauled me into his body so I could feel how much he wanted me. His touch wandered down and lifted the skirt of my dress.

I wasn't wearing underwear, and cool air kissed my bare skin.

He traced patterns of desire across my cheeks and down the backs of my thighs until he was spreading me open.

I flattened my palms against the stone, wanting something solid to grab onto, knowing I was about to be shaken to my core. Sparks of excitement shot through me when I heard him unzip, and then I felt his erection nudging me.

"I don't know what fucking game you're playing," he gritted out.

He sank slowly into me, filling me from behind. It was

almost too much, but when Hadrian placed a hand at the small of my back and leaned me against the terrace wall, I stretched to accommodate him.

I felt him everywhere, my body perfectly in tune with his. I'd been ready for him since I saw him that afternoon, and I was eager for the pleasure he could give me.

He thrusted and groaned, and his fingers wandered toward the seam of my legs to flit across the bundle of nerves waiting for attention.

With a small cry I erupted around him, but he continued to drive himself into me. It felt like a punishment—for what I couldn't say.

His lust for me was unyielding and with each plunge he branded me, sending me closer to another precipice. When I cried out that I was coming again, he gripped my hips and rammed himself against me. After a moment, Hadrian slid out of me, taking his heat with him.

In a state of pure exhaustion, I rested against the terrace wall and pressed my cheek to the cool stone. I closed my eyes and let my breath ease as I slowly drifted down from the height of pleasure.

I felt him gently tug my skirt back down to conceal me and then he took my hand and helped me stand.

His shirt collar was open at the neck and his suit jacket was wrinkled, but he'd tucked himself back into his trousers.

Without a word, he led me to the table and helped me to my seat before taking his own. He cut into the wedge of hard cheese, placed it on a cracker, and handed it to me.

"Thank you," I said and then took a dainty bite.

He stared at me across the table, his expression reserved. "You're not the same as you were four days ago."

"What do you mean?" I asked. "We just—"

"I'm not talking about sex. I know how your body

reacts to mine. I'm talking about the fact that you're treating me with cool detachment."

"I'm not mad at you, if that's what you think."

He shook his head slowly. "I left almost as soon as I brought you here. I haven't called or texted in four days and you act like you don't care. Furthermore, you didn't send me a slew of texts wondering when I'd come home."

My brow furrowed. "Was I supposed to? I'm not your girlfriend. You don't owe me anything, Hadrian. We have a contract. What you do with your own time is none of my business."

"You're doing it again."

"Doing *what* again?"

"Not acting the way I expected you to."

"Sorry, I'll try to be better about that," I said with a grin.

He pointed a finger at me. "Stop it."

"Stop *what?*" I demanded. "I'm just being me. I'm being honest. If you want me to pretend to be mad at you for leaving me alone on this gorgeous island with more than enough things to occupy my time, I guess we could role play. I didn't know you were into that."

"I don't like this side of you, Eden."

"What side of me is that?"

"This cool, flirtatious side of you. You're acting like a Rex girl."

"I *am* a Rex girl."

"During our time together, you've never behaved like one. Your reactions to me have always been honest—and for lack of a better word—volatile."

"So you *did* think I was going to be upset that you didn't communicate with me for four days, didn't you?"

"I told you as much," he groused. "You continue to surprise me."

"You're not a man who likes surprises," I stated. "You were surprised that I called you on your shit. You didn't like it, so you left."

"Called me on my shite?" he barked. "I don't have shite."

"Oh, honey," I drawled condescendingly. "We *all* have shit. Even handsome billionaires."

"Careful, Eden," he warned, a muscle in his jaw ticking.

"Careful what?" I demanded, rising from the table. "Should I be worried that you might nullify the contract and send me home? Go for it. You want me to be your plaything? Fine. You want to pick me up whenever you want and then set me aside like a toy? Fine. But if you thought leaving me alone for four days without a word would make me sit and pine for you, you picked the wrong Rex girl."

I swept from the rooftop terrace in an emotional blaze, made even angrier when I realized Hadrian had been inside of me not that long ago and the proof of him was running down my leg, reminding me that I was nothing more than a whore.

I woke up to a pair of wild, blue-gray eyes.

"Gah!" I reared back into my pillow, trying to put distance between Hadrian and me.

Sunlight filtered through the glass doors leading to the balcony, bathing the room in a fresh morning glow.

"How did I get here?" I asked in confusion. "I distinctly remember falling asleep on the theater-room couch."

"You did. I carried you to the bed. You didn't even notice."

I lifted the sheet and saw that I was still in my pajamas from the previous evening and let out an exhale.

After leaving Hadrian on the rooftop terrace, I'd showered in an attempt to remove his touch from my skin, but it hadn't worked. I still remembered the feel of him, the scent of him.

"How long have you been awake?" I asked, blinking the sleep from my eyes.

"A few minutes," he replied.

"Why were you watching me sleep?"

"Curiosity."

"About?"

"How you managed to fall asleep after our fight."

"Brandy."

"You drink brandy now?" he asked.

"I finished off the last of your scotch in the decanter while you were gone. I had to settle for the brandy." I stared at him for a moment and stated, "You were up most of the night."

I didn't wait for confirmation because I didn't need it. His sleepless night was in the shadows under his eyes.

He rolled over onto his back and lifted his arm to prop it behind his head. I made no move to scoot closer.

"I pride myself on being a man who can read a person within the first few seconds of meeting him. You are a constant surprise and that's…unnerving. I don't ever feel like I have a grasp on who you are."

"It's more than that, though. Isn't it?"

"What you said in the pool, about the void—I didn't like it. It struck a nerve because it was true."

"So you left."

"Aye."

With a sigh, I admitted, "It did sting that you left without a word and didn't contact me. But it reminded me of what we are. I'm a Rex girl and you're the man who bought me for six months."

He was silent for a moment as his gaze searched my face. "You won't even concede that you were aloof?"

"What we did against the terrace wall…that was me aloof?" I asked with a roguish smile. When he didn't grin at my teasing tone, I sobered. "While we're attempting to hold each other accountable, will you concede that you fucked me against that wall as a form of punishment?"

"Punishment," he said in surprise. "For what?"

"For me not sitting and pining for you while you were gone. For me not sending you text after text begging you to come back. For not acting like you expected me to."

"Only if you concede that you were acting cool and flirtatious because you were trying to prove that you could play the true part of a Rex girl."

"I concede," I said easily. "What about you? Do you concede?"

He lifted his arm and I snuggled into him to rest my cheek against his chest. I waited for him to tell me he yielded, but I was waiting in vain.

He quelled the long silence when he said, "My mother died during childbirth."

His hand drifted up and down my arm in a dreamy caress, and I cuddled deeper into his embrace.

"She was a teen runaway. Nothing out of the ordinary. I don't know who my father is. When they filled out the birth certificate, she was already dead… Anyway, I was taken to St. Michael's, an orphanage in Lerwick. The nuns there named all the male babies that came to them after Roman emperors. I don't know why. Maybe they wanted to give us strong names since we'd come to them with nothing. Maybe they thought we'd have a chance at feeling powerful during the course of our lives."

I lifted my face so I could rest my chin on his chest and stare at him. "And Rhys? Was that your mother's last name?"

He nodded, his eyes meeting mine.

"Why are you telling me this?" I asked him.

"Because you were honest with me this morning," he said softly, his brogue rumbly and thick. "You didn't have to be. You could've kept your guard up. Lord knows I would've understood why. I brought you here and then left you immediately."

Something finally clicked into place, an understanding of the enigmatic man whose bed I was in and whose arms I found pleasure in.

Everything in Hadrian's life, from his business dealings, to conversations with people…it was all transactional. Hadrian didn't know how to trust someone unless they offered him something he perceived as valuable in return.

My honesty, as he called it, was worth something to him. And so he'd shared a part of himself with me.

I stroked my fingers up his chest to cup his raspy cheek and then sank into his strawberry blond hair.

In that moment, I realized who Hadrian truly was: an orphan who'd never had unconditional love. How could he have? He hadn't known his own mother. She'd never gotten to watch him grow from boy to man. Whatever his course in life, he had done it without family.

"Eden?"

I met his bold stare and said simply, "Kiss me."

There was nothing boyish about the way he made me quiver. There was nothing boyish about the way he rolled me over, using his brute strength to pleasure me. There was nothing boyish about the way he slid inside me, so deep I wondered if he was settling himself in my heart.

I wanted to unravel every part of his past, each new secret a treasure revealed. I wanted to keep him safe and give myself to the raw beauty that we created when we were together.

And when I tightened around him, climaxing, I let him see the tears that seeped from the corners of my eyes.

I let him see the part of me that really mattered.

Chapter Twenty-Two

The next few days were spent in a blissful, dreamy state of pleasure and companionship. We didn't venture far from Hadrian's bed. We were cocooned in safety, and in the privacy of his bedroom, we could express ourselves the best way we knew how—by using our bodies. Neither of us were yet comfortable expressing deeper feelings and secrets, and usually we were able to skirt around them. But after Hadrian told me about his mother, there was a tender peace between us, an understanding that we didn't have to share everything all at once. That would come naturally with time, and we would hoard our pasts like dragons guarding gold, with each story told, each secret unveiled like a prize to be won.

Hadrian never slept the entire night next to me. His energy was dynamic and limitless. Was his drive something he'd been born with? Or was it something that had been chiseled into his psyche over time as he attempted to compensate for all the things he'd never had? I wondered if his inability to rest stemmed from his desire to prove his worth. Not to the world, but to himself.

He was his own master. He did not hold council with confidants. The few phone calls he'd taken while we were hidden away had shown me that.

There was nothing soft about him. He was demanding in his existence. In bed, and out of it.

One clear morning a week later, Hadrian introduced me to one of his horses, a black stallion named Midas. It was a temperamental beast, and Midas tossed his glossy head and kicked the barn door with impatience as we stood at his stall.

"I'm pretty sure Midas is your spirit animal," I teased. "You guys have a lot of the same characteristics."

"Such as?" he asked.

"Tempers, for one," I said. "You're both very vocal and demanding about your wants and needs."

"Speaking of needs… Midas has been lonely," he explained, and then placed his hand at my waist to guide me to the next stall over that held a chestnut beauty with a white speckled flank. The horse looked at Hadrian with her lovely dark brown eyes and came to him when we arrived at the stall.

"I let him choose his companion. I had dozens of fillies brought here for Midas. He ignored every single one of them—except for her. He pranced around in front of her, and she couldn't have been less interested. He liked her immediately, and there was no hiding it."

I grinned.

He arched a brow. "I know what you're thinking, and you couldn't be more wrong."

"Maybe this horse is *my* spirit animal," I joked.

Hadrian offered me a carrot and gestured with his chin to the mare. "What did you name her?" I asked. "She's so regal."

"She doesn't have a name yet. Would you like to do the honors?" he asked with a wry grin.

I tried to stem the rapid beat of my heart. "You want me to name her? Are you sure?"

He nodded.

I reached my hand out, palm flat, and the mare devoured the carrot and then nudged my shoulder in an obvious demand for another. When I didn't oblige fast enough, she bumped her nose against me again.

"She's pure trouble," I said with a laugh as I gave her another carrot.

"Definitely," Hadrian agreed, coming to stand closer to me, so his side was pressed to mine. He stroked his hand down the mare's neck.

Midas didn't like losing Hadrian's attention and gave a loud whicker.

"She's definitely gonna cause an uproar." I stroked my hand down her silky nose. "You're such an Eris."

The mare tossed her head again.

"Do you like that name?" I asked. "Eris?"

She repeated the action.

"All right then. Eris it is."

"Eris?" Hadrian asked.

"The Greek Goddess of Discord," I said.

"I don't know why, but it feels like a bad omen," Hadrian said.

"You're being superstitious," I said as I patted Eris's neck.

"Are you ready for your first riding lesson?" he asked.

With the help of the stable master and Hadrian, I was able to mount Eris with very little trouble or embarrassment.

"She's a natural," Airik said.

Hadrian nodded, a slight smile on his face.

Airik handed me the reigns, but he remained close in case Eris decided to pitch a fit. It turned out to be completely unnecessary. From the moment I settled on her back, it was as though we'd become one entity. She was naturally in tune with me, and I felt the same with her.

"For someone who's never ridden a horse, you look like you were born to it," Hadrian said, mounting a newly saddled Midas.

His words dug deep into my soul, and I thought instantly of my mother. I remembered the bedtime stories she'd told me about a young woman riding bareback across the hills of the Italian countryside by the light of the full moon. They hadn't been fabricated stories after all, but memories from her youth. Perhaps riding horses was in my blood.

I caught Hadrian watching me, his expression carefully blank. "What are you thinking about?"

Stroking Eris's neck with one hand and holding the reigns with the other, I said, "I was thinking about my mother. She loved horses. Come on." I flashed an overly bright smile. "An island like this must have a pirate cave somewhere."

"A pirate cave? Really?"

"I'm imaginative. Humor me," I teased, gently prodding Eris with my heels. I had to get away from Hadrian's prying gaze.

Memories of my mother assailed me. Not even the crisp sea air that teased the hair at my temples or the lush beauty surrounding me could divert my thoughts.

Her smile, somehow open yet mysterious. Her golden-brown eyes that flashed like lightning when she was angry. The way she'd start yelling at me in Italian and then switch to English mid-sentence. The way men had always stared at her wherever we'd gone. Not even the lines of exhaustion and years of arguing with me had marred her natural beauty. It had only enhanced it, lending a certain fragility to her. It tacitly called out to men to protect her, but she'd never let them. She was stronger than any of them anyway, they just didn't know it.

I heard the faintest sounds of Midas's trotting hoofbeats, and Hadrian appeared next to me. A sigh of appreciation escaped my lips before I could stop it. His stern expression and the way he handled his mount had me shivering in appreciation.

When he looked at me, his eyes were fierce and brooding.

"You've been having nightmares."

His words jarred me out of my fanciful mood. "What? No. I don't have nightmares."

"Aye, you do."

"I think I'd remember having nightmares," I countered. "I don't even remember dreaming, Hadrian."

He raised his brows. "Do you think I'm lying to you?"

"No, but—"

"You thrash and mutter in Italian. The moment I pull you into my arms, you go limp and you whimper. Do you know what you whisper against me?"

I shook my head, suddenly so afraid that my throat began to tighten.

"*Mama.*"

"You think I'm crying out in my sleep for my mother?" I asked bluntly.

"I don't think. I *know.*"

I looked away from him to stare at the waves lapping at the sand.

"I told you about my mother," he reminded me.

"You did," I agreed.

"Very few people know about her. I don't ever speak about her."

"We have that in common, then," I said.

"You could tell me. About yours."

"No."

"What do you think I'm going to do with the knowledge, Eden? Use it against you?"

The only thing he'd used against me was my own desire, and I couldn't really be mad at him for that.

Had I used Hadrian's past against him? No. It had only made me understand him better. It had made me yearn to know him even more. It had split something open inside of me, a canyon of need and want, but the legacy that was in my blood and the ripple effect that my mother's actions had caused had to remain a secret.

"Eden?"

His voice was soothing, like the gentle purls of ocean waves. I let it swell over me.

"She committed suicide," I said softly, forcing myself to say it out loud.

"Jesus," he muttered. "Did you—were you the one who—"

"No," I interrupted. "I wasn't the one who found her. I got a phone call."

Hadrian looked like he was about to pull me off my horse and onto his lap. I was afraid that if he did that, I'd give in and tell him everything. I could not fall apart, no matter how comforting he had been, no matter how instinctively I felt protected by his breadth and strength.

If I did that, I would lose my ability to remain safe in anonymity.

No. I would be safer alone, even though I didn't want to be. I reinforced my emotional walls that were in danger of tumbling down.

I maneuvered Eris away from Midas which gave me a moment to compose myself for the inevitable questions Hadrian would ask.

He did not disappoint. "Did she tell you why? Was there a note?"

I nodded, knowing I needed to skirt the truth, or bend it. I grasped at the only straw I had. "She never got over my father's death. She went on as long as she could, I guess. But in the end the pain of it was too much."

He nudged Midas closer to Eris, close enough that he could take one hand and cup my cheek. "There's more to it, isn't there?"

I blinked in surprise. "What do you mean?"

"I mean it's tragic that you lost your mother. It's tragic *how* you lost your mother, but I can read you, Eden. There's more to it than that. I'm sure of it."

He was like a hound on a scent.

"We were estranged," I admitted. "I hadn't spoken to her in years. Guilt, Hadrian. What you pick up on is guilt."

His eyes saddened. "I know a thing or two about guilt."

A serene ride on the beach lifted most of the melancholy from the atmosphere, and by the time we returned to the house for lunch, my spirits had lifted almost completely. Ingrid greeted us with a smile and hot sandwiches—her version of a Philly cheese steak, but with mutton.

"Bran is asking when you're coming to visit," Ingrid said as she set down a napkin in front of Hadrian who'd taken a stool at the counter. "He wants to show you what he can do with a football."

"Who's Bran?" I asked as I lifted the sandwich to my mouth.

"My youngest grandson," Ingrid explained. "He worships the ground Hadrian walks on."

The faintest trace of color appeared high on Hadrian's cheekbones and he kept his eyes downcast. "He's a good lad," he muttered.

"Where is Bran?" I asked with sudden interest.

"On the next island over. His parents tend to the livestock," Ingrid said. "You haven't seen the neighboring islands yet, have you?"

"Not yet," I said.

She looked at Hadrian with an accusing look. "Have you kept the poor girl chained to your bed?"

I choked audibly on my sandwich as my cheeks flamed. I attempted to chew quickly and swallow.

"If you were anyone else," Hadrian said mildly, "I'd tell you to mind your own business."

She let out a delighted laugh and they both smiled. It was nothing short of familial, the way they spoke to one another.

Hadrian took a sip of water from his glass and cleared his throat. "If Eden wants to spend the afternoon being subjected to your family's scrutiny, then we'll come and see them."

I shot Ingrid a look. "Oh, yeah, I definitely want to see the other islands."

"Don't say I didn't warn you," Hadrian said with feigned darkness.

After we finished lunch, we took a power boat to a neighboring island. We stepped foot onto the beach as a gaggle of children ran to greet us, the adults following at a more sedate pace.

Hadrian wrapped his arm around me and then introduced me in Norwegian. Ingrid's family called out greetings in English, their smiles open and welcoming. It took all of my willpower not to gawk as they treated Hadrian with casual affection.

The few teenage girls in the mix hung back, appearing enthralled and yet nervous about Hadrian's brutal virility. I felt their plights like they were my own. I understood their confusion. Hadrian's presence was naturally overwhelming, even to a grown woman.

A young boy, who had to be Bran since he had a soccer ball tucked underneath his arm, darted forward to boldly stand in front of Hadrian. He craned his neck back and said, "You owe me a rematch."

My gaze darted from the boy to Hadrian, who was grinning down with a smile I'd never seen across his face. I couldn't place it, but it was genuine, open, and full of yearning.

"You sure you're ready for a rematch?" Hadrian asked, rolling up the sleeves of his button-down shirt.

"I've been practicing," the boy said.

"Good," Hadrian said. He looked at me. "Would you like to play?"

I shook my head and lifted my foot to show him a boot. "I'm not really dressed for it."

He grinned. "I guess you'll have to cheer me on from the sidelines."

I rolled my eyes. "I'll be cheering for Bran."

Bran glanced up at me and grinned, revealing the gap from a missing tooth. He hastily brushed a long mop of dark hair out of his eyes. "I'm going to win for you, then."

I tried to hide my smile at Bran's bold arrogance but failed and let out a laugh. When he was finished with his proclamation, he latched himself to Hadrian's side and gazed up at him in boyish worship and imitated Hadrian's natural swagger.

Ingrid linked her arm with mine and took it upon

herself to be my shadow. The pack of Ingrid's family began to walk across the beach. The shore disappeared into a tree line and a path cut through to an area I couldn't yet see. We strolled through foliage until we came to an open clearing. Homes that looked like cottages one might see eight hundred years ago dotted the glade. They didn't have straw thatched roofs, but they were built from stone and massive wooden timbers.

"Was this island inhabited before Hadrian bought it?" I asked Ingrid.

She shook her head. "No."

"Oh," I said with a frown. "The homes... They look..."

"They're completely modern on the inside," she said with a wry grin. "But Hadrian wanted this land to appear untouched. So he had the homes constructed to resemble an old Scottish village. They're well insulated and we have modern amenities. On the other side of the trees behind the homes, you'll find the farm with all the livestock and the greenhouses."

The wind changed, and I wrinkled my nose when I smelled proof of the animals.

Hadrian jogged over and interrupted my conversation with Ingrid when he wrapped me in his arms and lifted me off the ground.

"What are you doing?" I demanded, embarrassed by his show of affection, and even more embarrassed when everyone fell silent.

"Kiss me for good luck," he commanded.

"You don't need luck," I whispered.

"Then kiss me because you want to."

I was smiling when our lips met, and even though we had an audience, Hadrian kissed me like we were alone.

When he set me down, I wobbled. His arms quickly

steadied me and then he chucked me gently under the chin. After a wink and a grin, he sauntered back to the field and to the kids who were impatiently calling for him to start the game.

I glanced at Ingrid who looked like she was about to say something.

"Please, whatever you're going to say, don't," I begged, hiding my head in mortification.

"I was just going to say that I enjoy seeing Hadrian happy."

Ingrid's family finally stopped gawking at the display they'd just witnessed. The men of the family brought out folding tables and chairs. A few of the teenage girls who had seemingly deemed they were too cool to play the game hung back and helped the adults cover the tables with tablecloths.

"We weren't ready for a get together," Ingrid explained, "but between all of us, we have enough refreshments and food for the afternoon."

"Can I help with anything?" I asked, hating that I was standing by, doing nothing.

She flung her hand in the direction of the stone wall that encircled the glade. "Go watch the game, and cheer for Hadrian every once in a while. It'll make him feel good."

The children surrounded Hadrian in the center of the big field. He reached into his pocket and pulled out a coin. Hadrian flipped it and when it landed on the ground, Bran and his teammates yelled in excitement.

A smile floated across my face when I looked at Hadrian. He laid his mock disappointment at the coin toss on thick, but then he turned to the few kids near him and said something which caused them to shout in a sportsmanlike war cry.

I wasn't a sports enthusiast by any means, but even I could tell that Hadrian was skilled. He wove and dodged, but he held back and mostly toyed with the kids to make them feel like they were beating him because otherwise there wouldn't have been much of a game.

"Eden," Ingrid called as she strode toward me with two clear plastic cups in her hands. She gave me one and then leaned against the wall to watch her grandchildren.

"Thanks," I said, taking a sip.

"Who's winning?" she asked.

"I think Hadrian's team, but I'm not sure. Sports aren't really my thing." I was spending more time watching Hadrian than following the game.

She gestured with her chin to the field. "Bran is really good, actually. I think he might be able to play professionally one day."

"Is he on a team now?" I asked. "I mean, he lives here. You all live here. How do you handle the isolation?"

"We take the helicopter," she said easily. "Anytime we need to go to Lerwick. We're not as isolated as you think. Besides, this is something of a paradise. If you haven't already noticed."

She called out to a weathered looking man who wore a cream-colored fisherman's sweater. He sauntered toward her and came to stand by her side. "This is my husband, Elgin. He doesn't speak a lot of English."

He was tanned from the sun, with crinkle lines at the corners of his eyes. The affection between them was obvious, and when Ingrid looked at him with love and devotion, something in my heart caught.

Elgin kissed his wife's cheek and then wandered toward the table laden with food.

"He's Hadrian's fisherman," Ingrid explained. "And more comfortable with fish than with humans. Don't take his lack of interest in talking to you personally. We're married, and though I know he loves me deeply, he hardly says more than a handful of words to me on any given day."

"I won't hold his tacit greeting against him," I assured her. "How long have you been married?"

"Forty years."

"That's—wow. That's not the norm."

"I know." She smiled at her fortune. "It takes a lot of work, a lot of patience, and a lot of humor."

I shook my head. "And being married to the right person."

"Yes, that does have something to do with it." Her gaze roamed back to her husband and she stared at him, seemingly lost in the feelings of a shared life.

"How did you meet Hadrian?" I asked suddenly. "I never thought to ask—and your whole family is here, living and working on his islands. It's got to be a good story."

She paused for a moment and then said, "Elgin and I used to own a fishing business in Norway. We only had three boats, and we were one bad storm away from losing everything. My children, their spouses, we were all dependent on good weather and a good haul year after year. Some years that didn't happen and profit was thin. We were a small, family run business. Over time, we simply couldn't compete with the bigger companies. We didn't have the capital to pour back into the business and buy more boats unless our prices went up, and since we couldn't produce like our competitors, we couldn't keep prices low. The profit margin was simply too small to stay afloat, let alone to turn a decent profit."

She stared at the field where her grandchildren played, her smile soft and dreamy. "Hadrian was dining at the nicest restaurant in Bergen when Elgin was trying to get the head chef to buy fish on contract to save the business. Hadrian was seated at a private table in back and overheard enough to ask Elgin to sit and speak with him. By the end of their conversation, Hadrian made him an offer to come here and work for him doing what he loved to do. When Elgin explained about the rest of the family…" She shrugged and smiled. "Hadrian told him to bring everyone and placed no restrictions on Elgin. As long as Hadrian has fresh fish to eat, Elgin can do what he wants. Sell the rest, trade it, whatever. My children didn't know anything about livestock or growing food when we came here. We were fishermen at heart, but we learned. We all learned. We were about to lose everything we had ever worked for. He saved us and gave us a new life."

"I know what that's like—to constantly be worried about money. You get a pit in your stomach. Right here." I pressed my fist to the spot below my ribs. "You wake up in the middle of the night, wondering which utility you're willing to have shut off until the next pay day."

She looked at me. "You're not what I expected."

"What were you expecting?" I asked with a smile.

"I'm not sure," she admitted. "Something else."

We fell silent and continued to watch the game. When Bran scored a goal, Hadrian dropped to his knees and gave a dramatic yell of defeat.

Bran ran around, high fiving his siblings and cousins as he crowed his triumph. When he was within range of Hadrian, Hadrian moved quickly and scooped up the boy and turned him upside down, causing Bran to shriek with laughter.

"He's good with them," Ingrid said.

"I never would've thought that," I confessed. My grin was so big I felt it take over my entire face.

Hadrian let out a booming laugh at something Bran

said to him and then his gaze found mine. The air teased his hair and even across the field, I could see the passion in his eyes.

My heart fluttered in my chest and my smile softened. Hadrian let Bran down to the ground. Bran immediately scrambled back up and demanded they get back to playing.

"He needs a family," Ingrid said, not taking her eyes off of Hadrian.

"Subtle," I said to her.

She let out a laugh. "I've never seen him like this, Eden. He's…different with you than he is with us."

"Different how?"

"He jokes and talks with us, but he still holds himself back. But with you…it's like he wants to be open but doesn't know how."

Her words made the shield around my heart shudder. Seeing him play with kids had already softened me toward him.

"Do you know how Hadrian and I met?" I asked her, pinning her with a stare. "Did Hadrian tell you?"

She paused for a moment and then replied, "He said Ramsey Buchanan introduced you when he was in the States. They're good friends, but I'm sure you know that already."

I clamped my lips shut. Ramsey had said he knew Hadrian personally, but I hadn't realized they were friends.

"Yes. Ramsey introduced us." It wasn't a lie, but it wasn't my place to be honest with her about the rest of it.

A rumble sounded in the distance and Ingrid looked at the sky. "Storm is going to blow in soon. We should pack up."

"Too bad. I was having a perfect afternoon," I protested. "It was really nice…" I shook my head, unsure of what I was trying to say. "It was nice to be around a family."

"I'm glad to hear that."

The game broke up, and Hadrian jogged over to me and Ingrid. "Storm is coming," he said to me.

"I've been told." I took his offered hand.

"I'll come in the boat with you," Ingrid said. "I have to prepare dinner."

"Not necessary," Hadrian said. "I'll cook for Eden."

I raised my eyes in surprise. "Oh, really? You're going to cook for me?"

He winked.

Bran and the other kids ran to say goodbye to us. "Next time you come over, you have to wear better shoes so you can play," Bran said, bouncing his ball from one knee to the other.

"Only if you're on my team," I said with a grin. "Because you totally thrashed Hadrian."

Hadrian wrapped an arm around my shoulder and hauled me to his side. He bent down and whispered in my ear, "You sure you don't want to be on my team? I can make it worth your while."

With one final wave, we headed down to the beach. We got back to Hadrian's home just in time—the sky opened up and unleashed one hell of a storm.

"You looked like you were having fun," Hadrian said as we walked into the den. He flipped on the gas fireplace and then turned to stare at me.

I plopped down on the couch and covered myself with the blanket. "Not as much fun as you."

He grinned. "I let Bran win."

"Uh huh."

Hadrian laughed and then took a seat on the couch.

He placed his arm on the cushion above me and draped his fingers so they grazed my shoulder.

"They really love you," I said softly, gazing up at him.

He studied me for a long moment. "Why do you say that?"

"Just the way Ingrid talks about you. And how the kids hang on your every word."

"She told you," he stated. "About how she and her family came here."

I nodded.

Something in my expression made his jaw clench and his eyes turn flinty. "Don't look at me that way."

"What way?"

"Like I'm some kind of savior. I'm not, Eden."

I placed my hand on his muscular thigh and felt the coiled tension just waiting to be unleashed. "Who are you trying to convince? You know what I noticed when you were with Ingrid and her family?" I met his gaze. "You were relaxed in a way I've never seen."

"What else did she tell you?" he demanded, his expression dark. "Aside from how she came here. I know she said more to you."

I hesitated. I doubted he'd appreciate Ingrid's honesty about what Hadrian needed. So I settled for a partial truth. "She mentioned Ramsey Buchanan. I had no idea you were actually friends."

"Aye, we're friends. Why does that matter?"

"Because he watched my interview with Genevieve," I explained, my heart hammering in my temples. "Did he— tell you about me?"

"No. Ramsey wouldn't do that. You're a Rex girl, remember? They don't bend the rules for anyone, not even me. Didn't Ramsey tell you that?"

"He did, but I—"

"Don't trust him?"

I nodded confirmation.

His smile was savage. "You don't trust anyone, do you? You fall into the trap every time, Eden. The more you attempt to keep me at bay, the more I want to know every-thing. Every secret, every desire. And Eden?" He leaned forward, his lips a mere whisper from mine, "I always get what I want."

Chapter Twenty-Three

It felt like I'd only just fallen asleep, sated and safe in Hadrian's arms when a hand pressed tightly over my mouth, instantly jarring me from a deep slumber.

I didn't relax, even when I realized it was Hadrian.

The storm that had threatened us in the afternoon had become an evening squall, and it continued to scream, battering the glass of the balcony doors with rain and wind.

It was almost completely dark in the bedroom, but there was enough glow from the moon beating its way through the storm clouds that I could see.

Hadrian loomed over me, and I could faintly detect the outline of him.

Without removing his hand from my mouth, he managed to drag me out of bed and then lowered me to the ground, shoving me beneath the raised platform.

No moonlight pierced the darkness under the bed. My naked body quickly chilled with fear even though I was pressed against the heated wooden floor.

The tempest raging outside had been muted due to the

double paned balcony doors, but suddenly the storm became a near deafening roar as the doors were thrust open.

Through the scream of the wind and the onslaught of rain, I could hear the smack of a fist meeting flesh. There was a hiss of pain and then a grunt.

I quickly covered my mouth with my hand and forced my terror down, refusing to let it escape.

Somehow, Hadrian had known an intruder was coming, though I hadn't heard a sound over the storm.

His home had been invaded.

How? Who was here? Who was Hadrian fighting?

My fear for him eclipsed all other emotions.

I hoped Hadrian's brute strength and the fact that he hadn't been caught by surprise would be his saving grace.

A boom of thunder echoed in the room and the resonance of rain hitting the stone balcony filled my ears.

There was another grunt, followed by a roar which resounded in my bones.

Hadrian had been injured.

I shivered and tried to keep silent when all I wanted was to go to him. But it wasn't safe yet.

All I could think about was the fact that he had protected me. The first thing he did was get me under the bed, shielding me from what was coming.

There was a crash, followed by rapid footsteps on the hard wood floor.

And then nothing.

Even after the echoes of the fight ended, I didn't move from underneath the bed.

A light turned on and black spots danced before my eyes. When my vision cleared, I could see Hadrian's ankles in my line of sight, but I still didn't budge.

I pressed my cheek to the floor, willing my heart to stop racing.

"Patrick," Hadrian clipped, "I had an intruder on the east side. He's escaped. Aye, I'm fine. No, don't bother. The storm… I think the bastard was waiting for something like this." He paused and then said, "Check the systems, though I doubt you'll find anything. If I had to guess, I'd say we're dealing with a professional. Let me know what you find… Yes, I injured him before he got away. Call as soon as you find anything."

I heard him set his phone down on the bedside table.

His tone when speaking to Patrick had been unlike anything I'd ever heard. It wasn't angry, but cool. Methodical. Like he was playing through the entire situation in his mind. Like he'd been giving a briefing of facts and hadn't just fought hand-to-hand combat with an intruder.

"Sterling, you can come out now."

My heart tripped in fear for an entirely different reason.

Hadrian had called me by my given name.

"Sterling," he said again but with barely leashed control, nearly yelling over the sound of the storm outside, "I'm not going to ask you again."

Swallowing my confusion, I crawled out. Adrenaline spiked my blood. Refusing to meet his gaze, I hastily pulled on the blue silk robe that rested on a chair in the corner of the room.

Hadrian sat on the side of the bed, his profile turned slightly toward me.

I was shocked to see a swollen lip, his bloody nose, and a crimson stained sheet he held pressed to his ribs.

My thoughts locked, and at that moment, nothing except tending to Hadrian's wound mattered.

"Hadrian," I shouted, going to him and kneeling down.

"It's just a scratch," he said, trying for a smile. It gave him a Joker-like appearance and caused me to flinch.

I wasn't sure what to say. I wasn't sure what questions I wanted to ask first.

"Is he gone?" I asked, gesturing with my chin to the balcony.

"Aye."

Nodding, I got up and went to shut the balcony doors. The sound of the storm faded immediately when I did. I latched them closed, but it seemed like a paltry defense after what had just occurred.

"I—who was he?" I asked, turning around to face him.

"Someone sent to kill me."

His casually spoken words made my blood turn to ice in my veins. "Why?"

"Because I have a lot of enemies, Sterling."

"But we're on a private island," I stated.

"No place is impenetrable," he replied with a negligent shrug. He stood up, looming tall and fierce.

"Let me see it," I demanded, shooting toward him, making sure I maneuvered around the puddles of water.

He slowly removed the corner of the sheet from his wound, and I saw a slice on the opposite side of his other scar.

"It's just a graze."

"Just a graze," I repeated, feeling tears threatening to spill from my eyes. Someone had hurt him, and I wasn't prepared for the anguish it caused me.

He pressed the sheet back to his wound. With a shaking hand, I grasped his elbow and urged him toward the bathroom.

"Are you going to play doctor? Patch me up?" he asked with a gruesome smile.

I didn't reply as I flipped on the light of the master bathroom. I waved him to sit down and he perched on the closed toilet seat, the sheet littering the floor as he continued to hold it to his side.

"Look in the medicine cabinet behind the mirror," he said. "There should be antiseptic and skin glue."

"He cut you. Why did he have a knife?" I asked, finding the supplies I needed. "I mean, why didn't he use a gun or something?"

"I didn't have time to stop and have a blether with him," he said darkly. "Can we hurry this along. I've got a mess to clean up."

"And I've got *you* to clean up," I snapped. "So you can just sit there and be pampered for like, five fucking minutes."

He suddenly smiled.

"What?" I asked warily. "What's that grin for?"

"You're worried about me."

"Uh, yeah." I hastily pulled back my hair into a lopsided messy top bun and then washed my hands. "I couldn't see anything that was happening. But the sounds…my imagination was in overdrive."

I brought my supplies to the end of the counter and then squatted down in front of Hadrian. I removed the sheet so I could get another look at the wound. It was no longer seeping and most of the blood had started to clot. It was clearly superficial, but I was still going to treat it like it was a life or death situation.

If it had been anyone else, they'd be dead. But Hadrian had enough skill to fight off someone he had referred to as a professional.

"Did you lie to me this afternoon?" I asked.

I tried to be gentle, and as I cleaned his wound he didn't wince or react.

"Lie about what?"

I blew on his injury, wanting the skin to dry before I glued it together. "You called me by my real name," I reminded him. "Ramsey told you, didn't he?"

"No. Ramsey didn't tell me."

When he refused to go on, I looked up at him.

"You're not going to like the answer," he said.

"Probably not," I said lightly.

"Your cell phone."

My eyes widened. "Oh my God. You've been monitoring my calls."

Tiffany had called me by my real name.

"You bastard!" I yelled, standing up and throwing the soiled wash rag into the sink. "All this time, you've been calling me Eden. You've been having a good fucking laugh at my expense, haven't you?"

"A laugh?" His face clouded with anger. "Every time I take you to my bed and I come inside you, I have to stop myself from crying out your name. Your *real* name." He stood up with the intention of crowding my space as was his natural inclination.

"Sit down!" I yelled. "And let me finish taking care of you!"

We glared at each other, breathing heavily. Another fight was brewing in the air, but there was something else, too.

Blood lust.

Someone had just tried to kill Hadrian, and he'd protected me. He'd acted like a warrior defending his queen.

"Who are you, Hadrian?" I whispered. "I have the right to know."

"You have the right to know?" he repeated. "How the hell do you figure that?"

"Someone came to your island to try and kill you. I happen to be staying with you. Don't you think I deserve a few answers?"

He fell silent, and I took the time to close his wound and bandage him up. He held his body taut, like at any moment he'd reach out and grab me. I could tell he was only a few moments away from losing his shit entirely.

"I met Ramsey Buchanan when I was sixteen," he said, shattering the silence. "I'd run away from Lerwick—the orphanage—more times than I could count. Eventually, they stopped coming after me.

"I lived in Edinburgh, on the streets. I was big for my age, even then. Anyone who tried to fuck with me learned quickly that I had a lot of rage, and no one to take it out on. I never started shite…but I ended it. A lot."

When he looked at me, it was like he was waiting for confirmation that I was listening. I nodded quickly.

He inhaled and went on, "One night, four lads a few years older than me thought they could take me on. Ramsey helped even the score." He smiled at the memory. "Here was this eejit with designer clothes and an expensive haircut with just as much rage as me. He had my back and never asked for anything. He just started hanging out with me. He'd disappear for a time and eventually come back. I found out he was doing the same thing—running away from home, looking for trouble for a few days. But he didn't know true struggle like I did. He wasn't built for living on the streets."

He shrugged. "Anyway, he came back one day and told me he met a couple of guys who ran an underground bare-knuckle boxing ring. He thought I could make a lot of money beating the shite out of rough men. And he was right." His smile at the memory dimmed.

"There was a girl," he said, his voice so low I had to lean forward to hear him. "An orphan girl two years younger than me named Finola. She's the one who introduced me to *The Last Unicorn* and King Haggard. We'd sit up in the belfry, hiding from the world, reading stories to each other to pass the time and escape the…"

He looked over my shoulder, going to a place I couldn't follow. "She'd get the dreamiest look on her face and tell me about all the places she'd go if she could, all the foods she'd eat if she had a million pounds. What life would be like if she were normal and not just a poor orphan." Hadrian came back to the present and glanced at me. "When she got placed with a family, I ran away to Edinburgh for good. There was no reason to stay there anymore. Finola was gone."

He scrubbed a hand through his strawberry blond hair. "I didn't expect her to find me a few months later on the streets. She told me her foster father made her uncomfortable. Staring at her. Touching her shoulder a little longer than was normal. Things she couldn't put into words, but she knew something was wrong. But she loved being in a home with a family so she didn't say anything. She didn't want to go back to the orphanage."

A sick feeling took up residence in my stomach, but I bit my tongue and let him continue.

"He snuck into her room one night." His expression went cold. "She sliced the bastard across his face with the knife I gave her as protection—just in case. They sent her back to the orphanage, of course, claimed she'd made up the entire story, but the father mysteriously didn't want to press any charges. He said she was crazy, and that was the end of it. No one looked into it further."

"What did Mother Superior say?" I asked, my heart breaking for a young girl I'd never met.

"I think she believed Finola, but what could she do?" He shook his head. "When Finola ran away, I think it was a bit of relief for all parties involved. Nothing would come it of it after that, no matter who said anything about it. The orphanage didn't look very hard for her. She was just gone."

He paused for a moment and then said, "I used to think I was brave. Beating the shite out of men. I was big, so what did I have to be afraid of? Finola was slim. Fragile. She needed to be protected. That's why she searched for me in Edinburgh.

"We slept on the same dirty mattress in the warehouse I'd made my home. I introduced her to Ramsey. Finola was never," he thought for a moment, "bitter. Never jaded. Never broken. She still had hope. Hope that life would eventually be kind to her, and that there was goodness in the world."

Emotion tugged at the back of my eyelids because I knew—*I knew*—the next part of Hadrian's story would gut me.

"She wanted to see me fight one night, and I let her. We took her down to one of the matches and of course I won—and while Ramsey was collecting our winnings, the lads who bet on their friend and lost, cornered Finola."

He boldly met my gaze, and the anguish I saw in his eyes was nearly my undoing. But if he could tell it, then I would be strong enough to hear it.

Hadrian took a deep, shuddering breath. "They cornered her and dragged her outside and raped her in the alley behind the ring—and then they slit her throat. Ramsey and I found her, eyes open, glazed over in shock."

He paused for a long while and then took a deep

breath and went on, "She used to carry around an old copy of *The Last Unicorn*. The book was lying on the ground in the alley, the spine split, and the pages torn out. She had silvery blonde hair. Almost white. Did I tell you that?"

I shook my head, stifling a sob that threatened to spill from me.

"Her hair was stained red from her own blood. The cream-colored pages of her book were splattered with mud and looked yellow in the dim streetlight."

He bowed his head and stared at his knees. "It's been twenty years, and I can still see her frozen in that moment. So clear. It never fades, Sterling. It just lives—" He pressed a fist to his heart. "I loved her. Her loss was…"

I had no words to offer him. No comfort to give. I could not ease the pain of his memory, of his first love's tragic death.

What would've happened if Finola had lived? Would she be here with him now? Would they have a family? Would they have made something beautiful together after coming from such brutal pasts?

Would Hadrian be the man he is now if he hadn't gone through such trauma?

"We found towels from the fight room to wrap Finola in and got her back to the warehouse without being seen. Even though we'd spent some time together, I didn't know who Ramsey truly was—the power of his last name. He made a call and a few hours later, we were in a car headed to Dornoch. We laid Finola to rest in his family's cemetery, and Ramsey introduced me to his father. He told us to go do what needed doing, and then Ramsey and I returned to Edinburgh and hunted every one of those fuckers down like rabid dogs," he said, his voice threaded with steel. "We spent four days finding them, and by the fourth night we had slit all their throats like they had done to Finola and left each of them on the doorsteps of their homes for their families to find. We pinned notes to their chests that said 'Rapist', so there would be no question about why they'd been killed. At first, the police thought a serial killer was on the loose, but everyone knew who those boys really were at heart, and the community quietly let the murders go unpunished. The police made it look like they were trying hard to find us and gave great quotes to the papers, but everyone knew it was all for show."

He clenched his hands a few times. "When we were done, Ramsey asked me to come back to Dornoch with him. He told me his father wanted to speak to me and—"

With a shuddering breath he said, "And my life was never the same again."

Chapter Twenty-Four

He finally got up and I instinctively backed away, but his attention wasn't on me. He all but fled to the bedroom, and I followed at a more sedate pace.

I sat down on the edge of the bed. I was exhausted from the events of the late night already, but it didn't feel like we were done. Not by a long shot.

Hadrian stood, clad in nothing but a pair of navy-blue boxer briefs. I wanted to hug him to me, but I wasn't sure he'd allow the comfort.

He went to the liquor cart and poured two drinks. Hadrian came toward me, holding out a glass. When I reached for it, my hand shook.

I grasped it but didn't drink. Instead, I stared into it like it was a crystal ball.

"You're afraid of me now," he said finally.

My head shot up. "What? No."

"You haven't said anything."

"You told me a lot," I reminded him. "I'm…thinking." I took a sip of my drink, wincing at the strong flavor of brandy.

Finola's death was tragic. I was glad Hadrian had delivered his own brand of vigilante justice with Ramsey. The world didn't need people who hurt the innocent.

"You have to tell me what's going on in your head, Sterling."

I arched a brow. "You seem very fond of using my real name."

He stared at me. "Of course I am. It's who you really are."

"You invaded my privacy," I lashed out.

"I'm a reclusive billionaire who has never brought a woman to his island, and there's a reason for that. I don't trust anybody."

Well, we have that in common, I guess. What else does he know about me?

What would he do if he found out the truth? Was I doing right by following the path my mother had instructed all along? Hide, get a new identity, forget my past and never tell anyone?

Be safe, be smart, and above all, survive.

"Sterling?"

"I understand why you monitored my calls," I said as Hadrian pulled me from my thoughts. "I'm sorry…about Finola."

Saying her name made it feel like her ghost was between us, that she was the true reason Hadrian was so closed off from the world.

He nodded once, his expression going blank.

"Why did you tell me about her, about how you—and the boys… You didn't have to."

He paused and took a sip of his drink. To stall for even more time, he flipped on the gas fireplace. "I wanted to. I wanted you to know what made me the man I am now."

"You've always been a protector, haven't you? Even when you were a kid."

"I didn't protect Finola—and I have to live with that every day for the rest of my life. She died because of me. She died because she knew me. If I'd sent her back to Lerwick where she was safe…"

"You were in love," I said quietly. "And she came to you because she would've rather taken her chances living as a runaway with you on the streets than being placed in another foster home where she wasn't safe."

He didn't seem to hear me or register what I'd said.

"I killed four lads."

"No. You killed four *rapists*. You did the world a favor."

"I slit their throats, Sterling. It was gruesome and brutal."

"You avenged her."

"I enjoyed killing them."

"Did you? Or did you enjoy punishing them for taking the woman you loved? Those aren't the same thing."

"I took pleasure in their pain. The fear in their eyes as they pissed themselves…the look on their faces as our blades met their throats. Aye." His gaze glittered. "I enjoyed it, because they deserved it."

I fell silent, turning over his words, examining them. I wasn't at all horrified by his confession, even though I should've been.

"You're leaving," he said suddenly.

"What?" I asked, shooting up from my spot on the bed.

He nodded. "As soon as the storm clears, you're getting on a helicopter to the mainland and then my plane will fly you back to Dallas."

"You can't—what?"

"I'll pay you the money from the contract. All of it." He clenched his jaw.

"Hadrian, stop," I whispered. "Why are you pushing me away?"

He glared. "I'm not pushing you away. I'm protecting you. Don't you understand? An assassin broke into my home—on my private island in the middle of nowhere—and he escaped. Which means he's still out there. He could come back to finish the job. Actually, I expect him to come back. You need to leave. You need to get as far away from me as possible."

Leave Hadrian?

Wasn't that the smart thing to do? But how could I do it?

The thought of leaving him was a punch to the chest and left me short of breath.

"You're not safe with me, Sterling. And I will not jeopardize your life. I've already lost one woman because I— you have to get as far away from me as possible."

For the first time since I'd met Hadrian, he looked unsure.

"Hadrian?" I peered into his eyes. "Do you like being with me?"

"That has nothing to do with it. I can't guarantee your safety here."

"Could you guarantee it when you offered me the contract?"

He clenched his jaw and then said, "You weren't in danger then. You are now."

He cared.

Hadrian Rhys cared about me.

Somewhere along the way, in our short time together, I'd managed to sneak past the fortifications guarding his heart.

Hadrian could protect me. He *had* protected me. He'd

shoved me under the bed and then fought off an assailant in the night.

"I can't imagine the pain you've gone through. Losing Finola the way you did…but I'm not her. Let me stay. Let me be here with you."

"Why would you knowingly put yourself in danger?" he demanded. "Do you have a death wish? Don't you understand? I'm cursed."

"You're not cursed, Hadrian," I said, my heart fracturing for the man standing in front of me, fracturing for the hurt he'd borne through the years.

"Aye, I am," he said, his tone emphatic.

"You live on an island, away from civilization. Why? To keep others out? Or to keep them safe from you?"

His expression cracked, finally showing the bleak pain shackled to his soul.

Only Hadrian could be the one to break free from it. I could be there to support him. I could prove to him I wasn't going anywhere, but that was all.

"You have no sense of self-preservation," he stated, his gaze flinty. "You're leaving the moment the storm clears, and that's final."

He marched to the balcony doors and placed his hand on the glass. His back was to me and his shoulders were tight with tension.

He was right. I didn't have any sense of self-preservation.

There had never been anyone in my past that elicited even a fraction of emotion that I felt for Hadrian.

I set my glass of brandy down on the bedside table, and with a boldness I didn't expect, I trekked across the bedroom floor to stand behind him. I brushed a kiss across the middle of his back and then pressed my cheek to his skin.

He tensed and then shuddered.

"You need me," I whispered.

"No," he lied.

"Well, *I* need you."

I thought he'd shrug me off, not wanting me to touch him, but he suddenly turned around to face me. He cradled my face in his hands. "Say it," he commanded. "Say it now or get out and never come back."

I swallowed, tears brimming in my eyes. I'd been fighting it since the moment I met him, the magnetic pull I didn't understand. The pull I thought was only lust.

But it was more.

So much more.

More than anything I'd ever felt in my entire life. Hadrian was my reason for being on Earth.

"I'm yours, Hadrian," I whispered, my throat tight with emotion.

"I'm not a normal man," he said, his voice so low I had trouble hearing him over the sound of the storm through the glass. "I can't promise you normal."

"What are you promising me then, Hadrian?" I asked, my heart thundering in my ears.

"The world, Sterling. I'm promising you the world."

His words lay at my feet, like a prize a warrior would offer his queen after a battle hard won.

Silence reigned between us.

"I don't want the world, Hadrian," I finally said, continuing to hold his stare. "I just want you."

He claimed my mouth.

I wrapped my arms around his neck, trying to get closer, trying to burrow into him. It would be different, this time.

His phone rang, pulling us out of the moment. Hadrian answered it.

"Patrick?" His lusty gaze remained on me while he listened to his head of security. "Aye. All right. I'll deal with it tomorrow morning."

He hung up and stared at the fireplace for a moment.

"Hadrian?" I prodded.

"Patrick found the intruder."

"In this storm? How?" I asked in shock.

"The infrared cameras picked up a foreign vessel in the outcrop on the other side of the island."

"Infrared cameras? Oh sure." I shook my head. "How did he get past your state-of-the-art security system? How did he manage to get here undetected?"

"I'll find out tomorrow morning when I question him," he said, clenching his jaw. "But he's clearly a professional, otherwise he wouldn't have gotten as far as he did."

"How are you going to—are you going to hurt him?"

"Hurt him?" His tone was arctic. "I'm going to kill him."

My breath hitched.

His expression hardened at the sound. "Are you sure you know what you're signing up for by choosing to be with me?"

I was silent.

"Sterling? Answer me," he commanded. "Answer me before I take you to bed."

"I don't know, Hadrian," I said softly, looking up at him through the sweep of my lashes. "All I know is that I want to be with you—and I'll sort out the rest as it comes."

He slowly untied the belt from around my waist and pushed open the robe, guiding it off me, and then urged me to the bed.

When I was naked and splayed out, he climbed onto the bed and placed a kiss at my navel. Then his lips dipped lower. Pleasure kindled between my legs as he feasted on me.

He grasped my hips and held me to him while his tongue danced and teased. My fingers sank into his hair, and I gave into everything I was feeling.

The rough whiskers on his jaw were their own form of torture. I was overly sensitive and when he swiped his tongue across the bundle of nerves between my legs, I erupted around him.

It was the fastest I'd ever come, my body primed for pleasure. Maybe I had a bit of blood lust of my own.

His eyes never left mine as he got up off the bed, only long enough to shed his boxers.

"Why are you so beautiful?" I asked, my gaze hungrily raking over him.

His lips curled in gratification at my question. "I was going to ask you the same thing."

He palmed his erection which seemed to grow even larger and then he crawled on top of me. My legs fell open in eager welcome and he thrust into me with one smooth, hard drive.

My body took all of him.

He stared into my eyes while he slowly drove in and out of me, never breaking contact. His hands wandered but his gaze did not. I felt him everywhere on my skin. Every touch was a burn, irrevocably branding me as his.

Hadrian angled his pelvis and ground against me with ruthless determination. His fingers played with my nipples, his lips kissed the side of my neck.

I grasped him to me, wanting us to come together.

"I'm close," I whispered.

Hadrian's thrust ceased as his mouth took mine in a ravenous kiss. I was just about to beg him to move again when he withdrew.

"What? What are you doing?" I cried out.

He grinned. "I want to try something else."

"Something else?" I repeated. "What do you want—"

He gently rolled me over so I was on my belly, and then he grabbed a pillow to nestle it under me, so my butt was angled in the air.

I realized what he wanted.

Apprehension coated my throat. "I've never done this before."

"We'll go slow. You say stop, we stop. Aye?"

I nodded. Nerves dampened my ardor.

Hadrian's chest covered my back, his face coming to rest in the crook where my shoulder met my neck. "Trust me," he whispered.

I nodded again and then lay my cheek flush to the bed and closed my eyes. The bedside drawer opened and closed. I looked up just in time to see Hadrian unscrewing a lid on a jar of coconut oil. He scooped out a dollop and settled it between his hands before putting them on me.

"Relax," he said.

"It's hard to relax when I don't know what's coming," I quipped.

His strong hands started at my neck and worked their way down. He kneaded the muscles of my shoulders and back, and every once in a while, he'd stop to place a kiss on my skin.

Lulled by his sensual, caressing touch, my eyes drifted shut and they didn't open—not even when he spread my cheeks.

He dribbled more oil onto my skin, letting it fall into crevices and creases. Every once in a while, he touched his finger to a place that had never been touched for pleasure before.

Hadrian nibbled on my shoulder as his finger gently

eased into me. I tensed immediately, not liking the pinch of discomfort, my untried body learning to make room.

"Easy," he whispered, gently easing his finger in and out of me.

I squirmed against his touch, not sure if I was trying to get away or wanting him to go deeper.

He withdrew completely and I feared he was going to replace his finger with something much larger, but he surprised me when he settled down next to me on his back.

"Come here," he ordered gruffly.

I removed the pillow from underneath me and tossed it to the floor before climbing Hadrian to straddle his body. I was still slick with want and oil and I grasped his erection and eased down on top of him.

"Kiss me," he commanded.

I leaned over and pressed my lips to his. While my body was drugged with pleasure and full of him, he slid his finger in me again. But something about this angle made it easier and excitement bloomed. So much so that I felt myself working him in deeper.

I was being filled in two places, and though it was only a small introduction of what could be, my mind went wild with fantasies.

Closing my eyes, I rode out the storm, clenching around his finger and erection. I gasped when Hadrian suddenly sat up with me still in his lap, his mouth drenching my neck and shoulders in kisses as he continued to undulate inside me.

With a moan of surrender, he finally came, grasping me tightly for a moment and then releasing me so that he could gently collapse against the pillows. I fell on top of his chest, my breathing erratic and scattered.

He swept away my hair and rested his hand on the back of my neck, urging me to look at him.

"Are you all right?" he asked, his eyes clear and intense.

"Yeah. Are you? I didn't hurt you?" I asked, my fingers drifting to his bandage.

"Hurt *me*?" he asked with a wry grin.

I rolled my eyes at his arrogance. It was clearly back, as though no vulnerability had passed between us.

"Did you enjoy it?" he asked baldly. "What I did to you?" His hand coasted over my hip to rest at the small of my back.

My cheeks flamed and I cleared my throat. "I think you know I enjoyed it."

He let out a laugh and leaned forward to brush his lips across mine. "I have a pretty good feeling you'll enjoy something much larger."

Embarrassment made me bury my head against his neck.

"Sterling," he said softly. "Look at me."

His tone and the use of my name had me pulling back to stare at him.

"You shouldn't ever be self-conscious with me. Nothing is off limits. Pleasure is pleasure and if you want something, ask for it. Aye?"

I nodded.

After he got up and washed his hands, he came back to bed and I snuggled up against him. His arm draped around me and his fingers stroked my spine.

"So, where does all of this leave us, Hadrian? I'm still a Rex girl and there is a contract between us."

"Damn the contract."

"I don't like the idea of being financially dependent on you."

"I guess that means you haven't bothered to check the bank account The Rex set up for you."

I looked up and propped my chin on his chest. "What do you mean?"

"The million dollars has been sitting in your account since the night you agreed to come to the island."

"What? The night we discussed the contract, you offered me a hundred thousand dollars for accepting. Why did you change the amount?" I asked in shock.

"I never had plans to keep you here if you didn't want to be. I didn't want the money to be the reason you stayed."

I stared at him in sudden understanding. "You wanted me to choose you, regardless of the money."

"Aye. And besides, a million dollars is pocket change to me. It was never about the money…for either of us."

I pressed my face to his chest again, loving the warm skin beneath my cheek. "Who is Ramsey's father?" I asked, changing the subject.

"Why do you want to know?"

"Because you said after you went back to Dornoch to talk to him your life was never the same again."

Hadrian paused for a moment, his hand tangling in my hair. "Ramsey's father was the man who taught me everything I needed to know about how to navigate the criminal underground."

My mind whirled with Hadrian's unveiling. "You're a criminal."

"Aye."

"What kind of…"

He stopped his tender love strokes and then gripped a handful of hair and gently forced my gaze to meet his. "It's better if you don't know."

I swallowed. "You're a criminal and a killer."

His expression hardened. "Now are you afraid of me?"

I paused before answering, brushing my hand across his chest. "No. I don't think I am," I admitted.

"Liar."

I glared in anger. "I'm *not* a liar."

"Then you like danger?"

"Hardly."

"Then why are you staying with me?"

I placed my hand on his heart. Not to push him away, but so I could assure myself that he wasn't a figment of my imagination that I'd dreamed up. That this man—this broken criminal—really wanted me.

"There's something special between us, and I want time to explore it," I said.

"That might be the most honest thing you've ever said to me."

There were still so many things left unsaid. The past I hadn't shared, and wishes for the future I desired.

But for the moment, I didn't need anything else except this time in his arms and the drums of our hearts beating as one.

Chapter Twenty-Five

We fell asleep sometime around dawn. I woke up again and found Hadrian standing over me, about to brush a kiss across my cheek.

I peered up at him. I'd taken out my contacts the night before, knowing my eyes would be gritty in the morning from lack of sleep.

"Your eyes," he whispered.

"Weird, right?" I asked.

"No, not weird. Unique. Like you."

"Don't get used to it. I prefer the contacts. Where are you going so early this morning?"

"To question the intruder."

Adrenaline pumped into my bloodstream and I was instantly alert and rolled onto my back, hiking the comforter up to cover myself.

A lot had transpired between us during the night. Hadrian was now dressed, his masculine form concealed. His expression was blank, and his eyes were clear.

"When I get back, we're going to talk," he said.

"Talk," I repeated. "About what? Didn't we talk last night?"

"There are still some things that need to be dealt with."

"Such as?"

"Your employment status with The Rex, for one."

"And?"

"Later. We'll talk later."

He leaned over the bed again and settled his lips on mine. He tasted minty and fresh, and I wondered how long he'd been awake—or if he'd even slept at all.

Hadrian pulled back, taking his warmth with him. The sensual haze remained.

"I'm afraid to leave you," he admitted.

"Why?"

His gaze was steady. "Don't come to your senses, please."

I frowned. "It's too early for word play."

"You're going to start thinking," he stated. "As soon as I'm gone, you'll start reevaluating everything."

I took a moment to study him. "Are *you* reevaluating everything?"

Hadrian stilled. "Damn right I am." My heart fell, until he continued, "I'm a selfish prick who should put you on the helicopter right now, but I can't bring myself to do it."

I beamed at him.

"Why are you grinning at me?" he asked.

"Some things are worth the risk, Hadrian."

"Your life isn't something I can risk." He cradled my head and kissed me hard. "Don't come to your senses," he said again when he pulled away. "I'll be back in a few hours. We'll talk about everything then."

I nodded and Hadrian released me and then stalked from the bedroom. The drapes were pulled back from the balcony doors and even though the sky was gray, it seemed like the storm had passed. I thought about going back to sleep, but my mind had kicked into gear.

I got out of bed and threw on a pair of navy-blue silk pajamas and then I went into the bathroom and put in my contacts. I slid on my slippers and then padded my way out into the hallway and down to the kitchen.

Ingrid was perched at the counter, sitting with her hands wrapped around a mug of coffee. It was still hot, and steam curled up around her faintly creased face. She looked pensive and didn't move when I came in. Only when I stood in her line of sight did she finally look up.

"Eden—er, Sterling," she corrected. Her face was awash with horror. "How are you? Hadrian told me about…I can't believe—"

I placed my hand on her arm to stop her stumbling speech. "I'm fine. We're fine." I went to the cabinet to retrieve a mug. "When did you learn my real name?"

"This morning. Hadrian explained who you are. Your Rex affiliation."

I thought about being embarrassed, but then I realized it was useless. We'd met how we'd met, and there was no use lamenting the fact that you couldn't change your history.

Your past didn't have to define your future.

"Sterling," she murmured.

"Hmm?"

"It suits you. Your name. You're definitely not an Eden."

"It doesn't alter your perception of me, does it?" I asked boldly.

"No."

I studied her for a moment and when I detected sincerity, I nodded.

"You don't seem shaken," she mused. "If it were me, I'd be hiding in the broom closet."

"I was terrified last night," I admitted. "But I've had some time to process."

Not to mention I was a bit distracted by Hadrian's honesty about his past.

Ingrid stared at me. "This has never happened before. No one has ever come to the island and attempted…You should leave."

I arched a brow. "Is this coming from you? Or from him?"

"Me."

"I can't leave him," I said softly. "I won't abandon him."

My heart felt like it was breaking inside my chest, cracking open to reveal all the feelings I'd tried to shove down inside of myself since my mother had died.

"You told me he needs me," I said to her. "Well, as it turns out, I need him. I just didn't know it."

"So, you're staying?" she asked with unconcealed hope.

Her tone gave me pause, and that's when I realized I wouldn't just be choosing to stay with Hadrian. I was choosing Ingrid, too. And her family, the island, and this secluded life.

My throat was suddenly tight with emotion I hadn't expected.

Just when I thought I'd have to flee and find some privacy to let out my feelings, Ingrid changed the subject. "Do you want breakfast?"

I shook my head. "No, thanks. I'm not really hungry. I think I'll walk on the beach and clear my head."

I went back to the bedroom and dressed quickly in warm clothes and comfortable walking boots. I grabbed my phone from the living room and then waved to Ingrid before heading out.

The air was cool but calm. Leaves and small twigs littered the sand from the previous night's storm. My hands quickly chilled and I stuck them in the pockets of my fleece-lined windbreaker as I walked, my thoughts swirling.

Hadrian is a criminal.

But somehow, that didn't matter to me. I was pondering a future with him. He was all I could think about. He was everything I had never even risked dreaming of, and more magnetic than any man I had ever known. My emotions were running rampant, and I knew I couldn't risk losing a chance to make a life with him.

As I went over the events of the last few weeks and previous night's attack, I realized that I couldn't knowingly keep him in the dark about why I'd needed a new identity. Lying by omission made me feel worse than becoming a Rex girl. He was determined to know everything about me. To keep it from him would sour the purity of our attraction. Every moment I spent in his arms made me feel cherished…loved. He'd shared his gruesome past, and if we had any chance at a real future together, then I had to share mine.

None of my logic or reasoning mattered.

I trusted him, and it was time.

I found a spot in the sand and sat on the beach. A short while passed and I was considering getting up and going inside when I saw Hadrian stalking toward me. He took a seat next to me, moving close enough to touch me, but he didn't. He brought his legs up to his chest and rested his hands on his knees. His knuckles were raw and enflamed. I wasn't sure if that had been from the night before, or if it was the result of his interrogation techniques.

How could someone with such a capacity for violence be so incredibly gentle with me?

I leaned my head against his shoulder.

"The intruder is dead," he stated.

I lifted my head and turned to look at him. "Dead?"

He nodded.

"Did you—"

"No. I didn't kill him." His tone was hard. "He cursed at me in Sicilian and then killed himself."

"He *what*? How?"

"He had a biologically implanted kill switch. High-level assassins use them to prevent themselves from being tortured for information. His was a very small glass cyanide capsule implanted at the base of his tongue. I was in the middle of…and he bit down hard on his tongue, breaking the capsule and releasing the poison, and that was it. Whoever sent him really didn't want anyone finding out who he was." His expression was grim. "If he hadn't killed himself, I would've broken his neck anyway."

I fell quiet once again as my mind whirled. What were the chances of a Sicilian hitman appearing on his island after my arrival? I had to tell him everything.

Hadrian brushed a battle-scarred hand against my cheek. "No one comes into my home to try and kill me and lives."

His intensity should've scared me, but it didn't.

"You have no idea who he is or who sent him, do you?" I asked.

"No, I don't. I can find out though. But it'll take some time."

I nodded and then looked away from him to stare out across the ocean.

He sighed. "You didn't change your mind about leaving, did you?"

"No." I dragged my fingers through the damp sand. "You might change your mind about me staying though… when I tell you the truth about who I am."

"Try me," he said, his tone surprisingly soft and tender, when moments ago he sounded like he wanted to go to war.

Nodding, I gathered my courage and began to tell him everything.

I started with my mother's funeral, my voice ringing out across the empty beach, fighting to be heard over the sound of the waves. The story leaked out of me as I purged the secrets of my soul—secrets I had been willing to take to my grave until I realized what he meant to me. I kept my eyes on the water, not wishing to see Hadrian turn away from me when he realized I was nothing but a burden.

When I was finished, I fell silent. I pulled my legs to my chest and rested my chin on my knees, almost perfectly mirroring his pose.

"Sterling," he said. "Look at me."

I reluctantly turned my face toward him but kept my cheek against my knee.

"You did the right thing by telling me. Now I can protect you."

"How?" I asked, my throat tight. "My family is dangerous."

He reached out to caress my jaw. "So am I."

Chapter Twenty-Six

I stared into his eyes. "You're not going to send me away?"

He frowned. "Why would I send you away?"

"Haven't I just become more trouble than I'm worth?"

He gently grasped my jaw, keeping my eyes on his. "What do you think last night was about?"

I swiped my tongue across my dry lips. "Someone tried to kill you. I don't know what you—"

"I meant after that," Hadrian said as he shook his head. "When I promised you the world. What the hell did you think that meant? That I would just get tired of you one day?"

My eyes dropped to the sand.

"No. You look at me. I need you to look at me, so I know you're listening."

I reluctantly returned my gaze to his.

"I will not abandon you," he stated fiercely. "I will not leave you to the mercy of your family or the Foscari. You are mine to protect. Do you hear me, Sterling? I really need you to understand how deeply I mean it."

The burden of my secret suddenly lifted from my

shoulders, and I bent my head and sobbed. I couldn't stop the tears of relief. Relief that I wasn't alone, that I'd finally found a man who wasn't just strong enough to shelter me from the oncoming storm, but who *chose* me.

Like I'd chosen him.

Hadrian stood and brushed the sand from his trousers. Then he reached down to grasp my hand, hauling me up into his firm embrace. Apparently that wasn't enough for him, because he lifted me into his arms and carried me toward his home.

I rested my cheek against his chest, the wool sweater warm under my skin.

"Ingrid made meat pies. Are you hungry?" he asked.

"How can you think about food at a time like this? I just told you who I really am, and you're sweeping it away like it's nothing."

He paused for a moment. "Is it surprising who you are? Of course, but in spite of what I've shared with you, you don't know everything about what it is I actually do for a living. Your family…are known to me. I've done business with them for years."

I lifted my head and peered at him in disbelief. "*What? You have?*"

We arrived at the stairs that led us back into his home. He set me down and then took my hand again as we made our ascent. "Come on. We'll finish this conversation in a minute. I need something to drink."

Once we were in the kitchen, I immediately went to the stove and put on the kettle for tea.

I leaned against the counter, trying to support myself with weak legs. "So, you do business with my family?"

"Aye," he said.

"What *kind* of business?" I demanded.

"Nothing that concerns you."

I looked at the tea kettle as I waited for it to boil. "My mother ran from the Foscari, but she made it clear that she was also running from her own family. She told me that I couldn't go to them for help, that it would be dangerous for me."

"You didn't go to them for help," he reminded me. "You came to *me* for help. And I can handle your family. You have to trust me."

I nodded absently. A part of me hated that I had handed over my problems to Hadrian. The other more rational part of me was glad that he was willing to deal with it on my behalf. My mother had fled because there hadn't been a way out of her predicament. Maybe turning to Hadrian, confiding in him, was the right decision to end the nightmare once and for all.

I momentarily pushed thoughts of my family away to address another matter that had yet to be settled between us.

"Hadrian?"

"Aye?"

"What am I going to do about The Rex?"

"What about The Rex?" His phone buzzed in his pocket. Hadrian pulled it out, read a text, and then typed out a reply.

"I became a Rex girl. I signed on the proverbial dotted line for a year."

"You're not a Rex girl anymore." He set his phone down on the counter and gave me his attention again. "It's already been handled."

A knot formed in my stomach. "What does that mean, exactly?" When he didn't reply, I pressed, "Hadrian. Tell me."

He ran a thumb across his chin. "When I transferred the money into your account I also settled with The Rex."

"Settled what?"

"You were never going back to The Rex, Sterling," he said calmly. "I wouldn't have allowed it."

"*Excuse me?*" I screeched. "You wouldn't have *allowed* it?"

"Before you get upset, let me explain. Even if you left here and decided not to stay the six months with me, I couldn't stomach the thought of you working at The Rex. So, I paid them not to take you back even if you wanted to go."

"Are you kidding me?"

"No. I'm not." His phone buzzed again, but before he could reach for it and dive into his text conversation, I grabbed it and held it behind my back.

"May I have my phone?" he asked in amusement.

"In a moment—after you explain things to my satisfaction."

"Speaking of satisfaction—"

"Hadrian," I snapped.

"Sterling," he mocked. "I always get my way. You should know that by now."

I bared my teeth in an angry snarl. "I am not a chess piece you can maneuver."

"I don't *maneuver*."

"No?"

"I tactfully manipulate."

"THIN. ICE."

His hand reached out to settle at the curve of my hip. "If you didn't want to stay, I would've let you go. It would've killed me, but I would have. I can't handle the idea of other men—of you with them."

I understood his possessive vein, but Hadrian couldn't make my choices for me.

"You need to promise me something," I said.

"What?"

"Moving forward, if you want me to do something, just ask. Don't go behind my back and pull my strings like some puppeteer."

"Just ask," he repeated. "That's all it would take?"

I nodded.

"Sterling?"

"Yes?"

"Will you kiss me?"

Before I could respond, he dragged me closer so that I was pressed against him. My arms reached up to loop around his neck, and I played with the hair at his nape. I stood on my toes, attempting to reach his mouth. "You're a fast learner."

When his mouth covered mine, I lost all rational thought. His arms tightened around me and it felt like he'd never let me go. I lost my desire to remain a separate entity, in spite of my hopes for the future.

Hadrian Rhys had scrambled my psyche, pulled apart my soul, and rearranged it to fit tightly into his.

We made it as far as the living room before he had me naked and bent over the couch. A Shetland tempest was nothing compared to us. We were cataclysmic, like an unstoppable storm.

When we collapsed to the floor, spent and shaking, Hadrian grabbed a woolen blanket and covered us before pulling me tight against him.

"Has it ever been like this?" I asked dreamily, my fingers stroking his chest. "With anyone else?" I closed my eyes and breathed in the perfume of pleasure in the air.

"No. It's never been like this with anyone," he said softly. "And I knew it the first night we spent together."

"Knew what?"

"I knew you were different."

After we recovered, we showered. We took our time, lathering each other's bodies, lingering with our touches and kisses. Then we laid in bed, facing one another as the rain beat against the balcony doors.

My hands wandered over his skin, lingering on his scar. His other fresh wound was bandaged again after our shower, but the pain of it hadn't slowed him down at all.

"Do they bother you? My scars?" he asked, his brogue rumbling like looming thunder.

To answer his question, I pulled back the covers so I could see him. And then I pressed a kiss to his healed mark before snuggling into his embrace.

His fingers plowed through my damp hair. I closed my eyes and gave into his pampering touch.

I slid my leg between his, angling to get closer, and when I did, I sighed in contentment. His fingers circled my neck, reminding me that I hadn't worn my necklace in days. Come to think of it, I couldn't remember the last time I'd seen it.

"Have you seen my necklace?" I asked.

"Aye. It's in my bedside drawer."

"How long has it been there?" I asked. "I don't remember losing it."

"You didn't lose it. I took it off of you on the yacht while you were asleep."

I smiled into his shoulder. "Of course you did."

"I kept telling myself that I only wanted to keep the necklace safe for you until you left, but I was lying to myself. I knew that bringing you here was the beginning of the end."

"The end of what?" I asked, propping my chin up to look at him.

His gaze softened. "My solitude."

He braced an arm underneath his head. Hadrian stared down at me with languid eyes, but another part of him seemed ready and eager for my attention. The sheet above his lower half was tented.

I reached underneath the covers and grasped him.

Hadrian closed his eyes, his jaw clenched.

He was like hot granite and my mouth watered in anticipation. I wanted to feel him at the back of my throat.

I removed the sheet so I could see him in all his naked glory. I glided my lips over him, causing him to groan. I strung out his pleasure and his hands clenched at his sides. Watching the big, brawny man lose control made me feel powerful in a way I'd never felt before.

I owned a part of him like he owned a part of me, and when he came in my mouth, I swallowed every bit of him.

His skin was flushed and damp, and I kissed his taut belly before resting my cheek against him.

"Have you forgiven me?" he asked.

"For what?"

"For my domineering nature?"

I let out a laugh. "I guess it comes with the package. The whole beautiful, protective, generous package."

"I've never heard myself described that way, but I'll take it."

"You're also broody and terrifying."

He grasped my hip and gently pulled me toward him. "I thought you weren't afraid of me. Despite what you know about me."

"I'm not. I feel…protected around you. I can't explain it."

He stroked my spine, and like a whip, his next words made their mark. "I've invited your family here."

My heart kicked up in fear, and I shot up off of his chest to stare at him. "What? Why?"

He pondered my question for a moment. "It's two-fold. Your mother's debt must be settled. You can't go through life on the run. How do you know you haven't made a mistake, just like Sister Agatha? You're not a professional, Sterling. You could have already done something you're not aware of that puts you…no, *us*, in jeopardy. Your family is powerful, and if there's any chance in the world they might piece together who you are…I can't risk it. We have to settle it now. But your family are also the kind of people who might know who tried to kill me—and why. The assassin spoke Sicilian just before he died. These men have ears to the ground in their own country. If they know anything about what happened, I need them to tell me."

Chapter Twenty-Seven

Fear slashed my insides as my mind churned over Hadrian's announcement. I attempted to slow my racing heart.

My mind kicked into survival mode and traveled every avenue of thought. I would come face to face with my family, the very people who were never supposed to know about my existence. The people my mother had warned me about.

This next part is the most important of all—you cannot go to my family.

But Hadrian would be waving me in their face.

I instinctively clutched him tighter. Even though I trusted him, I was afraid, and we lay there in silence until I fell into a restless sleep.

A few hours later I awoke, my heart thundering in my chest. The alarm clock on the bedside table read 3:15. I didn't need to reach out to Hadrian's side of the bed to know he was gone. A patch of moonlight speckled the floor and my sluggish brain managed to piece together that the drapes on the balcony doors were pulled back.

I could see Hadrian's stark form through the glass, and I blanched when I realized he was bare-chested. The weather in Shetland had been steadily getting colder, and I couldn't imagine being out in the elements without being properly dressed. It had been raining only a few hours ago and the air was no doubt still cold.

I flipped on the bedside lamp and sleepily stuck my feet in the pair of slippers at the edge of the bed. After I got up, I grabbed the tartan wool blanket from the back of the leather couch, turned on the gas fireplace to dispel the chill in the air, and then went out onto the balcony.

Hadrian sat in a patio chair, not noticing my intrusion. Without a word, I placed the blanket around his shoulders. He grasped the edges and pulled it closer to him. I was just about to leave him to his thoughts, when he reached out and dragged me onto his lap. As I settled in his embrace, he nestled us under the blanket and I shivered from the coolness of his skin, even though we were cocooned in tartan.

"Stay with me," he said. "I don't want to be alone right now." There was a long pause as his skin began to warm beneath the blanket and then he said, "I dream about her. About finding her in the alley…"

I placed my forehead against the side of his head and closed my eyes. I couldn't imagine the type of nightmares that plagued him. But I understood wanting to change the past.

Lightning flashed over the ocean. The storm wasn't over after all.

"Come back to bed, Hadrian," I said quietly.

"I'll be there in a bit."

~

Ingrid served us breakfast on the balcony, but before she left, Hadrian told her to prepare for the visitors coming in a few days. She inclined her head and told him she'd see to it before leaving us alone.

I picked at the eggs in front of me, but Hadrian ate with verve and quickly cleared his plate. He dabbed his mouth with the linen napkin and then set it aside. He grabbed his steaming hot coffee and lifted the mug in his hand before looking at me.

"Is there something wrong with your food?" he asked.

I shook my head.

"Then why aren't you eating?" he demanded.

I picked up my fork and cut off a bite of egg before placing it in my mouth. I chewed for a few moments and then swallowed, and as much as I wanted to force another piece into my mouth, my stomach rolled at the thought.

"Are you all right? You look pale," he said, his hand reaching out to touch my face.

"I'm fine," I said and then forced a smile. "Didn't sleep well."

He nodded, his brow furrowed. "You're not having regrets about telling me who you are, are you?"

I adamantly shook my head.

"Then what is it? Tell me so I can alleviate your concerns."

"If only it were that easy." I'd had Ingrid bring me tea instead of coffee, and I took a sip of the soothing chamomile. "It's overwhelming, Hadrian. I've been on the run since I was a child, even though I didn't realize it. Then my mother killed herself. I spent months living in motels trying to figure out how to get a job under the table without providing any information and blew all the cash she left me. When I finally found work, it only paid for a shitty basement apartment and Ramen noodles. There were some days I ate one meal… It was so hard, you don't understand—"

"*I* don't understand? I lived on the streets of Edinburgh and fought for my money."

"You're right, I didn't mean—"

"You're not alone in this, Sterling. The nightmare is over now."

"Is it?" My brow wrinkled as I turned pensive. "I didn't expect to care about you, Hadrian. Now that I do, I'm afraid I made a mistake by staying. What if you're in danger because of me? I couldn't bear it if anything happened to you because of who I am. I never should've taken this contract. I never should've let it get this far."

He leaned back in his chair and studied me. "Do you really think you had a choice?"

"What's that supposed to mean?"

"I mean, there isn't anything I wouldn't have done to seduce you into coming to my island."

"I should've done more to resist you."

"It's impossible to resist me."

I smiled absently as I sipped my tea. If only I was a normal girl, and I'd come here without any baggage. My situation had complicated our lives together.

"We need to discuss how things are going to go when your family is here," Hadrian said. "I've invited them to discuss what happened to me, but I haven't mentioned you yet."

I let out a slow exhale. "So they don't know about me?"

"No. I'll call you Eden in their presence up until it's time to discuss your situation. You will stand by my side and act as my hostess."

"Do we have to tell them?" I exclaimed. "I mean, they don't know about me. Maybe they'll never find out about me."

Hadrian leaned over and placed his large hand on my arm. "I told you: You can't live your life on the run. What would that look like for us? Hmm? You, stuck here on my island because we don't know if there's a trail? The rest of your life spent making sure the Foscari don't ever learn of your whereabouts? No, Sterling. We're going to tell your family and I'm going to pay whatever it is I have to pay to buy your freedom, and then we get to move on with our lives."

I set down my mug and got up from the table. I perched in his lap and wrapped my arms around him, needing the strength of him to be real. "I don't know what I did to deserve you, Hadrian Rhys."

His large hand stole across my back. "And here I was, thinking the same thing about you."

The air between us had changed. There were no longer any secrets. The veil had been lifted, and we were together as one.

United.

Committed to each other in a way I'd never expected.

I trusted him implicitly. I trusted him to protect me from the ruthlessness of the *Compagnia Bianca de Falco*.

He took me to bed, a relentless, feral beast. It was as if he was proving to me and to himself that he was the one in control. I cried out and tightened around him from the all-consuming pleasure, giving another piece of myself to Hadrian. In his bed, I found honesty and truth. I found absolution and safety. I found what I hadn't ever expected to find.

A few days later, I stood slightly behind him, prepared to greet the four Moretti men that Hadrian had invited into his home. Wind from the sea whipped the hair I had tied back into a ponytail across my shoulders as Hadrian and I waited on the roof.

"Even though the Moretti and I have a mutually beneficial business relationship, I would never call Angelo a friend. He would never call me a friend either, and it's rare that these men do business with non-Italians."

"So, why *do* they do business with you?"

He shot me an amused look. "Power is power. Even they can't deny that. I'm not a billionaire by chance, Sterling."

Was Hadrian's power enough to get me out of this clusterfuck of a situation?

Helicopter engines growled into existence, and a silver metal beast appeared in the sky as the beating of its rotors sprayed mist through the air. It landed on a giant "H" on Hadrian's helipad.

The door of the helicopter opened, and a man wearing a three-piece gray suit climbed out.

Huge. Bold. He strode with purpose, embodying wealth and luxury. His dark hair had threads of gray at the temples and was tastefully gelled off his forehead. His face betrayed no emotion whatsoever as he approached Hadrian. His skin was a naturally healthy bronze, and though his brow was furrowed with wrinkles, I couldn't tell his age.

Three men dressed in a similar fashion trailed behind him, all with the same dark hair and eyes.

The helicopter's rotors flattened, and the wind and sound diminished at once as the engines began to settle in a high-pitched, dying whine.

Hadrian grasped the man's outstretched palm when he was within distance.

"Thank you for coming on such short notice," Hadrian said in flawless Italian.

"My pleasure," the man returned politely as his dark gaze slid to me.

Hadrian reached behind me to drag me forward so he could drape his arm around me in a show of possession. "This is Eden."

The man held out his hand, and I set my palm against his. His skin was warm and smooth. "Angelo," he greeted in English. "Pleasure."

"The pleasure is all mine," I replied, trying not to gape at the man who was my uncle.

Angelo peered at Hadrian's battered face. "What happened to you?"

"I'll explain later. You're welcome to speak in your native tongue while you're here," Hadrian said. "Eden speaks fluent Italian."

I detected a flicker of interest enter Angelo's expression before he hid it. "We will discuss pleasantries in English and business in Italian. You are our host, and I will honor you by speaking in your native tongue."

Hadrian nodded.

Angelo dropped my hand and turned to the men behind him. "My younger brother, Nico. My heir, Luca. My second eldest, Tor."

The three men inclined their heads, but otherwise remained silent. Nico was thinner than Angelo, his nose more aquiline. He wasn't nearly as compelling to look at. Luca and Tor resembled their father, but while Luca's face appeared open and curious, Tor's remained shuttered. He stared at me underneath thick dark brows, and I had to stop myself from shivering. There was something unnerving in his solid, milk-chocolate gaze.

I tried not to stare at the men I was related to, but I kept stealing glances in an attempt to take them in.

Hadrian had informed me that no business would be discussed until pleasantries and decorum had been exchanged.

"We have refreshments waiting for you on the rooftop terrace," I said with a red-lipped smile. "The rain will hold a bit longer. Would you like to take a few minutes and enjoy the view?"

I felt Hadrian's coiled tension like it was my own.

He turned his attention to Nico, and then Angelo swooped in immediately and offered me his arm in a gesture of old-world, gentlemanly charm. My hand trembled when I touched him.

"Hadrian didn't mention a woman would be here with him," Angelo said. We glided away from the helipad toward the other side of the roof.

He didn't sound upset, but he was clearly fishing for information. "And he definitely didn't mention it would be a woman who speaks Italian."

I forced a smile but didn't reply. It was better to say as little as possible. Fear—and revulsion—were dueling inside of me. This man, Angelo, was my mother's older brother. Instead of protecting her, he'd gone along with their father's edict and attempted to marry her off to the Foscari.

I hated him.

Everything about him and what he stood for was vile. I hated that he was the head of the Moretti family and with his power he could control the outcome of my life.

Hate was better than fear, but I commanded myself to stay calm. No good would come of letting my emotions get the better of me. Hadrian would take care of the situation, and then I'd never have to see these people ever again.

One end of the rooftop deck had expensive lounge chairs nestled underneath a small white tent. A man in a black chef's coat and hat stood behind a long rectangular glass table with at least ten chafing dishes. A server waited at a portable stainless-steel bar with his hands behind his back in a show of stoic professionalism.

Ingrid had ensured everything was ready for Angelo's impending arrival. Because money was no object when Hadrian wanted something, it had all been handled quickly and without issue.

"We have everything you could want," I said to Angelo, guiding him to the bar. "Italian sodas, amaros—"

"I don't want to eat and drink the same things I'd eat and drink at home," Angelo said, interrupting me. "I'm not in Italy, am I?"

I blinked, unprepared for such a twist. "I thought you'd want to be comfortable—"

"I'm always comfortable," he said, his tone dark. "Except when someone tries to think for me."

He stared at me and I stared back. Out of my peripheral vision, I saw Hadrian gesture to the chef. The other men clearly didn't share Angelo's feelings and instead took the offered plates.

I looked at the bartender and said, "Two glasses of SINNERS, please. Three drops of water in each."

The bartender quickly made the drinks and handed them over.

Angelo lifted the glass of scotch to his nose and inhaled and then took a sip. I watched him roll the liquid gold around his mouth, but he still didn't show any emotion at all.

I took a small sip of my own drink despite the fact that I planned to remain sober. I didn't want alcohol to nourish my rage. I had to keep my head about me.

Time in Hadrian's presence had begun to change me, and I now enjoyed the bold, peaty flavor of SINNERS scotch.

Without a word, Angelo left the bar and went to recline in one of the comfortable chairs. His sons were already sitting with plates of food resting on their laps.

Nico stood at the edge of the rooftop deck, gazing out across the horizon, but then eventually wandered to the lounge furniture and took a seat. Ignoring the men, I went to the table of food and made myself a plate of homemade burrata and heirloom tomatoes. I thanked the chef with a smile and then took the plate to the balcony and rested it on the wall. I was in the middle of chewing when Luca, Angelo's heir apparent—and my cousin—came to stand next to me.

The ocean air whipped his dark hair and the sunlight highlighted his patrician nose and sculpted mouth. He looked at me and grinned.

I gazed at him, wary.

"Eden," he said, my name rolling off his tongue, "tell me something."

I arched a brow and waited.

"You're not really as compliant as you appear to be, are you?"

"What makes you think that?"

He cocked his head to the side and examined me. "I can see the fire in your eyes."

I didn't like that he was attempting to figure me out. "You have far too much Italian charm."

"An Italian can never have too much charm," he quipped. "Besides, I get it from my father. DNA doesn't lie."

I looked in Hadrian's direction; he was engaged in conversation with Nico and Angelo.

"How did you meet Hadrian? He's something of a recluse, no?" Luca asked, pulling my attention back to him.

"Ramsey Buchanan introduced us."

Luca nodded slowly. "Ramsey. Yes, that makes sense."

"You know Ramsey?"

"I know Ramsey," he repeated. "We have…history."

What history could Ramsey Buchanan possibly have with The White Company? I wondered.

Luca nodded toward the ocean. "It's beautiful."

"It is."

"I'm not sure I could stand the weather here, or the fact that it gets dark early in the winter."

"Getting dark early in the winter also means it stays light late in the summer."

"Have you been here through a winter?"

"Not yet."

"But you're staying."

"I'd like to," I answered truthfully.

Something passed between us, but I wasn't sure what it was. Luca hadn't come right out and asked who I was to Hadrian, or what I meant to him, but his curiosity was palpable.

"I've never been to Italy," I said in an attempt to turn the conversation. "What's it like where you live?"

"A quintessential postcard. Vineyards as far as the eye can see. The earth…it smells like—like warmth, and you can tell that it's alive. It's nothing like this wild, barren country."

Despite my desire to remain aloof, I had Luca's undivided attention. He wasn't the only one who was curious though, so I inquired, "And your home? Is it as imposing as Hadrian's?"

He smiled. "Yes, but in a completely different way. It's

a sprawling estate that sits at the top of a hill. At night, the sky is so clear you can ride a horse by the light of the moon."

I could picture it clearly in my mind's eye. A chill went up my spine.

With bold familiarity, he reached over to my plate and plucked a slice of tomato and stuck it in his mouth. Luca radiated the seductive charm and sensual pleasure that could only come from a man of his background. It had been bred into him, and he could no sooner change it than he could the color of his hair. He was one of those men who enjoyed being around women in any capacity. He wasn't hunting me the way aggressive men had done in the past, even though he didn't know I was his cousin—and I knew that was his true power. He had the ability to hide his intentions behind a veneer of good humor and indolent indifference, but I knew what was beneath his facade.

"How old are you?" I asked him.

"Twenty-eight."

"Your father doesn't look old enough to have a twenty-eight-year old son."

"He married young," he said with a shrug.

"Do you have siblings? Aside from Tor?"

"A younger sister. You're an inquisitive woman…"

"Just trying to make polite conversation."

"In that case, it's my turn to ask you some questions."

"You've already asked me some questions," I pointed out.

"Humor me."

He took another slice of tomato, and I smacked his hand before I could stop myself. "Get your own."

"But it's so much better from your plate." He winked. "Hadrian mentioned you speak Italian."

"That's not a question."

"Luca," Angelo called to his son. "Join us."

"Ah, just when I was getting somewhere, my father summons me," Luca lamented with a mocking bow, which instantly made me grin.

I breathed the scent of the ocean in deep, holding it in my lungs before releasing it to steady my nerves. For one brief moment, I'd forgotten that Luca was a Moretti. His urbane charm had lulled me into an easy banter. I hated that I'd forgotten, and I hated that I wanted to know more about him and his family.

My family.

I was just about to cut another bite of burrata when Hadrian called my name.

It was an edict. A dictum.

I held in a frustrated sigh and went to him. There was no empty seat next to Hadrian, and just when I thought I would have to stand behind his shoulder, as Nico stood behind Angelo's and Tor behind Luca's, Hadrian reached his arm around my waist and pulled me onto his lap.

I kept my face devoid of expression even though annoyance surged within. Hadrian was publicly staking his claim, and in that moment, I was a Rex girl once again.

Angelo stared at me for long enough to make me uncomfortable, but when he finally spoke, he addressed Hadrian. "She reminds me of Barrett Campbell."

It was subtle, the tension of Hadrian's thigh underneath me. "She's nothing like Flynn's wife," Hadrian said, his hand stroking my back.

"It was a compliment," Angelo stated. "Barrett is in a class above the rest."

"She is," Hadrian agreed.

Angelo suddenly smiled. "If Barrett were ever to be in

the position of becoming a widow, I would pursue her. Even though she isn't Italian. For her, I'd overlook that flaw."

The wind changed, bringing with it the aroma of an oncoming storm, signaling the end of our time on the roof.

"I'll show you gentlemen to the dock," Hadrian said, gently patting me into standing. "Your guest house is on another island so you can enjoy your privacy. Take some time to settle in. The boat will come for you tonight at seven to bring you here. Dinner will be at seven-thirty in the dining room, and then we can discuss why I've asked you to come."

"Thank you for the view," Luca said with a wink at me. "The ocean was lovely, too."

I stoically stared at Luca as Hadrian's arm tightened around me. I placed my hand on his chest in a delicate but pointed signal to stand down.

"I told your beautiful companion about our home," he said. "She didn't seem impressed."

Hadrian's grin was fierce. "She doesn't impress easily."

"If you'll excuse me," I said, moving away from Hadrian. "I'll leave you men to it. Feel free to continue discussing me when I am no longer within ear shot."

I turned and headed to the door that would lead me to the stairs into Hadrian's home. Even though the wind kicked up, I could still hear Angelo's voice as he said, "She *definitely* reminds me of Barrett Campbell."

"What are you doing? Why is Ingrid cooking? That's Paulo's job," Hadrian said not half an hour later when he entered the kitchen.

I gently grasped Hadrian's arm and led him away while Ingrid called out commands and barked orders like a drill sergeant. It was uncharacteristic of her, but Paulo and his crew jumped to, not at all bothered to do her bidding. There was something endearing about Ingrid's ability to take charge, and it made me smile.

"We made a mistake offering the Moretti Italian cuisine."

"How do you know that was a mistake?" Hadrian asked as we entered the den. "I didn't hear any complaints."

I went to the liquor cart and poured two glasses of amaro. I handed him one and then sat down on the couch next to him.

"Angelo made it clear when I was talking with him at the bar. We will never do better than they can do themselves. Not when it comes to Italian food. So, let's not compete. Let's show them something different."

"Different like Scottish cuisine different?"

I grinned. "No. Ingrid's cooking different."

Hadrian smiled back. "Aye." He pulled me into his side, and I kicked off my heels so I could curl into him. "How are you? Are you okay?"

"I guess. I can't believe I just met my family and they don't even realize who I am. I'm so…" I paused thoughtfully. "Angry, Hadrian. I'm *so* fucking angry. I hate them so much. I hate them for the way I grew up, for the fact that they gave my mother over to the Foscari and that because of them she chose to run. But you know what I hate more than all of that?"

"No, what?"

"I hate that I'm so damn curious about them."

Hadrian's hand stroked up and down my back. "I don't like how he looks at you."

"Luca? You don't need to worry about him. He's a harmless flirt. All part of the Italian charm. Besides, that'll change when he realizes we're related."

"Not Luca. Angelo."

My heartbeat escalated. "How does he look at me?"

"Like he's trying to piece you together. He can't take his eyes off of you. Even when you were standing on the terrace talking to Luca, Angelo's attention always came back to you. It's not sexual with him, it's something else."

"Do you think he knows who I am?"

"I don't know. How much do you look like your mother?"

I shook my head. "Not very much. I guess I resemble my father. I wouldn't know though, having never seen any pictures of him."

We sipped our amaros and enjoyed the reprieve from our guests. I was still uneasy that Hadrian knew the truth about me, and yet I felt like I was able to finally speak freely, without concern.

"Nico and Tor don't say much," I said.

"They're second in commands. They're meant to watch and protect. To remain vigilant and get their hands dirty when it's necessary. Angelo and Luca lead."

"I didn't quite understand what my mother meant until now."

"What do you mean?"

"She tried to explain as best she could in the letter about bloodlines and legacies. But meeting Angelo and the rest of them, I finally get it. It's the way they carry themselves. Like they've never been told no…like they're part of something ancient and sacred. It's more than just a high opinion of self-worth. It's like they rule the world…"

He snorted. "They're modern Romans—and you're right, they've never been told no."

"If they've never been told no, then how will you be able to—"

He placed his lips on mine and silenced my concerns. When he pulled away he said, "I'll take care of it. They might be modern Romans, but I'm a modern Viking."

Chapter Twenty-Eight

My dress dipped low in the front showing off the swell of my breasts. The back was cut into a "V", which bared the golden skin of my shoulder blades.

Hadrian stood behind me in an immaculately tailored suit, tracing the curve of my neck with his finger. My hair had been put up to draw attention to my curves.

"How do I look?" I asked his reflection.

His eyes were dark. "Almost perfect."

"Almost?" I repeated in mock outrage. "Do you know how long it took me to do my hair and makeup?"

He grinned, and from his inner breast pocket, he revealed a long skinny jewelry box. He flipped it open and presented it to me. It was a delicate, diamond leaf tennis bracelet that appeared to resemble leaves on a vine. He quickly fastened it around my left wrist and then kissed my palm while I gaped at him.

"That's not all," Hadrian said, heading to his night-stand drawer. He pulled out a fine box and showed me a matching set of earrings and necklace. "The jewelry will be all you're wearing when I fuck you from behind later tonight."

I wobbled in my heels as he approached me. "Jesus, Hadrian."

Grinning, he nipped my shoulder. "Sterling?"

"Hmm?"

"Are you ready?"

Was I? Not even a little bit. I wasn't prepared to tell my family the truth, but the sooner it was out in the open, the sooner it would be behind us.

"What happens if they don't believe me?" I asked, my voice low.

"If they don't believe your words, then you'll show them your eyes. It's an undeniable Moretti trait."

"And then what?"

"Then they leave, and our lives return to normal. Dinners on the terrace, helicopter rides to Lerwick to go exploring, taking Aegir out and sightseeing the other islands. Whatever we want, Sterling."

I shook my head and pressed my hand to his lapel. "No, I meant, what does this mean for me and my family? You have business dealings with them, but I don't want them in my life, Hadrian."

"Then they won't be." He took my hand and brought it to his lips. "After tonight, you'll never have to see them again if you don't want to."

Our moment was interrupted by a knock on the door. Hadrian called, "Come in," and Ingrid popped her head inside.

"They're here," she announced.

"Thank you. We'll be right out."

The door closed, giving us privacy once again. Shivering in trepidation, I quickly put on the earrings and necklace, and then Hadrian escorted me out of the bedroom to the den. Feeling the need to be protected, I appreciated his possessive touch now more than ever.

I forced a megawatt smile for our guests, who were already waiting in the den. Hadrian released me and then Luca took my hand and brought it to his lips in greeting, which made Hadrian take an unmistakable step closer to me.

"Gentlemen," I welcomed. "Good evening. What can I get everyone to drink?"

I went to the liquor cart after taking their orders, and I wasn't surprised when Luca sidled up next to me.

"Your boyfriend doesn't like me very much," he said.

"He's not my boyfriend," I said automatically.

"Oh?" His eyes scanned my ears. "Nice earrings."

"Thank you." I handed Luca his Compari and soda.

"If he's not your boyfriend, what is he?"

"That's none of your business."

He took a sip of his drink and then sighed. "Can I give you a word of advice?"

"I'd rather you didn't."

Luca blinked and then a crack of laughter escaped his lips. "All right then."

"How's the guest house?" I asked.

"Very comfortable. A home away from home."

"Why do I remind your father of Barrett Campbell?" I asked, my gaze sliding to a distant Hadrian. He was conversing with Nico and Angelo, and Tor sat by himself slightly farther away. Definitely the broody silent type.

Luca smiled slightly and his eyes took on a dreamy quality. "Barrett Campbell is the only woman to ever put my father in his place. Hadrian's wrong, you know."

"About?"

"You and Barrett do have a lot in common. My father

paid you the highest compliment when he said you were like her." He peered at me. "Have you met her?"

"No."

"But it was Ramsey Buchanan who introduced you to Hadrian?"

"Yes," I said, brow furrowing. "What does that have to do with anything?"

"Flynn and Ramsey are as close as brothers. I would've thought you'd have met her."

He was digging for information and not being at all subtle about it.

Ingrid appeared in the den, wiping her hands on a dishtowel. Her eyes caught mine, and I was grateful for a reason to flee the conversation.

"Dinner is ready," I announced to the room.

Hadrian arrived at my side and escorted me into the dining room. The table was set with a red satin tablecloth and white china. He helped me with my seat and then took the spot at the head of the table. Angelo sat at the other end. Luca was across from me on Hadrian's left, his brother at his side. Nico took the chair at Angelo's left, which put him next to me.

A bouquet of purple sterling roses rested in the center of the table. I looked at Hadrian who inclined his head and then winked.

I placed my napkin in my lap, unable to stop the rush of pleasure from Hadrian's subtle tribute to me. Pleasure mingled with anxiety.

The first course was served along with crisp white wine.

"This is delicious," Angelo declared, taking another spoonful of soup. "I'm impressed."

"It was Eden's idea for a menu change," Hadrian said easily.

Eyes turned to me. "I can't take any credit for the food. It's all Ingrid."

The table was relatively silent, devoid of conversation. Hadrian sat, his body erect, and I knew he wanted to get to the heart of the matter and discuss why they were there.

But Angelo showed no inclination to do business. He was enjoying his meal, and nothing important would be dealt with until the coffees and brandies were poured.

Even though I had no inclination to be sociable, the suspense was killing me, and I decided I'd rather make polite conversation than sit in silence with my inner turmoil.

I looked at Luca. "You mentioned riding horses at your home. Do you still ride?"

He nodded. "We've got an impressive stable. What about you? Do you ride?"

"I'm new to it," I admitted. I reached over and placed my hand on top of Hadrian's, which rested casually on the table. "Hadrian bought a mare for his mount, Midas, and he let me name her. I've been riding her most mornings, when the weather holds."

Luca looked at Hadrian and then back to me. "You let her name your mare?"

"It made her happy," Hadrian said with a negligent shrug. "And besides, it's her mare now."

"What did you name her?" Tor asked, breaking his silence. His voice was as dark as Luca's was light. It was clear he wasn't used to conversing, and as Angelo's second son, he didn't have to be affable or charming.

"My brother has a way with horses," Luca explained with an amused grin.

Luca teased his brother with good-natured affection, yet Tor didn't appear to hear him, nor did he engage.

"I named her Eris," I said. "The Goddess of—"

"Discord," Angelo finished.

"She nipped my shoulder when I wouldn't give her a carrot," I said, forcing a grin. "The name seemed obvious to me."

"Midas likes his spirited mare," Hadrian said. His tone was overtly suggestive, and heat crept up my neck when his eyes blatantly caressed me.

It made me think of his promise earlier when he'd given me jewelry, and I couldn't stop the flash of desire I felt between my thighs.

"She's the kind of mare that's full of adventure," I said. "Hadrian has been very generous to me."

The table fell into a companionable silence as we continued to eat.

Luca broke the quiet when he said, "I'm dying of curiosity. I know *Papà* always insists on waiting until dessert to discuss business, but I'm from a different generation, and I think we should get to the point of our meeting."

"Your generation has no patience," Angelo remarked with amusement. "But I have to say I'm also intrigued enough to dispense with ceremony. I'm ready to proceed."

He looked at me, but I made no move to get up.

"She stays," Hadrian said quietly, his voice steel.

"Are you sure?" Angelo asked.

"Aye. I want her to hear all of it."

"All right then." He leaned back in his chair and waited for Hadrian to speak.

"A few nights ago, an assassin broke into my home," Hadrian began, switching from English to Italian. "It's never been done before. You know the precautions I take to prevent things like that. The assassin and I fought— hand to hand—he escaped, but not without injury. My head of security was able to find him before he got off the island. When I went to question him the next morning, he broke a cyanide capsule inserted into his tongue. He cursed at me in Sicilian before he killed himself. He died before I learned anything of value."

Hadrian's fist rested next to his plate, and he slowly unclenched it. "So, my question to you is, who is desperate enough to kill a man as powerful as me even though I have a dead man's switch in place?"

I frowned, not understanding the term.

"Sicilian…do you think it's one of the five families?" Luca asked after a moment. The question wasn't directed at Hadrian, but at his father.

Angelo slowly scratched his clean-shaven jaw. "Perhaps."

"Are you sure it was Sicilian?" Luca asked.

"Of course I'm sure," Hadrian said, his face clouding with annoyance. "Who would stand to gain the most from my death?"

"The Lanzas are the only one of the five families that are Sicilian," Nico said.

"It wasn't the Lanzas," Angelo rebutted. "The head of their family just died and now his sons are fighting amongst each other for the right to lead. They wouldn't benefit from Hadrian's death." He paused for a moment and then said, "It couldn't have been the Foscari, either. If they'd wanted something done, they would have done it themselves. They'd never send a Sicilian to do their dirty work."

I reached for my glass of water with the intention of taking a long sip to steady my nerves, but instead of grasping the stem, my fingers fumbled, and I knocked it over.

Angelo's eyes locked onto mine and for a brief moment, my heart felt as though it was going to burst out of my chest.

Luca jumped up immediately, grabbing his napkin from his lap and hastily covering the spill.

"I'm sorry," I whispered.

"No harm done," Luca said absently, tossing the soiled napkin on the table.

I rose from my seat with the intention of getting Luca a clean linen. As I headed to the china hutch, my back was to the table, giving me a moment to compose myself.

"That leaves only the Sforza or the Borgia," Hadrian said after a spell of silence.

I opened the drawer and pulled out a napkin and brought it to Luca. He smiled his thanks, and I reached around him to grab the wet napkin and remove it from the table.

"It's not the Sforza," Nico piped up. "They wouldn't do anything that takes time away from expanding their fashion empire. It's already worth over a billion dollars and they're not prone to violence anyway. It doesn't make sense for them to make a move like that."

"It's without question the Borgia," Tor said firmly.

Everyone turned to look at him. His brother peered at him in curiosity. "We're leaning that direction, clearly, but how do you know for sure, Tor," Luca asked. "It could be another lesser known aristocratic family trying to make a name for themselves and worm their way to the top."

"The Borgia have no code of honor." Tor shook his head. "About a year ago, the Borgia were caught human trafficking through the ports by members of an Italian Secret Police organization. I wouldn't put it past Carlo Borgia to make a deal with the government. Think about it, how do you save your own skin? You turn in a bigger fish—a rival."

"But how does killing Hadrian help the Borgia?" I

asked in confusion, my stomach turning at the thought of human trafficking.

Hadrian looked at me. "I'm an *utpresser*, a professional blackmailer. If I die, everything I know about the five families will become public. That's the dead man's switch. If anyone kills me, a whole slew of people go down in flames."

"But why would the Borgia be okay with their own secrets coming out? That's what would've happened if the assassin had been successful, right?" I asked, still trying to piece it all together.

Angelo picked up the thread of conversation. "If the Borgia got immunity from the government, they don't care about their own secrets coming out and it will leave the other four families vulnerable. It will take time to verify this. But if it's true, it needs to be handled delicately and quietly."

"We can handle it quietly if you want, but an example needs to be made," Hadrian said, his tone dark.

Angelo nodded. "It will be done."

"Good." He paused. "There's another reason why I invited you here. It wasn't just about the assassin."

All eyes were on Hadrian, giving him their undivided attention.

"I also invited you here to reunite you with your kin."

Nico's brows snapped together.

"Kin?" Angelo repeated. "What are you talking about?"

Hadrian looked at me and gave a nod.

I took a deep breath and after a moment I said, "My name isn't Eden. It's Sterling. And my mother was Violetta Moretti."

There was a stunned silence in the room and then Nico

erupted. "Impossible!" His body quivered as though he was barely able to control himself.

Angelo's face was inscrutable. He stared at me and then glanced at Hadrian. When his eyes came back to mine, he said, "Child, I don't know what you're up to, but you had better explain yourself. Where is my sister? If you know—"

"My mother is dead. You are Angelo Moretti, and within you flows the blood of the *Compagnia Bianca del Falco*. My mother fled Italy after the Foscari murdered my father, Gianni Russo. She went to the United States and raised me in secret. I've spent my entire life on the run, but it ends here and now, and I can prove to you who I am."

Angelo's expression contorted as he struggled to process what I'd just told him, and as he was about to say something, Hadrian raised a hand and said, "*No.* Wait. She'll show you."

I looked to the ceiling and removed my right contact lens. I blinked a few times to clear my vision, and then lowered my gaze to reveal a brilliant turquoise blue eye to the room.

Angelo flinched. Luca gasped. Nico gripped the edge of the table. Tor didn't react at all.

I took out my left contact lens in the same fashion, uncovering a green eye the color of peridot.

The Moretti men stared at me in shock.

Angelo swallowed a few times, clearly attempting to find his voice. "When did Violetta die?"

I glanced at Hadrian, silently calling on his strength. "A little over a year ago."

"How did she…" Nico trailed off, sounding drained of all his energy.

"She took her own life," I swallowed, "to protect me. She was afraid the Foscari would find me…and she warned me not to come to you. But here we are, and I have to know; did you know that she was pregnant when she left Italy?"

"No," Angelo said. "We had no idea. Neither did the Foscari. They've been looking for Violetta, and as far as we knew, they never caught up with her. Our business with them ended after she slighted their family, and we haven't been in contact with them for years. She embarrassed us in a way you can't understand. She spat on the legacy of generations past. She turned her back on family for the love of a man who was unworthy, and by doing so she has dragged the Moretti name through the filth."

"*Papà*," Tor said.

"Yes, son," Angelo said with a nod at his second eldest. To me, he stated, "We have a chance now to make things right for generations. *You* will help us make things right."

The finality of his statement sent a pit of despair deep into my belly. He finally rose from his seat, as did Nico and Tor.

Hadrian's voice lashed like a whip. "Sterling was not raised by the *Compagnia Bianca del Falco*. She is under no obligation to honor her mother's pledge." His jaw was tight with anger.

"But she is Violetta's daughter, and the Foscari *deserve* restitution," Angelo said.

"There is another option," Hadrian said, taking my hand and pulling me to his side. He didn't wait for Angelo to speak, "You have a daughter. Marry her to the Foscari. Sterling is already promised. To me."

I inhaled a sharp gasp at Hadrian's public declaration. His words resounded through the room even after he fell silent. The two men at the opposite ends of the table stared at one another.

"I like you, Hadrian," Angelo said finally. "I've always

admired you—what you've built, coming from nothing. But as powerful and wealthy as you are, you are not one of the five families of Italy, and you don't understand our code of honor. It doesn't matter how many islands you buy or how much wealth you acquire, you will never be one of us. You will never be good enough to marry a Moretti."

"I don't think I've made myself clear," Hadrian stated, his eyes turning feral. "Sterling will leave this island over my dead body."

They continued to stare each other down, two allies who had become opponents.

Because of me.

Angelo turned his chin ever so slightly, diverting my attention.

In one expert, calculated move, Luca stood from his chair and darted toward Hadrian, striking him hard and fast in the throat. While Hadrian was stunned, Luca produced a syringe and plunged it into the side of Hadrian's neck.

Hadrian's left hand went to his throat as he gasped for air and after a few seconds, his eyes rolled into the back of his head. His palm slid from mine and I gulped in terror as his body slackened, slumping against the arm of his chair.

"What did you do?" I whispered in horror.

"He'll live, Sterling. But you're coming with us," Angelo said, straightening the cuff of his shirt. "Nico?"

Before I knew what was happening, Nico all but launched himself toward me. His hand clamped around the back of my neck and he squeezed once hard enough to make me light-headed and then he let go. Then he tapped his thumb hard and fast against my temple.

Everything went dark.

Chapter Twenty-Nine

I rolled over, expecting to feel Hadrian in bed next to me, but his side was cold—which suddenly made me lurch up in fear.

I was not in Hadrian's bed.

I was no longer in Hadrian's home.

My breaths came in spurts, and I focused on drawing air into my lungs. Terror, unlike anything I'd ever known before, pierced my soul.

Now I was under the control of my family—family that had driven my mother to flee her home. Family that had stood by and let my father be murdered in cold blood.

God, no.

I lifted my knees to my chest. I was on a comfortable four-poster wooden bed with blue and gold paisley drapes. A rope of golden threads kept the draperies from closing. I reached out to touch one of the tassels.

Hadrian.

I clenched my fist and shoved it in my mouth, biting down hard on my knuckles, refusing to scream.

Hadrian.

A bout of longing hit me so deep that it felt like it had cleaved me in half, and I sucked in a breath of air.

He had claimed me. He promised to protect me from my family. He would come for me.

All I had to do was hold on and trust him.

My heart stuttered in my chest, and then like a stick trapped in the spoke of a wheel, my world came to a grinding halt. A cold blanket of shock enveloped me.

It was as if I'd lived through enough tragedy, enough pain, enough guilt, and my mind had finally said *enough*.

Daylight streamed through the large glass windows in the room. I untangled my limbs and climbed out of bed, realizing I was still in my dress and jewelry from the previous evening. Only my heels were missing.

I walked to a set of glass doors that led to a stone balcony and looked out. A sprawling, manicured garden went on for as far as the eye could see. It reminded me of the garden at The Mansion, the place I'd spent my first night with—

I doubted the doors were unlocked; why would my family take any chances that I might escape?

I was my mother's daughter, after all.

My hand went to the doors anyway. Surprise sparked inside of me when they opened freely, and I stepped out onto the balcony and took a deep breath of warm air. I smelled earth and soil, not ocean and mountains.

I had no idea of my exact location—Luca had never mentioned where in Italy he lived. Yet when I breathed in, the scent of vines tickled the back of my throat and I knew instantly I was in the home my mother had grown up in.

The land called to me. It was innately in my blood, and though I'd never visited the vineyards, or been weaned on the stories of my ancestors, something clicked into place inside of me. A feeling of belonging, a kinship.

I heard the faintest sound of the bedroom door opening but refused to turn to see who'd come. Leather soles padded across the wooden floor before halting a few feet behind me.

"You're awake," Luca said as he came to stand next to me on the balcony.

I touched the side of my head where it was sore from Nico's strike. "What happened? How did I—"

"Family secret," he said without smiling. "Every Moretti knows specific pressure points that will either result in death, or unconsciousness."

"Every Moretti male, you mean?"

"Yes." He stared at me pensively. "Cousin—"

"*Don't* call me that."

"But we are cousins," he said.

"No. I am no more than a pawn to you."

Anger and hatred ripped through me, but it wasn't a hot, blistering ember. It was a ball of ice, and it continued to spread through my body, freezing everything that had once made me, *me*.

"So? What will happen now? Are you and your father going to keep me locked in this room?" My tone was bitter, but Luca didn't rise to the bait.

"The doors aren't locked, but times have changed. We won't lose you like we lost Violetta. You have no allies here, no money, nothing. If you run, we will hunt you down and bring you back. You will marry Raphael Foscari and unite the Foscari and the Moretti once and for all."

"*Fuck you*, Luca. I'm not a Moretti. You are not my people."

His eyes hardened. "Do you know why I'm up here with you instead of my father or my brother? Because unlike them, my heart isn't dead. I saw the way you and Hadrian looked at each other. I'm sorry there was nothing to be done about it. If I were in charge of the family, I'd —" He abruptly cut himself off. "This is out of my hands. I am my father's son and I *am* a Moretti." His tone turned frigid as he went on, "Your life is at stake, Sterling. If you accept your fate, if you align yourself with us, if you make good on your mother's unfulfilled promise, then you will live a good life. The Foscari will treat you the way you were always meant to be treated—as a Moretti married into their own family."

"You want to give me to the people that murdered my father and hunted my mother," I lashed out.

"You only have to fear them if you are their enemy, and right now you are. So, make this right." His hands dropped from my shoulders. "You have two choices, Sterling. You can marry Raphael Foscari. You can give him heirs. You can be treated as a queen. Or…"

"Or?" I prodded.

He turned his attention to the gardens. "Or I can leave you unattended for a few minutes. You're on the sixth floor. Your only way out of this is death. I hope I've made myself clear."

I blinked. "Jump? You expect me to jump?"

"No. I don't expect you to jump. You're a Moretti. I expect you to survive."

We stared at one another, bound by blood. My kin.

"Hadrian will come for me," I vowed. "And when he does, you will beg for mercy, Luca."

"Accept your fate, Sterling."

I turned away from him and gripped the stone balcony, swallowing the rage that threatened to overtake me.

The Moretti expected me to marry a man who was not the one I loved, or die by my own hand.

They were cruel and calculating, and Hadrian had

underestimated their reaction to finding out who I was. He thought he could use power and wealth to save me.

He was wrong.

"I'll send someone to help you bathe and dress," Luca said, interrupting my thoughts.

I frowned. "Why?"

He righted his shirt cuff. "Family meal."

"I'm not hungry."

"It doesn't matter," he stated. "*Papà* has requested your presence."

When he stepped away from the balcony and headed into the bedroom, I called out to him, "You're the most dangerous of all, Luca."

He didn't stop his long stride to the exit, but I knew he heard what I said.

Luca *was* the most dangerous. His power wasn't derived from violence alone. He had the ability to seduce with charm and humor. He didn't need to use his fists; Luca was a master manipulator. A natural orator. A true Roman Caesar.

Forty minutes later, I looked at my reflection in the mirror. I had concealed my eyes since I was a child, and now I was baring them for the world to see. They might've been a part of my legacy, but they were foreign, even to me.

Luca came to escort me to the formal dining room. As we walked down the lavish staircase, I took in the beauty of The White Company ancestral home. Irreplaceable Renaissance art hung on the walls, ornate rugs covered gold inlaid marble floors, and gleaming wooden furniture spanned fashions over the course of hundreds of years. The worth of each piece would be incalculable to all but the world's finest antique dealers.

The wealth was so encompassing that I briefly

wondered if I'd entered a different time. It felt like a different world. A world not even Hadrian had been a part of.

The thought of him sent a stab of yearning through my belly.

The wooden doors of the dining room were already open, the occupants seated at their places. At the head of a long wooden table was Angelo. Two spots on his right were vacant, while the two seats to his left were occupied. Tor sat at his father's left elbow and a young woman, who couldn't be any older than sixteen perched next to him.

My eyes skimmed over Tor's cold expression and then settled on the young woman, who wore a dusty pink dress. She shot me a tentative smile, but I refused to smile back.

Luca helped me with my seat.

"Sterling," Angelo greeted. "You look lovely."

I didn't give a damn what he thought about how I looked. "I thought you said this was a family meal? Where's Nico? Or should I say, *Uncle* Nico?"

"Nico doesn't live here," Angelo explained, not at all perturbed by my attitude. "He lives with his wife, Beatrice, and their four children on their own estate. This home is for the first-born son and his family. You'll meet Beatrice and your cousins in a few days."

I reached for my napkin just to have something to do.

"This is my daughter, Gisella," Angelo said with a smile at his youngest child.

"It's a pleasure to meet you, Sterling," Gisella said. "Your Italian is flawless. How did you learn to speak it?"

"My dead mother taught me," I stated coldly.

She didn't react, but still, I instantly felt remorse for lashing out at the young girl. It wasn't her fault she'd grown up a Moretti.

Angelo ignored my remark as though I had said

nothing of importance and rang a small brass bell that rested by his plate. A few moments later lunch was served. Cured meats and cheeses, warm bread and olive oil, sautéed escarole and broccoli rabe, grilled calamari and octopus, platters of meat and fish.

I couldn't help the maniacal laugh that escaped.

Luca glanced at me and frowned. "What's so funny?"

"Is this a welcome home feast?" I asked, a gruesome grin stretching across my face. "What's the point of this charade?"

"Charade?" Angelo repeated. "It's no charade. You're family. And families dine together."

"We're *not* family," I gritted out.

I was on the verge of taking a butter knife and jabbing it into Luca's thigh, but I thought better than to draw blood at the table. In one swift move, I stood up, knocking my chair over and rushing from the room.

No one stopped me.

I had no idea where I was going, but I passed a maid dusting a priceless antique vase resting on a wooden credenza and asked her how I could get outside. She pointed the way to a set of double doors that led out into the gardens. They were even more magnificent to behold from ground level.

Greedily gulping the fragrant air, I tried to stem the rapid beat of my heart. My blood simmered in my system, but at that moment I chose to nurture it instead of shoving the feelings away. I would gladly give the Moretti my rage, but they would not conquer me nor spill my tears.

I found a stone bench in front of a fountain depicting a bearded god wearing a crown, holding a naked woman. It was so beautiful that it nearly brought my emotion to the surface, but I got control of myself. I took a seat in front of it, not caring that the white dress I wore would be smudged with dust.

"It's a version of the Rape of Proserpina," a timid voice said from behind me, making me jump.

I turned to look at the intruder. Gisella had walked on light steps. She reminded me of a doe, watchful, careful, quiet.

She lifted a plate of food in her hands. "I thought you might be hungry. I didn't mean to—"

"Thank you," I said. "That was thoughtful of you."

Gisella came to the bench and took a seat next to me and handed me the plate. It had olives and other antipasti, foods I could eat with my fingers.

Despite my situation, I wasn't immune to the scent of food. I would need sustenance if I was going to go another round with the Moretti men.

"I'm sorry about your mother," she said.

I nodded absently, feeling a fresh coat of tears breach my eyes. "I'm sorry for the way I spoke to you back there."

"I understand why you did. I'm a Moretti."

"Apparently, so am I," I joked.

She didn't laugh. Gisella nibbled on her plump bottom lip. She was pretty, but her beauty was subtle and unripe. She had the flush and slender features of youth, but in a few years, she would be a beautiful woman.

"How old are you?" I asked suddenly.

"Sixteen."

"Sixteen," I murmured with a shake of my head.

"Be careful, Sterling," she said. "Don't anger him."

"Angelo? It's a little late for—"

"Not my father. Raphael Foscari. You don't know what he's capable of…"

"What? What do you know about him?" I asked.

She was just about to reply when Luca called, "Gisella? *Papà* wants you to return to the table."

Gisella stood up and brushed the wrinkles from the skirt of her dress. With one final look at me, she left, passing Luca as she went.

Her brother reached out to touch her arm, holding her for just a moment as he leaned down to whisper something in her ear.

She smiled up at him with such a look of trust I wanted to scoop her up into my arms and protect her. She was a fawn in a glen of wolves.

I didn't even hear her footsteps as she strode away.

Luca stood near me with his hands in his trouser pockets.

"I'd like to be alone," I said, turning my back to him and focusing on the fountain.

The artist had taken great creative liberty with this version, because there was no fear or revulsion on Proserpina's face. In fact, the look she gave Pluto was nothing short of carnal.

Luca didn't bow to my demand. Instead, he took a seat next to me on the bench. "What did Gisella say to you?"

"She brought me food and said she was sorry about my mother." I picked up a seasoned olive and placed it in my mouth.

"Is that all?"

I chewed and removed the olive pit before answering. "Yes, that's all." I looked at him and frowned. What was he driving at? Did he suspect that Gisella had warned me about Raphael?

She hadn't needed to warn me. My mother had told me what the Foscari were capable of—murdering my father in cold blood, hunting her tirelessly for years.

How had she found the strength to go on? All she had

was Sister Agatha, and then it was just her, alone in the world. A mother with nothing more than the determination to protect her child.

I had Hadrian. I just had to wait. I could withstand anything, knowing he would come for me.

"Your fiancé will arrive tomorrow," Luca announced.

I stood up from the bench and flung my half-eaten plate of food into the fountain.

Chapter Thirty

After my reprieve in the gardens, I went back to my bedroom, refusing to spend any more time in my family's presence. A servant brought me dinner on a tray, but I didn't touch it.

I went to bed, hugging a pillow to me and crying. Deep, bone wrenching sobs. I had only been on my own for one day and already I felt myself breaking.

I needed Hadrian. I needed his arms around me, his strength, his power. I needed him to sweep me away from this horrible nightmare that had become my reality.

Sometime around dawn, I finally fell into a fitful sleep, only to be awakened a few minutes later by a female servant bringing me a breakfast tray. Even though I felt nauseous, I managed to choke down a homemade chocolate-filled *sfogliatella*.

I decided to sit and have tea on the balcony and try to collect my thoughts when Luca entered my bedroom without bothering to knock.

I glared at him. "There's this thing called privacy. You can't just barge in here like that."

"You're not afforded privacy anymore," he stated.

"I hate you," I seethed, ready to chuck the delicate china teacup at him.

"You've made that clear." He straightened his tie. "Raphael Foscari will be here within the hour. I suggest you make yourself presentable."

"Or what? He'll send me back to the factory and ask for a new Moretti brood mare?"

His jaw tightened. "He's graciously decided to marry you despite the fact that you're not a virgin."

"How wonderful for me." I took a sip of my tea, wishing it didn't taste so bitter on my tongue.

Luca stalked toward me and in spite of my temper, I had to stop the tremble of fear that washed through me. My anxiety was for naught though, because all he did was reach out to gently cup my chin and force my face up to his for examination.

"You didn't sleep," he stated. "And your eyes are bloodshot."

I batted his hand away. "It's hard to let my guard down in a prison. Doesn't matter how nice the mattress is."

"One hour," he reminded me, taking a step toward the door. "Don't keep him waiting. He won't like it."

Luca left, leaving me alone.

I gently set the teacup down and ran to the bathroom, throwing up the contents of my stomach, hating that nerves were getting the better of me.

Where are you, Hadrian?

In the armoire were dozens of dresses in my size. I was surprised Luca hadn't picked out a garment for me. What should I wear to meet the man my family was going to marry me off to?

I thought about Gisella's warning. It wouldn't do well to flaunt the fact that I wasn't a virgin.

Something demure then, but definitely not white.

I choose a champagne colored dress that neither completely concealed nor hid my attributes. It was form-fitting at the bust but flared at the waist. I hung it up on the back of the armoire door and then went to shower. I didn't bother blow drying my hair, choosing instead to pull it away from my face and pin it into a bun.

Shadows under my eyes were stark in contrast to my pale cheeks. I used the makeup products to conceal my sleepless night and blush to bring life back into my face. I coated my lips in a rosy gloss and then slid into the dress. A pair of matching heels completed my outfit.

There was a knock on the door, followed by a female servant entering. "Sorry to intrude, Miss. Your uncle bade me to come get you. Mr. Foscari is waiting for you in the salon."

"Thank you," I murmured.

Nodding, she retreated, but left the bedroom door open.

With one final look in the armoire mirror, I steeled my nerves and went downstairs.

Raphael Foscari stood at the mantle, speaking in low tones to Angelo. Both men's gazes turned toward me when I arrived in the doorway of the salon.

Luca and Tor were seated on an antique white settee, but they both rose like gentlemen when I entered the room.

It was clear I was there to be presented.

A Moretti woman on the altar of sacrifice.

A gift for a man and no more.

Raphael was a handsome man in his mid-forties. Golden skin, tall, blond. But there was a calculating gleam in his blue eyes, and I would never forget the words in my mother's letter. She'd warned me about the Foscari. I would not be deceived by physical beauty.

He was everything Hadrian was not.

Raphael pushed away from the mantle and strode toward me. My gaze tracked him, and I met his eyes when he stopped in front of me.

"She has the Moretti trait," he said, addressing Angelo, but his attention remained on me. "It's unique, and I approve of it."

"She will be a credit to you," Angelo stated.

A serpent of rage coiled around my heart, but I kept my expression serene.

"I'd like to walk with her in the gardens," Raphael said, still addressing Angelo.

"Absolutely," Angelo said. "It's best if you get to know one another."

Get to know one another?

"Shall we?" Raphael asked, offering me his arm. His voice was velvet richness, so very unlike Hadrian's bold brogue.

I remembered Gisella's warning again and took his arm reluctantly. He led me from the salon, and out of the corner of my eye, I saw Luca watching me intently. I couldn't discern his look, but I realized it didn't matter.

I was on my own.

As I held his arm, Raphael rested his hand on mine, and we turned down a long hallway. Only when we were out of sight did his hand tighten on mine in a clear show of force. Instead of taking me toward the double doors that led out into the gardens, he changed course and shoved me into a bathroom.

My heart tripped in terror.

Raphael shut the door and then with a sinister twist of the lock, blocked the exit. I barely registered the black and white marble tile floor of the guest bathroom or the gleaming wood of the walls. The attractive man before me smiled, an evil coil of his lips.

"You're beautiful. Like your mother."

I swallowed but didn't reply.

"You're also a whore, just like your mother. Sharing a bed with that Scottish brute." He took a menacing step toward me. "I will *not* be shamed again."

He reached into his trouser pocket and pulled out a long skinny device wrapped in a foil packet. "You're going to take a pregnancy test. Now. While I watch."

"I'm not pregnant," I protested. "There's no need for—"

He backhanded me across the cheek, the force of it so strong my head snapped to the side and my eyes watered. "You will not talk back to me. *Ever.* Now lift up your dress and pull down your underwear."

When I stared at him fright, he took another ominous step toward me. "Don't make me tell you again."

Shocked into submission, my head still reeling from his blow, I hastened to do his bidding. With supreme embarrassment, I lifted the skirt of my dress and slithered my panties down around my ankles.

I heard the crinkle of the wrapper as Raphael opened the pregnancy test and then he shoved it at me. Keeping my head bowed, my heart thundering in my chest, I moved to the toilet and peed on the stick.

After setting the test on the sink counter, I drew up my underwear. I tucked myself into the corner and waited.

Raphael's eyes were trained on the stick as were mine, though I knew the result. There was no way I was pregnant. I'd been on birth control since before I'd slept with Hadrian.

My heart continued to drum as one pink line of the

test slowly began to appear on the tiny screen. I let out a slow exhale, my gaze swiveling to Raphael.

But he wasn't looking at me. His eyes were still focused on the test, which he slowly lifted in his hand to show me.

Another pink line had appeared.

"Like I said. A whore," he said with ominous precision.

"I—"

In one swift move, he punched me hard in the belly. I buckled forward and almost fell over, but he pushed me up against the wall with his free hand, and then hit me again so hard I thought I was going to vomit. I doubled over in pain with my arms around myself in a futile gesture of protection, and I began to sob.

"You won't embarrass me the way your mother did," he spat. "I will not be made a fool of twice. If by some miracle your bastard isn't dead yet, it *will be* after the wedding. You'll get an abortion, and then I'll sow my own seed within you."

Gasping for air, tears streamed from my eyes, sending makeup cascading down my face. I bowed my head, not wishing to see his depraved expression.

"You'll say nothing of this to your family, or I'll kill you and make it look like an accident."

Raphael leaned down to grasp my arm and hauled me up to a standing position. Nausea swam in my belly.

"You look pale, *mia dolce*. Wash your face and then go upstairs. I'll explain to your family that you needed a moment of privacy. Don't worry, I'll tell them that we get along famously and later tonight, we will toast our long and fruitful marriage. And you *will* convince them that's the truth."

Chapter Thirty-One

Raphael let me out of the bathroom, and I escaped to my bedroom. I shut my door and then ran to the mirror. My cheek still throbbed and it was red, but it didn't look swollen.

Thank God. Raphael might've found a way to blame that on me, too.

I gripped the counter and struggled to keep my emotions under control.

I was pregnant.

I carried Hadrian's child, and I didn't know if Raphael had just—

If circumstances had been different, I would've been overjoyed. But hearing what Raphael planned to do had my insides cramping.

I was lightheaded and in danger of passing out.

No. I would not be weak. I would not give in to my desire to faint, to mentally check out for just a few minutes.

This wasn't just about me anymore, and I had to figure out a plan to survive.

I wasn't physically strong enough to protect my unborn

child from Raphael's malevolent intentions. He'd already beaten me.

If I was still carrying Hadrian's baby—

"Sterling?" Gisella called. "Sterling, are you all right?"

I pinched my cheeks to give myself some color, wincing at my tender skin. "I'm fine. I just needed a minute."

When I couldn't hide any longer, I left the bathroom and met Gisella's penetrating expression. Her eyes searched my face, trained on the cheek Raphael had hit.

She inhaled a shaky breath. "You can't go downstairs looking like that."

"It's that noticeable?"

She nodded. "Stay here. Let me get you some ice. Hopefully that will take care of it by dinnertime… *Papà* invited him to stay for the evening meal."

I swallowed. "How did he—I mean, were you in the salon when he returned?"

"Yes."

"How did he look?"

"As though nothing had transpired at all," she blurted out, her eyes wide.

I let out a choked sob. "He's a monster."

"I'm sorry," she whispered brokenly.

"Why are *you* sorry? It's not your fault. You didn't do this."

She bit her lip as her eyes filled with tears. "We were tentatively engaged. I was too young to marry him, and then you…"

"Showed up out of the blue." I dragged the younger girl into my arms and held her tightly. My mother hadn't been able to protect me from the Foscari, and I might not be able to protect my unborn child from them either. But at least I was able to protect this sweet, innocent girl from marrying a sadist.

After a moment, she pulled away and swiped at the tears on her cheeks. "Let me go get you that ice."

"Thank you," I said.

Gisella and I spent the afternoon holed up in my room. Her company was a welcome distraction from my disorderly thoughts and current situation. No one came looking for us until it was cocktail hour. A servant knocked on my door and told us our presence was required downstairs.

"Gisella," I said to her before we left the sanctuary of my bedroom. "Do me a favor."

"What?" she asked, peering at me with her golden-brown, fawn-like eyes.

"Keep your distance from me, okay? I don't want to give Raphael any reason to—I don't want anything to happen to you because of me. Do you understand?"

Nodding, she replied, "I understand."

"How's my cheek?" I asked her.

"Hardly noticeable."

We walked down to the salon together, and I was careful to remain aloof. When we were in the doorway, Raphael turned to look at me.

"You look refreshed," he commented.

"My afternoon nap was invigorating," I said with a bland smile. "Thank you for understanding my need for space."

Any shrewd observer could look at me and know I hadn't napped, and that I was boldly lying to cover something up. But I was in a room full of Moretti who wanted this marriage to go through, so they smiled and pretended to believe me.

"I was just discussing wedding dates with your uncle. The ceremony will take place a week from today."

"You must bring your family to stay," Angelo said to Raphael. "We'll have a long overdue celebration."

Angelo held out his hand to Raphael, who didn't hesitate to take it, but they did not shake. Instead, they wrapped their hands around each other's forearms, grasping one another in a silent vow. A new alliance to be sealed with my marriage to Raphael, and the birth of a child that would carry the blood of both Foscari and Moretti.

The butler appeared in the doorway of the salon to announce that dinner was ready.

"You go ahead," Raphael said to the other occupants. "I'd like a word with my fiancée."

I tried to stop the shiver of apprehension that crawled up my spine. Angelo left the room first, followed by Luca and Tor. Gisella was slower to depart and when she did, she threw a casual look at me over her shoulder before disappearing.

When we were alone, Raphael took a threatening step toward me. "A servant told me you spent the afternoon with your cousin."

"I did." I swallowed my nerves and clenched my hands into fists, but I kept them at my sides.

"Did you tell her what happened between us?"

"No. She doesn't know a thing."

He pinched my chin and turned my head to the side, inspecting the cheek he'd delivered vengeance to.

"It's not swollen," he murmured. "Excellent. Shall we go to dinner?"

Once again, he offered me his arm. I didn't hesitate to take it. I would do nothing to incite his wrath.

Where are you, Hadrian?

Dinner was an oddly lively affair. Even though Raphael was a sociopath, he was a charming one. He drew everyone individually into conversation at one time or another, and laughter was rampant.

I remained quiet, attempting to keep the rich meal in my belly. I ignored the wine that was set at my plate, wishing I could partake. But if there was the slightest chance Raphael hadn't made good on his promise, that I was still carrying Hadrian's child, I would do everything within my power to protect it.

After the cannoli were served and devoured, Angelo asked, "Would you like a brandy and cigar, Raphael?"

Raphael dabbed his lips with a linen napkin before setting it aside. "Thank you, but no. I should be heading home." He looked down at me. "Come, Sterling. See me out."

He helped me rise from my chair and then we swept from the dining room, away from the prying eyes of my family.

When we stood on the front steps of The White Company's ancestral home, Raphael's driver patiently waited for him in the front seat of a silver BMW sedan.

Raphael gathered me into his arms. "You pleased me tonight. I have no doubt that when you're my wife, you will be a beautiful adornment at my table."

A scream lodged in my throat as Raphael dipped his head. Hysteria threatened to overtake me. I knew what was coming, and that refuting it would cost me, so I closed my eyes and pictured Hadrian as Raphael's mouth covered mine.

His tongue darted between the seam of my lips. I nearly gagged on the overwhelming taste of caramelized onions and heady red wine from my family's vineyard.

He ground his pelvis against mine, letting me know in no uncertain terms that it didn't matter if I wanted him or not. He wouldn't care about my pleasure when he rutted between my thighs.

His fingers plowed into my hair, tearing the pins from

my bun. My scalp burned from his grip when he tilted my head back and forced me to meet his gaze.

"I should've fucked you in the bathroom," he growled. "Fucked you like the whore you are."

"Why didn't you?" I demanded before I could stop myself.

His clasp on my hair tightened, but I refused to cry out in pain, even as tears sprung to my eyes. Raphael leaned down and pressed his cheek to mine. To anyone watching the scene, we might've looked like two lovers locked in a passionate embrace. But the words he whispered in my ear belied the truth.

"Because when I fuck you," he said, his voice low, "I'm going to take my time, and I'm going to make it hurt. And just when you think I've had enough, I'm going to do it all over again until you're pregnant."

Bile surged up my throat, but Raphael released me. I gulped breaths of air voraciously, trying not to let him see my fear, but it didn't matter.

Raphael knew—and he smirked when he saw the terror on my face.

He pulled out a jewelry box from his suit breast pocket. "Your engagement ring."

When I made no move to take it, he opened it himself and took it out. He grabbed my hand and shoved the ring onto my finger. It was a gaudy, overpowering diamond set in a classic gold mount.

A symbol of my bondage.

"From this day forward, if you ever take off this ring, I'll cut off your finger."

With a jaunty chuck underneath my chin and a dazzling smile, he turned and waltzed down the front steps, whistling as he went.

His driver jumped out of the car and hastily opened

the back door for his master to climb in as Raphael approached.

Raphael's face appeared through the side window. He blew me a kiss when they departed.

I pressed my clenched fist to my heart, staring at the retreating lights of Raphael's car. He was gone for now, but his terrifying presence remained.

When I started to shiver in the cool air, I turned to head up the steps and stopped. Luca stood in the doorway.

I wondered what he'd seen, and whether or not he knew the truth. It didn't matter.

"Come into the salon," he said quietly. "We'll have a drink."

I trekked closer to him, and just when I was about to pass him by, I spit in his face.

"*Fuck you*, Luca."

Chapter Thirty-Two

I was alone after an exhausting day and finally had a measure of privacy. I slipped into the en suite bathroom of the room I was staying in and locked the door for good measure, even though I knew it would do nothing to keep anyone out.

I turned on the shower and stripped off all my clothes. Every inch of my body was sore. The lack of sleep had taken its toll, along with the sheer emotional upheaval and Raphael's beating. Before stepping under the water, I looked at myself in the mirror. My gaze dropped to my flat belly and I slowly stole a hand across it.

"Are you still there?" I whispered, my heart beating with hope.

When I was finally under the showerhead and the warm water poured over me, I fell apart. I cried for all the terror I'd felt over the last couple of days. I sent up a fervent prayer that Hadrian was on his way, and I wondered why it was taking him so long to come for me.

Exhausted, I turned off the water and stepped out of

the shower. I grabbed a white fluffy towel and quickly dried off before wrapping it around me.

When I left the bathroom, I drew to a halt and gaped in surprise. Tor sat at the edge of my bed. He didn't look at me when I entered; his body was hunched over as he leaned his elbows on his knees.

"What's with you Moretti men?" I demanded, tightening my fist around the towel I wore. "You just show up in my bedroom like it's your right."

Tor didn't supply a rebuttal. He got up off the bed and stalked to the balcony doors and peered out. "Get dressed. I want to show you something."

"It's late, Tor, and I'm tired."

"It won't take long." He looked at me over his shoulder, his eyes glittering in the low lamp light.

"What's this about?" I asked.

"You'll see. You won't get rid of me, so you might as well give in. Don't bother with outdoor clothes. We're not leaving the house."

Reluctantly, I went to the dresser and discreetly pulled out a pair of underwear and a set of blue silk pajamas. I headed back into the bathroom to change, wondering what the hell was so important that Tor—silent, stoic Tor—had to show me.

"I'm ready," I said when I opened the bathroom door.

Nodding, he headed to the exit of the room, not bothering to look behind him to see if I was following.

The house was quiet. Tor took the ornate staircase to the first floor, and I thought we'd turn in the direction of the salon where the family usually congregated, but he surprised me when he headed the opposite way.

The massive, austere, ancestral home was a labyrinth that I was sure each Moretti knew like the back of their hand. When we arrived at a heavy wooden door, Tor pushed it open and went in first. It was a library—the gargantuan wood-burning fireplace had not been modernized and was at least ten feet tall. Leather bound books lined the shelves, and I wondered if they were all for show, or if people ever actually read them.

"This is the sanctuary," Tor explained. "This is where the men of the family come to discuss the fate of Italy and the legacy of the *Compagnia Bianca del Falco.*"

I didn't bother holding in the eye roll. "It looks like any other library on a grand estate. You couldn't show me this tomorrow?"

When I made a move to leave, he reached for my arm and stopped me.

"There's a purpose to this room. One you need to understand," he said, his voice gravelly and low, like he was unaccustomed to speaking for prolonged periods of time.

Tor walked to the far wall and pointed to the painting of a handsome man with tan skin and a short, silver beard. He sat atop a black stallion and he was dressed in chain mail armor. On a flagpole attached to his horse and braced by one of his hands, flew a deep red flag with the image of a white falcon on a coat of arms.

"We can trace our lineage back to this man," he said, gazing up at the painting, his dark eyes glowing with pride. "Alfonso Moretti."

I looked at the painting again, studying it. Through the generations, the Moretti men still carried the hearty stamp of Alfonso's features. Aristocratic brow, patrician nose. Alfonso's chin was concealed by his beard, but I didn't doubt that it was as robust as the vitality emanating from him.

"The falcon…I always wondered why the literal translation of the *Compagnia Bianca del Falco* is The White Falcon

Company. How did it become known as The White Company? What happened to the falcon?" I asked.

"We actually don't know. Our coat of arms shows the white falcon, but through the generations the falcon was dropped from the translation and we became known simply as The White Company."

Tor moved to the next painting and the next, depicting every first-born son and leader of The White Company. There were sixteen in all.

"Where's Angelo's painting?" I asked.

"His will go on the wall after he passes," Tor explained. He looked up at the most recent painting. "Our grandfather, Antonio."

My mother's father.

"You look like our grandmother," Tor said.

I absently reached up to touch my nose and then let my hand drop.

My curiosity ran rampant, and I wanted to see paintings of the Moretti women. What of them? Were they all pawns like I'd become, or had any of them risen above their own oppression?

Here, in the sanctuary, the legacies of men reigned.

"Why did you bring me here, Tor?" I asked, my voice soft.

"One day, my brother will replace my father as the head of this family. One day, I will stand as his second in command. I will do *anything* to protect him and our legacy. Choose wisely, Sterling."

My heart lurched. "What do you mean?"

"You are a Moretti. It's your duty to honor and serve your family. It's been that way since you were born, whether you knew it or not."

The anger that had been simmering inside me finally ratcheted up to a boil. "It's an honor to *serve* my family?"

"Yes. It is."

"You're delusional. All of you are," I spat.

Without waiting for his reply, I fled the library and returned to the illusion of refuge in the confines of my bedroom.

I was trapped by my Moretti blood.

Power, bloodlines, archaic alliances…that is all my family—and the other four families—care about.

My mother had tried to warn me. Nothing else mattered to these people.

As soon as my wrath had come, it leaked out of me like a deflating tire. I crawled into bed and pulled the covers up to my chin before leaning over to turn off the bedside lamp.

I slid my hand over my belly and let it rest there.

I didn't care about the Moretti legacy.

I cared about my own.

I slept deeply and without interruption. Long after dawn had come and gone, I finally awoke. I stretched leisurely in bed, wincing at my sore and bruised body. When I got up, I sucked in a quick breath, feeling a cramp low in my stomach.

Padding my way to the bathroom, I focused on breathing and trying not to panic. But concern gave way to horror when I saw drops of blood in my underwear.

Had Raphael gotten his way? Was I having a miscarriage?

My mother had been a devout Catholic. She had turned to The Church when she needed help. I turned to her God now, praying for the safekeeping of my baby, praying for strength.

There was a subtle knock on the bedroom door. I expected it to be a servant with a breakfast tray, but when I called, "Come in," it was Gisella who entered. She was dressed in expensive riding clothes and her glossy dark hair was pulled back into a ponytail.

"Good, you're awake," she said with a shy smile. "I was worried that you were still sleeping."

Forcing my expression placid, I shook my head.

"You look like you slept. Did you?" she inquired.

"I did."

"Do you want to go riding with me this morning?" she queried. "It's a gorgeous day."

I would've loved nothing more than to go with her, to feel the wind on my cheeks and the warm scented air in my lungs. But I was too fragile to entertain the idea of fun.

"I'm not in the mood to ride, but I think I'd like…" I frowned.

"Sterling?" she pressed. "What's wrong?"

"Nothing." I inhaled a shaky breath, but it did nothing to calm the nausea. I turned quickly and dashed for the bathroom, making it to the toilet and throwing up bile.

I vaguely realized that Gisella had followed me into the bathroom and shut the door. "Oh, Sterling… Are you—"

"No. It's just nerves." I looked her in the eye. "Do you understand, Gisella? It's only my nerves."

She nodded slowly. "Nerves. Got it."

"No one can know about my nerves," I stated. "It would be catastrophic for me."

"Does your fiancé," she whispered, "know about your nerves?"

"Yes. He knows."

Gisella leaned her head against the door and closed her eyes. Finally, she opened them and stared at me. "Get dressed and meet me in the gardens."

Before I could reply, she ran out. I brushed my teeth and then splashed some cold water on my face. I was already having morning sickness, which meant I was farther along in my pregnancy than I had realized.

It must've happened the first night I was with Hadrian.

My life had changed then, and I hadn't even known it.

I dressed quickly, feeling the walls closing in on me.

There were no servants in the hallway nor any looming Moretti men, and I was able to escape to the gardens. I found Gisella on the stone bench in front of the fountain and took a seat next to her.

"Here," she said, handing me a biscuit wrapped in a paper napkin.

"This is becoming a routine of ours," I said dryly.

She smiled. "I brought you some weak tea." Gisella looked around and once she ensured we had privacy she spoke again, only this time her voice was lower. "One of the maids has four children, and she swears the cure for morning sickness is a biscuit and weak tea."

"Thank you," I said, feeling tears sting my eyes. "Why are you helping me?" I picked at the biscuit and placed a piece in my mouth to settle my stomach while I waited for her to reply.

She nibbled her lip in pensive thought. "I heard what happened to you. I mean, how you were…taken."

"Who told you?" I asked.

"Last night, my brothers were in the sanctuary talking with my father. I was passing by and overheard…"

I couldn't help it; I grinned. "You mean you were spying?"

"I prefer snooping," she said, pretending to be offended, but then she spoiled it by letting out a giggle. "They mentioned Hadrian."

My heart lodged in my throat. "What did they say?"

"They're wondering why he hasn't come for you." Her brown eyes stared into mine. "They expect him to come."

"So do I…"

"Tor said he'll come 'because he's Hadrian Rhys'. What does that mean?"

"If you'd met Hadrian, you'd understand. Did they say anything else?" I pressed. "Please, Gisella. If you know—"

"*Papà* and Luca think he—they think he might be planning something. They sounded afraid…"

A grin spread across my face. "They *should* be afraid."

Chapter Thirty-Three

"Who *is* Hadrian?" Gisella asked, her voice filled with awe.

What could I say to a sixteen-year-old?

She may have been just sixteen, but she was a Moretti. She deserved to be protected, but I wouldn't treat her like some sheltered, spoiled child.

"He's a professional international blackmailer with ties to the criminal underworld," I said.

Her mouth formed a silent 'oh'.

I shrugged. "You asked."

"I didn't think you'd really tell me," she said with a laugh.

Sunlight caught the diamond on my finger, and I absentmindedly fiddled with the vulgar bauble.

Gisella reached for my hand and lifted it to stare at the ring. "Do you think…"

"Hmmm?" I looked at her when she trailed off.

"Do you think this was the ring he'd have given me if I'd been the one to marry him?"

"Probably," I admitted.

I thought of the diamond jewelry Hadrian had

bequeathed me. It was still resting on the nightstand in the guest room.

"I wonder if his first wife wore the same ring," Gisella said, dropping my hand and gazing at the fountain.

"First wife?" I asked quietly. "He's been married before?"

She nodded, her eyes sad. "He married her soon after your mother left. She died only a few years into their marriage."

"Any children?"

"No."

"How did she die?" I asked, a knot of horror forming just below my breastbone.

"In a car accident. I don't know much about it. It was kept quiet…"

Kept quiet.

"What's he like?" Gisella asked.

"Who? Raphael?"

"Not him. Hadrian."

My entire body softened when I thought of him. "What's he like," I repeated. "He's indescribable."

"Try," she said in amusement.

I squeezed her hand, knowing she was trying to distract me from the horrors of my situation.

"He's," I began, "*big.*"

"Big?" She raised her eyebrows.

"Tall and muscular," I said. "Beautiful."

Ruthless.

I closed my eyes so I could picture him. The smile that came to his lips when I surprised him with my sassy attitude. The breadth of his shoulders when he slid into me. The scars marring his body. The rough, callused hands that touched me with reverence and passion. The strawberry blond hair of his warrior ancestors. The blue-gray eyes that held so much pain.

The wind changed and I could almost smell the scent of rain blowing in from the ocean, and it reminded me of his skin in the early Shetland morning.

But when I opened my eyes, all I saw was the Rape of Proserpina, carved in a fountain that rested on my family's land.

Talking about Hadrian would only remind me that he hadn't come for me.

"What happens to you, Gisella?" I asked, changing the subject.

"What do you mean?"

"Now that you're no longer embroiled with Raphael, do you have a choice? Can you marry someone you love?"

Her eyes grew despondent. "I'm a Moretti. I'm not given the luxury of marrying for love."

There was a commotion coming from the direction of the house, followed by a woman calling out.

"What's going on?" I asked, swiveling around, but I saw nothing.

"Aunt Beatrice has arrived," Gisella said, standing. "To begin the preparations for your wedding."

I sat up most of the night, the balcony doors open, listening to the sounds of the countryside. It was a complete departure from the noises of Hadrian's island, I mused.

No ocean waves, no impending storm.

The tempest had come and destroyed everything already. There was nothing left.

As I closed my eyes and let the moonlight bathe my

face, I imagined Hadrian's hard, naked body curling around mine.

As soon as Beatrice had arrived, I'd been told to go to my room so that I could be measured for my wedding dress and trousseau. It had taken all of my willpower not to vomit or spew nasty words at the woman who cinched a measuring tape to my waist and bust.

My aunt was a short, no-nonsense woman who'd become the matriarch of the family after Angelo's wife had passed away. She planned the weddings, orchestrated the baptisms, holidays, and other family gatherings.

My wedding to Raphael would happen.

I'd pled a headache and escaped dinner. They didn't need me to enjoy meals, so long as I didn't fight the wedding planning.

I thought of my mother. How strange it all was—I had wound up in the home she'd grown up in, and I was engaged to the man she was supposed to marry.

Every ounce of anger I'd held onto where she was concerned evaporated. As my hand settled on my belly, I understood her. I understood all of it. She'd done everything in her power to protect me.

My soul split open and I wept for the woman who'd given me everything. I forgave her for the impossible choices she'd had to make in order to survive, in order to ensure *I* had survived.

"I'm so sorry, Mama," I whispered.

A breeze brushed past my cheek and I closed my eyes, pretending it was a caress from her.

Pretending we'd been able to make amends while she'd been alive.

The breakfast tray arrived almost the moment I opened my eyes. They were gritty from lack of sleep, but I gladly took the discomfort. I'd laid my past to rest the night before, and in the light of day, I felt restored.

After placing the tray on the balcony, the servant left. I got up, waiting for the bout of morning sickness to pass.

I hoped Raphael had failed.

I went to eat my breakfast on the balcony. If only I wasn't a prisoner, I might've enjoyed the view. If only I could pretend I was a pampered guest, not a bartering chip.

There was a knock on the bedroom door, and despite my predicament, I smiled. It was Gisella, no doubt.

"Come in," I called.

My smile died when I saw that it was Luca.

"Oh good, you're here," I said snidely, turning away from him. "I would like to enjoy my breakfast alone, please."

He didn't address my snark when he came to my side and sat down in the chair next to me. In a bold gesture, he reached over to my plate and picked up the half-eaten pastry and took a huge bite.

"So, this is where all the *sfogliatella* have gone. Does the cook have a soft spot for you?" he asked, smiling.

My eyes narrowed. I didn't appreciate his charm, now that I knew what lie beneath it.

"Why are you here?" I demanded.

"I wanted to tell you that Raphael and his immediate family will arrive the day before the wedding. The servants have already started airing out the guest rooms."

"Lovely," I said, my tone as scathing as I could make it. "I *can't wait* to see my fiancé again."

It was on the tip of my tongue to ask Luca what he knew about Raphael's first wife, but I didn't expect him to tell me the truth. Nor did I think it was a wise idea to alert him that I had an ally in their midst, one of their own.

Gisella was mine to protect, and at the moment, her friendship was the only thing keeping me from going stark raving mad.

"Tor told me he took you to the sanctuary last night."

I raised my eyebrows. "Yeah. It was *so* interesting seeing the Moretti men through the generations."

"I can tell by your cynicism that you could give a fuck about your own legacy."

"Well, you're no dummy, Luca. I'll give you that."

I looked away from him to stare out across the balcony. I loathed the beauty and serenity here. It was nothing but a mockery.

"You'll be expected to join us for meals when Raphael is here." His edict shattered whatever tranquility I'd managed to hold onto.

"I serve at the pleasure of the Moretti," I drawled. "I'd bow, but that would mean standing. If that's all, you can leave." I lifted the cup of tea to my lips in supreme dismissal.

"That's not all," he said. "I know you're holding out hope that Hadrian will come for you, but he won't."

"Goodbye, Luca."

His gaze remained trained on me, scanning both of my eyes.

"I knocked him unconscious with a simple tranquilizer, Sterling. I guarantee you it wore off in just a few hours, even for a man his size. I didn't kill him. If he was going to come for you, he would have already. He doesn't love you."

I couldn't stop my heart from staggering in my chest. But I refused to give this man, *this Moretti*, the pleasure of thinking he could control the outcome of the situation.

A beastly grin spread across my face. "If you believed

that, Luca, you wouldn't have gone through the trouble of coming here and saying a word about it." I leaned forward in his direction. "You're not a man who's used to fear, but you fear Hadrian's wrath. I can see it in your eyes… Like I said, you're no dummy."

He rose gracefully to his feet and headed for the door. Just when I thought he was going to leave without replying, he stopped and said, "You keep reiterating you're not a Moretti, but even now, with your back to the wall, you won't admit defeat. You're a Moretti through and through."

The click of the door told me I was finally alone.

I gripped the priceless, delicate teacup between my fingers, the handle snapping off in my hand.

Chapter Thirty-Four

That night, Nico arrived with his four sons to stay at The White Company home. I watched Nico interact with his wife. There was genuine affection between them, and even though they physically didn't look like they belonged together—Nico was tall and slender while Beatrice was short and round—they had the kind of relationship that came from years together raising children. Their sons were strapping young men with olive colored skin and dark eyes. They looked like they'd have been more at home plowing a field than wearing suits in a formal dining room, but from their bold features there was no doubt that they were the next generation of Moretti.

"No wonder the Moretti marry off their daughters," I said to Gisella that night as we walked into my bedroom. "They're so few and far between. The Moretti spawn boys like it's their job."

Gisella grinned and helped me pull back the covers of the bed, removing the accent pillows and moving them to the chair in the corner. "You would think they'd revere us more, instead of using us as puppets."

"You'd think," I agreed dryly.

I thought of the baby I carried. Hadrian and I hadn't discussed having a family—our relationship had just begun. But I couldn't ever imagine him marrying off his daughter to solidify an alliance.

I looked at the young woman who'd been unfailingly kind to me. Most of the time, I forgot that we were cousins or that almost a decade separated us. I gazed at her for a moment, biting my lip and turning pensive.

She stared back at me. "What? Why are you looking at me like that?"

I walked to the bedroom door and turned the lock, hoping for a bit of privacy. I waved her to the bed and then followed. She slipped off her heels and then curled her legs underneath her when she took a seat.

"I feel like I can trust you," I said to her, pitching my voice low to ensure that in case anyone was walking by, they would only hear the muted murmurs of conversation.

She nodded. "You can. I'm really—I'm sorry for the reason you've come here, but I'm glad I've gotten a chance to meet you."

I grabbed her hand and gave it a squeeze. "Do you want to stay here and live this life, Gisella?"

Her eyes widened. "What do you mean?"

"I mean, do you want your family to decide who you marry and for what reason?"

"I don't have a choice, Sterling."

"Yes, you do." I took a deep breath. "When Hadrian comes for me, I'll have him pay restitution to your family or whatever to—"

Her expression hardened, making her look older. "You're delusional if you think that. What happened when my father found out you existed? You—half Moretti, with tainted blood. If Hadrian thought that he had enough money and power to save you from this, then he was wrong. My father will not let me marry a commoner, or even a powerful Italian of my own choosing. Don't you get it? We don't have a choice. We're women."

Gisella stood up, visibly upset. She scrambled to pick up her shoes. "I don't know how to tell you this, Sterling, but I think you're not fully aware of the situation you're in. Hadrian isn't coming for you. Based on everything you've told me about him, he would've been here already. So, what happened to him? Think about that and be honest with yourself."

There were only two options: He'd decided not to come for me, or he was dead.

When she saw my face, she nodded. "Exactly. You get it now. I admire your unwavering belief in him. I do. But really, Sterling. At this point you're just being foolish."

She took her heels and went to the door. "Raphael is coming here in a few days. Hadrian isn't coming to save you, and your child…accept the truth."

Gisella went to leave and then turned the lock and opened the door. Before she headed out, she threw me a look over her shoulder.

Pity.

A sixteen-year-old girl pitied me.

After the door shut, I took a moment to myself. Whispering to hear the sound of my own voice I said, "I'm not delusional. He's coming." I slid a hand across my stomach and looked down. "He'll come for us both. You'll see."

Days passed in a whirlwind of morning sickness and wedding plans. I kept to my room, refusing Gisella's overtures of friendship.

I felt stupid for confiding in a teenager—not because I thought she'd blab to her father about what I'd said, but because I couldn't stand the naked sorrow on her face every time she saw me.

It only strengthened my resolve.

Maybe I *was* delusional. But if I didn't have faith that Hadrian would show up and save me, then I had to contemplate the horrors of marrying Raphael Foscari.

The day before the wedding finally arrived, and there was still no sign of Hadrian.

I graced the stone steps of The White Company mansion, flanked by Luca and Tor. Angelo and Nico stood above me at the crest of the short staircase. We appeared a united front as the Foscari band arrived.

A line of black town cars drove up the long driveway and Raphael was the first one to climb out. I made no move to step down and greet him. Fear curled through me.

With a not-so-subtle prod from Angelo, I slowly descended the stone steps to approach Raphael.

I wasn't physically strong enough to handle a man like him, and he'd already tried and convicted me of my mother's crimes. On top of that, I would marry him with another man's child in my belly.

With that realization, I knew what my future held. He'd ensure I lost this baby, impregnate me as soon as he could, and when I gave him his desired heir, he would find a way to get rid of me.

When I stopped in front of him, he reached out and grasped my hand, pulling me to his side. His touch wasn't gentle, and I had to stop myself from flinching. "I've missed you, *mia dolce*."

I swallowed my revulsion and forced a docile smile.

We walked up to the steps of the mansion. Raphael held out his palm to greet Angelo. Angelo took Raphael's arm in his grasp, but his jaw was clenched taut from my obvious reluctance to greet my fiancé.

Raphael's three younger brothers had come with him. After the introductions were made, we all went to the salon to partake of refreshments.

Conversation was stilted and formal. Gisella shot me another commiserating smile that I ignored.

"You're looking pale," Raphael said, reluctantly pulling my attention from surveying the room. His hand was tight on my elbow as he steered me to a corner where we had a bit more privacy. "Are you still carrying that reprobate's baby?"

I brought a glass of chilled water to my lips and nodded, unable to speak the words.

His gaze remained passive. "Pity. Would you like to hear about your new home?" Without waiting for my answer, he went on, "I have a place a few hours from Venice. Have you ever been?"

I shook my head.

He took my hand and stared at it, his thumb skimming over the delicate bones of my wrist. "I have a townhouse in the city. I'll take you there. We'll eat fresh seafood and watch the boats pass all day long. We'll drink wine and sunbathe on my terrace. I'll show you where Marco Polo lived, and we'll walk through the square of the Basilica di San Marco. You'll breathe in the beauty of Venice in all its glory. And when the leaning bell towers chime in unison on Sunday, you'll know you're in one of the greatest cities in the world. I'll take you there the morning after our wedding night —after the doctor I'll have waiting at my home removes any trace of that Scottish bastard from your womb."

He took a step closer, his hand crushing my fingers.

"And when you're healed, I will take you morning, noon, and night, and you will cry out that you love it."

I couldn't stop the bile from surging up my throat, but if I embarrassed myself by vomiting on Raphael, there would surely be hell to pay when we were alone, away from the watchful eyes of my family.

"Excuse me," I whispered. "I need to use the restroom."

Raphael's grip tightened a fraction and then he released me.

I set my glass of water down on a coaster that would protect the antique table's varnish and headed for the door.

Luca was standing by the exit, talking with one of Raphael's brothers when he noticed my movements. "Where are you going, cousin?"

"I need to use the restroom," I said, far more calmly than I felt.

Luca's gaze searched my face and then darted to Raphael. He slowly stepped out of my path, clearing the way for me.

I didn't look behind me as I all but ran from the room. No doubt I would've seen the sickening twist of Raphael's lips.

When I made it to the privacy of my bathroom, I closed the door and slid down against it. I brought my legs up to my chest and rested my forehead on my knees.

And then I wept.

Because on the morrow, I would marry a monster.

And Hadrian hadn't come.

Chapter Thirty-Five

Blazing torches guarded the patio while we dined alfresco. The table was laden with a cream-colored tablecloth and white bone china. I sat next to Raphael while servants poured us wine from the Moretti vineyards.

Conversation was lively and everyone was boisterously animated—everyone except me.

Raphael's menacing presence dampened any chance I might've had of enjoying the meal. The toasts began after the main course was cleared. Every male stood and raised a glass to the joining of the Moretti and Foscari families by marriage, a calculated ending to years of strife between them.

Dessert was served. I kept my gaze trained on my plate so I didn't have to see the smiles resulting from my sacrifice.

Lost in inner turmoil, I flinched when I felt Raphael's hand settle on my thigh in a possessive hold underneath the table.

When Lorenzo, Raphael's brother, stood to make the

final toast of the evening, Raphael's fingers wandered toward the apex of my thighs.

I instinctively clamped my legs together, but my unwillingness only made Raphael intensify his effort. It was clear that he wouldn't stop until he had what he wanted.

As his brother droned on in Italian, Raphael's gaze shifted and momentarily rested on me. He arched a brow and we silently battled.

With a shaky exhale, I unclenched.

Raphael's smile was triumphant, and he was so consumed with thoughts of touching me, he didn't notice when I grabbed my dessert fork. Lifting the edge of the tablecloth so that I could see his hand, I jabbed the utensil into the fleshy skin between his thumb and forefinger.

Raphael snatched his hand back and recoiled away from me in an instinctive full body retreat, causing his knee to hit the underside of the table with a dense thud. Glasses trembled and liquid sloshed; silverware clattered against china.

His reaction caused Lorenzo to stop mid-speech, and everyone at the table turned to look in our direction. I picked off the corner of the lemon ricotta cake and stuck it in my mouth.

"Delicious," I murmured and then smiled.

Out of the corner of my eye, I saw Raphael's jaw clench. I looked at him. "Is it not to your liking, my love?" I purred. "Try the chocolate raspberry torte. It might be more your style."

Raphael struggled to maintain control of his emotions. Eventually the color in his face returned to normal. He smirked at me. Only his eyes betrayed the truth, and they promised retribution when we were alone again.

My bladder was full, but I refused to leave the table. I would not give Raphael the chance to corner me.

Angelo must have sensed something was out of place and finally interrupted Lorenzo by rising and saying, "Gentlemen, I think it's time we retreat to the sanctuary for amaro and cigars."

One by one the men stood and left the table. Raphael rose and then leaned down to whisper in my ear before he left. "Sleep well, *mia dolce.* Tonight will be the last night you sleep alone."

He brushed his lips against my cheek and then followed Nico inside.

I shuddered in loathing.

Only Beatrice, Gisella, and I remained. The Foscari hadn't brought any wives or female relatives to the celebration. It only emphasized how little they valued their women.

"Would you like another slice of cake, Sterling?" Beatrice asked.

I shook my head and stood. "No, thank you. If you'll excuse me, I think I'll head up to bed."

They both watched me, their eyes drilling into my back as I retreated.

I entered the house and heard laughter from the sanctuary. I took the servant's staircase to the second floor and slipped into my room, locking the door and sliding to the ground.

When the house had been quiet for hours, I was finally able to sneak out of my room undetected. The night was cool, my senses in tune with my surroundings. There was enough moonlight to pad my way to the stables. When I arrived, I waited to see if a sleepy stable master would appear and alert Angelo that I wasn't in my bed, but no one came.

As I walked through the stalls, I took an instant liking to a sorrel colored mare with white socks and patches of white on her flank. I saddled her, sending up a thought of gratitude that Hadrian had introduced me to the world of riding horses.

I guided the mare from her stall and out of the stable. After quickly mounting her, I urged her to a trot, leaving behind the vineyard. Once we had trotted clear of the stables, I brought her to a canter, and when she fell into a rhythm without hesitation, I knew I could trust her. The light of the moon lit the path forward and after a moment, a surge of adrenaline pumped through me and I brought her to a gallop, soaring across the hills of my ancestral home.

The wind tore through my hair and cut at my cheeks as hooves left their marks in the soil beneath us, beating a pattern into the earth that resounded in my eardrums as I rode. I breathed in life in all its glory—shoving away the anger and sadness, knowing those two useless emotions wouldn't bring back the dead, or change the outcome of tomorrow.

After a while, I slowed the mare to a canter and then to a trot, allowing her to catch her breath. Sweat had formed beneath the saddle, and the smell of wet leather struck my nose. We came to rest on a hilltop, and then I turned my face up to the sky to stare at the stars.

I looked at the moon, wondering if my mother could see me. If she knew that I was here in this place. I was more connected to her in death than I'd ever been in life.

Reluctantly, I guided the mare back toward the stables, prepared to meet the wrath of the stablemaster or one of my cousins, but still, no one came to greet me. I removed the saddle and brushed the mare down while she was still damp. Then I gave her a few carrots and held my head close to her, offering her a whisper of thanks.

I trekked to the house; the sound of my boots muted

from the dirt of the earth. When I arrived at the back door, Angelo stood there, waiting for me. He was my enemy, a traitor, and I would not hide my disdain for him.

"Do you know what would've happened if it had been your fiancé who found you riding instead of me?" he asked, his voice dangerous in the shadows.

"But he didn't, did he?" I snapped.

"You could've broken your neck." His tone was menacing. "You risked *everything* we've been trying to accomplish between our families for twenty-five years, all for a midnight ride."

"Don't worry, your precious legacy is still protected."

I swept past him and padded quietly up the stairs. I slipped into my room and closed the door. I was just about to remove my riding shirt when I saw a silhouette on my bed, and I nearly let out a yelp.

But the moonlight poured through the doors of the balcony and as my eyes adjusted to the light in the room, my heart slowed when I realized it was only Gisella.

"You nearly gave me a heart attack," I said, hand to my chest.

"Sorry," she said softly. "I didn't mean to—I'm sorry."

I knew she was apologizing for more than just startling me. I nodded. "What are you doing here? It's late."

She got up off the bed and gestured toward the bathroom. I followed her. She flipped on the light and when I entered after her, she shut the door.

Gisella was wearing a pair of satin pink pajamas with her initials monogramed at the breast pocket. She reached up to her neck and removed a dainty gold chain from around her neck and then held it out to me with her palm closed.

"What's this?" I asked with a smirk. "My something borrowed for tomorrow?"

She flipped her hand open. On the gold chain was a small, rectangular emerald pendant, the size of nickel.

Gisella paused, looking pensive. "It's poison."

I blinked. "*Excuse me?*"

Without hesitation she continued. "In this pendant there's a secret cavity that contains a liquid neurotoxin that's found in the spines of a certain exotic fish. Once ingested, it will enter the bloodstream, paralyzing the diaphragm within minutes. The victim will die of respiratory failure," she explained. "There's no antidote, it's more potent than cyanide, and it doesn't show up on a tox screen." She took my palm and set the necklace into it and closed my hand. "All you have to do is unscrew the top and then—"

"Are you suggesting I poison Raphael?"

"No. I'm suggesting *you* take it."

"*What?*" I breathed.

"Getting rid of Raphael won't solve anything—not for you," she said. "*Papà* will just marry you off to Lorenzo, and your baby will suffer the same fate. Make no mistake, Sterling, any man you wind up with will kill Hadrian's child. *Your* child."

My eyes narrowed. "All this time, I thought you were sweet and naive. Where did you get this?"

"It doesn't matter. I'm giving it to you. What you do with it is your choice."

"But if I take it…" I said slowly. "Then *you* will have to marry him."

"There are some things worse than death, Sterling. He won't hurt me like he'll hurt you. I'm not Violetta's daughter, and like it or not, in his eyes, my blood is pure."

"All this time, I thought I had to protect you. But you don't need my protection at all, do you?"

Gisella flashed a sympathetic smile and then left. She'd entered the room a girl but left a woman.

I slipped the necklace over my head and contemplated my choices.

After a moment, I left the bathroom and tread softly to the bed. Climbing under the covers, I curled into a ball. I stared out the windows and waited for the dawn.

Beatrice entered my room a few minutes after sunrise, followed by three female servants who would help me dress for my wedding.

One of them went into the en suite bathroom and drew me a bath, liberally sprinkling the water with citrus and vanilla essential oils. With a hand covering my mouth to shield a yawn, I padded my way into the bathroom.

"What did you do? Stay up all night?" Beatrice asked, looking me over. Her pudgy fingers clasped my chin as she turned my head for her inspection. She leaned forward and sniffed. "And you smell like horse sweat and leather."

"I went for a midnight ride," I said with a wide smile.

Her mouth pinched into a formidable expression. "Explains the smell—and the clothes." Her grip was strong as she began to undress me.

Servant's hands guided me into the bath. I closed my eyes and let them wash my hair and body. They scrubbed me until my skin gleamed and then they had me stand. They wrapped me in a towel and dragged me to the vanity.

Beatrice noticed my necklace and lifted the emerald vial for inspection. I cursed my stupidity for wearing it but remembered that the poison inside was hidden from plain view by the colored stone. But still, what if she—

"This is beautiful," she said. "Where did you get it?"

"Gisella lent it to me. It's my something borrowed for the day."

She nodded. "It's good that you're wearing something from a family member. I'm glad you're settling in."

I let out a slow exhale and my heart rate began to return to normal.

Beatrice orchestrated the women to curl my hair and pin it up away from my face. I hadn't bothered asking about my wedding dress, assuming it would be something beautiful, white, and lace.

I was surprised when Gisella entered my bedroom carrying a purple satin gown without a train.

Purple. A symbol of Roman royalty.

Gisella hung the gown up on the armoire door and then turned to face me. Her dark hair had been schooled into a sleek side ponytail and curled. She wore a rose-colored dress that was feminine and youthful. To think, if my family hadn't discovered my existence, she would've had to marry a man over two decades her senior.

Her gaze dropped to the necklace she'd given me, and she met my eyes. "Raphael wanted me to give you this," she said, handing me an earring box. I opened it. On black velvet lay a pair of heavy gold chandelier earrings accented with brilliant diamonds. It was another adornment for his soon-to-be trophy wife.

An hour later, I was standing in my bedroom, alone. I looked in the full-length mirror.

A Roman empress.

I'd never wanted to be an empress.

I just wanted to be Hadrian's.

Thoughts of my own suffering dwindled when I thought of the man I loved.

What happened to you, Hadrian?

The gold earrings were heavy at my ears. My different colored eyes glistened with unshed tears. I only had to be strong a little while longer…

A knock resounded on my door and then it opened. Angelo stepped inside.

I had no father to give me away, to walk me down the aisle and entrust my life to another man. No mother to dab the tears at her eyes as she wept with joy when I said my vows. I was alone on a day that should've been one of the happiest of my life.

"It's time," he said, and then extended his arm to me.

I glanced at it but didn't move to take it.

"Sterling," he said softly. "Come."

I took his arm reluctantly, the core of my being solidifying in hatred.

Angelo and I left the room and took the stairs before venturing down a long hallway to a set of doors that led outside. Raphael and I would be married outdoors with the scent of the hills and the vineyards surrounding us.

When we stepped into the bright daylight, I could make out Raphael's tall blond form at the end of the aisle. He stood with Lorenzo next to him. A priest in traditional ceremonial garb waited with them.

A wedding between the Foscari and the Moretti would finally commence. Both families had waited twenty-five years to form an alliance, and there seemed to be a collective holding of breaths that wouldn't release until the union was complete.

I was surprised to see only about thirty guests sitting in folding chairs on both sides of the aisle. I looked at Angelo inquisitively.

"Why are there so few people here?" I asked. "Isn't this *the* wedding of the generation?"

"The wedding is intimate, and only close family from both sides are here. When Raphael takes you to his home after you become his wife, there will be a reception with hundreds of people, full of prominent guests. It's the way of things."

I took a bouquet of white and purple roses from Gisella.

A stringed quartet lifted their instruments and began to play a tune I didn't recognize. Gisella walked down the aisle ahead of me, and when she'd made it to the altar, she took her place across from Raphael's younger brother.

With a deep breath, I let Angelo guide me down the aisle.

If only the people watching me knew that I was pregnant with Hadrian's baby…

My gaze remained focused on Raphael. I couldn't detect any emotion on his expressionless face. He looked solemn and commanding. For once, no cruelty graced his distinguished features.

It was a lie.

Angelo took my hand and placed it in Raphael's, and then he went to his chair in the front row next to Luca.

The priest began the ceremony, and after a few short minutes of speaking, we all took Communion. We recited our vows, and Raphael's hands tightened on mine as he slipped a wide gold band onto my finger.

Bringing my knuckles to his lips, he then turned us to face our families, who'd been grave and proper. They suddenly cheered in a decidedly inelegant and highly emotional fashion.

It was done.

I was now Sterling Foscari.

"Now we feast," Angelo stated, standing up and waving his hand toward the wedding tent and the tables lined with red and purple tablecloths, wine glasses, and bone china inlaid with gold.

Raphael escorted me to an isolated table which had

only two seats so we could speak to each other privately, yet its position allowed us both to remain a centerpiece for our families to observe. Raphael pulled out my chair for me and I took a seat. When he was settled next to me, a wedding attendant poured us two flutes of Prosecco.

"Will you excuse me for a moment?" I asked him. "I need to use the restroom."

When I made a move to stand, he reached out to grab me with his injured hand. "Serve me first, and then I'll think about allowing it. Or, I might let you piss yourself in embarrassment."

I thought of the power that dangled around my neck, and my thoughts went to my mother.

We were the same, she and I.

She'd ended her life to save mine. And now I was going to do the same. Better my child and I went together, than be forced to endure the cruelty of Raphael Foscari.

If I lived, Raphael would take Hadrian's child from me. He'd give me another, an heir of his own, but that child would never be mine. It would be a Foscari, nurtured on savagery.

I'd married the devil, and Hadrian hadn't appeared like a knight in shining armor to rescue me. For all he knew, he was dead.

I was truly and completely alone.

There was no longer a choice. I'd go to the bathroom, and when it was clear I'd been gone too long, Raphael would come in search of me.

I thought about the expression he would wear on his face, his cheeks mottled with anger when he found me dead on the bathroom floor on our wedding day.

A small dish of seasoned olives rested in the middle of the table. I reached for it and scooped out a spoonful and placed the olives on Raphael's plate. When I set the bowl down, I looked at him. "Do you want me to cut your meat for you too, little boy? We could play the airplane game—"

Raphael's rage got the better of him, and he grasped my wrist in an unrelenting grip. When he did, my lips perversely curved with pleasure, knowing he could only hurt me for a few more minutes.

"Get out of my sight," he spat. "And when you come back, you will control yourself, or I'll make damned sure you never misbehave again."

With a bold gesture, I took Raphael's flute of Prosecco and took a long swallow.

Liquid courage for what I was about to do.

I was just about to take my leave of the table when someone strolling through the vineyard caught my attention.

My heart drummed in my ears when I recognized a familiar form. A genuine smile of relief flitted to life on my face, and the hair on my neck stood up.

Hadrian Rhys had come for me.

Chapter Thirty-Six

Conversation and laughter ceased as Hadrian strode between the tables of the wedding feast. He was under-dressed in black trousers and a white button-down shirt open at the collar and rolled up to the elbows, showing off fair skin and muscular forearms. I watched intently, and immediately noticed that he was moving slowly, seemingly unwell.

I heard nothing over the sound of my own rapidly thumping heart, and it was little more than good fortune that I remembered not to squeeze the flute in my hand. I set it down on the table, my hand shaking.

A few of the Foscari men rose, ready to pounce on Hadrian as he strolled by, looking decidedly unconcerned.

"Sit down!" Angelo barked at his family, and when the Foscari made no move to listen, Angelo spat again, "Hadrian Rhys is *not* to be harmed!"

Hadrian placed his hand on his heart. "Angelo, I'm touched."

The Foscari lowered themselves back into their chairs one by one but remained alert and watchful.

When Hadrian came to our table, he stopped. His gaze raked over me, hungrily. And then he arched a brow, an appreciative smile drifting across his face.

I bit my lip to stop my answering grin and then said, "You're late."

Hadrian laughed as we continued to ignore the wedding guests. "I had a wee bit of trouble getting here. I had a horrible allergic reaction to the tranquilizer, and I'm still not fully recovered." He turned, and when he saw Luca, his gaze halted. "It's a good thing you didn't accidentally kill me. My dead man's switch was nearly activated."

Hadrian's focus came back to Raphael. He plucked the flute I'd abdicated and raised it in the air and then took a sip.

"Crisp. Light. Expensive. Perfect for a fall wedding."

My eyes continued to drink him in, finally noticing that he was thinner than he had been eight days ago. I wanted to ask how he'd gotten through security and into the wedding. I wanted to reach out and touch him, to assure myself that he wasn't a dream.

But I recognized the cold mask of indifference he wore on his face.

He was livid.

Raphael took my hand in an unconcealed show of dominance.

I struggled to breathe, trying to force air into my lungs to keep myself from fainting.

Hadrian set the empty flute down onto the table and studied me. "Are you all right, *yarta*?"

My heart warmed from Hadrian's Shetlandic endearment of sweetheart, and I nodded. He'd said it to me once in the throes of passion and explained later as we were falling asleep what it had meant.

Hadrian surveyed the wedding guests, turning his back on Raphael. I wanted to warn him that Raphael was the kind of man who wouldn't hesitate to stab someone in the back, but Raphael made no move.

Hadrian and Angelo stared at one another coldly. They were calculating, weighing their options and studying each other's facial expressions, trying to discern if one had an emotional advantage over the other, wondering who would act first.

"She's right, you know. You're too late," Raphael voiced. "Our marriage vows have been spoken. The ceremony is over."

"Has your marriage been consummated?" Hadrian demanded. "If not, it can be annulled. Or I can just kill you right now and make it easy."

"But Hadrian, I haven't yet had the opportunity to sample her charms." Raphael reached out and dragged a finger down the column of my neck to rest on my collarbone. "Based on her reaction to my kisses, I know I'll have her begging for my cock."

Hadrian's eyes never left Raphael's face. "You'll regret your words, Raphael, I promise you that. Sterling, you're coming home. Come with—"

"She's *my* wife now. She doesn't belong to you any longer," Raphael stated.

Hadrian dismissed Raphael and faced Angelo to address him again, but this time his tone was sinister. "You came to my home as an honored guest, as a friend. You didn't even know of Sterling's existence. She is Moretti born, but she didn't grow up in your world. You came to my island and stole what doesn't belong to you. You have insulted me, and I question your honor as a Moretti, as the head of the *Compagnia Bianca del Falco*."

Wedding guests stage-whispered to one another, their

excitement palpable, but Angelo's gaze was inscrutable. He remained frozen, like a statue in a museum.

Hadrian continued, his voice thunderous without needing to shout. He stared straight at Angelo and said, "I challenge you for the right to claim what's mine: Sterling Moretti. I make that challenge by demanding a fight to the death."

After a few moments of silence from Angelo, he finally spoke. "Twenty-five years ago, my sister, Violetta, dishonored my family when she broke her betrothal to Raphael Foscari. She married a man beneath her station and fled the country. Today, her daughter has become a Foscari. The woman you claim is no longer a Moretti. Our debts have been paid, and the union of families is now complete. It is up to her husband to decide if he wants to fight for her."

Hadrian rotated once again, this time to address Raphael. "Then I challenge *you* to a fight to the death for Sterling."

"A fight to the death?" Raphael spat. "I could kill you from here." His hand gripped the steak knife that rested next to his plate, a tacit threat.

"You could try," Hadrian agreed easily. "But you won't. And even if you were successful, it would be your own undoing considering what I know about your family."

"You're not even a worthy opponent." Raphael laughed but it wasn't in humor and it grated my ears. "My family have been assassins for generations. You're no match for me. You're a peasant who thinks he's a king."

Hadrian's smile was slow and vicious. "The world is made up of peasants and kings. But I am no king. I'm an *emperor*. A conqueror. And I'm not asking you to fight to the death, I'm commanding it. And you'll accept, because if you don't, I won't just destroy the Foscari, but every single one of the five families. Her life is worth more than even that to me, so don't think I won't do it."

Hadrian's gaze never wavered as he continued to stare at Raphael. "If you're willing to fight for her, I'll turn off my dead man's switch. If I lose, you get Sterling, and the information I have on the five families dies with me. Your empires will be safe. But if *I* win, you die today, Sterling is mine, and her debt is cleared forever."

Raphael glanced at Angelo who ever so slightly inclined his head in agreement.

My husband raised his brows and looked down his aristocratic nose at Hadrian. "Your challenge is formal?"

"It is," Hadrian ground out.

"To the death?"

"Aye. To the death."

Raphael took a sip of Prosecco and then set the glass down and began to loosen his bow tie. "So be it."

~

Hadrian had come for me.

Just when I'd given up all hope, he'd come for me.

And now I was terrified I would have to watch him die.

It didn't matter that Hadrian had fought an assailant hand to hand. Raphael Foscari came from an ancient family line of assassins, and Hadrian was still unwell, putting him at a severe disadvantage.

And yet I meant enough to him that he'd laid his cards on the table, and he was willing to risk everything for me.

Hadrian had made a phone call to an attorney on a secure phone and ordered him to temporarily disable his dead man's switch. When it was done, we left the wedding reception. Gisella walked by my side as we strolled through estate, past the vineyards to a fighting ring that resembled an ancient Roman amphitheater.

The Foscari and the Moretti assembled on opposite sides of the arena.

I sat on an ornate wooden throne on the ground level, between both sides. With my hands clenched in my lap and my back straight, I waited.

Hadrian stood in the center of the ring. He was shirtless, his fair skin bright in the autumn light. The bandage from the wound the intruder had inflicted to his side was gone, but I could still see his scars. He was huge, but with his shirt off, his weight loss was pronounced.

Raphael was also bare chested. Though tall, he was significantly leaner than Hadrian. His golden skinned body was unblemished, but I didn't discount his rage.

I couldn't look at the man I'd been forced to marry and think of him as anything but a monster.

A monster who stepped out of the fighting ring and boldly stalked toward me and kissed me.

With tongue.

In front of Hadrian.

When Raphael pulled away, I looked at Hadrian out of the corner of my eye. His jaw was clenched, and fire was in his eyes.

Raphael would fight dirty. I expected it, and judging by Hadrian's expression, he expected it too.

Angelo rose from his seat high above the arena, and after the crowd fell silent, he called out, "You have both vowed in front of witnesses to fight to the death for the honor of claiming Sterling, a woman of Moretti blood, now carrying the last name Foscari. There are only three rules. Opponents must fight without the use of weapons of any kind, retreat is not an option, and the fight is to the death. Do you both agree?"

"Aye," Hadrian stated.

"Yes," Raphael replied.

"Shake hands," Angelo commanded.

In spite of his anger, Hadrian reached his hand out, but Raphael simply spat at Hadrian's feet and backed away from him, craning his neck and stretching for what was coming.

Nico stood at a large bronze gong that hung at the far corner of the arena. It was six feet in diameter, engraved with a falcon, and raised on its own wooden platform. The Moretti had clearly been settling scores through hand-to-hand combat for generations. Without hesitation, Nico took a mallet to it once, and the resounding din signaled the beginning of the fight.

Hadrian and Raphael began to circle one another, sizing each other up. Hadrian was raw, brute strength. Raphael was trim, but tall and strong enough to pose a real threat.

For a few moments, it looked like they were both frozen, suspended in time, and then they attacked each other with violent intensity.

The smacking sound of flesh meeting bone turned my stomach, but I refused to react, refused to show any emotion.

Hadrian's head snapped to the side when Raphael's fist collided with his jaw. It knocked him off balance, dazing him for a moment. He recovered quickly and lunged at Raphael, whose skin had turned damp with sweat, glistening on his marvelous body in the sun. I noted with a clear sort of detachment that he, too, was beautiful.

Dangerous, beautiful men.

I only trusted one.

I only loved one.

Raphael dodged Hadrian's assault by jumping aside

and then he began circling again, staying out of Hadrian's reach. He grimaced and then stated for all to hear, "I'm going murder your unborn child while it's still in your woman's belly. And then I'm going to fuck her on your grave."

I didn't take my eyes off the battle, not even to look at the members of my family to see their reaction to Raphael's declaration.

Upon hearing the words, Hadrian froze just long enough for Raphael to kick his leg out from under him. With a roar of pure, unadulterated rage, Hadrian fell down. Raphael launched himself on top of Hadrian, pinning him on his back and then went straight for the wound the assassin had inflicted on Hadrian's side. He winced in pain as Raphael beat the tender spot with all his might.

Hadrian was losing the battle. Time slowed down and I felt every blow delivered. Felt them in my bones.

Hadrian attempted to push Raphael off him, but he was already exhausted. Raphael punched Hadrian hard in the nose, and with a sharp crack, blood began spurting from his face.

The wind changed direction, bringing the scent of dust and tangy copper to my nose.

Raphael shifted tactics and dug an elbow into Hadrian's throat, rearing back and striking down hard to try and crush Hadrian's windpipe.

It was life and death now, beyond making a point or punishing each other for past grievances.

Hadrian managed to block Raphael's elbows and reared up off the dirt to press his body to the older man, closing the distance and eliminating Raphael's ability to strike. Raphael spun and landed a solid blow to Hadrian's broken nose.

After a bellow of pain, Hadrian somehow found a vestige of strength and arched his back, flinging Raphael up in the air slightly. Hadrian succeeded in getting his legs out from under Raphael and then locked them around the other man's neck to choke him.

My heart pounded as I watched Hadrian become the aggressor, managing to flip the leaner man beneath him and press him to the ground. He curled up on top of Raphael and used his hands to pull Raphael's head close to him, strangling him between his legs and arms. Blood from Hadrian's shattered nose dripped down his face, spattering Raphael like a violent painting.

It was Hadrian's turn to say something, but I couldn't hear what he said. Whatever passed his lips made Raphael renew his struggle.

He clawed at Hadrian's face in a blind rage, a fight for life itself, but Hadrian turned his cheek before Raphael could dig his fingers into Hadrian's eyes. He took a gouge from Raphael's fingernails as he attempted to rear back. Raphael then grabbed a handful of dirt and threw it in Hadrian's face. He instinctively let Raphael go and rolled off him to put distance between them while he attempted to recover his sight.

Raphael scrambled to his feet and then lifted his foot. He arched his leg back like he was going to kick Hadrian. I winced in anticipation, but my mouth parted when I saw Raphael reach down with his right hand and pull something from the heel of his boot.

The knife glinted in the early afternoon light, and a startled gasp escaped my lips. I wasn't the only one who made a noise of surprise.

I hadn't noticed when Gisella had come to stand by my side. I lifted my hand up to her and she clasped it, linking her fingers through mine. I squeezed the dainty bones of her hand, not caring that I felt them crunch.

No one made a move to stop Raphael, despite the obvious violation of the rules.

No one wanted Hadrian to win.

No one but me.

Hadrian surged to his feet and rubbed his eyes just before Raphael lunged at him with his knife. Hadrian's arm whirled downward, deflecting the blade from sliding between his ribs. But then Raphael changed his plan of attack. Gripping the blade tightly in his hand, he sank to a crouch and lunged past Hadrian, slashing his left hamstring. The knife made contact and Hadrian's scream of rage and pain echoed through the arena as he sank to one knee, blood emitting from his open wound.

Raphael rose, standing over Hadrian a few feet from him with an expression of victory on his face.

Hadrian's teeth were clenched, and he struggled to remain upright, his face muddied with dirt and blood.

I willed his eyes to meet mine so I could tell him I loved him.

But he never looked in my direction, and when Raphael's arm came down with the intention of ending Hadrian's life, I closed my eyes.

There was a collective gasp from the audience and the unmistakable sound of a man wheezing in pain.

Gisella murmured, "*Sterling.*"

My eyes flipped open and my jaw dropped. I expected to see Hadrian bleeding out, blood staining the dirt beneath him.

Instead, I saw Raphael's blade sticking out of Hadrian's left pectoral, and Raphael laying on the ground a few feet away, striving to get back on his feet.

Hadrian's wound looked deep, but I didn't know if it

was fatal. He remained on his knees, staring at the blade. He peered at it curiously, like he wasn't sure how it had gotten there or how he was still alive.

Raphael finally regained his stance and took a few steps closer with the intent of finishing the fight and ending Hadrian's life.

He reached for the blade stuck in Hadrian's chest.

Hadrian suddenly moved, alert and with the precision of an experienced killer.

In two swift motions, he yanked the blade from his own flesh and then impaled Raphael under the breastbone, burying the knife to the hilt.

Hadrian gruesomely twisted the blade and then yanked it out.

Blood gushed from Raphael's wound like he was a stuck pig.

A look of complete disbelief washed over the Foscari's face and he fell to his knees, realizing that Hadrian had pierced his heart. He sat for a moment and then went ghost white and fell backward into the dirt, lying motionless.

Hadrian collapsed to the ground in the opposite direction, the blade still in his hand.

I leapt from my chair and flung myself over the two-foot wall, my purple dress ripping along the hem.

When I got to Hadrian's side, I dropped to my knees and leaned over him. His eyes were halfway open and caked with dirt and blood, but a triumphant smile drifted across his face.

"You will not die," I commanded.

"I wouldn't dream of it," he assured me.

I pressed a gentle kiss to his lips. "They didn't think you'd win," I whispered.

"I know." He peered at me, his eyes closing as unconsciousness came for him.

"What did you whisper to Raphael?" I demanded.

"I told him that when he was dead, I was going to pry every one of his teeth from his head and string them into a necklace for you to wear."

I wrinkled my nose. "Seriously?"

"Viking," he reminded me.

I rose and stood next to Hadrian. My eyes met Angelo's and then landed on each member of my family, one by one. And then I surveyed the Foscari, who were waiting to see what would unfold next.

"Foscari blood has been spilled today," I said, my voice ringing out like a bell. "It's over. On your honor you will not violate your oaths. I denounce the Foscari name. I am Sterling Moretti of the *Compagnia Bianca del Falco*, and I choose Hadrian Rhys. I carry his child."

I kept my attention on the crowd, watching as they hung on my every word.

"I will accept your pronouncement, but you must seal it in blood," Angelo stated. "It's the blood within you that brought you to this place. Spill it here and now, and it will be done."

I bent down and gently took the blade from Hadrian's hand and then sliced my palm. The pain was sharp and instant. I closed my hand, letting blood well, ignoring the agony. Slowly, I rose, blood dripping onto the arena floor as I held my hand out by my side.

Angelo nodded. "Now it is done. Any Foscari who breaks the blood sacrifice, know that it will be a declaration of war on the Moretti."

I looked to the Foscari—to Raphael's brother, the next in line.

"Do you accept?" I prodded Lorenzo.

"Yes," he said simply. "But Raphael has dishonored our family by breaking the rules during mortal combat. The tables have turned, and you have every right to demand restitution for his failure to honor them. That is a stain on our family name that we do not accept." He paused for a moment, his brow furrowed. "I wish for peace between our families, now that Raphael is gone."

"Let it be done then," Angelo replied.

Tension eased out of me though I refused to let my shoulders droop. I nodded, and then grasped the hem of my ruined wedding gown and tore a strip from it so I could wrap it around my bleeding palm.

While the Foscari and the Moretti were rising from their seats and talking amongst themselves, I went back to Hadrian's side and squatted down next to him.

His eyes were cracked open, a gruesome smile stretched across his face. "I had no idea you were such an orator."

I shot him a wobbly smile. "Neither did I."

"Why didn't you tell me you were pregnant?"

"I didn't know until a few days ago."

A dreamy expression flashed across his face. "Oh," he said, right before he passed out.

Chapter Thirty-Seven

I turned my face to the sky, letting the moon kiss me in greeting. I was alone on the balcony while Hadrian slept soundly in bed.

He'd been transported back to my ancestral home where a surgeon had tended to his injuries. He'd stitched what could be stitched, repaired what could be repaired. Due to the slashing of his hamstring, Hadrian might never walk normally again, the doctor had said.

Only time would tell.

He had a broken nose, cracked and bruised ribs, a concussion, a sliced hamstring, and a deep stab wound.

And he was still recovering from an accidental poisoning.

He was lucky to be alive.

We both were.

The surgeon had seen to my hand after he'd tended to Hadrian, and then he'd taken the time to examine me. I was healthy, and I cried when the doctor said he believed my baby was healthy as well.

Reluctantly, I went into the bedroom, but left the

balcony doors open to allow fresh countryside air to circulate. Fragrant beauty was carried on the wind.

I touched Hadrian's forehead and then slid my hand down to his chest. He wasn't hot, and I hoped that meant the antibiotics were working their magic, but it was still too soon to tell.

"Think you can slide that hand a wee bit lower?" came his throaty growl.

I yanked my hand away. "You're supposed to be asleep."

"How am I supposed to be asleep when you're groping me?"

"I'm not groping you," I said.

"Aye, and that's the problem." He cracked his lids. "Can I have some water?"

I nodded and then went to the bedside table and turned on the lamp. I poured him a glass. He was already propped up against the pillows, so it took very little effort to get the liquid and pain pills into him.

"I can't believe I'm accepting hospitality from the men that stole you from my own home," he stated. "I wish we were back on my island. I don't trust your family."

"That makes two of us," I remarked dryly. "But you're not well enough to travel. You need to rest, Hadrian."

"Where are they?" Hadrian asked.

"Where are what?"

"The rings that cheating, lying, bastard slid onto your finger?" His blue-gray eyes were stormy with anger.

"I gave them to his brother when they carted his body from the arena. You don't know this, because you passed out, but I spit on his corpse." I raised my eyebrows. "Does that make you happy?"

"Hardly," he snapped. "I was supposed to be your first and *only* husband. That fucker beat me to it."

"You also made me a widow," I pointed out dryly. "Besides, the Foscari are devout Catholics and we never consummated the marriage, so…"

He paused for a moment, mulling over his next words. His tone was tempered when he said, "There are some things we need to say to each other. Aye?"

I nodded warily, not at all looking forward to our discussion.

"You have to know that I was coming for you. You trusted that, didn't you, Sterling?"

"I did," I promised. "I had faith that you were on your way. Only…"

"Only what?" he prodded.

"Luca told me that he'd only given you a tranquilizer, and I thought for sure you had a plan up your sleeve. But then you didn't come for me for eight days, Hadrian."

"My plan was trying to stay alive," he remarked snidely. "Ingrid found me vomiting and swollen on the floor, barely able to breathe. It wasn't a moment too soon. Had to take the helicopter to Lerwick. They killed Patrick when he tried to stop them from taking you off the island."

I nodded and fell silent.

"Tell me the truth, *yarta*. Did you ever doubt that I'd come for you?"

"I did today," I admitted and boldly met his eyes. "You don't know what he was capable of, Hadrian."

"Tell me." His voice so gentle I wanted to weep.

"After he told Angelo he'd marry me, he forced me to take a pregnancy test. I didn't know, Hadrian, I swear it. He tried to kill our child. He beat me and threatened my life if I told my family. And he—he told me after he married me, he'd take me back to his home where there would be a doctor waiting for me to…"

I broke down, sobbing with my face in my hands. I vaguely realized that Hadrian tugged on my arms and soon I was crying against his chest, my cheeks stained with fear and relief.

I wasn't sure I could admit the rest; the necklace Gisella had given me, the absolute desolation I felt and the destruction of hope, my willingness to go to the grave so that Raphael couldn't take anything more from me.

"His death was too quick," he said, brushing his lips across the top of my head. "I wish I had the chance to kill him all over again and make him suffer."

I swiped the tears from my skin and lifted myself up, mindful of his injured body. "I think it happened the first night we were together."

"At The Mansion?" he asked.

"Yes. I was on birth control. I didn't—"

"It's not your fault. Clearly, I have the seed of a warrior."

I snorted. "Really, Hadrian?"

"You're crying all over me. I'm trying to make you feel better. You need to laugh, aye?"

I let out a rueful chuckle and shook my head.

"You didn't ask me how I feel about it," he pressed.

"How *do* you feel about it?" I bit my lip but wasn't able to hide my worry.

"I didn't want bairns," he said slowly. "I never thought I'd have a family. But I didn't expect to meet anyone like you, Sterling."

"You don't have to stay with me," I blurted out. "The threat of my family is over now. I can live my life out in the open. I can raise the baby and—"

"Woman," he said with a rueful shake of his head, "I told you I wanted to give you the world and then fought to the death for you gladiator style. If you can't figure out that you'll never be alone again, then I don't know what the hell will convince you."

My smile quivered. "Does that mean—you love me?"

Hadrian let out a laugh and then winced. "You're dense. Do you know that?"

I reached out and gently stroked his cheek, feeling the beginnings of a beard. "Do you truly love me? My family is made up of ruthless mercenaries…"

"Say the word, Sterling, and I'll go to war."

I blanched. "War? What do you—"

"I promised to protect you and I failed. They almost killed me by accident. They stole you from my home. They married you to a sociopath to further their own gain. Should I go on? Do I need to? Aye, say the word and I'll wipe the *Compagnia Bianca del Falco* off the face of the earth. Honor be damned."

His vow shook me to my core. "I hate my family," I said slowly. "I hate what they did to my mother. I hate how I was forced to grow up. I hate everything they stand for." I paused, weighing my options. I thought of Gisella. Innocent, beautiful Gisella, with a constitution of steel. She didn't deserve the hell Hadrian could rain down on her.

"I want nothing to do with them—except for Gisella," I voiced. "She was my confidant while I was here, and she never betrayed the truth of my pregnancy. I can't knowingly have her harmed."

"I could spare her," he said easily. "I could kill the rest of them. Hell, I could call the Italian government and have them take care of it for me. I wouldn't even have to lift a finger."

I shook my head. "Violence begets violence. It has to end or we'll never have a moment of peace."

He paused, lost in thought. "My business relationship with them is done. I'll keep the information I have on them secret, but only so I can use it against them should they raise a hand to me or mine ever again."

Hadrian reached out and gently grasped my chin and forced me to meet his gaze. Silvery moonlight cast shadows across his face.

"I came to protect you and bring you home." His hand dropped to slide down my arm and then covered my belly. "I'll always protect you."

The first few days after he was injured, I didn't leave his bedside. But inevitably, Hadrian told me that he wasn't going to die and that I needed to leave the bedroom and stretch my legs.

There were plenty of female servants who volunteered to keep vigil, bringing him anything he needed, and spoon-feeding him broth and bread.

"I don't think you need me at all," I remarked dryly when I gently crawled into bed one night, pressing a kiss to his brow.

His eyes were closed, but he smiled. "They might feed me and be willing to give me sponge baths, but none of them give me what I really need."

"A warm, naked body on top of yours?"

He chuckled. "They might, if I asked."

"You're so full of yourself, Hadrian Rhys. It's a good thing I'm not the jealous type."

Hadrian started to recuperate under the solicitous care of the *Compagnia Bianca del Falco*, but even when he was resting, I refused to dine with my family. I accepted their hospitality in the form of food and enough time for Hadrian to heal so we could travel back to his island, but no more than that.

My family was dead to me. All except Gisella, who often popped her head into the room I shared with Hadrian, asking if I wanted to go for walks or horse rides while he was napping. I said yes to the walks but refused to ride. Now that I knew the baby was healthy and safe, I wouldn't do anything to jeopardize it.

Each night, Hadrian stole a touch across my naked body, resting his hand on my belly.

I'd just woken from an afternoon nap when there was a slight knock on the door. I hastily got up and pulled on a robe and looked at Hadrian who was still fast asleep.

I opened the door to see Luca at the threshold. I stepped into the hallway and closed the door behind me, so as not to disturb Hadrian.

"*Papà* requests your presence at dinner tonight," he said.

"I'm busy," I said, crossing my arms over my chest.

"Sterling, please," he said, his voice and expression vulnerable. He ran a hand through his dark hair.

"Please, *what*?" I snapped. "I've been here for days and no apology has passed your lips. Not yours, not your brother's, not your father's. You married me off to a sociopath—and for what?"

"Why didn't you confide in me?" he demanded. "Why didn't you tell me you were pregnant?"

I raised my brows. "Aside from the fact that Raphael threatened my life if I told you? I still had hope that Hadrian was coming for me, so I wasn't going to do *anything* to endanger my own safety or the life of my child."

"Sterling, I—"

"Which brings me to another point," I interrupted. "You wanted me to believe that Hadrian *wasn't* coming for me."

"At first I thought he would, but after days of silence I

didn't think he was coming," he stated. "I've never—I've never witnessed that kind of love and devotion before."

"My mother sacrificed her life to protect me. Hadrian fought to the death for me. You, Tor, all of you did *nothing* to protect me. You know what I think, Luca Moretti? I think Moretti men are fucking *cowards*. Get out of my sight. You make me sick."

Without waiting for his response, I opened the door and went back into the bedroom. I slammed it shut, my breath coming in rapid pants.

"If I hadn't already been awake, that crashing door would've done it," Hadrian said. He was propped up in bed, and though his expression was amused, his eyes coasted over me, as if looking for physical injuries.

"I'm sorry," I said, immediately contrite. "How are you feeling?"

"Fine."

"Did you hear my fight with Luca?"

"I think the entire house heard your fight with Luca."

I rubbed my third eye. "Angelo wants me to have dinner with the family. He used Luca as his messenger."

Hadrian paused for a moment and then said, "Luca came to see me."

"What? When?"

"A few days ago. You were out with Gisella." His eyes met mine. "We discussed…things."

"Things? What kind of things?"

"Don't judge your cousin based on your uncle's actions. He could no more go against his father's demands and edicts than you could."

"Are you saying—are you saying I should *forgive* him?"

"I'm saying Luca isn't—he's not as archaic as Angelo. He's willing to flex with the times."

"He's still a Moretti."

"Aye."

"He still wants to further his own family's power."

"Aye."

"Stop saying *aye*," I barked.

"Your temper and high blood pressure aren't good for the bairn, *yarta*." He patted the spot on the bed next to him.

I reluctantly went to him, dragging my feet.

"You want what's best for Gisella, don't you?"

I looked at him in confusion. "Of course I do."

"What would you be willing to do so that she might be able to marry for love? Hmm? Angelo—he's too myopic in his world views. But Luca…Luca has the desire to listen. I thought you should know." He leaned his head back against the pillow and smiled at me.

"How many drugs are in your system?" I asked. "You're far too levelheaded, and dare I say, docile?"

"Docile? Come here and I'll show you docile."

I shook my head. "The doctor said—"

"Hang the doctor. It's been far too long since I've slid inside your—"

"I guess I have no choice but to go to dinner," I said, rising off the bed before Hadrian could lean over and pull me to him. "It's for your own health."

Panting, Hadrian leaned back against the pillows. "Bring me dessert, aye?"

Angelo set down his near empty wine glass and looked at me. "Would you like to join Luca, Tor, and me in the sanctuary for after dinner drinks?"

"I'm pregnant," I reminded him. "And I thought only men were welcome in the sanctuary."

"I'll have a servant bring you hot chocolate," Angelo said, ignoring my snarky tone. "And as far as the sanctuary goes…there are some matters that need to be addressed and it's where we do family business."

"Can I come, *Papà*?" Gisella begged with wide eyes.

"Maybe when you turn eighteen," he evaded.

With a feminine pout that would only refine with age, she got up from the table. She kissed her father's cheek and then went to Luca and flicked his ear.

"Irreverent *fragolina*," he teased.

She stuck out her tongue and then went to Tor, who she hugged from behind. Finally, she winked at me and then skipped from the dining room, leaving me alone with the Moretti men. I couldn't believe she was the same young woman who'd given me a vial of poison I still wore around my neck. She was a chameleon—and then a terrifying thought entered my mind.

What if I had been wrong? What if it wasn't Luca that was the most dangerous of all? What if Gisella had learned enough at her age to blend into any environment, moving seamlessly from one place to the next with no one knowing who she truly was at any moment?

I've underestimated her, badly.

The four of us retired to the sanctuary. The men took their seats—Luca on the light blue couch and Angelo in one of the highbacked chairs by the lit fireplace. I took the matching chair across from him. Tor poured three glasses of fifty-year old ruby port.

A servant knocked on the door and was told to enter. She came in and placed a silver tea tray in front of me on a wooden table. The aroma of hot chocolate hit my nose and I couldn't help the sigh of appreciation.

"Thank you," I told her.

She nodded and then discreetly left.

"The Foscari have been in contact," Angelo said, breaking the silence.

Anger came swift and fast, but I shoved it down. There was no use discussing it. The fight was over. Hadrian had won. At a great cost to himself, but he'd won.

I was free.

"What did Lorenzo have to say?" Luca asked. He took a sip of his port, eyes on his father.

"They've confirmed it was the Borgia who sent the assassin to kill Hadrian. They've offered their aid in dealing with them."

"What's the plan?" Tor asked, his dark eyes glittering with the desire to deliver retribution.

"We'll torch their ancestral home and kill Carlo. We'll leave Carlo's sons alive to bear the shame of their family name, but their business will move elsewhere, and they'll be impoverished. We won't hear from them again, and when it's done, there will be only four families."

"What about Francesca," Tor voiced.

Angelo took a long swallow of his port before replying. "There will be another marriage…"

"Oh?" Luca asked, his cheeks suddenly flushed in the dim light of the sanctuary.

"Yes. *You* will marry her," Angelo said. "It will keep the Borgia from retaliating."

Luca stared at his father and for the first time since I'd known him, I felt like I was seeing who Luca really was. Hadrian's words about my cousin came back to me.

A flash of anger and hatred burned in Luca's eyes but disappeared just as quickly.

"Do I have a choice in the matter?" Luca asked, his voice tight.

"It's past time you marry and do your duty in producing a Moretti heir."

Father and son never took their eyes off one another. Finally, Luca raised his glass in the air. "To my future wife."

Tor glanced at his brother, but then he drank the rest of his port in commiseration of his brother's toast.

Luca finished his drink. "You'll see to the arrangements? You'll let me know when to put the call out to our men?"

Angelo nodded.

"Fine." Luca stood and with a chin nod at me, he left the room. Tor also rose, and without so much as a fare-thee-well, stalked after his brother.

"That was sneaky and rotten of you," I said.

"I do what has to be done for the family," Angelo said, peering into the fire.

"Right, the family," I said. I leaned my head against the chair in sudden exhaustion.

"You're a Moretti. Whether you want to be or not. Even when you marry Hadrian, you will still be a Moretti. You will *always* be a Moretti."

"And therefore a pawn in your elaborate chess game? I reject the burden that comes with the Moretti name."

"It doesn't matter what you want. Blood is blood."

"Did you love my mother?" I asked suddenly.

"Of course I loved her. She was impossible not to love."

"And yet her happiness was never a thought, never considered."

"*My* happiness was never a thought, never considered." His eyes darkened. "I had an arranged marriage. The only happiness that came from that union were my children. That's all Moretti—or any of the five families—can hope for."

I shook my head. "Sad. So incredibly sad. Lives

wasted. And for what? Arranged marriages, unions that breed only hatred."

"You won't change our ways, Sterling."

"I know," I said.

"Then what is it you want?"

"I'm lost to you," I said. "I want Hadrian, and he wants me."

"That's already been decided," Angelo stated.

"I'm carrying his baby. You have no claim on my child. If I bear a son, he will not become a Moretti mercenary. If I bear a daughter, she will not be a pawn to marry off."

Angelo didn't reply right away. Finally, he said, "All right. This child, and any other you bear, will be in control of their own lives."

"Why should I trust you?"

"You shouldn't. But I won't cross your future husband again. Even now, he could be planning retaliation. I don't want any Moretti blood spilled over a vendetta. It's too precious to waste."

We fell into a pensive silence. I sipped my hot chocolate, wondering when I could escape the tragedy that was this room.

Angelo's eyes softened when he looked into the fire again. "Will you tell me? Where she's buried?"

I swallowed. "Why?"

"So I can bring her home. Where she belongs."

"She took her own life," I reminded him. "Doesn't that violate the sanctity of The Church?"

"I think God will forgive her for protecting her child." He paused. "Besides, it's the family crypt and we have different rules than The Church."

I told him the name of the town where she'd been laid to rest.

"Thank you," he said, voice grave.

"You're welcome."

We would never be close—my uncle and I—there was too much between us. But there, in that moment, we both silently drank to the life of a woman we'd both loved and failed to protect.

In that moment, we were family.

Chapter Thirty-Eight

I woke up in the middle of the night, wondering what had caused me to stir. I reached for Hadrian, surprised that he was gone. How had he managed to get himself out of bed without me knowing?

I looked to the balcony doors. They were open, and moonlight streamed into the room, but I couldn't see him out there. I was just about to get up when the bedroom door opened.

Letting out a squeak in surprise, I hastily pulled the sheet up to my chin. But it was only Gisella and Beatrice.

Beatrice hit the light switch and the room brightened.

"What the hell are you doing?" I asked Beatrice. "It's the middle of the night!"

My glare transferred from my aunt to my cousin, both of whom were in formal wear. "What time is it? Why are you dressed like that?"

Gisella and Beatrice exchanged a smile.

"Where's Hadrian?"

"It's just past midnight," Gisella said. "Do you want to

wear a sheet to the party, or would you rather wear a dress?"

"Party? At this hour?" I asked.

"Family only," Beatrice said. "Come on, everyone else is already dressed and waiting."

My sluggish mind refused to comprehend what was going on, but I let them pull the sheet away from my body. I didn't bother with modesty as I slid into undergarments and then the dress Beatrice had pulled out of the armoire.

It was a red, strapless confection and hit just above the knee. I thought about pulling my hair up but Gisella shook her head. "Leave it down."

Beatrice brushed it until my locks were glossy.

When I slid into the matching red pumps, I looked to them for inspection. "I don't have any jewelry," I said.

"You don't need any," Beatrice said with a smile.

I followed them out of the room, my curiosity growing as we headed not to the salon, but to the back door that led to the vineyard.

My breath caught when I saw Hadrian under the moonlight, dressed in a tuxedo. He was using a cane to stand upright, but his smile was boyish and devoid of pain as he looked at me. Hadrian stood on a wooden pavilion graced with fairy twinkle lights and long tapered candles.

My cousins and uncles were with him, and I couldn't stop the sense of pride I felt when I saw him towering over them all.

Beatrice went to join her husband and Gisella clasped her hand with mine and together we walked toward my groom.

As I strolled down the aisle, my gaze drifted over Nico and his sons.

When I arrived at the altar, we halted. Gisella

embraced me and whispered in my ear, "Be happy, cousin."

Tears glistened in my eyes when I nodded at her, a smile pulling across my cheeks.

Hadrian took my hand. "Surprise."

And there, under the full moon, on the hills of my ancestral home, I married Hadrian Rhys.

The family dined outdoors underneath the canopy of stars. Hadrian's smile was bright and easy when he leaned toward me and brushed his lips across mine.

"Why didn't you let me in on the secret of our midnight wedding?" I asked, breathless.

"I had this planned long before I knew about your family," he said softly. "Only I wanted to marry you on the beach of my island. And for the record, I never planned on *asking* you to marry me."

I arched a brow. "No?"

"No." He grinned, shattering the solemnity of the moment. "I always planned on *telling* you that you were going to marry me."

Letting out a chuckle, I looked down at the ring. Hadrian had slid a cushion cut amethyst flanked by diamonds and set in yellow gold onto my finger.

"Before all of this," I said, waving to the hills and my family dining and conversing at a table not far away, "when were you planning on telling me to marry you?"

"As soon as The White Company left," he said. "They sort of…spoiled my plans."

"That soon?" I asked breathlessly.

"I didn't want to wait." His gaze softened. "As soon as

you told me the truth about who you were, I knew I wanted you. Forever."

We shared a tender look.

"My best friend missed my wedding," I groaned. "She's going to kill me."

"She can get in line," Hadrian said with a chuckle. "Ingrid is not going to be happy either. We'll make it up to them. Though Ingrid's idea of a wedding is a wee bit different than you might expect…"

"Different how?"

"Let's just say it's less wedding and more Viking fertility ritual."

"Wow, okay…but I'm already pregnant," I pointed out.

"We could still have the celebration. It involves bonfires, a psychotropic drink, and animal pelts. Though I think you should forgo the psychotropic drink."

"Sign. Me. Up."

Hadrian's crack of laughter echoed into the night. "Tiffany should come to the island. I'd like to meet your friend."

"She'd like to meet you, too."

His expression sobered. "Everything that I have is yours."

I couldn't stop the hammering of my heart as his words penetrated. "Some people would call you foolish for saying that."

"Some would," he agreed. "But I knew from the beginning it was never about the money for you. I was never going to let you leave me. I'll fight for you every day if I have to. I'll protect you. I'll love you. I'll make you happy, Sterling."

"My mother was wrong," I said quietly.

"Oh? What about?"

"She told me all I had to do was survive. But that

wasn't enough, Hadrian. I had to fall in love—I had to have a reason for living."

With stars in my eyes and a dreamy smile on my lips, I leaned over to kiss my husband, the love of my life, the man who had fought for me, and who would fight for me always.

No woman could wish for anything more.

Epilogue

Three months later

I stood on the balcony that overlooked the ocean. Winter air cooled my heated cheeks but did nothing to douse the flame of desire that burned brighter now than ever before.

The sound of tumultuous waves hit my ears, making me smile.

I heard his soft footsteps, slow, labored. Hadrian was still healing.

His arms enveloped me from behind, tucking me into his protective embrace as his flaming red beard rubbed my cheek. "What are you doing out here?" he asked, his voice husky with sleep and passion.

"Aside from freezing?" I turned my face toward his for a kiss. When we pulled away, my head felt light, and I was fizzy with happiness.

I leaned back against his chest, letting the poignancy of

the moment wash over me. His hands slipped down my body to gently rest on the swell of my belly.

"Are you happy?" he asked.

"Delirious," I admitted. "You?"

He paused long enough for me to look up at him and arch a brow. Hadrian grinned down at me and placed a kiss at the tip of my nose. "I'm not a poet, aye? Give me a minute to find the words."

I inclined my head but refused to turn my gaze away from him. His nose had healed, but it was slightly more crooked than before. His body had new scars, but he had survived.

Hadrian Rhys.

Warrior. Lover. Husband.

And soon to be father.

"There's no amount of wealth that can ever buy what we have," he said. "Money. Power. None of it matters. Not without you."

He let me go, but only so he could swivel me to face him. "I had a house, but you made it a home. I had a life, but I wasn't really alive."

His hands stole down my body to rest again on my stomach.

The symbol of our love.

"The world is made up of peasants and kings," he said.

"And you're an emperor?" I asked with a winsome smile.

"No. Just a man," he said, his voice raw, aching. "Just a man who was lucky enough to find heaven on earth."

Additional Works

The Tarnished Angels Motorcycle Club Series:

Wreck & Ruin (Tarnished Angels Book 1)
Crash & Carnage (Tarnished Angels Book 2)
Madness & Mayhem (Tarnished Angels Book 3)
Thrust & Throttle (Tarnished Angels Book 4)
Venom & Vengeance (Tarnished Angels Book 5)

SINS Series:

Sins of a King (Book 1)
Birth of a Queen (Book 2)
Rise of a Dynasty (Book 3)
Dawn of an Empire (Book 4)
Ember (Book 5)
Burn (Book 6)
Ashes (Book 7)
Fall of a Kingdom (Book 8)

Others:

Additional Works

Peasants and Kings

About the Author

Wall Street Journal & USA Today bestselling author Emma Slate writes romance with heart and heat.

Called "the dialogue queen" by her college playwriting professor, Emma writes love stories that range from romance-for-your-pants to action-flicks-for-chicks.

When she isn't writing, she's usually curled up under a heating blanket with a steamy romance novel and her two beagles—unless her outdoorsy husband can convince her to go on a hike.